WITH

D1150545

THIEVES OF MERCY

A Novel of the Civil War at Sea

James Nelson

CORGI BOOKS

THIEVES OF MERCY
A CORGI BOOK : 0 552 15098 3

First publication in Great Britain

PRINTING HISTORY
Corgi edition published 2005

1 3 5 7 9 10 8 6 4 2

Copyright © James L. Nelson 2005

The right of James L. Nelson to be identified as the author of this work has been asserted in accordance with sections 77 and 78 of the Copyright Designs and Patents Act 1988.

This book is a work of fiction. References to real people, events, establishments, organizations or locales are intended only to provide a sense of authenticity, and are used fictitiously. All other characters, and all incidents and dialogue, are drawn from the author's imagination and are not to be construed as real.

Condition of Sale

Set in 10.5/12pt Galliard by
Falcon Oast Graphic Art Ltd.

Corgi Books are published by Transworld Publishers,
61–63 Uxbridge Road, London W5 5SA,
a division of The Random House Group Ltd,
in Australia by Random House Australia (Pty) Ltd,
20 Alfred Street, Milsons Point, Sydney, NSW 2061, Australia,
in New Zealand by Random House New Zealand Ltd,
18 Poland Road, Glenfield, Auckland 10, New Zealand
and in South Africa by Random House (Pty) Ltd,
Isle of Houghton, Corner Boundary Road & Carse O'Gowrie,
Houghton 2198, South Africa.

Printed and bound in Great Britain by
Cox & Wyman Ltd, Reading, Berkshire

Papers used by Transworld Publishers are natural, recyclable products made from wood grown in sustainable forests. The manufacturing processes conform to the environmental regulations of the country of origin

To Jonathan Bonaventure Nelson,
my beautiful boy

Ere we were two days old at sea, a pirate of very warlike appointment gave us chase.

Finding ourselves too slow of sail, we put on a compelled valor, and in the grapple I boarded them. On the instant they got clear of our ship, so I alone became their prisoner.

They have dealt with me like thieves of mercy . . .

SHAKESPEARE, *HAMLET*,
ACT IV, SCENE 6

ACKNOWLEDGEMENTS

Once again, I owe a great deal to Ed Donohoe, my friend and steam wizard. Thanks as well to a good friend and a wonderful novelist, Van Reid, for all of his support and, specifically, for suggesting some of the moments in this book. Thanks to Randy Smidy and Dave Frink for the steamboat information. Thanks to George and Amy Jepson and Tall Ships Books for their support over the years.

At HarperCollins, once again, I am grateful for the help of David Semanki and Hugh Van Dusen.

And in particular, I would like to thank Nat Sobel for everything he has done for me during my first decade as a writer.

And last, I would like to thank Lisa Nelson for . . . well . . . you know . . .

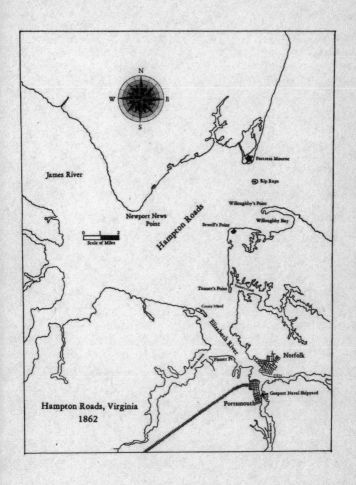

N

W   E

S

James River

Fortress Monroe

Rip Raps

Newport News
Point

Willoughby's Point

Hampton Roads

Sewell's Point

Willoughby Bay

Tanner's Point

Craney Island

Elizabeth River

Norfolk

Fort

Portsmouth

Gosport Naval Shipyard

Hampton Roads, Virginia
1862

0   1   2
Scale of Miles

THIEVES OF MERCY

PROLOGUE

The completion of the iron-clad gunboat at Memphis, by Mr Shirley, is regarded as highly important to the defenses of the Mississippi. One of them at Columbus would have enabled you to complete the annihilation of the enemy.

Stephen R. Mallory,
Secretary of the Confederate Navy,
to General Leonidas Polk

It was nighttime in the shipyard, the working day long over. But there were men there still, nearly fifty men, standing around in the dirt and sawdust. The air was damp and warm, alive with summer bugs and the sounds of frogs and the lap of water. Just to the north, the lights that climbed up the steep banks and low hills along the Mississippi showed where the city of Memphis was still awake, like the soldiers at Agincourt, too restless to sleep on the eve of battle. To the men in the shipyard, the city might as well have been Agincourt, it felt so far removed.

The men were shipwrights and house carpenters. They were blue-water sailors and river men and black gang. They were from Charleston and New Orleans, Yazoo City and Memphis and Richmond and Mobile, all the states that now formed the Confederate States of America, and a few transplant Yankees thrown in.

There was John Shirley, dancing from one foot to another. There was Ruffin Tanner, his wounded arm still bound with a white bandage. There was Hieronymus Taylor, chief engineer, leaning on a crutch, his splinted leg thrust out in front of him. The glow of his cigar looked like a signal lantern. Red at the masthead.

At the head of them stood Lt. Samuel Bowater, Confederate States Navy. Thirty-five years old, a fifteen-year veteran of the United States Navy, where, after some brief action as an ensign during the Mexican War, he had spent his time visiting foreign ports and seeing that the various ships aboard which he served as lieutenant were clean to navy standards. There had not been much more to do in the old navy.

Bowater smoothed his moustache and goatee, stepped off to the right to get a better look at the ship. The half-dozen men behind him carried torches that spilled their light over the shipyard, the sawmill, the piles of unused timber, the hastily built shacks to house the blacksmith's and carpenter's shops, the looming hull of the vessel.

Good. She looks good, Bowater thought. But she was not finished. She had been slated for completion in December of '61, and now it was June of '62 and she was far from done.

It was not for want of trying. It was for want of everything else: iron plate, bolts, machinery, wood, manpower. Timber came from five different sawmills, iron from all over the Confederacy. The first load of bolt and spike iron was taken before it even arrived, not by Yankees, but by officers of the Confederate States Navy who reckoned they had a better use for it.

Despite the pleas of contractor John Shirley to Stephen Mallory, and Stephen Mallory's pleas to the army to detail a minimum of one hundred men with shipbuilding experience to the project, the shipwrights arrived in Memphis in twos and threes. Shirley made use of house carpenters, day laborers, anyone who knew which end of the hammer to hold.

Given all that, it was something of a miracle what Shirley had accomplished. Two ironclads, nearly complete, built in Memphis on the low banks of the Mississippi. The *Arkansas* and the *Tennessee*.

Of the two, the *Arkansas* was much further along, her woodwork all but done, her iron plating bolted on as far as the main deck, her engines on board, if not in place. Bowater looked at the empty ways on which she had been built. The grease from her launch still shone in the light of the torches. They had slid *Arkansas* into the river and towed her south to Yazoo City. Away from the onrushing Yankees, General Halleck and Commodore Davis and his fleet of ironclad river gunboats coming down from the north, Farragut coming up from the south. Towed her to the heart of the Confederacy, away from the anaconda, squeezing tighter.

But the *Arkansas* was not Bowater's concern. His was the *Tennessee*. His third command.

It was just over a year before that he had joined the Confederate Navy, right after witnessing the bombardment of Fort Sumter in his native Charleston. Bowater was a Southern man, a Southern gentleman, but at the time he was also an officer of the United States Navy. He had sworn an oath to that service, and gentlemen of the South did not break oaths easily.

He went with his state, in the end, and with his new country, and had been given command of the CSS *Cape Fear*, an armed tug, which had been shot out from under him in the naval skirmish in Albemarle Sound in North Carolina. He and his men had been transferred *en masse* to Yazoo City to form the crew of the ironclad *Yazoo River*, which had met her death at New Orleans, fighting to stop Farragut's fleet from pushing up from the delta to take the Crescent City.

Now Farragut was at New Orleans, that city in Yankee hands, and once again Bowater's men had been moved as a unit to their next ship. The *Tennessee*.

The white pine planking of her hull looked orange in the light of the torches, her topsides all but lost in the dark. She was framed in oak and planked with pine but there was no iron plate on her yet. The iron was not even there – it was still on the Arkansas side of the river, still waiting for payment. *Tennessee* was a turtle without a shell.

She was not huge, by ironclad standards. One hundred and sixty-five feet long, more than one hundred feet shorter than the CSS *Virginia*, the former *Merrimack*. Thirty-five feet wide. Her waterline, scribed in the planking, was visible six feet above Bowater's head. She was not huge, but she would have been powerful. She might have changed the entire strategic situation on that part of the river.

Son of a bitch, Bowater muttered. He was dragging his feet now, and there was no call for it.

He was not the only Confederate officer there. The provost marshal for the city of Memphis stood nearby, watching, his gray frock coat unbuttoned in the warm night, arms folded with mounting impatience. It was by his order that they were there, doing the job they were doing. But it was not the provost's ship. He did not share Bowater's feelings. He coughed impatiently.

'All right, you men.' Bowater turned to his crew behind him. 'Go ahead.'

The men with the torches stepped forward, solemn, as if they were part of some religious service. They spread out along the length of the hull and thrust the flames into the bales of cotton stacked under the wooden hull, cotton soaked in turpentine.

All along the length of the *Tennessee* the flames of the torches swelled into flames like campfires and then like bonfires as the cotton was engulfed. The flames rose up and threw their light all over the shipyard, lighting up the watching men so they were all bright light and dark shadow, flickering over the far ends of the shipyard.

Bowater stepped back. The heat was already too much to bear. He could see the planking on what would have been the ship's wetted surface turn black. The caulking between the planks began to burn and then the planks themselves flared as the heavy timbers began to catch fire.

Bowater heard the limping gate of Hieronymus Taylor as the chief engineer stepped up beside him. 'Well, goddamn me, Cap'n,' Taylor said around his cigar, his accent thick New Orleans. 'There goes your third ship.' He pulled out a flask of whiskey, took a drink, handed it to Bowater. Bowater took it, put it to his lips, and took a big mouthful, a thing he would have considered unthinkable a year before. Captains did not drink with the crew. Samuel Bowater did not drink whiskey from a flask. He did not drink with the likes of Hieronymus Taylor.

It had been a long year.

'Seems the life span of your ships just gets shorter and shorter all the damn time,' Taylor observed, taking the flask back.

'Don't see how it could get much shorter than this, Chief.' They had been there for less than a month, working like madmen to get the ship in the water. Finishing her was not even a consideration, they hoped only to get her floating, so that like her sister ship *Arkansas* she might be towed away.

It was June fifth, and the *Tennessee* was still on the stocks and the Yankees were just up the river. The following day there would be a battle, a river battle that would determine whether Memphis would be in Union or Confederate hands.

If the Confederates won, and if they could hold the Yankees at bay, then there was still a chance that they could get the *Tennessee* in the water and downriver to safety.

But if the Union won, then Yankee shipwrights would complete the *Tennessee* with an efficiency that the South could not match, and the trim little ironclad would be used against her own people.

It was a gamble over who would win the river fight, and everyone knew which side was the odds-on favorite, so before the battle even started they burned the ship on the ways.

CHAPTER 1

Latitude, elevation and rainfall all combine to render the Mississippi Valley capable of supporting a dense population. As a dwelling-place for civilized man it is by far the first upon our globe.
Harper's Magazine, February 1863

It was a month before the burning of the *Tennessee*, and ten hours after he met the man, that Samuel Bowater first saw someone smash a chair over Mississippi Mike Sullivan's head.

The one doing the smashing was Ruffin Tanner, a blue-water sailor of nearly twenty years' experience, who had been with Bowater since Bowater had commanded the *Cape Fear* in Norfolk.

Tanner was a powerful man, certainly as strong as Sullivan, though not nearly as big. The chair, however, was a meager affair, with thin turned legs and a cane seat, and it shattered over Mike's thick head and wide shoulders like a china figurine and did little more than slew his slouch hat around, leaving Tanner red-faced and gripping the two smashed back rails.

It was two days before that chair-smashing,

all-hands-in brawl that Bowater finally heard from the Navy Department in Richmond.

After the Battle of New Orleans, after the *Yazoo River* had been battered to death by Farragut's big ships, Bowater and his remaining men had returned to Yazoo City. They had no other place to go, and the Yankees were still far from that Yazoo, so it seemed like a good choice. Bowater began to send telegraphs off to Richmond, looking for instructions.

On the third of May, word arrived.

Lt. Samuel Bowater, CSN
Yazoo City, Mississippi

Sir:
You and those men still under your command will proceed with all possible dispatch to Memphis, Tennessee, where you will assume command of the ironclad *Tennessee* currently building there. You will exert all possible effort in the completion and fitting out of that vessel. Recent events along the Mississippi have made it imperative that this iron-clad sloop of war be readied to meet the enemy.
Respectfully,
Stephen Mallory
Secretary of the Navy

Bowater read the words with some skepticism. Sometimes it seemed as if Mallory believed that call-ing a ship an ironclad would make it so. The last time Mallory had ordered him to command an 'ironclad' it had turned out to be a broken-down side-wheeler with pine board and cotton bale bulwarks, a 'cotton-clad.' It was a near miracle that they had managed to turn her battered topsides into an iron casement, and Bowater reckoned that his supply of miracles was pretty well played out.

And so he stood in the telegraph office and looked for a long time at the words, until he heard the telegraph operator start to clear his throat in a nervous sort of way.

Ironclad . . . recent events . . .

Bowater could not fault Mallory for his understanding of the tactical situation, even if the Secretary had been mistaken in thinking the chief threat to New Orleans was from the north, and not the Gulf. It was true that Farragut's big men-of-war, built for fighting the British on the high seas, were utterly unsuited for river work. But the Union admiral had managed to drag his heavy squadron bodily over the shallow bar at the mouth of the river and blast his way past the forts and the smattering of Confederate ships defending the river below the city.

Now Farragut was probing upriver, but the farther north he came, and the more the water level continued to fall, the more unwieldy his fleet became.

Flat-bottomed, paddle-wheel-driven, ironclad gunboats. Those were the ships for this river fight. A new vessel for an unprecedented type of warfare.

Mallory knew it, was trying his level best to make it a reality. The Yankees knew it as well, and behind their effort was an almost unlimited industrial capacity. So, for the first year of the war, while the Confederacy struggled to get even one operational ironclad on the Father of Waters, the Union built seven. Those ships, the 'City Class' gunboats, were fighting their way south, accompanying the Union Army sweeping along the shore.

Bowater left the telegraph office, wandered along the streets of Yazoo City, still considering the 'iron-clad *Tennessee.*' What, he wondered, would greet him on his arrival in Memphis. How would he get there?

'Reckon we best get to Vicksburg.' That was Hieronymus Taylor's pronouncement, upon learning about the orders. Taylor was a riverboat man, an engineer out of New Orleans who had joined the navy to avoid a possible draft, and for the possibility of killing Yankees, which he found very appealing. He was a part of the world of the Mississippi River, as alien to Bowater as the moon.

'Vicksburg,' Bowater repeated.

'Best place to find a boat goin north. Ain't a damn thing movin on this here backwater. We best get to Vicksburg before goddamn Farragut does.'

The next day they found a tug that would take them to Vicksburg, and Bowater herded aboard it the thirty-six men still under his command.

He felt like a schoolteacher at times, or the head of an orphanage, with his charges to care for. He had men but no ship to house them, no galley to feed them. It was like having a company of infantry, but infantry were prepared for such living, they had tents and knew how to cook rations. Sailors without a ship were lost men. They looked to Bowater for guidance, but Bowater did not know much more about such things than they did. He had never been in that situation before.

They steamed down the Yazoo River, crowded on the deck of the tug, turned south where the Yazoo met with the Mississippi River. Just above the city, the river took a sharp turn so that for a time they were actually steaming northeast before turning one hundred and eighty degrees. Around the low, marshy point was the city of Vicksburg.

The hills of the town rose up from the water's edge, steep and terraced, a formidable defensive position. The 'Gibraltar of the West,' as it was popularly called, a name that carried no small amount of hope for the city's ability to withstand invasion.

From the deck of the tug, as the pilot jockeyed her into the dock, Bowater could see brown patches of turned earth scattered over the high bluffs. Artillery positions set up to command the river below. Confederate gunners could set up a plunging fire that even ironclads would have a hard time surviving. If there was any city that could hold out against the Union's two-pronged attack, it would be Vicksburg.

And that was good, because soon Vicksburg and Port Hudson would be the only points on the Mississippi that were not in Union hands. They would be the citadels that would deny the Yankees control of the entire river, from the headwaters to the delta.

'Goddamned Yankees can't have control of the Mississippi. They can't,' the pilot said to Bowater, speaking around a large wad of tobacco and ringing *all stop* down to the engine room.

'No,' Bowater replied, though he did not know if the man meant that the Confederate Army would prevent it or that a just God would not allow it to happen.

Bowater led his men onto the dock. He did not know what to do next, so he sent them to find some dinner and forbade them to drink, while he went to see about their transportation. He gave the orders in a tone that implied he had the whole thing figured.

'Chief Taylor, come with me, please. Tanner,

you're in charge until my return.'

Bowater led Taylor down along the waterfront, and when he had put some distance between them and the men, he stopped and Taylor stopped as well. Bowater had been saddled with Taylor as engineer since his first command in the Confederate Navy. Taylor had a genius for irritating him, but he also had a genius for engineering, could keep machinery running with a near magical efficiency; the two nearly canceled one another out.

'I'm not certain how we should go about securing passage to Memphis,' Bowater said. 'I know you are quite familiar with the shipping around here. I would appreciate your thoughts on the matter.'

Taylor nodded. 'Beats me,' he said. Insubordination, infinitely subtle. That was Hieronymus Taylor's forte.

Bowater pressed his lips together, preventing himself from speaking. Taylor was going to play this one for all it was worth. The river and its people were a community, a waterborne society, about which Bowater knew nothing. He was as lost here as Taylor would have been at the grand Charleston balls or theater performances that were part of Samuel's former life.

And so Bowater resisted saying the first thing that came to mind, which was a rebuke involving several animal similes, because, infuriating as it was, he needed Taylor's help.

'You are more familiar with Vicksburg than I am. How do you think we should proceed?'

'Well . . .' Taylor rocked back on his heels, looked up at the high bluffs. 'Normally there'd be a power of traffic runnin up and down the river. But hell, this don't hardly look like the Vicksburg I know. People rushin all over, ain't but half the number of boats you normally see dockside.'

Bowater had been to Vicksburg only a few times, but he too recognized the difference. The city was preparing for an attack, aware as the Union was of the strategic importance it held. There was a different feel to the place, a desperate and determined feel.

'I guess we had best just walk on down along the docks, ask around,' Taylor said.

'Very well,' Bowater said. He had been hoping Taylor would have a line on a ship, perhaps know someone who could help, but in the end he had suggested the one thing that Bowater had already considered.

Well, that was a damned lot of crow I ate for nothing.

They continued on along the waterfront, considering the various side-wheelers and stern-wheelers and screw tugs, searching for a vessel that looked to be getting under way soon. Bowater walked with purpose. Taylor ambled along with hands in his pockets and a cigar between his teeth.

The voice, when it called out, was so loud it seemed to boom at them from several directions. 'Hieronymus Taylor! You damned, dirty dog!'

Bowater looked around. It was like trying to determine what direction a bullet came from. Taylor's face lost its amused expression and he said, 'Ah, hell . . .' as Mike Sullivan appeared on the hurricane deck of a side-wheeler, wearing dark braces and a checked shirt stretched over his big chest, a battered sack coat. He was waving a sweat-stained slouch hat, grinning through a massive and untamed beard.

'Taylor, you wait right there, you dog!' he called

and hurried down the ladder to the main deck, stepping easily onto the wharf, moving with a grace Bowater found surprising.

Sullivan hurried up, grinning wide. He was even bigger than Bowater had thought at first, over six feet and approaching three hundred pounds, but there was nothing flabby about him. He reached out his hand, took Taylor's, which Taylor offered with a half-hearted gesture, shook it hard.

'Hieronymus Taylor, you son of a bitch! Ain't seen you in . . . hell, must be a year at least. Not since we whipped your ass in that run to Natchez.'

'We beat you by thirty-four minutes,' Taylor said through clenched teeth as his arm was worked like a pump handle.

'Like hell . . . well, maybe.'

Taylor turned to Bowater. 'Captain, this here's—'

The big man turned to Bowater, held out his hand. 'Mike Sullivan. They call me Mississippi Mike Sullivan.'

'No one calls you Mississippi Mike Sullivan but you,' Taylor said.

'Pleased to meet you,' Bowater said, shaking hands. Mississippi Mike had about him the faint odor of whiskey and cigars and coal dust and turpentine.

' 'Course you're pleased to meet me! Heard tell of me, no doubt. Hardest drivin, hardest drinkin, most dangerous son of a whore riverboat man on the Western Waters.'

'Impressive *curriculum vitae,* skipper, but no, I'm afraid I have not heard of you.'

'He ain't from around here, Sullivan,' Taylor said.

'Oh, that's it. Should have guessed from that fancy-lady way you talk. Must be from the goddamn

28

moon, ain't heard of Mississippi Mike Sullivan.'

Sullivan let go of Bowater's hand, turned back to Taylor, squinted at the shoulder straps on his uniform frock coat. 'Taylor, what the hell is this? What are you, on the Sanitary Commission or some damned thing?'

Taylor stiffened and said, in as matter-of-fact a tone as he could manage, 'As it happens, Sullivan, I am a first assistant engineer in the Confederate States Navy.'

Sullivan paused as if he was too stunned to speak and then he burst out laughing. He laughed from his ample gut, the way a grizzly bear would laugh if it could. He laughed for a long time, until he was red in the face, gasping for breath, as Bowater and Taylor stood silent and annoyed.

'First assistant engineer?' Sullivan said, trying to breathe. 'What the hell is that? They let you run the ash hoist, or you gotta be promoted to full junior engineer to do that?'

Taylor nodded, worked the cigar around in his mouth.

'Chief Taylor is lead engineer on board my command,' Bowater explained. 'First assistant is just a navy designation.'

'That a fact?' Sullivan wiped a tear from his eye. 'What command is that, Captain?'

'The ironclad *Tennessee*, building in Memphis.'

Sullivan's eyes went wide. 'The ironclad *Tenn*—' At that he howled again, bent over double, laughing so hard he looked like he would pass out.

'You don't need to help my case no more, Captain, thanks anyway,' Taylor said.

Sullivan straightened. 'How long you been the captain of the *Tennessee*?'

'I have just received orders now.'

'You're a long damned way from Memphis, Captain, if you don't mind my makin that observation.'

'We are attempting to secure passage, Sullivan, and we have no more time to waste conversing. Good day.'

Bowater stepped away, but Sullivan said, 'Now wait, Captain,' and his tone was more conciliatory. 'This here's your lucky day, because the fact is I'm takin my steamer up to Memphis. Leavin tonight.'

'Well, ain't that a coincidence,' Taylor said. 'Don't reckon we need any part of what you're up to.'

'Now hold on, Chief,' Bowater said. He did not want Taylor to toss away an easy solution to their dilemma just because he didn't care for this 'Mississippi Mike.' Bowater didn't care for him either, but he could tolerate him for the length of time it would take to steam to Memphis.

There was also some satisfaction in overriding Taylor.

'You're heading up to Memphis tonight?' Bowater asked. 'Are you hauling freight?'

'Deserting to the Yankees, most like,' Taylor offered.

'Now lookee here, Mr First Assistant Engineer Hieronymus Taylor, Confederate States Navy, you ain't the only one fightin this here war,' Sullivan said. 'Fact is, I am captain of the side-wheel ram *General Page,* the pride of the River Defense Fleet, true Sons of the South and the foremost defenders of this here river.'

'That a fact?' Taylor said, and now it was he who

was smiling, grinning around his cigar, but Sullivan did not seem to notice.

'That's right, boy,' Sullivan said, tapping Taylor on the chest with a finger like a sausage. 'We are an independent branch, we answer to the general of the army in the Mississippi Department, and we don't take orders from no navy peckerwoods.'

Indeed, Bowater thought. The River Defense Fleet certainly did not take orders from naval officers, peckerwood or otherwise. Or from anyone else, for that matter.

Part of the fleet had been at the Battle of New Orleans. They had refused to cooperate in the organized action against the Yankees and had contributed absolutely nothing to the defense of the forts. The only thing they did that Bowater was aware of was to accidentally set their fire rafts alongside Fort Jackson's wharf, blinding the Confederate gunners but neatly illuminating the fort for the Yankees. That was what the War Department got for the one million five hundred thousand dollars they spent establishing the River Defense Fleet.

'River Defense Fleet, huh? Oh, brother, now I *am* impressed, "Mississippi Mike," ' Taylor said. 'Captain Bowater, I think we best look for more suitable transport upriver.'

'Hmmm,' Bowater said, stalling. It was only a ride upriver, for God's sake, a little over two hundred miles, two days' steaming at the worst. They could endure Sullivan and the River Defense Fleet for that long. What harm could come of it? 'Actually, Chief, I believe we'll accept Captain Sullivan's offer.'

'Whatever you say, Captain,' Taylor said. He looked amused.

'Sure you will,' Sullivan said, giving Bowater a good-natured slap on the back, just the kind of *bonhomie* that Bowater despised. 'The *Page*'s the fastest damn boat on the river, and I'm the best damn pilot. We'll be pickin up a barge tonight, and then it's off to Memphis.'

'Very good, Captain,' Bowater said. 'If my men can be of any assistance in your navigation, let me know.'

'Oh, I reckon y'all can be of assistance, suh, absolutely.' The jolly tone had left Sullivan's voice, as if he was forcing himself to be sincere. 'I imagine you are some eager to get to Memphis and take command of your . . . *ironclad.*'

Then like steam through a cracked pipe, the laughter burst out of Sullivan's mouth and he doubled over again.

CHAPTER 2

I will here state that the river defense fleet proved a failure. . . . Unable to govern themselves, and unwilling to be governed by others, their total want of system, vigilance, and discipline rendered them useless and helpless when the enemy finally dashed upon them suddenly in a dark night.

Major General M. Lovell to
General S. Cooper, Adjutant and
Inspector General, Richmond, Virginia

Even before the shooting started, Bowater guessed that his blue-water sailors and the riverboat men would be an uneasy mix.

Taylor put that concern in his head. It was just after Bowater ushered his men into what had been the *General Page*'s first-class passengers' salon back when the River Defense boat *General Page* had been the civilian riverboat *Lisa Marie*.

The navy men took seats at the tables along the port side. Taylor sat down beside Bowater, his frock coat unbuttoned, his cap tilted back, three days' growth of beard on his face. Taylor seemed more relaxed in some ways, being back on his native Mississippi. And in some ways he seemed less. There seemed to be some turmoil of the spirit raging in the engineer's soul, which, like most things about Hieronymus Taylor, was of no interest to Bowater.

'Captain,' Taylor drawled, 'I reckon a warnin is in order. I know there are certain . . . aspects of my personality that you find objectionable. Fair enough. I'm a river rat, and you're . . . well . . . not. But the boys they got working this bucket, they're somethin else.'

'In what way?'

'Well . . . they ain't real refined. Not like me. And they don't like the navy, and they don't like deep-water sailors, and they don't like much of anything else. We just got to see our boys don't get baited into doin somethin stupid.'

Bowater was digesting this when the door burst open and the crew of the *General Page* spilled into the salon. They were big men, with wool pants and checked shirts or patched dungarees held up with braces, bearded or with thick moustaches, sweat-stained caps and hats pushed down on their heads. They were a loud and aromatic bunch, cheeks bulging with tobacco. They were a well-armed bunch too, with pistols and bowie knives hanging from belts.

Bowater felt his men tense as the riverboat men, twenty-five or so in number, took over the salon. They carried pails full of food and they sat at the once fine tables on the starboard side and laid into their meal. They ate without talking, the only sound the loud chewing and smacking of lips. They took no notice of the navy men.

34

Suddenly one of the riverboat men leaped to his feet. 'Son of a bitch, look at that one!' he shouted, jerking his pistol from his belt. Bowater stood quickly, unsure what was happening. His hand reached for his own gun, a .36-caliber Navy Colt, finely engraved, a gift from his father.

Before he could even pull the gun the river man started firing, blasting away at the salon's forward bulkhead as half a dozen of his compatriots leaped to their feet, guns clearing holsters. Up against the bulkhead, the largest rat that Bowater had ever seen raced side to side, panicked by the bullets shattering the wood around him.

'Hold still, you little puke!' another of the riverboat men shouted, fanning the hammer of his gun. Bowater's eyes moved from the rat to the firing squad and back. The animal froze, stood on hind legs, and then seemed to explode as a bullet hit him square, but that did not slow the gunfire. In seconds the place where the rat had been was reduced to a ragged, stained hole in the bulkhead, and it was only when hammers fell on empty chambers that the guns were holstered and the men returned to their meal.

In the quiet that followed the fusillade, Bowater waited for someone to comment, but no one did. He turned to his own men, who were all on their feet, eyes wide, pistols held limp in the hands of those who had them. All looked stunned, save for Hieronymus Taylor, who did not appear to have moved.

'They ain't real refined, like I said, Captain,' Taylor explained.

Then the door burst open again, and Mississippi Mike Sullivan stood framed against the blue evening light outside. 'What the hell is all this shootin?' he yelled into the salon, then charged in, very like a bull. The men at the tables did not even look up.

'Rat,' said the one who had fired the first shot. His mouth was full of beefsteak and the words were muffled. He swallowed. 'Son of a bitch rat.'

'Rat!?' Sullivan shouted. 'You're shootin at a god-damn rat?' He crossed the room in five steps, planted a brogan on the shooter's chair, and sent him flying. The man landed in a heap, scrambled to his feet, pulling a bowie knife as he did, a foot-long blade with a hand guard that made it look more like a short sword than a long knife.

The rest of the river men leaped to their feet, tumbling chairs to the deck, forming a rough semicircle.

Sullivan charged across the room. 'We got guests aboard here, you dumb bastard!' he bellowed. His right foot came up and kicked the man's hand hard and the knife flew away and Bayard Quayle of Bowater's crew had to flinch to avoid being hit. Sullivan hit the shooter hard in the stomach, doubling him over, shoved him to the floor, pulled his own pistol, aimed it at the man.

'Get up, Tarbox,' Sullivan growled and the man on the deck stood up slowly. He stepped over and retrieved his knife and sheathed it and Sullivan put his pistol back in his holster because somehow they both knew the fight was over. The river men picked up their chairs, and resumed their meal.

'Did you git the sum bitch?' Sullivan asked.

'Yeah, I got him.'

'Come here,' Sullivan said and he led Tarbox over to Samuel Bowater. 'Captain Bowater,' Sullivan said in a formal tone, 'I'd like you to meet my first officer.

36

This here's Buford Tarbox, and he's a hell of a river man when he ain't bein a dumb-ass, shootin up rats in front of guests.'

'Honored to meet ya,' Tarbox said, sticking out his hand, and Bowater shook, too stunned by it all to do anything else. 'Pleased to meet you,' he replied.

'Captain Bowater and his men is takin passage up to Memphis with us. They are the crew of the *ironclad Tennessee*,' Sullivan explained.

'The *ironclad Tennessee*, is that a fact?' Tarbox said with something like a half grin appearing through his thatch of beard.

'That is a fact,' Sullivan said. 'Now show these boys some goddamn courtesy and get em somthin to eat, you hear? And don't shoot nothin else.' Sullivan touched his hat to Bowater and disappeared. When he was gone, Tarbox shouted, 'Hey, Doc, get these here fancy navy gen'lmen some grub!'

Tarbox picked up his chair and resumed his place at the table, while the one called Doc, wearing a stained apron, rose from his seat, conveying with every move, every nuance of expression, how much he resented the task.

Ten minutes later, pails of food were set on the tables occupied by Bowater's men, and Doc went back to eating, without ever saying a word to any of the navy men, or even making eye contact. Bowater's men were too hungry to care. They tore into the food in a manner that made the riverboat men look civilized.

The sky was coal-tar black when they finally got under way, approaching midnight, and the frenetic energy of soon-to-be-embattled Vicksburg had slowed considerably. One by one the lamps that had lit the waterfront were extinguished, dark and quiet settled over the docks, the hiss of steam engines and the squeal of hoisting gear died away, the rumble of carts on cobblestone, and the shouting of motivated men tapered off and disappeared.

By 11 P.M. the loudest place on the waterfront was the big saloon on the main deck level of the *General Page*, where the crew of the riverboat had finished supper and moved on to whiskey, which made the otherwise taciturn men quite vocal, shouting, bragging, lying. The General Pages drank, smoked, chewed, and played cards. They ignored the blue-water men, who resented it, especially as it meant that none of the copious amount of whiskey flowing to starboard was finding its way to port.

The *Page* was a side-wheel steamer, one hundred and eighty feet on deck, around six hundred and fifty tons, not much different from hundreds of other riverboats that ran on the western rivers, hauling passengers, cotton, and mixed freight. Her twin paddle wheels were driven by a massive walking beam engine, a single cylinder driving a diamond-shaped rocking arm, the 'walking beam,' that in turn rotated the paddle-wheel shaft. The engine was a huge affair, the walking beam mounted on top of a thirty-foot-high A-frame that went right through the hurricane deck, the uppermost deck, on which the wheelhouse sat.

Her conversion to a man-of-war had not been extensive. A heavy iron ram was bolted to her stem, just under the water. A metal shield that looked more like a cowcatcher than anything else was mounted on her bow and backed up with compressed bales of cotton. That offered some protection to the men working the ten-pound Parrott rifle mounted forward. On her stern she carried a thirty-two-pound smoothbore cannon, used to discourage pursuit. Unlike the crowded men-of-war to which Bowater was accustomed, there was a lot of room left over for the crew.

Bowater stood at the salon door and looked out at the few lights still burning in the city. *What the hell is the wait?* he wondered. They had had steam up for hours; he could not understand why they remained tied to the dock. Unless Mississippi Mike Sullivan didn't think his men were drunk enough yet.

He heard steps from forward and Sullivan's hulking frame materialized out of the dark. 'Captain Bowater!' The big hand swung around and smacked Bowater on the shoulder. 'You ready to get under way?'

'And have been for several hours.'

'I know, I know, damned irritatin. You ain't a river rat? Ain't spent much time on the Old Miss?'

'No, my experience with the river is limited.'

'Well . . . it's all tides and currents, that's what's holdin us up. Tides, currents . . . whole different world on the river.' He pushed past Bowater, into the thick fog of tobacco smoke in the salon. 'All right, you sons of bitches, let's get this bucket under way! Come on, go!'

The riverboat men, who looked as if they would never obey any authority, obeyed Mississippi Mike. They leaped to it, pushed their way out of the salon, ran to stations. Within half a minute, only Bowater's sailors were left in the big space, the smoke hanging like the ghost of the men who had been there.

'Captain, you come up to the wheelhouse with

me. Man such as yourself got to be where the action is!'

A part of Bowater did not care to be in the wheel-house with Sullivan, but the other part was flattered to be asked. And he reasoned that he should take any opportunity to learn more about the operation of shallow-draft, side-wheeled vessels on a river – so unlike anything his previous experience or training had prepared him for.

'Very well, Captain Sullivan, I thank you.' He followed Sullivan up the ladder to the wheelhouse, a boxy structure with windows on three sides sitting on top of the hurricane deck. Leaning on the wheel, which was five feet tall, was one of the river men. He was smoking a cheroot and digging at his nails with a bowie knife. He acknowledged Sullivan with a nod of his head.

Sullivan seemed to build momentum, like a beer wagon careening downhill. 'Stop prettifying yourself and grab that wheel, Baxter, we got us a barge to pick up.' He stepped out of the wheelhouse door, bellowed, 'Let 'em go! Let all them damned fasts go!' He rushed back into the wheelhouse, shouted, 'Let's get them buckets turning!' He grabbed the bell rope, gave a jingle and rang two bells, and a moment later the paddle wheels began their slow turn in reverse. He was shouting orders at Baxter, two feet away, when the answering ring came from the engine room below.

The *General Page* backed out into the river as Sullivan raced from side to side of the wheelhouse, stepping out on the deck, now to starboard, now to port, shouting into the dark, keeping up a running commentary. He was a tornado, exhausting just to watch, grinning wide with the sheer joy of having the riverboat moving under him.

Baxter, by contrast, said nothing, stared straight ahead through the glass, puffed the cheroot. He seemed not even to notice Sullivan, and the constant stream of instructions that Sullivan poured on him seemed to have no effect on his steering whatsoever.

In that way the side-wheeler swung away from the dock and turned her bow downstream.

'Ooowee, we goin now, Cap'n Bowater, we surely are!' Sullivan pulled a cigar from the pocket of his sack coat, stuck it in his mouth in a gesture that reminded Bowater very much of Hieronymus Taylor. Sullivan was grinning. Bowater could not remember the last adult he'd met who greeted life with such pure exuberance as Mississippi Mike Sullivan. There was something enviable about it.

'What brought you down to Vicksburg, Captain?' Bowater asked.

'Cracked bearin on the starboard paddle shaft,' Sullivan said, still moving from side to side across the front of the wheelhouse, his eyes everywhere. 'Been up around Fort Pillow since . . . hell . . .'

'March,' Baxter supplied.

'March. Waitin for our chance to get at them damned Yankee gunboats, them turtles. I'm gonna be mighty angry if they whipped them Yankees while we was down here. All right, Baxter, here we go.'

Sullivan rang one bell, *slow ahead*. Bowater peered out the window, trying to see what Sullivan saw, but it was all black waterfront to him.

'Hard a'port,' Sullivan said. He rang *slow astern*. 'Hell, Cap'n Bowater, we're doin all kinda good for the navy tonight,' he continued, eyes fixed on the shore. 'Bringin the crew of the *Tennessee* upriver. Gettin this here coal barge for what's left of the Confederate Navy fleet, up there at Memphis.'

'Navy fleet?' Bowater asked. 'Not the River Defense Fleet?'

'That's right.'

'Well . . .' Bowater paused while Sullivan raced out onto the hurricane deck, then raced back into the wheelhouse. 'I didn't realize there were any naval forces left up there.'

'Oh, hell, yes, Cap'n. A few. And of course the *Tennessee,* and her sister ironclad *Arkansas,* they'll need coal, soon enough. Navy fellow there heard I was comin down to Vicksburg, why, he asked would I pick up this barge for him. "Pleased to help," I said.'

'That's good to hear, Captain. We're all fighting the same war, after all. We're often too quick to forget it.'

'Amen to that, Brother Bowater. Come left, you blind, poxed son of a whore!' That last was shouted at Baxter, who was coming left even as Sullivan said it. Baxter emitted a little puff of smoke from his cheroot, like a miniature steam engine, kept his eyes forward.

Sullivan rang *all stop,* then a jingle and a bell for *slow astern.* He stepped out into the dark, looked aft, and this time Bowater followed him out onto the deck. In the light of a few feeble lamps on shore he could make out a barge tied alongside a wall, a train sitting on a siding, and sundry tugs lying against a wooden dock.

Sullivan raced back into the wheelhouse, rang *all stop.* The *General Page* shuddered slightly as the stern came against the barge.

'Come on down, Cap'n Bowater. Let me show you how we make these barges up, Mississippi style.'

Bowater followed Sullivan down the ladder to the boiler deck, then down to the main deck and aft. The *General Page*'s stern was hard against the barge and the riverboat men were swarming over it, running lines to the big bollards on the *Page*'s fantail.

'Hey, what the hell you doin?' The voice came from the dark, from the shore. Bowater looked past the barge. A man was standing there, on the far side, on the edge of the wall. He was just visible in the light of the lantern he held in his hand.

'Pickin up the barge, here!' Sullivan shouted back.

'Like hell! Who are you?'

'Got Captain Bowater here, of the Confederate States Navy!' Sullivan shouted across the heaps of coal.

'Who?'

'Hold your horses there, brother!' Sullivan shouted, then turned to Bowater. 'Cap'n, go over there and explain to that chucklehead, will you?'

'Explain what?'

'You know, about the coal for the navy, and the *Tennessee* and all. How we're all fightin the same war.'

'But—'

A heavy line sailed over the taffrail and Sullivan grabbed it up, pulled it over to the starboard bollard. 'Go on, Cap'n, tell him how this here coal's for the navy. Best hurry or sure as hell we'll miss the tide!' he shouted while straining against the rope.

Bowater stepped over the rail, onto the barge, made his way around the edge with one foot on the caprail and the other on the heaps of coal. He crossed around to the seawall, stepped up to face the man with the lantern.

'Who are you? What do you think you're doing?' The man with the lantern had the look of a watchman, too old and sodden for any other work. He appeared to be leaning on a cane, but up close Bowater saw it was a shotgun.

The watchman glared at Bowater. His eyes moved over the gold-embroidered ornament on Bowater's cap, with its single star, fouled anchor, and wreath of oak leaves. He squinted at the shoulder straps on his gray frock coat.

'My name is Bowater, Lieutenant Bowater of the Confederate States Navy.'

'That a fact? What're you doin?'

'Ahh . . .' Bowater was not sure. 'This barge, apparently, is bound for Memphis. For the naval force there.'

The watchman frowned. 'Supposed to be picked up tomorrow. Bound for Natchez.'

Bowater felt the irritation mount. Why was he talking to this man, and not Sullivan? 'I know simply that I was told the barge is intended for the navy at Memphis.'

'All right then, let's see your papers.' The watchman sighed.

Papers? Bowater thought. *My commission? What papers?*

'Ya got papers, ain't ya? Receipt, contract for the barge? Didn't Mr Williamson give you no papers?'

This was idiotic and Bowater was about to say as much when he heard the churning water sound of the *General Page*'s paddle wheels beginning to turn hard, and the side-wheeler's steam whistle howled. Bowater looked over, startled. The barge was pulling away from the wall, he could see the black space opening up, the chasm between barge and wall and the dark water at the bottom. The whistle stopped and Sullivan's voice boomed over the sound of the paddle wheels, shouting, 'Come on, Cap'n! Jump for it, you'll miss the damned boat!'

Bowater looked from the barge to the watchman to the barge. 'Hold her there, you thievin son of a bitch!' the watchman shouted. The shotgun thudded on the packed dirt as he let go of the barrel, grabbed hold of Bowater's collar. Bowater knocked his hand aside, sprinted for the wall. He launched himself off, was flying through the air, when it occurred to him the barge might be too far away already.

It wasn't. He landed hard, fell forward, hands down on the lumps of coal. He scrambled to his feet, scrambled up the hill of coal. The night was filled with a flash like lightning, the boom of the shotgun going off. A swarm of buckshot hit the coal just at Bowater's left hand, spit fragments of the black rock into his face. He scrambled on, up over the coal pile and down the other side.

The barge was still up against the *General Page*'s transom, and Bowater grabbed hold of the rail and pulled himself over. Ruffin Tanner was there, helping him over, and Francis Pinette. Further forward, standing in a clump and out of the way, were six of the riverboat men. They were smiling, enjoying the show.

'Oooweee!'

Bowater and his men looked up. Mississippi Mike Sullivan was leaning on the hurricane deck rail, grinning down at them. 'That was a hell of a jump,

Cap'n! I surely did not think you would make that!'

Bowater felt his eyes go wide, his mouth fall open. He was incapable of speech.

Sullivan leaned farther over the rail. 'Damn, Cap'n, you are completely covered in coal dust! You could do a minstrel show, right here!'

Bowater's hands were trembling. He felt the words rise up from his throat. 'You . . . son . . . of . . . a . . . bitch!' He charged forward, raced for the ladder to the hurricane deck.

Samuel Bowater knew about killing. As a young ensign he had killed Mexicans. He had killed hostile islanders in the Pacific, slavers in Africa. In a year of warfare, Bowater had killed Yankees. But each time, every time, he had killed because he had to, because it was his duty. He had never actually wanted to kill anyone. Until now.

CHAPTER 3

SIR: We have some information today that the enemy is about moving, and his forces are said to be large and his transports very numerous at Old Point [Virginia]. I trust you will be able to penetrate and defeat his designs.
Very respectfully, your obedient servant,

Stephen R. Mallory
to Flag Officer Josiah Tattnall,
Commanding Naval Forces, James River

Wendy Atkins looked at the letter in her hand. Crumpled and stained, smudged, wrinkled as if it had been wet, subject to the hard use of the Confederate Postal Service. Postmarked Yazoo City. Written by Samuel Bowater.

In front of her, on the bed where she and Samuel had made love her first and only time, a carpetbag sat open. Its gaping mouth begged to be filled, but Wendy hesitated. *What to put in it? Can I really do this thing?*

She had met Bowater one year before. A mutual love of painting had led them both to the little waterside park in Norfolk, a lovely view of the river that begged to be rendered on canvas. He had been put off by her, which was no surprise. Her brashness was an organic part of her, like her long, dark brown hair, and it overpowered any natural charm she possessed. She had offered her criticism of his work, which he most certainly had not requested. She delighted in his discomfort.

She had always been like that. She had always shocked people with her outspoken manner, her boldness. She did it to keep people away, like a rattlesnake shaking its tail. She did it because she was so terrified of being ordinary that she had to make herself extraordinary, even if it meant making herself obnoxious.

But their lives, it seemed, were made to intersect. Wendy met an engineer named Hieronymus Taylor, who helped her to live out a dream she had long held, to sail aboard a man-of-war in combat. It was a thing she had wanted ever since, as a little girl, she had sat on the floor of her father's library and read romantic stories of great naval heroes and their victories in glorious battle.

Taylor snuck her aboard his ship dressed as a common sailor. One thing that Taylor had failed to mention – the captain of the ship was Samuel Bowater. She had seen him, calm as if he was painting a picture, in the middle of the bloody combat. She had been revolted, terrified, intrigued. The emotional wounds of all she saw that day took months to heal. She fled Norfolk for her family's home in Culpepper.

It was late fall when she returned to Norfolk, a very different person. Things did not seem as frivolous as they once had. Her experience in battle had focused her mind beautifully. She volunteered as a nurse at the naval hospital.

In that capacity she met Samuel Bowater again, when he was brought it on a stretcher, fresh from Hatteras Inlet, his leg and arm so torn up that he nearly lost them both. Wendy nursed him back to health. She fell in love with him. And he with her.

It was in February that Bowater came to her there, in the little carriage house in which she lived, behind the Portsmouth home of her aunt Molly Atkins. He came from the fight at Elizabeth City, a fleet battle between gunboats in which he had seen things that wrenched him down deep. He asked her for canvas and paint and for hours he poured his grief out with oils and brush. And when he was done, and that horror was exorcized, as much as it could be, they lay down on the bed on which her carpetbag now rested and consummated the tumultuous thing that had been brewing between them for eleven months.

Soon after, he was reassigned to an ironclad in Mississippi. He fought in the losing effort to stop the Yankees from coming up the Mississippi River from the Gulf, Farragut and that bunch.

For two weeks after the battle, Wendy had walked around numb, as if she were encased in glass, her mind dulled to the grief and anxiety of not knowing. And then, on the eighth of May, the letter arrived and she knew that Samuel Bowater was safe, as of eight days earlier. He was in Yazoo City.

She had to go to him.

She went to her wardrobe, pulled out a plain gray dress, folded it, stuck it in her carpetbag.

This is insane.

How could she travel to Yazoo City, a woman by

herself? It would be madness at any time, but now, with the entire nation at war, it was beyond the pale.

But yet . . . War brought with it a certain insanity, as if the old rules did not apply, as if she could do things she would not otherwise have dreamed of doing. Hadn't she dressed as an apprentice sailor and snuck aboard a man-of-war, actually taken the wheel in the middle of a sea fight? How, in a sane world, could that have happened?

She could go to Yazoo City. It was just a matter of courage. Did she have the courage.

'No,' she said out loud, 'I do not have the courage.' *But I'll go anyway.*

She packed the rest quickly: dresses, chemises, stockings, her painting smock and her paints, a tiny canvas she had primed the day before. She looked at the window, more as a matter of habit than in hopes of seeing anything. It was around nine o'clock at night, full dark, and all she could see was her own reflection in the glass.

Dear God, I look a misery. The days of anxiety had not been kind to her. She was twenty-seven, not a young girl anymore, and the years were starting to show.

'I guess I had better get Samuel to marry me,' she said out loud, 'or I'll be an old maid soon enough.' She smiled as she thought of the two of them, she and Aunt Molly, living out their dotage together, old maids with white hair. People would whisper about them. Children would start rumors that they were witches.

She could imagine the two of them growing old together. They had got on well in the two years that Wendy had been with her, staying in the carriage house. Molly was lively and fun, and they understood each other's need for occasional solitude.

Indeed, they did not grow tired of one another because they did not see much of one another. Molly was always on the move, and there would sometimes be weeks in which Wendy was certain Molly had not come home, but she was never sure. Molly never announced when she was leaving and did not announce her return. One day she was around the house, one day she was not. But Wendy lived happily in the little carriage house and enjoyed Molly's company when it was there, and she did not ask questions.

Wendy finished packing, then pulled a simple traveling dress over her chemise, no crinoline, which she avoided in any event. She took the money that she had hidden in her sock drawer and stuffed it down into the carpetbag. She sat at her familiar desk and wrote a short note to Aunt Molly, explaining things matter-of-factly, and left it on her pillow. She took one look around the carriage house, a place she had come to love, then tied a simple bonnet on her head, turned down the lantern until the flame was extinguished, and stepped out into the night.

It was dark and warm, springtime in tidewater Virginia, Thursday night, and the city was a frenzy of activity. McClellan was on the Peninsula, pushing for Richmond, and it was generally believed that the Yankees would soon be crossing Hampton Roads and landing on the Confederate side of the water. All that morning and afternoon they had heard the boom of the Yankee guns as the men-of-war in Hampton Roads shelled Sewell's Point.

Rumors drifted like clouds over the city: the

Yankees would overrun them, the Yankees would be beaten back by Confederate troops even now being sent from Richmond, the mighty ironclad *Virginia* would destroy any vessel attempting to ferry troops, as she had destroyed *Cumberland* and *Congress* just a month before.

Those stories had pulled Wendy's emotions one way, then another, until finally she was so sick of the back-and-forth that she dismissed them all, out of hand.

But from the sounds that came out of the night she could tell that the rumors still found true believers. Portsmouth and Norfolk across the river were being abandoned; the signs and the noise of flight were all around. The clatter of hooves, the rumble of wagons and carriages, the huff and hiss and roar of the trains filled the night. Soldiers and civilians, they were all on the move.

For a second Wendy just stood, felt the handle of her carpetbag in her sweating palm, wondered what she should do. She had reckoned on getting a train and had not considered the possibility that she would not be able to. Still, she could think of no better plan, so she took a deep breath and headed down the flag-stone path to the gate in the picket fence.

'There's a war on, haven't you heard?' The voice came from behind her, soft and feminine, and it startled her as if a hand had grabbed her ankle. She gasped, jumped, whirled.

Aunt Molly stepped out of the shadows of the rhododendron bush that huddled against the carriage house. 'Are you fleeing from the Yankee vandals, dear?' she asked.

'Oh—' Wendy needed a moment to collect herself.

She pressed a hand to her throat, took a deep breath. She could feel her heart thumping in her chest. 'Oh, Molly, you scared me half to death! How did you—'

'You left your curtains open, dear. I've been watching you pack like a madwoman for the past hour. I suppose I got curious.'

'Oh. Well . . . with all the rumors . . . and such . . . of the Yankees coming, I thought perhaps I should go back to Culpepper . . . be with my family . . . my mother. You understand.'

Molly took a step closer and smiled. She was ten years older than Wendy, never married, which put her solidly in the category of spinster aunt.

Why she had never married, Wendy did not understand. She was a beautiful woman, her hair thick and blond, her skin pale and smooth as that of a woman half her age. In coloring she and Wendy were nearly opposites, but in temperament they were more alike than any other two members of the family. That was the real reason that Wendy's parents had objected so vociferously to her coming to live with Molly. They did not think their daughter's behavior needed further reinforcing.

'You're worried about your mother?' Molly asked.

'Yes . . . and, you understand—'

'Wendy, darling, that is just such horseshit in so many ways.' Molly's vulgarity made Wendy blush, not for the first time. The words sounded so odd spoken in Molly's lilting voice, the soft tidewater accent. In truth, Molly was Wendy to the third power, the woman Wendy wished she was, but did not have the grit to be.

'How can you say that? How—'

'Wendy, you spent an hour staring at that letter from your sailor, and then you started packing. You might as well have shouted out your intentions into the night. And you didn't even have sense enough to close your curtains.'

Wendy felt her eyebrows come together, her lips press tight. 'Fine, very well, I am going to go to Samuel. You won't stop me.' She was impressed with her own determination, her tone of defiance, even as she spoke.

'No, I won't stop you,' Molly agreed. 'I just want to be sure you'll make it there alive.' She took two steps forward, her hand lashed out, grabbed the handle of the carpetbag, yanked it from Wendy's grasp. She moved so fast Wendy only had time to gasp, and then she was standing there empty-handed.

'All right,' Molly said. 'Now I have stolen your bag. But that's no great concern, is it, because your money is hidden on your person. Right?'

'Oh . . . ah . . .'

'Your money is in your bag? All of it?'

'Well, yes.'

'Very well. So now you are a penniless woman, far from home and friends. And now I am a filthy lecher who is determined to have his way with you. And you do what?'

'Scream?'

Molly nodded. 'Scream as you pull a gun and shoot me?'

'Pull a gun? Dear Lord.'

Molly shook her head. Her expression showed incredulity, amusement, pity. 'My dear, you have a lot more courage than you do sense. That's how I knew you weren't going to Culpepper, because going to

54

Culpepper would be the sensible thing to do, but it would not be the courageous thing. As it is, you'll be lucky to make it out of Virginia alive.'

Wendy felt the tears coming and she wiped them aside. She was frightened, frustrated, uncertain. She stood there in the chaotic night and she felt like a stupid little girl caught trying to run away from home.

'Oh, come now.' Molly stepped up and put her arms around Wendy and Wendy buried her face in Molly's silk dress. 'I shouldn't have said you lack sense, that's not true. You just want for experience.' She let Wendy cry for a minute more before adding, 'We'll be all right. We'll find your sailor boy.'

Wendy let the tears come, let the fear and uncertainty of the past two weeks flow out and soak into Molly's dress.

Then, as she felt the tears ebb, another thought vied for her attention. *Did she say 'we'?*

Molly, it turned out, did say 'we,' and she meant 'we,' literally. She parried Wendy's protests like a fencer, turning each argument aside. 'No, no, Wendy dear, it is not an imposition, it is an adventure. Besides, I don't want to be left here in Norfolk with those damned Yankees overrunning the place. It wouldn't be safe for a single girl.'

She presented her arguments as she led the protesting Wendy up the flagstone path to her own house and in the back door that opened into the kitchen. A bulging carpetbag sat on the table. Molly was already packed.

She set Wendy's bag down beside her own. 'All right, Wendy, get your money out of your bag.'

Sheepishly, Wendy fished around for her little

bundle of Confederate bills. She found them near the bottom, pulled them out, handed them to Molly.

Molly began dividing up the bills like a card dealer. 'Unbutton your dress, dear,' she said, and then, sensing Wendy's hesitation, looked up and said, 'Go ahead.'

Wendy cleared her throat, reached a tentative hand to the buttons on her dress, and began to undo them, feeling the snug-fitting fabric fall away. She had got to just below her breasts when Molly said, 'That's fine. Now here . . .' She handed Wendy one of the three piles of bills into which she had divided her niece's net worth. 'Stick this in your dress, right on your boobie.'

'Molly!'

'Come along. At least anyone who finds it there is someone with whom you are quite intimate. I assume you trust your sailor boy not to steal from you?'

Wendy felt her cheeks burn but said nothing as she positioned the bills.

'One stack to port, one to starboard, as your sailor might say.' Molly waited while Wendy secured the bills, buttoned her dress back up.

'But why not put all the money in there?' Wendy asked.

'My dear, you don't want to have to go fishing around in there every time you need some cash! Besides, if you are robbed, it is important to have something to give, or else the robber will become more aggressive in searching. Now, have you ever fired a gun?'

'A gun? No . . .'

'Very well, then, you had better have the little one.' Molly put her foot up on a chair at the kitchen table and pulled up her dress. Silk stocking came up to her thighs, covering well-formed calves. Around her right thigh was a thin leather belt from which hung a small holstered derringer. Molly unbuckled the belt, showed it to Wendy.

'Molly, where did you ever get such a thing?'

'A single girl has to look out for herself,' Molly said. 'Now come with me.'

She led Wendy outside again, into the dark yard. 'You must always treat a gun as if it was loaded. Don't ever point it at a person unless there might be a genuine need to shoot them.'

Wendy nodded. Things were moving too fast for her to put words to them.

'Here.' Molly handed her the little gun and Wendy took it, held it carefully as if it were made of delicate china. 'Hold it with authority, like you mean it,' Molly advised. 'You won't break it. Now, go ahead and shoot the rhododendron.'

'Shoot . . .'

'Go ahead. That little thing won't do any harm.'

Wendy nodded, held the gun out the way she had seen her father do it, looked over the barrel at the dark shape of the rhododendron. She squeezed her eyes tight.

'Wait, wait! Don't close your eyes.'

'Oh.'

Wendy aimed again, this time focused on keeping her eyes open. She pulled the trigger. The derringer fired with a sharp crack, a flash like a photographer's flash powder, and a satisfying kick that bent her arm at the elbow so the gun was by her head. A week before, a gunshot would have attracted quite a bit of attention in Portsmouth, but now no one took notice. It was not the first gunshot they had heard that night.

Wendy grinned and looked at Molly. Molly said, 'Very good, dear. In any event, if you have to use that, it will no doubt be at close range.'

They went back in the kitchen. Molly showed Wendy how to load the diminutive gun, then they strapped it to Wendy's leg. She liked the feel of it, the weight, the secret menace. By outward appearance she still looked like a helpless woman. No one but Molly knew her lethal secret. She liked that.

Molly fetched a little silk drawstring reticule. She pulled it open, withdrew another gun, an odd-looking thing with a barrel that consisted of six barrels mounted around a separate shaft. 'They call this a "pepperbox,"' Molly explained as she checked the load in each barrel. 'Six shots in revolving barrels.' She explained it as if she were discussing the latest fashion from Paris.

'But see here, Wendy. The gun is always a last resort. Once a gun is pulled, things change, and it is often hard to extract yourself from the situation. Talk is always best. Talk yourself out of any circumstance, and pull the gun when you have no other choice.'

Wendy nodded and wondered where Molly had ever picked up such practical advice. She recalled the time Molly had taught her her secret recipe for pickle relish. Her tone of voice, the manner of her speech, were just the same as they were now. Guns, apparently, were as familiar to her as condiments.

Molly put the pepperbox back in the reticule and hung the bag on her arm. She picked up her carpet-bag and Wendy did the same.

'Shall we go?' Molly asked.

Wendy nodded. Once again, words abandoned her. She was not sure what to say. It was perhaps the strangest evening of her life. It was perhaps the most exhilarating.

CHAPTER 4

[U]nless some competent person of education, system, and brains is put over each division of this [River Defense] fleet it will, in my judgment, prove an utter failure. There is little or no discipline or subordination — too much 'steamboat' and too little of the 'man-of-war' to be very effective.

Major General M. Lovell
to General G. W. Randolph,
Secretary of War,
Confederate States of America

Samuel Bowater ran forward, reached the bottom of the ladder leading to the hurricane deck, pivoted around the rail, and raced up. He hit the upper deck running, passed the walking beam working up and down like a teeter-totter, made straight for the wheelhouse. A lifetime of his father's strict instruction concerning the conduct of a gentleman, fifteen years of observing the decorum expected of a naval officer, were all obliterated by blind rage. Mississippi Mike Sullivan had set him up, played him like a flute. No one had ever done that to him before.

He reached the wheelhouse, threw open the door. He was breathing hard. In the window on the opposite side he caught his reflection, the picture of a feral and frightening thing, like one of Mr Darwin's ape-men. But Sullivan was not there.

'Where – where the hell is Sullivan?' Bowater gasped.

Baxter, still at the helm, looked over at him. The cheroot was shorter now but still smoldering. His face was almost expressionless, maybe a bit amused. Men in a rage, looking to kill Sullivan, were probably common enough.

'Salon,' he said, nodding in that general direction.

Bowater cursed, slammed the door, stamped back across the hurricane deck. Sullivan must have gone down the starboard side ladder while Bowater charged up the port. He felt the fury ebb as he took the steps of the ladder fast and hit the main deck below. By the time he reached the salon door, his mood had changed from an irrational hysteria to a more controlled fury.

He kicked the door in, stamped into the big room. Oil lamps on the bulkheads lit the place with a warm, dull light. The riverboat men seemed to be celebrating, holding bottles aloft, shouting, while Bowater's men stood in a tight and angry cluster to starboard.

'Captain Bowater!' Mike Sullivan extracted himself from the crowd, crossed the deck with hand extended. 'Captain, that was a damn well-done thing, back there!'

The *bonhomie*, which would have irritated Bowater at any time, now made the fury boil again. 'You bastard!' he shouted, taking a step toward Sullivan, so

61

they were face to face, though Bowater had to look up to meet Sullivan's eyes. 'You son of a bitch, you played me . . . help you . . . steal a goddamned . . .'

'Ah, hell, Captain, we was just havin some fun! How we do it, here on the river. Come on, now, have a drink and forget it!'

Sullivan held up a bottle. Bowater drew back his arm and hit Sullivan in the face, as hard as he was able to drive his fist, hit him right in the jaw. The pain in his hand was like an explosion, as if he had shattered every bone clear up to his elbow.

Sullivan pivoted around and staggered back, but he did not fall, which was bad, because Bowater had reckoned on laying him out flat with that one blow.

The river pilot turned back to Bowater, blood running from his mouth, and his face was hard to read. Bowater shook out his hand, gasping at the pain, and got ready to take Sullivan on as he came. He had not been in a fistfight since his first year at the Navy School, but he was ready. The blood was up.

The sullen tension in the salon broke like a thunderstorm and the space was filled with shouting and pounding feet. Bowater's blue-water sailors stormed across the cabin, leaping over tables, snatching up chairs, howling like banshees, and the riverboat men raced to meet them halfway, and then they were into it.

Sullivan straightened, balled his hands into fists. Behind him Bowater saw Ruffin Tanner, holding the back rails of a chair in both hands, drawing it back like he was swinging a baseball bat.

The chair came around, describing a wide arc, and hit Sullivan on the neck and shoulders, exploding into fragments, knocking Mississippi Mike sideways and a bit off balance.

Sullivan wheeled around to face this new threat. Tanner was standing there with the shattered remains of the chair in his hands, like twin clubs. He swung for Sullivan's head and Sullivan snatched the chair rail in midswing, and while his arm was up Tanner drove the other rail into Sullivan's gut, like he was thrusting a cutlass into him. Sullivan doubled over, and as his face came down it met Tanner's knee coming up.

Damn, Bowater thought. His past fistfights were more gentlemanly affairs, boxing, really. This was a brawl, ugly and brutish.

Sullivan staggered, but still the man did not go down. He made a wounded and cornered animal sound, swung a big paw, and connected with Tanner's head, sending the sailor sprawling back into Seth Williams and one of the riverboat men, who were bound together with left arms while they flailed at one another with their right fists. The three of them fell in a heap on the deck.

Bowater understood the rules of engagement now. He cocked his arm, ready to smash Sullivan on the neck, then considered what that would do to his shattered hand. He cocked his leg instead to give him a solid kick in the lower back, when out of the corner of his eye he caught an image of a man sailing through the air, actually airborne, a flash of red-checked shirt and thick beard coming at him, and then the man hit him at waist level and carried him down to the deck.

They came down in a tangle of confused limbs, with no room to fight. Bowater might have had only a half-dozen fights in his life, but he had years of fencing, and that gave him an instinctual sense for an opening. He saw one now, slamming the man's face with his left elbow, one, two, three solid blows before the riverboat man was able to extract himself. Bowater rolled on his back, planted a foot on the man's chest, and sent him sprawling.

Scrambling to his feet, Bowater shouted in agony as he thoughtlessly put his weight on his right hand. The salon was a battlefield now, blue-water sailors in their bibbed pullovers mixing it up with the wild men of the *General Page,* clusters of fighting men, knots of two and three hammering with fists and parts of broken chairs. A table flew across the room and brought Dick Merrow down, and the sailor took one of the riverboat's black gang down with him.

Bowater gulped air, considered shouting for the men to stop it, but that was absurd, he could see it. They would stop when they could no longer move.

This is insane!

And then from his right, unseen, a fist came around and plowed into Bowater's stomach, doubling him over. Bowater flung himself shoulder first into his attacker, bringing them both down to the deck. With his left hand he snatched up part of the chair Tanner had hit Sullivan with, all concern for the relative sanity of the situation lost in his powerful need to hit the son of a bitch who had punched him.

At the moment that Tanner's chair met Sullivan's unyielding back, Hieronymus Taylor was standing in the clear space between the boilers and the massive frame of the *General Page*'s engine. He was listening to the *Page*'s chief engineer, the short, wiry, nearly bald – save for a fringe of greasy hair around his head

– Spence Guthrie. Guthrie was complaining, not an unusual circumstance. This time the subject was shortages in Memphis: coal, boiler plate, machine shops, piping, sheet lead, prostitutes.

Taylor's eyes wandered over the main steam line, caught the little bits of rust lurking against flanges. His ears heard, along with Guthrie's litany of complaints, a noise from the crosshead that was not quite right. The *pssst* and thump of steam and piston told him that somewhere an alignment was off, just a bit. But it was not his engine room.

'Got three spare fire tubes. Three. And when they's gone, goddamned if I know where we'll get more,' Guthrie was saying. He turned to the fireman. 'Come on now, get that damper open, all the way! She'll take three more pounds of pressure or I ain't Spence Guthrie!'

Taylor's eyes flickered over the steam gauge mounted on the face of the scotch boiler. The needle was creeping up toward fifteen pounds per square inch, though Taylor was certain the boilers were not meant to run much more than ten.

'Three more pounds, Spence? Gonna pop them safety valves, ain't ya?'

Guthrie snickered. 'Would, if the safety valves wasn't tied down! Best part about bein part of this army fleet. No damned inspectors crawlin around the engine room, tellin ya this and that. Man can do what he wants, engine room's his castle, way it should be. You must get an earful on them navy boats, huh?'

Taylor shook his head. His eyes moved to the top of the long, narrow locomotive boilers that provided steam to the walking beam engine. He could see the tatty bits of twine tied around the lever arms of the safety valves, preventing them from opening under the pressure of excess steam. He looked back at the steam gauge, the needle creeping up as the furnace sucked air into the fire. 'On them big ships, maybe, but I don't get bothered much. Old man don't know enough engineering to stick his nose in.' By 'old man,' Taylor meant Bowater, who was six years his junior.

'Well, you know Sullivan, he can't keep his god-damned nose outta my business. But I just give him a swift kick in the ass and it's settled.'

Guthrie and Mississippi Mike Sullivan had been together for the past year, but Taylor had known them both much longer than that. Sailors and black gang moved in and out of the universe of riverboat men on the Mississippi, but at the center of that universe was a core of pilots and engineers and captains who had been drifting around the river for years. They were a small town. They knew one another.

Taylor nodded absently. 'Uh-huh. Sullivan can use a swift kick, now and again.' The needle in the pressure gauge was trembling around fifteen pounds per square inch.

It was the first time Taylor had been in an engine room since abandoning the crippled *Yazoo River* below New Orleans. He had started that fight as chief engineer, ended it as a coal passer, the last man standing. An exploding boiler had done in the rest of the black gang at the very moment that Taylor had been crammed in a far corner of the room, fixing a broken fire pump, out of the way of the blast. It fell to Taylor to finish the work the explosion had left incomplete, and with a shotgun he had killed the shrieking, scalded human forms that were all that was left of two of his men. One of them, James Burgess, as close to being a friend as any man Taylor had known.

Taylor forced his eyes from the gauge. Beads of sweat were standing out on his forehead. It was well over one hundred degrees in the engine room, but the sweat he felt on his face and palms, on his back, was something different. A cold sweat. He could smell himself.

'Got to get the hell outta Vicksburg, ya see?' Guthrie was still talking. 'On account of how we commandeered that coal barge, and thank your skipper for his help. Back off on the steam once we gets up around the bend.'

Taylor nodded again. Suddenly he was not feeling well. He heard a thump on the deck overhead and it made him start. Then he heard another, and with it a muffled cry and he cocked his head, turned his ear to the fidley, that open space above the engine room that ended with the cabin roof above.

There was a fight going on, a brawl topsides. Taylor recognized the sounds – he had heard them often enough, on riverboats and in taverns and on waterfront streets. It was easy enough to guess who was doing the fighting and why. As every river man knew, when salt- and freshwater mix, it causes a chaotic, roiling effect.

'Gotta go, Spence. I'll stop by later,' Taylor said quickly and headed up the ladder.

'What the hell's your hurry?' Spence called to his back. Guthrie had not heard the sounds of the fight over the hiss of steam, the roar of the boiler, and Taylor did not enlighten him.

He stepped out of the fidley into the night air and

breathed deep. He had left his gray uniform frock coat on the workbench below, and his white cotton shirt was wet with perspiration. It was fifty degrees cooler topside than in the engine room, and though the night was not cold by any means, Taylor shivered. He was glad to be on deck.

He hurried down the side deck, the sounds of the fight loud now. He could hear breaking furniture, cursing, shouting, the thump of bodies hitting structural members of the vessel. He burst through the door into the salon, into a world of chaos.

The fight was fully under way, with sailors and river men flailing away at one another, men rolling on the deck, swinging roundhouse punches, biting, kicking, clawing. Hard to see who was winning. No one.

To his right, Taylor saw Angus Littlefield, rated seaman, with arms pinned behind him by the one they called Doc, while another of the riverboat crew was beating him senseless. Taylor had no concern for Littlefield one way or another – it was how he felt about most sailors – but now Littlefield was one of his people getting whipped by two of them.

He shouted and flung himself at the cluster of men, pushing Littlefield out of the river men's grasp as he elbowed one and drove a fist into the jaw of the second, the kind of move that takes dozens of brawls to master.

Littlefield went down, so did the man holding him, but the man punching came up with a boot in the stomach and Taylor was doubled over. But he knew what was coming, stumbled aside, felt the second kick swish by his head and miss. He straightened. The kicker was off balance now, and Taylor's fist plowed into his hedgerow of beard.

The man went down and Taylor pounced on him.

Taylor's fists fell like hammer blows, too fast for the man to fend off. Over twenty years of wrenching in engine rooms had rendered his hands and arms powerful. He felt his control slipping, slipping. A brawl was supposed to be cathartic, but now every blow he struck just ratcheted his fury up further and further. He was shouting, 'Son of a bitch! Son of a bitch!'

A brogan connected with his left side, knocked him off the bleeding man he had been pummeling and onto the deck. The foot hit him again, in the stomach, but his muscles were clenched and he hardly felt it. The river man kicked again. Taylor caught the foot in his arm, pulled, and the man went down, and Taylor was up and on him, kicking him again and again, shouting incoherently. The room seemed to resolve into shades of red, and his screaming seemed to meld into the shrieks of James Burgess an instant before the silencing blast of the shotgun.

The man on the deck was curled up, fetal position, and Taylor's kicks were landing on shins and arms, so Taylor stopped kicking him, grabbed him by the hair, and pulled him half to his knees. He grabbed the collar of the river man's filthy checked shirt, held it with the iron grip of his left hand, and began to hammer the man's face with his right, and there was nothing the man could do to stop him, so powerful and relentless was Hieronymus Taylor.

Taylor no longer had any sense of what was happening, of the fight around him, of the noise, which had fallen off to nothing, he could only keep hitting and screaming. He felt hands on his arms and his shoulders, pulling him back, and he jerked and twisted and flailed out, but the hands had him tight, pulled him away until his grip on the riverboat man's shirt was broken, his bloody face out of reach.

The hands pulled him back, and he twisted and saw that it was Ruffin Tanner holding him on one side, blood streaked across his face. On the other side, Dick Merrow, his gray bibbed sailor shirt ripped halfway in two. And still Taylor fought.

'All right, Chief, all right!' Tanner shouted. 'Fight's over, damn it!'

Taylor stopped flailing. The room came back into focus. He could hear his own breath, the loudest thing in his ears. The hands were still holding him tight, and he twisted, angry and resentful, and they let him go.

He looked around the room. The chairs and tables were everywhere, not one still standing. The men had stopped fighting now. Bloody men, hurt men, some nursing limbs or holding handkerchiefs against bleeding wounds.

They were looking at him. Looking at him like he was some kind of lunatic. In that place of insanity, they were looking at him as if he had done something savage and inhuman. He turned from them all and stormed out of the wrecked salon.

CHAPTER 5

Captain Lee: . . . I must begin by saying that we were preparing for evacuation [of Norfolk] 10 or 12 days before it took place. General Johnston . . . was fearful that the abandonment of the Peninsula would necessitate the evacuation of the navy yard.

Investigation of the Navy Department,
Confederate States of America

Wendy let Molly lead the way to the train station. More than lead, Molly seemed to tow her along, like a tug with a ship on the hawser. It was not the first time Wendy had felt that way, like an awkward, wind-bound ship to Molly's nimble, powerful towboat. That was how frenetic Molly could be. Even when her aunt was not physically pulling her by the arm, Wendy felt dragged along by the vortex of her energy.

They walked to the train depot. It was pointless to try to get transportation. That much was clear once they maneuvered through the smaller side streets in which Molly's house was hidden and came out on Water Street. Streetcars stood abandoned, their traces lying empty before them as if in surrender. Wagons heavy loaded with furniture and children, entire households, rattled for the roads north to Richmond. The waterfront was crowded with steamboats and sailing vessels, fishing smacks, coasting schooners, all scrambling to get under way. It was the Exodus, minus Moses, minus the hope of a Promised Land.

'I am not optimistic, dear, about what we will find at the train depot,' Molly said, but her lack of optimism did not slow her down. They walked down the dark street, the river to their east, brick buildings like a wall beside them. Wendy felt the weight and steady thump of the gun on her thigh and she liked the sensation. She remembered Samuel's hand running over that same spot of skin.

They were still a block distant from the train station when they were forced to slow down by the wide stream of people all flooding in the same direction. People hustled forward with hands straining to grip bulging bags, packages held under arms. Carts were chockablock in the road, and all the drivers could do was yell and curse at one another because there was no place for any of them to go. On the sidings, which Wendy could occasionally glimpse between the brick and wooden buildings, train cars jerked and stopped, rolled and stopped, to the hiss of steam and the rumble of iron wheels on tracks.

The crowd grew denser as they approached the station, the center of the universe of flight, and progress slowed until it was near a standstill, a mere shuffling toward the steps of the clapboard-sided building.

'Molly, this is hopeless,' Wendy said, speaking loudly to be heard over the mass of sound from the crowd, the carts, and the trains.

'Perhaps,' Molly said. 'Let's get inside and see. I know some people. They might help.'

'But how will we ever . . .' It did not seem possible that they could even get into the station, but before she could finish her question, Molly advanced, moving like a fox through the undergrowth, slipping sideways through gaps in the throng, exploiting every tiny opening in the pack of refugees. Her elbows flailed like offensive weapons, her carpetbag a battering ram, opening the way with just enough subtlety that the people she pushed past could dismiss the assault as an accident, if they were feeling charitable. Most of them, of course, were not feeling charitable, but by the time the curse left their lips, Molly was well past them.

Wendy could do nothing but follow close behind, keeping in Molly's wake, stepping along before the parted waters closed up again.

For all of Molly's aggression, it still took them fifteen minutes to cover the hundred yards from the edge of the crowd to the platform of the station, where the real chaos was taking place. The bedlam in the streets did not compare to the insanity on the platform, with men pushing and shoving for trains, packing aboard until the number of people jammed into each car was laughable, and then a few more shoving in.

They were soldiers mostly, gray-clad, carrying packs and rifles. Officers in frock coats with swirls of gold on sleeves, sergeants shouting in hoarse voices. If there was some order to it all, Wendy could not see it.

Why are the soldiers getting on the trains? she wondered. If indeed the Yankees were coming to

Norfolk, shouldn't the soldiers be there to meet them?

Molly stopped at an office door, a nondescript door that would pass unnoticed if one were not looking for it. She knocked, hard, waited, knocked again. They waited. Molly let out a breath of exasperation.

'Who are we looking for?' Wendy asked. The night was growing more bizarre, with her slightly eccentric but generally harmless aunt now displaying resources and a determination that Wendy had never seen before.

'Alvan Reid. The stationmaster. But he seems to be—'

The door opened and a man in his mid-forties or so, a very haggard-looking man in shirtsleeves and unbuttoned vest, his thick brown hair wild, his moustache slightly askew, peered out uncertainly, like an animal peeking out of its hole to see if it is safe to come out, if the dogs are gone. He saw Molly and his face brightened a bit, or at least for an instant looked less miserable, and he opened the door wider and waved them in.

It was quieter in the office, the din of the platform muted a bit by the thin walls. 'Molly, it is grand to see you, but you can forget it.'

'Forget it? Alvan, dear, you do not even know why I am here.'

'Certainly I do. You're looking for a seat on a train out of here. It has been the same all day. But I fear the army has taken over all the trains. There are only soldiers riding tonight, and those who have managed to associate themselves with the army in some way.'

Wendy spoke at last. 'But why are the soldiers

leaving? If the Yankees are coming, shouldn't the soldiers stay?'

Alvan looked at Wendy as if he was surprised she could speak. 'Soldiers are going to Richmond. The Union Army is on the Peninsula and marching for Richmond, and all the troops around are being sent there to defend it. Leave us to the Yankees, we don't matter, they need every man to protect the damned politicians in Richmond.'

'Now, Alvan,' Molly continued, her tone soft and persuasive, 'I know these soldiers are taking up a lot of room, but surely there's—'

'I said forget it, Molly, I meant forget it. It's out of my hands. The damn army's taken over the platform and they're deciding who goes and who doesn't. I'm just trying to keep the trains running, and even that's more than I can handle.'

He reached out a hand, laid it on Molly's shoulder, and when he spoke again his tone was different. Kinder. 'You know I'd help you if I could, Molly. You before any of the others come see me today, and there's been a power of 'em. But there's nothing I can do.'

Molly nodded, resigned. 'Very well. Thank you, Alvan, I know you'd help if you could. Godspeed.' She turned to Wendy. 'Let's go, dear, we'll have to find some other way out of town.'

They pushed their way off the platform and out of the station, and the going was a bit easier moving against the crowd than pushing through it. They didn't even try to speak until the station was two blocks behind them and the mob sparse enough for them to walk side by side.

'Well, that was a lot of effort for nothing,' Molly

said. 'I'm sorry, dear.' She was still walking with purpose.

'It's quite all right, Molly. How do you happen to know the stationmaster?'

'Oh, you know how it is, one meets people . . .'

'I see,' Wendy said, though she didn't. Wendy had never had that capacity. Too abrasive, too forward, she rejected people before they rejected her. She had somehow always thought her aunt the same way. They were, were they not, the closest in temperament of all the family?

Perhaps not.

There seemed to be so many truths that Wendy was now finding were not true at all.

They walked back the way they had come, past the side road that led to Molly's house, and continued on. 'There are other ways out of town,' Molly was explaining. 'But not by road. We can't very well walk, and I suspect the roads are completely jammed with wagons and such and they'll all just sit there until the Yankees come and shoo them all home.'

'Yes,' Wendy said. What else could she say?

They walked in silence for a while, and soon they were walking by the ten-foot-high brick wall that separated the town of Portsmouth from the shipyard. The shipyard was generally called the Norfolk Navy Yard, though it was not in Norfolk. Its official name was the Gosport Naval Shipyard, though it was not in Gosport either, but rather Portsmouth.

They came at last to the wide wrought-iron gate that marked the entrance to the shipyard. They were accustomed to seeing guards there, bored-looking teenagers in butternut, leaning on their rifles or on the wall. But not tonight. Now there was a detail of a dozen soldiers and a lieutenant in charge of them, and they looked as if they were taking their duty very seriously.

Not so seriously, however, that they could resist a few appreciative glances as Molly, and Wendy behind her, came to a halt in front of them.

The lieutenant stepped forward, gave a little bow, doffed his hat. 'Ladies, how may I assist?'

'I would like to see Captain John Tucker, of the navy,' Molly said, very businesslike. 'Is he within?'

The lieutenant smiled. 'I believe he is within, ma'am, but he's a bit busy right now.'

'He will see me. Please inform him that Molly Atkins is at the gate.'

Molly stopped, as if no more need be said. The lieutenant began to smile again, amused and patronizing, and then the smile died as the possibility dawned on him that Molly was something more than a camp follower. He hesitated; his eyes shifted left and right. He made a decision. 'Johnson, go and find Captain Tucker. Tell him there is a Molly Atkins here.'

Johnson saluted and ran off into the dark shipyard. 'So, Lieutenant,' Molly said, and her voice was all sweetness now, 'whatever is *your* name?'

There were questions that Wendy wanted to ask, questions piled on questions, going right back to Molly's brandishing that first pistol, but she could not ask them, standing there in front of the navy yard. In any event, Molly gave her no chance as she carried on her flirtation with the lieutenant.

By the time Johnson returned with a naval officer following behind, the lieutenant would have torn off his right arm if Molly had asked him to.

'Mo – Miss Atkins, a pleasant surprise.' Captain Tucker was tall, with dark hair and long side whiskers that ran up into his moustache and along the side of his mouth, so that only the hair on the chin was missing to make it a full beard. He bowed, took Molly's proffered hand.

'Captain, the lieutenant here has been most gracious, but is there a place we might speak?'

Tucker threw a glace back over his shoulder. Lights were moving like fireflies in the shipyard, and a world of noise was coming out of the dark, men shouting orders, large things moving, the sounds of a shipyard being dismantled.

'Ah, yes, I suppose . . .' Tucker said. 'Won't you follow me?'

'Certainly. Wendy, may I present Captain John Tucker? Captain, this is my niece, Wendy Atkins.'

Tucker nodded, too distracted to take any great notice. The lieutenant barked, 'Johnson, Quigley, get the ladies' bags!'

The soldiers snatched up the carpetbags as Tucker led the way into the shipyard. Molly turned to Wendy and said, *sotto voce*, 'You can see they don't call Captain Tucker "Handsome Jack" for nothing.'

Wendy smiled, nodded, followed behind Molly, unsure of how a rash decision just a few hours before had led her to that place.

They crossed the cobblestone-paved ground, and the farther they got into the yard, the more pronounced the sound of chaotic flight. It was the same within the walls of the yard as it was in the town outside, except that the chaos in the navy yard had more of a feel of organization. Methodical chaos.

'They reckon the Yankees'll be here any day,'

Tucker explained as they walked. 'We could defend this yard if we wanted to, but Richmond doesn't believe it, so we're taking everything that can be moved and we'll leave the rest.' He shook his head. 'Absolutely shameful.'

They came at last to a brick building, an office building, and Tucker led them inside, down a hallway lit with a series of lamps, into what Wendy assumed was his own office, a cluttered desk, papers piled on chairs, on top of file drawers. A young midshipman was pulling armfuls of documents from the drawers and stuffing them into crates on the floor.

'Fletcher, leave us for a minute,' Tucker said and the young man disappeared.

Tucker cleared off two chairs, gestured, sat behind his desk.

'All right, Molly,' he said.

'John . . .' Molly paused after the familiar address, gave the name a teasing quality. 'Wendy and I are trying to get out of Norfolk. Before the Yankees arrive. There's no getting on the trains, and the roads are impossible.'

For a moment they were silent, the implied request hanging in the air. Then Tucker said, 'Do you want me to get you on board a naval vessel? Molly, you can't possibly think—'

'Not a naval vessel, silly. Surely there are tugs and transports and things. What are you using to carry all your loot to Richmond?'

'Well, there are transports, but—'

'John . . .' Again Molly paused, and Wendy could only shake her head in admiration. Molly could do with words what Wendy strove to do with painting, applying the subtlest shading, pulling nuance out of the mundane, infusing every bit of it with meaning that was clear to anyone alert and intelligent enough to grasp it.

'John, you know it would not be good for the Yankees to find me here.'

Tucker was silent for a moment. 'No,' he admitted at last, and Wendy understood enough of the conversation to realize she was not really following it. *Why wouldn't it be good? Are the Yankees going to rape and pillage?* Surely they would not, and even if they did, why should Molly think she warranted special treatment? And why might Tucker agree?

'But Molly, I don't think the Yankees will be looking . . . for you . . . in particular.'

Molly sighed. 'I would not have thought so a month ago. Now . . . ?'

No, Wendy thought, *they are having a conversation on an entirely different level, like they're talking in code.* She looked at her aunt, with her lovely full lips, her little nose in profile, and wondered who the hell she was.

Tucker shook his head. 'Molly, I understand your situation, but you must understand mine. There is just no possibility—'

Footsteps clattered down the hall outside and the fragile tension of their negotiation collapsed as Tucker turned his head to the closed door. A fist rapped on the frame.

'Come,' Tucker called. Wendy saw a cloud of irritation sweep across Molly's face, and then she resettled herself, adjusted her skirts, and with that resettling, her face fell back into its usual expression, one nearly devoid of emotion, save for a slightly pleasant, not too inquisitive look. It was the expression Wendy had fixed in her mind when she thought of Molly. Now she wondered if perhaps even that expression carried more nuance than she had ever guessed at.

The door opened, and a man in the frock coat and cap of a Confederate Navy lieutenant entered, saluted. A handsome man, early thirties, perhaps, with a bold dark moustache the same color as his dark brown eyes. 'Sir, I'm back from Sewell's Point.'

'Tell me what's happening,' Tucker said. The lieutenant's eyes darted at the two women. 'Molly Atkins, Wendy Atkins,' Tucker added, 'may I present Lieutenant Asa Batchelor? Go ahead, Lieutenant, it's all right.'

'Ah, yes, sir . . .' Batchelor began, unsure. 'The Federals opened up a little after noon and the forts replied as best they could but of course they're all but deserted. The Federals continued until the *Virginia* came up, around two-thirty.'

CSS *Virginia*. Wendy knew her well. Everyone around Norfolk did. Since March of that year, so did everyone in the Western world. She was an ironclad man-of-war, a battery of ten heavy guns housed in a nearly impregnable casemate, built on the hull of the former United States steam frigate *Merrimack*.

A month before, she had mauled the Federal blockading fleet in a day-long, bloody rampage, had been absolute master of Hampton Roads until the Union ironclad *Monitor* arrived. Since that day, it had been an uneasy stalemate between the two novel ships.

'Was the *Monitor* there?'

'Yes, sir. *Monitor* and four of their smaller steamers.

81

They did considerable damage to the fort. Set the barracks on fire. Reckon they're still burning. As soon as *Virginia* steamed up, well, they all up-anchored and skedaddled back across the Roads.'

Tucker nodded. 'No fight?'

'No, sir. *Monitor* doesn't care to tangle with the *Virginia* anymore, it seems.'

Tucker nodded again. 'No troops? Did they seem as if they were interested in putting troops ashore?'

'No, sir, not that I could see. No boats from any of the ships. Guess maybe they were just testing the strength of the forts on the point.'

Tucker frowned. Molly spoke. 'Whatever is the matter, Captain Tucker?' It sounded silly, a woman and a civilian asking after military affairs, and so it seemed odder still when Tucker answered her with no hint of condescension.

'The Federals are going to put men ashore somewhere, and soon, I imagine. We need to keep *Virginia* safe, she's the most powerful weapon we have. We can't afford to let her get trapped between the Yankees ashore and the Yankee fleet in the Roads.'

'So send her away,' Molly said. 'Send her up the James to Richmond. Defense of the river will be as important as the defensive lines on shore.'

'We can't.' Tucker smiled. 'We need her here. She's the most powerful weapon we have. Besides, *Virginia* might be able to stop the Yankees from taking Norfolk. McClellan nearly canceled his whole campaign for fear of *Virginia*.'

'The Yankee soldiers are only vulnerable to *Virginia* when they are landing,' Molly said. 'She can do nothing to them once they are ashore. What you need to know is when and where the Yankees will land, so you can stop them, or at least hold your beastly iron ship here until the last moment.'

'Exactly.'

'Well,' Molly said, as if the answer was obvious, 'why don't you ask me to find out for you?'

Tucker leaned back in his chair, regarded Molly for a moment. 'I thought you wanted to get out of Norfolk,' he said at length. 'Now you're offering to stay?'

'I'll stay long enough to tell you when and where the Yankees will arrive. I'll find that out in exchange for your promise that Wendy and I are on the boat that takes you out of here.'

Tucker looked at Batchelor. Batchelor looked baffled, and Wendy was glad to have company in her confusion.

'I don't know . . .' Tucker said. 'If you were going to New York, perhaps. But you're too well known around here, particularly among the navy men. You said yourself you wouldn't be safe—'

Molly dismissed that with a wave of her hand. 'I'll be safe, don't you worry. I have Wendy here, and Wendy' – Molly's voice dropped to a whisper – '*has a gun!*'

Tucker laughed and then Batchelor laughed and finally Wendy thought she saw the humor in it and she laughed too. And then Tucker said, 'Very well, Miss Atkins, if you reckon you can fulfill your part of the bargain, you have a deal. What do you need?'

'Well' – Molly ran an appreciative eye over Lieutenant Batchelor – 'why don't you give me this handsome young officer and let him attend to my needs?'

83

'Very well,' Tucker said. 'Lieutenant, please attend to Miss Atkins. Get her whatever she wants, within reason.'

'Ah . . . yes, sir,' Batchelor said.

'Good.' Molly stood with the satisfied air of someone who has won an auction. 'Let's get moving. Wendy, come with me, darling.'

Wendy stood more slowly. 'Where are we going?'

'I'm not entirely certain, dear,' Molly said, 'but I suppose we'll go and ask those vile Yankees what their intentions are.'

CHAPTER 6

I trust that the results to be derived from this [River Defense] fleet will compensate for the out-lay, but unless some good head is put in charge of it I fear such will not be the case. The expenses for outfit, payment for ships, and month's wages will consume one and a half millions.

Major General M. Lovell
to General G. W. Randolph

The morning after the brawl, Bowater woke with an unaccustomed stiffness in his arms and legs. He could feel the tender places on his body, like patches of punky wood on an old boat. He sat up with a groan and a difficulty that belonged to a much older man. He braced himself on the edge of his bunk with his right hand, then jerked the hand back as the pain shot right up through his arm.

He closed his eyes, let the pain settle. He did not want to look at the hand but knew he had to. Finally, he opened his eyes, examined his outstretched fingers, his palm, and the back of his hand. It was swollen nearly double what it should be, and stained an unnatural yellow and purple. He flexed his fingers. He could move them all, but not much, and it hurt like hell when he tried. At least he could move them, which meant they were not broken. He thought.

Goddamn it . . . He stood and shuffled to the small mirror mounted on the bulkhead, found that he could not walk without limping. Sullivan had given him one of the first-class passenger cabins, which was not what Bowater would generally call first class – it hardly compared to his second officer's cabin aboard the USS *Pensacola* – but it was better than the bedroll on the deck that the men had for quarters.

Samuel stared in the mirror, saw shades of his father staring back. It was in the eyes, the set of the mouth, the slightly weary, slightly haughty expression. His father wore a neatly trimmed beard and moustache, pure white, while Samuel wore a moustache and goatee, which were still dark brown, shot through with only a few strands of white.

He shook his head, washed his face as best he could with his left hand, dismissed the idea of shaving. He pulled on his pants and his shirt. It took him fifteen minutes to button them, fifteen painful, frustrating minutes, but there was no chance that he was going to ask for help.

At last he pulled on his frock coat and set his cap on his head. His muscles were warmed by the activity, the stiffness worked out of them, and he could walk with no discernible limp.

He did not know what would greet him on deck, but he was not optimistic. There was civil war raging right on the decks of the *General Page*. The night before, the much-injured combatants had crawled off to their various places to heal: two sullen, angry gangs of men with a big score to settle. The war had not been decided.

Perhaps they were going at it already, taking up where they had left off. But Samuel couldn't hear the sounds of a fight, and he had to imagine that most of the others, like himself, weren't feeling much like fighting at the moment.

Maybe Sullivan was going to put the *General Page* against the bank and boot them all off, leave them stranded in some fetid swamp.

He cursed himself, as he opened the door onto the side deck, for putting himself and his men at the mercy of a man such as Mississippi Mike Sullivan. Then he cursed Mike Sullivan and Hieronymus Taylor and the world at large.

It was quiet on deck, just the creak of the big paddle wheels, the squeak and groan of the walking beam on the deck above, the rush of water along the sides. Bowater looked out over the great brown expanse of river water, the lush green shore far away.

There was no fight that he could hear.

He made his way down the side deck to the first-class passenger's salon, last night's battlefield. He reckoned breakfast was out of the question, for him and his men, anyway.

At last he could hear voices and he paused to gauge their timbre. Loud, boisterous, but not angry. Not the sounds of conflict. He wondered if his own men were collected someplace else on the ship. Aft on the fantail, perhaps.

Perhaps. But first he had to look in the salon, as much to demonstrate that he was not afraid to show his face in there as to look for his crew. He took a breath, pushed the door open.

The sight that greeted him was not the one he would have expected. Indeed, it was the one scenario he had not even considered, his men and the riverboat men all eating their breakfast, clustered around the damaged tables and occupying the surviving chairs, or sitting on the deck, backs against the bulkheads. It was not blue-water men to port, riverboat men to starboard, but all of them mixed up, some talking, some eating, some sucking on cheroots. There was not a bit of animosity in the air. Quite the opposite. The atmosphere was, if anything, congenial.

'Here, Captain, come on over here,' Hieronymus Taylor called from across the room. He was seated at a round table with Spence Guthrie, the *Page*'s chief engineer, and First Mate Buford Tarbox. Being as the *Page* was a man-of-war, Tarbox probably should have had the title first lieutenant, or executive officer, but Bowater could not bring himself to think of the man in that way.

Bowater pushed his way through the men, trying not to limp, trying not to look surprised. One of the riverboat men at a nearby table stood and pushed his chair up to Taylor's table so that Bowater could sit.

'Thank you,' Bowater said, sitting carefully. Doc, still clad in his filthy apron, appeared out of nowhere and set a plate of fried eggs and bacon down in front of him. Bowater nodded his thanks. He picked up the fork and slipped it under the table, and with the tail of his frock coat he scrubbed it as hard as he could.

'Captain, good day to you,' Tarbox said, scraping a lucifer on the table and sparking up a cheroot. 'We had us a pretty good run overnight, considerin we was draggin that barge you commandeered. Be right

88

up with Greenville by the middle of the forenoon watch.'

'Indeed.' Bowater tried the eggs. Not bad. He was very hungry.

'These gentlemen been telling me about the paucity of supplies to be found in Memphis,' Taylor said. 'It don't look too encouraging, I got to say.'

Bowater nodded, his teeth working on a piece of bacon. Behind him, the salon door opened and Mike Sullivan's voice roared through the cabin. 'Whoa, you dirty dogs! Y'all get on deck, a clean sweep fore and aft! Y'ain't on a goddamned yachting holiday!' There was good humor in his voice, and his men leaped up, and Bowater's men leaped up too, and tumbled out on deck, and Bowater wondered when they had begun taking their orders from Sullivan.

He had the sudden, disturbing thought that perhaps the fight had not really happened, that it had been a dream, or something worse.

'Captain Bowater!' Bowater swiveled to see Sullivan stepping up to their table. 'How's the hand this morning?' He was grinning wide.

'The hand is fine, thank you, Captain,' Bowater said, with coolness and just enough courtesy to avoid the taint of rudeness. He wished there were a way to discreetly slip his hand – which was decidedly not fine, and looked it – under the table, but it was too late for that.

'And how are you this morning, Captain?' Bowater asked, looking Sullivan up and down, looking for some sign of damage done in the brawl, but he could see nothing. He would have liked to think that the force needed to smash his hand as badly as it was would be enough to break Sullivan's jaw, but apparently not. If there was a bruise, it was hidden beneath thick beard.

'Goddamn it,' Sullivan roared, 'but there is nothing like an all-hands-in brawl to clear the air, ain't that a fact?'

The other river rats, Taylor, Guthrie, and Tarbox, all nodded. Sullivan slammed a big hand down on Bowater's shoulder. 'Glad we got that over with, Captain. Like pulling a tooth, it hurts for a bit, but damned if it ain't a relief after. Puts the hands in a good mood, like the fine weather that comes in on the tail of a storm.' He put a hand on his jaw, worked it back and forth. 'Be a relief when I recover from that mighty wallop you gave me.'

Sullivan grabbed up one of the empty chairs, spun it around so it was back to the edge of the table and sat down, his arms, as big as most men's legs, resting on the back. Bowater noticed for the first time that he was holding several slim, paper-bound books.

'Gentlemen.' Sullivan looked to Bowater, then Taylor. 'Didn't get a chance to show y'all these here.'

Sullivan tossed the books on the table. Taylor made no move to pick one up, so Bowater did. He looked at the cover. He was not sure what to make of it.

'It's one of those dime novels, isn't it?' Bowater asked. 'I've heard of these, never seen one.'

'Never seen one?' Mike asked with theatrical incredulity. 'Where the hell you been livin, brother?'

'In civilization. The English call them "penny dreadfuls," do they not?'

'Devil take the rutting English, this here's good ol' American lit-rit-ur.'

Bowater read the title: *The Further Adventures of Mississippi Mike Sullivan, Riverboat Man!* The cover

90

was a pen-and-ink drawing. A fellow who looked passably like the Mississippi Mike seated beside him, though trimmer, his beard more under control, was knocking a savage-looking seaman back with an uppercut to the jaw. Behind him, a black man with a slouch hat on his head and a gun in each hand fired away at cutlass-bearing cutthroats. The caption underneath read, 'Mississippi Mike dispatched the Captain of the River Pirates while his sable pard held the crew back with pistols blazing.'

Samuel Bowater burst out laughing. It was a spontaneous reaction, a pure expression of his regard for this unique form of 'lit-rit-ur.'

'It's somethin, ain't it?' Mike was grinning ear to ear, not in the least put off by Bowater's reaction. 'Now you see why the name Mississippi Mike's so goddamned famous all up and down this here river.'

Tarbox was reading one of the books, running his finger left to right and mouthing the words. Taylor had picked up another, was thumbing through it. 'You write this yourself, Sullivan?'

'Hell, no! As if I got time. I'm too busy doin amazin things to write about 'em. No, I jest put down some descriptions of my adventures, like I done with them river pirates, and I send 'em off to New York City. Publisher's got some Jewish fella, he writes it up all pretty, and next thing, folks all over the country's readin about Mississippi Mike.'

Bowater looked up and caught Taylor's eye. A shared sense of amusement passed between them, a mutual understanding such as they rarely experienced. Bowater knew that Taylor would find the penny dreadful as ludicrous as he did.

'This here war must be a great inconvenience to your literary aspirations,' Taylor drawled.

'It ain't makin things easy, I can tell ya,' Mike said. 'And they's gonna be some damned disappointed readers, if they don't get the further adventures of Mississippi Mike.'

Bowater opened the book to the first page.

The name of Mississippi Mike Sullivan is known along every watery mile of the river after which he is called. From the docks of New Orleans to the granaries of St. Paul, Minnesota, the people on the river know Mike as the hardest driving, hardest drinking, most dangerous son of a gun riverboat man on the Western Waters. Everywhere, men know to stay on his good side, or stay out of his way. It was a lesson the river pirates learned the hard way, but they learned it well.

Bowater grinned. *This just gets better and better.*

'So this . . . *contretemps* . . . with the river pirates, this was a thing that happened to you. And your' – Bowater referred back to the cover – 'your "sable pard"?'

'You're damn right it was. Sons of bitches tried to rob me. Taught 'em good. Oh, sure, there's some stuff in there's stretched a bit. And the "sable pard" stuff, that makes them abolition kangaroos in New York get all excited, shows 'em we know how to treat darkies down here. But mostly it's all true.'

Bowater nodded. He flipped to the middle of the book.

*Mississippi Mike slipped silently into the river,
and parting the waters with broad strokes of his
powerful arms, closed silently with the
unsuspecting pirates' paddle wheeler. He took a
firm grasp of the anchor chain, hauled himself
out of the water, until, catlike, he eased himself
over the rail. He paused, alert to any possible
danger. All was silent. The guard on the main
deck had not seen him.*

'Come on now, Sullivan.' Bowater looked up.
'When was the last time you moved "catlike"?'

'Never mind about that, it don't make no difference. Captain Bowater, might I have a private word
with you?'

Bowater leaned back, alert to any possible danger.
'I suppose,' he said.

'I'm obliged, surely am.' He stood and Bowater
stood and Mike led him out on the side deck and forward to the master's cabin. Sullivan held the door
open, and Bowater stepped into the mahogany and
red velvet lined sitting room. Scattered around the
space were worn, velvet-upholstered chairs and
various spittoons, the brown splotches evidence of
poor marksmanship. In Rio de Janeiro, on his first
cruise after the Navy School, Bowater had been
talked into visiting a brothel with his shipmates.
Sullivan's cabin was very reminiscent of that place.

From the hurricane deck, eight bells rang out. End
of the morning watch, 8:00 A.M. Footsteps thudded
on the deck overhead, muffled voices called out.
Sullivan gestured toward a chair. Bowater sat, his eyes
drawn to the painting on the wall. A reclining
nude. Like the French nudes from the Romantic

movement, Bowater thought, as interpreted by some randy hack.

'Beauty, ain't she? Wrestled a whorehouse bouncer for her.'

'Very nice. She fits in well. Thematically.'

'There, ya see, that's it.' Sullivan took a chair facing Bowater. He leaned forward, elbows on his knees.

'What's . . . it?'

'Well, you. You're a man of letters, I can see that. Can toss around a word like *thematically* like a preacher spouting scripture. A man of good education.'

'I am a graduate of the Naval Academy,' Bowater confirmed.

'Sure. But that don't mean you ain't an educated man, a man of letters, fellow who knows his way around a book.'

'Wel . . .'

Sullivan did not let him continue. His enthusiasm was building in a way that Bowater now recognized. 'See, here's the thing, Cap'n. This war's gonna be the end of them Mississippi Mike books. Jest too damned hard to git anything to New York City nowadays. And besides, them fellas in New York, they don't know a walking beam from a flying cow chip. Their hearts ain't in it. Mine is. I want to write these here books myself, see? But I ain't a man of letters. I'm a hard drinkin, hard fightin river rat, but I don't know nothin about writin up a book.'

'You forgot "most dangerous son of a gun river-boat man on the Western Waters." '

'Yeah, that too. But I ain't a scribbler, see?'

Bowater could see where this was going. 'But Captain Sullivan, I was under the impression that these books were no more than a retelling of actual events in your life. Why not just write them down as they happen?'

'Hell yes, sure, I could do that. But there has to be a real story, see? Can't just be a bunch of crazy things happenin. It needs a . . . what do you call it . . .'

'Plot?'

'Exactly! See, that's what I'm talkin about. We need a big story, and then all the amazin things I get into, well, they all fit into the story, like planks on a hull. Understand?'

Bowater nodded. Sullivan, like any real raconteur, had an instinctual understanding of storytelling and narrative structure. But somehow it was now 'we' who needed the plot.

'This sort of thing isn't really in my line,' Bowater said.

'Oh, I understand. I didn't reckon you could write a whole book, not as good as this fella been writin my stories. I just thought maybe you could give me a hand, a few ideas, maybe.'

'Hmm.' Bowater ran the fingers of his right hand gingerly through his goatee, over the stubble of two days' growth on his cheeks. 'All right. Perhaps I can help.'

Sullivan nodded, sat up, like a big dog anticipating a treat. 'Good, good. We need some kind of plot, you know, so as all this stuff makes sense.'

'All right, I'm thinking . . .' Bowater looked off to the middle distance, trying to keep his eyes from the nude's breasts. He assumed a thoughtful expression. 'Let's say . . . Is your father still alive? In the books, I mean?'

Sullivan frowned. 'Yeah. Ain't really been no mention of my pa.'

'Good, good. Perfect. Let's say ... Mississippi Mike's father is a riverboat pilot. Best on the Mississippi, except for Mike. It's where Mike learned the trade.'

Mike Sullivan was nodding.

'He runs one of the biggest stern-wheelers on the river. Great boat. Now, one day, his father dies ...'

Sullivan was nodding harder.

'Now, say the first mate is Mississippi Mike's uncle, his father's brother, and he gets the captaincy now. Everyone thinks that Mike's father died naturally, but Mike knows different. Mike knows it was his uncle, done murdered his pa.' Bowater found himself slipping into the vernacular.

'That's good!' Sullivan said. 'But how do I – how does this Mike Sullivan know that?'

'Well ... I guess he would figure it out somehow. Or ...'

'What?'

'What if ... yes, that's good! What if Mike's father's ghost were to show up, tell him the truth?'

Sullivan's eyebrows came together. 'His pa's ghost?'

'Yes, his ghost. Oh, readers love to see ghosts in books.'

'They do, huh? All right, so this ghost shows up, tells Mike what happened.'

'How about if Mike's sable pard sees the ghost first? Say his sable pard is on anchor watch, and the ghost shows up, and his pard knows it's Mike's pa?'

Sullivan nodded. 'Them darkies is scared to death of ghosts.'

'Exactly! That's what would make the scene so effective.'

96

Sullivan smiled wide. 'I like it, Captain Bowater, goddamn me if I don't! So then . . . what? Mike goes after his dirty rotten uncle, beats him with fists like boulders?'

'No, no . . . Mike's too smart for that. He has to make sure.'

Sullivan looked serious now, overcome by the weight of their artistic endeavors. 'All right, how does he do that?'

Bowater shook his head. 'That's all. I can't come up with any more right now. One can't force the creative process.'

'No . . . one can't,' Sullivan agreed. He stood and crossed to a small table where a bottle of whiskey and a few glasses stood on a silver tray. 'Like a wet there, Captain? Celebrate our partnership?'

Bowater glanced at the clock on the wall: 8:36 A.M. But the rules of civilization, he was finding, did not seem to apply on the Father of Waters.

'Love one, Mississippi Mike. Love one.'

CHAPTER 7

Telegram
Washington, May 6, 1862
The Norwegian corvette Norvier *is expected to
arrive at Hampton Roads with the Norwegian
minister on board. Has she yet arrived? If not,
telegraph me when she does, and inform the
commander that the Norwegian minister will
visit him at Hampton Roads.*

Gideon Welles, Secretary of the Navy,
to Flag Officer L. M. Goldsborough,
United States Navy

Wendy Atkins had a disconnected, free-floating feeling, like one of those hot air balloons that had slipped its tether, drifting along with the currents in the air, unable to direct or even predict in what direction she would be blown.

She wanted more than anything to grab Aunt Molly by the collar, to pull her into a private room, shut the door, make her answer the thousand questions that the last few hours had created. Her connection to the navy, the reasons she might be in danger, the very idea of wheedling from the Yankees the place where they would land troops.

Put all together, the disparate bits of information seemed to form a picture of what Molly was, although it was not a picture that Wendy could believe.

But Wendy did not have the chance to ask, or even to express surprise at the developments or question Molly's judgment or inquire as to their immediate future, because things were still unwinding too fast for her to pause. She had got no further than to stammer, 'Should I . . . shall I . . .' when Molly said, 'You must stay with me, dear. If we are separated now we will never find one another. It is always that way, for all the careful plans one lays. So stick by me, and I'll tell you the part to play.'

And that was it. Twenty minutes later they were seated in a dark coach, side by side, and facing a professionally detached Lieutenant Batchelor as they rattled north out of Norfolk.

They rode for a long time in silence, Molly staring out the window at the lights and the crowds in the streets, until at last the insanity of the town gave way to the dark of the country, and only the blue moonlight illuminated the low marshy land and the hard-packed, dusty road. And only then did Molly speak.

'This sort of thing . . .' she said, and for the first time Wendy heard a note of defeat in her voice, and it made her wonder what conclusions she had reached during her long silence. 'This sort of thing is so very dependent on time. Lots of time, one needs lots of time, and that is what we do not have.'

She sighed, and with that sigh seemed to expel the

gloom, and she seemed much brighter when she turned to Lieutenant Batchelor and said, 'Now, Lieutenant, you must tell me everything that you know about the situation in Hampton Roads.'

Batchelor began his briefing, professional and methodical. He told of Union forces under McClellan overrunning Yorktown behind the retreating Confederates, of Yankee ships moving up the York River, with the James denied to them by the presence of CSS *Virginia*.

'We are gravely outnumbered on the Peninsula,' Batchelor said. 'If there were anyone in command of the Union forces besides McClellan, they would be in Richmond by now. I hope all Yankee generals are as backward as the "young Napoleon."'

Batchelor described the Yankee men-of-war, the big ocean-going steam frigates, and the smaller river vessels, and the Confederate river forces that opposed them, mostly small converted civilian craft, save for the mighty *Virginia*.

'The *Virginia* draws twenty-two feet, but the pilots assure us that if we lighten her some we can get her up the James River. Right now she's the only thing stopping the Yankee boats from sailing up the James. That's why the Yankees are going up the York. Tattnall made a try at getting *Virginia* up to the York. But he couldn't do that without sinking or taking the *Monitor,* and the Yankees won't let him get close enough to their precious boat to try.'

During the entire lecture, Molly just listened and nodded and seemed to work each bit of information around in her head, like a wine taster ferreting out the subtleties of the drink. At last she said, 'Very well, then.'

'Do you have a notion of what you will do?' Batchelor asked.

'No. Is there anything else you have not told me?'

'I don't believe so. One of our people tells us a Norwegian corvette is expected in the Roads. She is carrying the Norwegian minister to Washington.'

'Really?' Molly said, and she leaned forward. This information, an afterthought for Batchelor, seemed to interest her more than the rest. 'What is the name of the ship?'

'The *Norvier*, I believe.'

'You believe?'

'She is the *Norvier*.'

Molly leaned back again, and again her eyes moved to the dark glass of the carriage window and she said nothing. They rode in silence for another twenty minutes before Molly turned back to Batchelor and said, 'Lieutenant, do you speak Norwegian?'

'No, ma'am.'

'You are formerly of the United States Navy, is that correct?'

'Yes.'

'Are there many in the United States Navy who speak Norwegian?'

Batchelor shrugged his shoulders. 'I knew of a few squareheads in the forecastle. Not many. Certainly no officers that I knew of.'

Molly nodded and looked out the window again.

They arrived at Sewell's Point somewhere around midnight. The air was thick with smoke, turning the black night sky into a swirling charcoal gray, lit up from below by the fires still burning – great heaped bonfires, ten feet high, with flames rising as high again, piles of burning wood which that morning had been the barracks for the garrisoned troops still left at the battery.

Wendy stepped down from the carriage, her muscles aching, more bone-weary than she could recall ever having been. She smelled acrid smoke and the rotten fish smell of tidal flats. The black men on the driver's seat hopped down and took their bags and they followed Batchelor through the rough gate of the battery.

The burning barracks threw enough light around the place that Wendy could see the full length of the fortress. Walls of logs and dirt lined the seaward side, facing Hampton Roads. Behind the walls, timber frame gun platforms, crude but solid, made up of thick, rough-cut beams, morticed and pegged, supported a succession of guns. The muzzles peered over the walls, *en barbette*, if Wendy understood the term correctly.

Men lay sprawled around the guns, and for a horrible second Wendy thought they were dead men, left to rot where they fell, but no sooner had the thought come to her than she realized that they were just sleeping, gun crews sleeping at their guns. In case of action, they would be right where they were needed, and with their barracks still burning, there was no better place for them.

'There's only a fraction of the original garrison left here,' Batchelor explained as he led the way up a ladder to the gun platform. 'Just enough to man a few guns, and I reckon those will be withdrawn in the morning.'

They stepped onto the rough wooden planks of the platform, and across to look over the parapet at the Roads beyond. The fire behind them made it difficult to see into the dark, but they could make out points of light here and there, anchor lights of the Union fleet, Batchelor explained, and the lights of Fortress Monroe across the water, a little less than four miles away.

Wendy pulled her eyes from the water to look at Molly standing beside her. Her aunt's face was grim, her lips set in a frown, eyebrows slightly pinched together.

'I don't think there's a damn thing we can do tonight,' Molly said.

'Too much chance of being shot in the dark,' Batchelor agreed.

'I hate to lose a moment, but there's nothing for it,' Molly said. 'Besides, I am too tired to think.' She turned to Batchelor. 'Lieutenant, I assume you have some accommodations that are appropriate for ladies?'

A tent was the best that could be produced, but it was a big one, a wall tent fifteen by twenty feet with two cots and a table, and it was fine with Wendy. She had been ready to lie down with one of the gun crews and sleep on the platform, she was so utterly exhausted. But even the siren song of the field cot was not enough to make Molly pause in her calculations.

'Wendy, dear,' she said as she sat on the edge of her cot, and Wendy sat on hers, and they unbuttoned shoes from aching feet, 'I forgot to ask you. Do you speak Norwegian?'

Wendy smiled. 'No, I am afraid not.'

'A shame. How is your French?'

'Not bad. I'm far from fluent, but I can get by.'

'*Écoutes*, Wendy,' Molly said. '*Peux-tu comprendre ce que je viens de dire? Pourras-tu le traduire?*'

Wendy smiled again. Molly's French was perfect, but her accent was very odd. Not French at all, nor that of an American speaking French. 'You said, "Listen, Wendy. Can you understand what I just said? Would you be able to translate it?" '

'Excellent,' Molly said. 'Now, come over here and sit by me. I must tell you what we are going to do in the morning, and then I will let you sleep.'

Wendy stood with difficulty, her muscles tight and aching, hobbled over to Molly's cot, and sat beside her. For the next hour and ten minutes, Molly laid out her intentions, quizzed Wendy, drilled her, instructed her. When she was done, Wendy retreated to her own cot. She lay down, let her muscles relax, and tried to let the sleep she so desperately craved wash over her, but for the next two hours she could do nothing but stare dumbfounded into the dark.

Wendy was dreaming of ships. She was dreaming about walking the deck of a ship under way, the short choppy sea slamming broadside against the hull, making the ship shudder, jarring her body as she tried to make her way forward.

She came from that dream slowly awake and realized that someone was shaking her. She opened her eyes. They smarted with fatigue. In the dim light of a single lantern she could see Molly standing beside her, shaking her gently.

'Rise and shine, dear.'

Wendy swung her legs over the side of the cot, rubbed her eyes. Her body ached; she was exhausted and confused. She had slept in her clothes in the hot, humid tent and she felt as if her whole body was coated in a layer of grime. Her dress was wrinkled and stained from climbing around the gun platforms and all the hard use it had received the night before.

'Aunt, I am an absolute fright. I trust we'll get some chance to freshen up and shift clothes?'

'No, no. You are perfect, my dear. Remember the part you're playing, and all you've been through. You look just the thing.'

Wendy knew she was right but she did not have the spirit to reply. Instead she stood and walked over to the basin of water on the nightstand and splashed cold water on her face, and that did much to revive her. Molly led her out of the tent. It was just before sunrise, and the sky was a predawn gray. A campfire was burning, a couple of men in shirtsleeves and kepis sitting on stools and staring into the flames. Lieutenant Batchelor, looking immaculate in his uniform, stood before the fire. A black man squatting by the flames was tending a big frying pan of scrambled eggs and bacon.

They ate, and Wendy felt her spirits rise again, and as the sky grew lighter, the day did not seem so horrible, the past twelve hours not so much a chaotic nightmare. She sat on a stool and enjoyed the quiet company and the bizarre turns of events and thought that everything would be all right. And then Molly said, softly, 'Time to go,' and Wendy felt her stomach turn.

The men in the kepis took the women's bags and they all followed Batchelor out of a small door in the seaward side of the battery. A makeshift dock formed a road over the mud flats to a place where the water was deep enough for a small boat to float peacefully at the end of its painter.

They made their way to the end of the dock and

then one of the men climbed down into the boat and the other handed the bags down.

'How are you doing, Wendy?' Molly asked in a low voice.

'I am frightened to death,' Wendy said. She thought she might throw up.

'This part is the worst. But remember, the whole thing might seem outrageous now, but outrageous will work for us. It's half measures that fail, half-hearted attempts at deception. If you don't have time for extreme subtlety, then it calls for a big show.'

The morning was beautiful, the sun just breaking the horizon, the sky lit up orange and yellow and light blue as the boat glided away from the dock, her bow toward the Union fleet.

The water in Hampton Roads was calm and dark, the ships riding at anchor peaceful and snug in the arms of the land, the bosom of Virginia, Wendy's native Virginia, her beloved state. For a moment Wendy was able to forget her worries and oppressing concerns, and enjoy with her painter's eye the scene unfolding around her.

And then, from far off, a cannon fired, muted but sharp enough to make her jump; then another gun went off and another. 'Oh!' she shouted involuntarily, looking around. Molly and the lieutenant were unmoved by the gunfire.

'Morning guns, Miss Atkins,' Lieutenant Batchelor said, his eyes on the distant fleet and Fortress Monroe. 'No reason for concern.'

'Of course,' Wendy said, and she could feel her face flush. She had heard morning guns often enough, living in Portsmouth.

I must calm down, she thought, and made a

conscious effort to breathe slowly and deeply, but quietly. She did not want the others to know she was doing so. She felt her stomach roll over, felt the film of sweat on her palms and forehead, little shooting jolts of electricity in her fingers and toes and her arms and legs. She wondered if this was what it was like, going to one's own execution, the terror and un-reality of it all.

She glanced at Molly. Her aunt was sitting upright, staring out at the Union fleet. She had a haughty, superior expression, a look of disdain mixed with anger, a look that took Wendy aback. Such arrogance did not seem terribly appropriate at that moment, under those conditions.

And then she realized – Molly was playing her part, assuming her character, becoming the woman she wanted the Federals to see.

Wendy looked across the Roads. They were still two miles from the USS *Minnesota*, flagship of the blockading fleet. A mile away was a small fort that from their vantage seemed to float in the water. 'Fort Wool,' Batchelor explained. 'It's built on a little rocky island called Rip Raps.' Could men with telescopes see them already, see their faces? No, it was not possible. Molly was preparing herself for the moment when they could.

'Wendy,' Molly said, her voice stern, *'you had best start thinking about what you will say when we are alongside the flagship.'* She spoke in French, in her weird accent. She spoke like an overly strict governess, a woman used to having her way. Wendy felt herself flush again, as if she had been scolded.

'*Oui, madame,*' she said, meeting Molly's eyes with an averted glance. Molly looked down on her with her imperious expression, and then, for just an instant, the arrogance was gone, and she smiled and winked. Just the length of a muzzle flash, and then Aunt Molly was haughty and arrogant once more.

That smile and wink lifted Wendy's spirits more than she would have guessed possible. It made her feel a part of what they were doing, not just someone being dragged along. It gave her a sense of camaraderie and shared adventure. It gave her hope. She sat up straight now, looked out across the water, considered who she was, and who she wanted the others to think she was.

They pulled for the Union ships as the sun lifted above the Chesapeake Bay and spread its light over the water and the low green shore. No one spoke, and the only sound was the creak and splash of the oars, the call of the gulls.

Finally, Lieutenant Batchelor spoke. 'Tug's under way. Seems to be making for us. To the right of the flagship.'

Wendy and Molly shifted their gaze. To the right of where the *Minnesota* lay tide-rode at anchor, a small vessel was churning toward them, under a great plume of black smoke. They could see the flash of white water kicked up by her bow.

'I better get this set,' the lieutenant said. He reached down to the bottom of the boat and with some difficulty extracted a long pole wrapped in white cloth. He stood, squeezed between the oarsmen, made his way to the bow. He unwrapped the cloth – a white flag affixed to a pole – stuck it in a socket at the bow. Satisfied, he made his way back to the stern sheets and took up the tiller again.

They continued their rhythmic pull to the flagship,

but it was soon clear that the tug would head them off. 'Sorry, Miss Atkins, there's nothing for it,' Batchelor said in a low breath. 'Reckon this tug was sent out to see what we're about. We'll have to talk to them.'

Molly nodded; her expression did not alter. 'Very well,' she said softly, her lips barely moving, though the nearest Yankee was still nearly a mile away. The degree of caution Molly exercised was not lost on Wendy.

This was not good, and Wendy felt her fear rise again, just as she had come to a place where she was ready to play her part. Their intention had been to get aboard the flagship, where decisions were being made. At two o'clock the next morning, Batchelor would come alongside to take them off. It did not seem much of a plan, but Molly assured her that there were any number of ways to get off a ship unnoticed, that under the guns of Fortress Monroe the Yankees would keep an indifferent watch.

But none of that would apply if they had to go aboard the tug. What intelligence might they gather aboard so unimportant a vessel? What if they were simply deposited behind Union lines and left there?

It took less than ten minutes for the tug to come up with the boat. Wendy could see the steamer throttle back, see her settle lower in the water as the speed came off of her.

The tug's wake reached them first and the boat rocked hard in the succession of waves. Wendy grabbed tight on the gunnel and felt her stomach convulse again. It was not seasickness, but the proximity of the moment, the instant she had been thinking of since she had sat on Molly's cot the night before.

The tug came up at a crawl, slowly enough to avoid swamping their boat. Wendy could see blue-clad sailors on board, some carrying rifles, a gun crew manning the big cannon in the bow. And they had only the white flag to protect them.

At last the tug came to a stop, ten feet away, and a man tossed a line, which one of the oarsmen caught, and the boat was pulled alongside the tug. Bearded, grim men looked down on them. Wendy felt her hands shake; sweat ran freely down her neck. Was she supposed to speak first? She had forgotten to ask, and now it was too late. She felt the sharp edge of panic at her throat.

Leaning on the tug's rail, an officer in a blue frock coat regarded the boat and the occupants. He opened his mouth, but before he could say a word, Molly seemed to explode. It was a full barrage of words, a broadside of anger and fury so startling and intense that it took Wendy a second to realize she was speaking French.

Wendy turned to her aunt, held up her hands as if to ward off the attack, said, 'Just a second, just a second, let me speak to them.' She said it in French. She had no notion of how she had remembered to do so.

'What is this?' the Union officer managed to get out.

Lieutenant Batchelor spoke next. 'Lieutenant, I got these here women on my hands, I do truly believe they belong on your side. This one,' he nodded toward Molly, who looked as angry as a wet cat, 'says she's the wife of some Norwegian minister. I got orders to take them to the flagship.'

The Union officer's brows came together. He looked from Batchelor to Molly and back, and Wendy recognized her moment.

'Sir, if I may,' she said, her tone tired and defeated. 'This is my aunt, Ingrid Nielsen. She is the wife of the Norwegian minister, who is due to arrive on the *Norvier*. A Norwegian navy ship, sir.'

Wendy paused, as if she thought that explained it. *Don't be too quick with answers,* Molly had instructed.

'So what are you doing here?' the Union officer asked.

'Oh, sir, we have had a horrible time. We . . . my aunt and I . . . were taking passage to America when we were captured by one of these horrid Rebel privateers. Sir, we have been forever trying to get to Washington, so my aunt might meet her husband.'

'You are not Norwegian,' the lieutenant observed. There was a hint of accusation in his voice.

'I am a Marylander by birth, sir, but have been in Europe these past years. I have been traveling with my aunt, sir, from Norway, where I was visiting, sir.'

The Union officer nodded. 'Why didn't you take passage on the *Norvier*?'

Wendy began to speak, but Molly cut her off with another tirade, a nearly hysterical shrieking, arm-waving harangue that covered Rebels, Yankees, Americans, ships, everything that had supposedly caused offense in the past month. She spoke in French, and Wendy understood now that the weird accent was Norwegian, or what Molly guessed a Norwegian accent to be.

Again Wendy held up her hands, silenced her. She felt bold, on her game. She was no longer afraid. She was taken with the spirit of the thing.

'Sir, do you speak French?' Wendy asked.

'No.'

'It's just as well. My aunt is . . . upset. These few bags are all we have left.'

'Why doesn't your aunt speak Norwegian?'

'She does, of course. French is the only language we have in common.'

The Union officer nodded. 'So what do you want?' He addressed the question to Lieutenant Batchelor.

'Best as I can understand it, this lady's husband is bound to Washington. I don't know nothing about this *Norvier*. Lady keeps sayin the ship's due here any day. Any event, she's got no business in the Confederate States. My commanding officer, he told me to get her to the Yankee flagship. Reckoned an admiral would know where she belongs.'

'You want me to take her?'

'No, sir. I just need passage under flag of truce to get her to the *Minnesota*. Lieutenant, I swear I will give the keys to Richmond to the Yankee admiral who'll take her off my hands.'

The Union officer paused and stared at the women, clearly unsure of what to do. This entire act was supposed to be played out alongside the flagship, where there would be officers who could make decisions, where two little women would seem rather harmless against the great mass of men and ship.

'Lieutenant, that cockleshell boat can't be too comfortable. I reckon the gentlemanly thing to do is to take these ladies on board.'

Wendy looked up. The man who had spoken was on the roof of the deckhouse, leaning on the rail. He had been watching the whole proceeding from up there. Wendy had not even noticed him.

'Yes, Mr President,' the lieutenant replied, crisp and quick.

Wendy stared at the man, stared in shock at the lanky form, the long, horselike features, the part sad, part amused expression on the face of President Abraham Lincoln.

CHAPTER 8

*Hope ere long you will be able to test with success
the efficiency of your boats, which are now the last
hope of closing the river to the enemy's gunboats.*
General G. T. Beauregard
to General M. Jeff Thompson,
River Defense Fleet

Hieronymus Taylor found himself wandering about
the decks of the *General Page*. He had some tender
spots from the previous night's brawl and he tried not
to let them show in the way he moved. He was
not bouncing back from the damage done the way he
had in earlier years. The fight had not chased away
the blue devils.

He climbed up to the hurricane deck, watched the
great walking beam go through its teeter-totter
motion, driving the side wheels that pushed the ship
north against the current.

He climbed up on the platform built on the
starboard wheel box, felt the paddle wheel vibrating
below him. He leaned on the rail and looked out
across the water. The town of Greenville was just

going out of sight around a point of land. Taylor knew a girl once from Greenville. Ended up as a whore in New Orleans. He tried to picture her face but couldn't.

After a while he sighed and stood up straight. The town was lost from sight and the banks were a wild tangle of marsh and forest and swamp. They steamed past wide rafts floating downstream, barely controlled by the long sweeps rigged out astern. In the middle of the rafts, makeshift shelters where men squatted around fires, cooked breakfast, and made coffee. They waved and Taylor waved back.

Tugs with barges pulling astern passed them as well, and paddle wheelers carrying Lord knows what. Two years before it would have been cotton, down-bound, and sundry merchandise coming up – foodstuffs and manufactures that could not be grown or produced on the plantations. But now? There were hardly any manufactured goods coming into the Confederacy through the coils of the Yankee anaconda, and King Cotton for export made it as far as New Orleans, and there it sat on the dock.

No, Taylor corrected himself, *not New Orleans.* New Orleans was a Yankee-held town now.

Taylor's despair became, in his mind, a boiler, steam building inside. The idea of the Yankees at New Orleans made the steam gauge jump, the needle quiver up in the regions of trouble. A good fight was supposed to be a safety valve, blow the excess steam right out. It had failed. It seemed the valve was lashed tight.

He climbed down from the wheel box, down to the main deck, drifted along the side of the deck-house. From the outside, the deckhouse of a

115

steamship looked to be a spacious affair, running almost the full length of the ship itself, but that was deceptive. The center third of the deckhouse was not a house at all, but a great open space above the engine room, called the 'fidley.' The fidley extended from the floor plates of the engine room, which were just below the lowest, or main deck, up through the boiler deck, which was next deck above the main deck, and up to the hurricane deck, two decks above, where skylights provided light to the black gang and air to the engines and boilers.

Taylor paused at the fidley door. The engine room was his domain, but now he felt some invisible force pushing him away, like trying to make opposite poles of a magnet touch.

Ain't my engine room, he thought. Engineers looked on their engine rooms the way women looked on their kitchens, or dogs on their yards, with a disdain for intruders who might interfere. The message was, 'I'll thank you to stay the hell out of here,' stated verbally or otherwise.

Taylor opened the fidley door, stepped inside. Intruder, perhaps, but Spence would wonder why he was not hanging around, because that was the other thing engineers did on some other engineer's ship, though they might hate it on their own.

The fidley door opened onto a catwalk above the engine room and a ladder down. Directly in front of him, taking up most of the fidley, was the massive wooden A-frame that supported the walking beam. It rose from its mounting blocks in the bilges below right up through the hurricane deck overhead.

For a moment Taylor stood still as the heat and the sounds washed over him – the dull roar of the fire in the boiler, the *pssst, pssst* of steam in the cylinder, the knocking of pipes, the creaking of the A-frame, the loud and profane voices of Mike Sullivan and Spence Guthrie as they screamed in each other's faces.

Oh, hell, Taylor thought. He turned for the door, but Sullivan's voice caught him before he could escape.

'Taylor! Taylor, you son of a bitch, come down here, talk some sense into this damn mule-headed . . .'

There was no escape now. Taylor turned back, climbed down the ladder to the floor plates. Sullivan and Guthrie were near the workbench, standing close to one another. Sullivan had his hands on his hips, Guthrie had his arms folded. Sullivan was sweating profusely, sweat running down his face and staining his river driver shirt. He was a big, angry man, unused to engine room heat.

'How can I help you gentlemen?' Taylor drawled. His eyes darted to the steam gauge on the boiler. Eleven pounds, well within specs. The safety valves were untied.

'You can help me stuff this fat bastard back up the fidley,' Guthrie said.

'Hieronymus, talk some sense into the man,' Sullivan said. 'He's got the damned safety valves tied down, which is fine when we really need it, but there ain't no call all the time!'

'Look at this!' Guthrie held up a fistful of old twine. 'This son of a bitch comes down here on my watch below, cuts them away! Like he got a right to make decisions here!'

Taylor had to agree with Sullivan. He was not as

117

enthusiastic as he once had been about tying safety valves shut. On the other hand, it was an offense against nature for the captain to come down to the engine room and interfere, particularly when the chief was not there.

He held his hands up, a gesture of surrender. 'I ain't got a dog in this here fight,' he said.

'What would you do, was you engineer?' Guthrie asked. The question was part challenge, part accusation.

'I would do as my heart commanded me,' Taylor said.

'Well, Guthrie here gonna do as I command him,' Sullivan said with finality. 'You keep them safety valves free unless I say otherwise, or by God you'll be on the beach in Memphis.' For emphasis he poked Guthrie in the chest with a sausage finger, then stormed off, leaving the engineer to hurl obscenities in his wake.

'Son of a bitch, big fat bastard, coming down here telling me what to do. To hell with him, the lazy . . . No, sir, he can go to the devil . . .'

Taylor was surprised. He would not have expected such good sense from anyone who called himself Mississippi Mike.

As Guthrie ranted and cursed – his verbal storm was his own personal safety valve, fully functional – Taylor's ears sorted out the various sounds of the engine and boiler rooms. He could not help it. He was not really even aware that he was doing it.

'. . . ain't nothin but a chicken, thinks his whole damn boat's gonna blow up . . .'

'You got a fire tube broken,' Taylor said.

'Huh?'

'I think you got a broken fire tube on the starboard boiler.' The fire tubes ran through the interior of the boilers, from one end to the other. The searing hot vapors of the coal fire in the firebox passed through the tubes and brought the water to a boil. Taylor could hear the irregular hissing and popping of spurting water on hot iron. When a tube was broken, water leaked from the boiler into the tube and into the firebox at one end, the smoke box at the other.

'Oh, horseshit, broken . . .' Guthrie said, with momentum still on his tirade, but he paused, cocked an ear, shut his mouth for a moment. 'Well . . .'

With a scowl and a spit into the bilges he stepped over to the starboard boiler and threw open the door to the firebox. The coal was laid out in an even bed, glowing white hot, the heat shimmering and rising and hitting Guthrie and Taylor like a solid thing. No smoke. The shirtless, black-smudged fireman knew his business.

Taylor peered over Guthrie's shoulder at the black circles that were the ends of the fire tubes. Third row down, second tube inboard, he could see the water dancing and sizzling and the gray vapor rising off it as the steam condensed. He opened his mouth, shut it, waited. A second later, Guthrie said, 'There's the son of a bitch . . . three rows down, second in from the starboard side . . .'

'Oh, yeah, sure enough.'

Guthrie straightened. 'Well, I guess we'll have to plug the bastard. Not like we got any spare tubes. Maybe when we're tryin to get up steam with one tube left, someone'll think to get us some more.'

Taylor nodded his understanding. He could see

that four other tubes were already plugged. 'I'll get the other end,' he said.

'Huh?'

'The plug at the forward end. I'll get it.'

'Why? You don't even work on this bucket, and you better thank Jesus you don't, son of a bitch rotten . . .'

'I know. But I reckon I best earn my keep.'

Guthrie shrugged. 'Have it your way, pard.' They went over to the workbench. Taylor shed his frock coat, pulled on heavy leather gloves. They assembled wrenches, plugs, nuts. Taylor took a lantern, knowing the feeble light of the engine room would not extend to the far end of the boilers. 'Let's do it,' Taylor said.

Guthrie stepped over to the after end of the boiler. 'Daniels, English,' he called to two of the firemen, 'git some fire hoses rigged an charged. English, you go an help Taylor, there.'

Taylor went forward, skirting around the long, low iron tank, tons of iron of unknown integrity containing within it enough scalding water and steam to kill every man in the engine room – boiler explosions, the great terror of the steamship, to be feared like the wrath of God and defended against with a similar religious zeal. Taylor once had looked on the possibility of a boiler explosion the way most men looked upon sin – as something to worry about unless it was inconvenient. But no more.

His feet crunched on bits of coal spilled from the bunkers up against the starboard side of the ship. He walked sideways, through the narrow space between boiler and bunker, leaning away from the hot iron. He could feel the sweat on his brow and hands and recognized that it was not the sweat made by engine room heat, even though it was one hundred degrees at least in that space. His hands would be trembling if he had not been gripping his tools hard.

He skirted around a stanchion and the wrench slipped from his hand, clattered on the iron floor plate. *Hell* . . . He bent over, awkward in that narrow space, the burning metal of the boiler right beside him, picked the wrench up with slick fingers. He continued on, came out around the forward end of the boiler. In front of him there was only the black void of the coal bunker.

He found a hook in an overhead beam and hung the lantern, then applied the wrench to the nuts that secured the access plate to the smoke box. He was aware of the quiver in his fingers. He could smell the sweat from under his shirt.

He paused for a moment while English dragged the charged fire hose forward and opened it, letting the water gush into the bilge. While Taylor was actually plugging the tube, English would play the water over his hands. Otherwise the heat would be unbearable.

Most . . . goddamn routine . . . fucking simple job . . . Plugging fire tubes. It was a common enough task. He could not begin to recall how often he had done it in the course of his career. But that was before he had seen the power of the beast steam let loose.

He took the nuts off, dropped two, had to fumble around to find them, cursing.

'You done, there?' Guthrie called from the other end of the boiler.

'Hang on, hang on, got a froze nut,' Taylor shouted back. He was surprised by the anger in his voice. He pulled the plate free, opening up the smoke box and the end of the boiler, with its rows of tubes.

Water hissed and spit, jetting from the broken tube, steam condensing into swirling gray clouds. *Ah, shit . . .* The boilers were tipped forward, ever so slightly. It might have been the way they were mounted, or the trim of the vessel, or any number of factors. But the majority of the water leaking into the broken tube was running down toward Taylor, dancing and flying in the heat and with the motion of the ship.

Taylor felt the sharp insect bites of boiling water droplets lashing his face. The heat from the fire tubes was overwhelming. He took a step back, turned his head away. His breathing was becoming fast and shallow. He did not have to do this. It was not his engine room.

But he knew he had to do it. Especially now, after his great show of casually volunteering for the job. And it was not a hard job, not a dangerous job. Routine. But here he was, standing in the jaws of the beast, approaching it, laying hands on it, and the hardest part was to resist conjuring up the image of what was left of the scalded James Burgess right before he shot him.

'What the hell you doin up there?'

'Hold your goddamned horses . . . I got it now!' Taylor shouted back. 'All right, English, go on.'

The fireman raised the stream of water until it was rushing over Taylor's hands and hissing and popping against the boiler. Taylor tried to breathe deeply but the breath wouldn't come. He stepped into the grip of the heat, blinking water from his eyes, trembling, flinching from the steam and the spattering boiler water.

He heard something clang, as if someone had hit the boiler, and it made him jump. English jerked, and the stream of water from the fire hose went wide. Water jetted from the fire tube, gushing out the end, falling on hot metal plates, sizzling, steaming. Boiling water splashed over Taylor's arms and chest, burned him right through his shirt. Steam whistled by his face. He felt his stomach convulse, he thought he might piss his pants.

'Oh! Oh, son of a bitch! Git that goddamned water on here! Git it on here, you stupid bastard!' He was shrieking at English, shouting like a madman. The fire tube had cracked more, perhaps cracked clean through. Guthrie had the plug in on the other side – the added pressure might have done it, or the jostling by Guthrie's wrench. Whatever. The smoke box was filled with jetting water, steam, vapor, and heat.

'What's wrong?' Guthrie shouted.

'Tube's . . . son of a bitch tube . . . is ruptured!' Taylor went in, blinking, squinting, face turned away, hands shaking, tears running down his cheeks. There was water gushing everywhere, coming from the fire tube, from the stream English was directing at him. The heat and the smoke filled his eyes. He went in with the cone-shaped plug held out like a sword, lunging at the spurting tube. He heard himself make a low, whimpering noise but it seemed like it was someone else making the sound. He jammed the plug in the end of the tube. The water and the steam stopped.

The heat from the fire tubes was overwhelming, a searing, clawing agony, even with the stream from the fire hose. Taylor knew he had only seconds to get the nut on before he would have to step back.

And then the plug would fall out and the water and steam would come and he would have to do it all again.

Don't drop the nut, don't drop the nut, don't drop the nut . . . Taylor held the plug with his left hand, the nut in his right. The water from the fire hose tried to jerk it from his grip. Squinting in the terrible heat, like being pressed against a griddle, he worked the nut on the threads, worked it around, waited for the threads to catch.

Come on, come on, come on . . . And then he felt the threads take, felt the satisfying action of nut and bolt working together. He cranked it down, hand tight, stepped back with a gasp of relief.

For a minute, two minutes, he just stood there, hands on hips, gasping air, hot air, but not the burning air of the smoke box. At last he stepped forward, put the wrench on the nut, tightened it down. 'All right,' he said to English, trying to sound as reasonable as he could, to compensate for his earlier hysteria. English directed the stream back into the bilge. Taylor put the access plate back on the smoke box, replaced the nuts. The heat fell off perceptibly.

'There you are! Hell, I thought you'd fainted from the heat!' Guthrie started around the boiler toward Taylor.

Taylor nodded, could not talk for a second. 'That . . . was a son of a bitch,' he said. 'Real spouter.'

'All right. Well, it's done. Thanks for the help.' There was a grudging sound to Guthrie's thanks.

'You're welcome.' Taylor had a sudden and overwhelming need to get out of the engine room, to stand on the deck, let the cool breeze run over him. To get away from the beast. 'I got to get some fresh

124

air,' he said, following Guthrie back around the boiler.

'Fresh air?' Guthrie exclaimed. 'What the hell kind of engineer are you?' he asked, but that was yet another question that Taylor did not care to explore.

The *General Page* was twenty-eight hours from Greenville to Memphis, steaming upriver against a one-to two-knot current, negotiating the wild, serpentine bends of the Mississippi River. Small towns and huge plantations slipped past, but the *Page* did not belong to the land. She was a citizen of another place, the riverborne community of the paddle wheelers and rafts and tugs and canoes that moved as languidly as the current on the wide brown water. The Mississippi River was like a whole other nation, with different geography, different customs, different history than the land through which it ran – one single, narrow, twisting nation smack in the middle of another.

Bowater was beginning to appreciate this unique quality of the river, to understand how the riverboat men came to be a separate breed from the deepwater sailors. During his long confinement at the naval hospital in Norfolk he had come upon and read a copy of Charles Darwin's new *Origin of Species,* and though he viewed the work as predominantly a bunch of irreligious claptrap, there had been a few ideas that he fixed on, and found intriguing.

He wondered now how natural selection might have led to the species of men who worked the river. Certainly, he thought, the environment of the river community would have weeded out his own species, or any species of man with any sort of refinement or sensibilities.

These pointless and meandering thoughts drifted through Bowater's head as he in turn drifted around the side wheeler, trying always to avoid Mike Sullivan, but still Sullivan hunted him like a hound dog on the scent of coon. Mississippi Mike was in a literary frenzy, so taken with the artistic merits and genuine originality of Bowater's ideas on plot and character that he seemed unable to concentrate on anything else.

Sullivan finally caught him on the fantail, caught him alone. A moment before, Bowater had been talking with Ruffin Tanner about allocating crew on the new ironclad, the *Tennessee*, once she was under way. As long as he was with someone else, Bowater knew he was safe, because Sullivan wanted to keep his literary aspirations secret, and would not approach if a third party was there.

But no sooner had Tanner left, and Bowater begun considering with whom he could speak next, than Sullivan appeared around the corner of the deckhouse. So quickly, in fact, that Bowater had to imagine he was lurking there, waiting for Tanner to leave.

'Cap'n Bowater, there you are! I been working like a sum bitch, wrote it up the way you said.' Sullivan was smiling wide, holding a sheaf of paper in his hand. 'Here, let me read you some—'

'Ahh . . .' There was no escape. Samuel Bowater had seen enough combat to know when there was nothing you could do but stand and take it. 'All right . . .'

Mike, grinning harder, held the papers in front of

him. ' "*The Adventures of Mississippi Mike and the Murdering Dogs,*" ' he read.

' "Chapter One – A Ghostly Tale. On the whole of the Mississippi, there ain't no one who dare cross Mississippi Mike, best of the riverboat men—" '

'Isn't anyone.'

'What?'

'There isn't anyone who dares cross Mississippi Mike. That's how it should read. Or better yet, there's no man who would dare cross Mississippi Mike.'

Mike nodded. 'Yeah, that sounds real sweet, like the way them fancy French whores talk. All right, we'll fix that up.' Mike licked the end of a pencil, scribbled awkwardly on the page.

> . . . *no man who would dare cross Mississippi Mike, best of the riverboat men. And of all of them, you'd reckon it was his kin would know best that the hardest drinkin, hardest fightin man on Western Waters was not a fellow to be done dirty. So Mike, being generous of spirit and not a fellow to think bad of another fellow, especially his kinfolk, never even thought that when his pa died it might have been at the hands of a murdering dog.*

'What do you think?' Mike asked.

'Good, good,' Samuel said. 'A little foreshadowing. Some nice alliteration. Is there much more of this . . . ah . . . introductory material?'

'No, no, I get right at it. Even used the names you come up with, for the other fellows. Here, listen up.' Mike cleared his throat and read:

This was in the early days, when Mississippi Mike had not yet got command of his own riverboat, but was mate on board the Belle of the West, *which his pa was captain on. Paddy Sullivan was the best riverboat man there was, until his son inherited that mantle and even surpassed the former.*

'I read that thing about "inheriting that mantle" somewhere, don't recall where, and I always liked it,' Sullivan explained. 'Is that all right – you know, borrowin' from another writer an all?'

'Generally, no, but I think we can let that stand. Go on.'

When Paddy Sullivan died, gentle in his sleep, it was a sad day on the river, and a sadder day for Mississippi Mike. But it was not for two months more, on a foggy morning watch, that Mike would find out the dirty deed that was done his pa.
The Belle of the West *was anchored just south of Natchez and waiting for the fog to lift, when Horatio, a free Negro and Mike's longtime pard, was on the deck watch.*
'You seen it? Two times you seen it?' Horatio asked his shipmates, Barney and Mark, who had the watch with him.
'That's right. We seen it twice. And if you don't believe in ghosts, pard, you best bet you would if you seen this.'
Horatio's eyes was like saucers. 'Oh, Lawd, I surely do believe in ghosts, and I surely hope we don't see one now!'

'Look, y'all!' Mark shouted.

*The three men looked up. Right out of the fog,
like a man-shaped cloud, and all shiny, stepped a
spirit from another world, a world of the dead!*

*'Oh, Lawdy, Lawdy! Dat surely is de ghost of ol'
Paddy Sullivan! An don't it look jest like him!'
Horatio held tight to his shotgun, his ebony finger
on the trigger, his eyes bulging from their sockets.*

'Talk to him, Horatio!' Barney whispered.

'No, suh, I ain't talking to no ghost!'

*'Go on!' Mark said next, pushing Mike's sable
pard toward the apparition.*

*Horatio held the gun in front of him and the
barrel trembled like a leaf in a breeze. 'What you
want, Paddy Sullivan?' he shouted in a hoarse
voice. 'What you coming around here for, scaring
decent folk?' Horatio spoke bravely, for even
though the Negro race is more afraid of ghosts
and such than regular folk, Mike's old shipmate
was no coward. But the ghost would not talk to
him, but instead floated free across the deck.*

Sullivan looked up. 'What do you think?'

'Excellent, Sullivan. Perfect,' Bowater said. He was
impressed. It was not nearly as awful as he had
imagined it would be, with a few bits that seemed
genuinely inspired. He could see his enthusiasm
reflected on Mike's face.

'Really?'

'Oh, yes. You captured the mood of the thing very
nicely. But see here, I had another idea, something
that might really give the book some bite, you know.'

'Yeah?' Mike took a step closer, a conspiratorial
move.

'Here's what I was thinking. How about if Mississippi Mike's uncle, along with becoming captain of the *Belle of the West* . . .'

'Yeah?'

'How about if he marries Mike's mother!'

Mike stood up straight, his eyes like saucers. 'Marries his *mother*?'

'Yes. Just think on it. Wouldn't that get Mike hot for revenge?'

'Yeah, it would do that . . .' Mike looked away, trying to absorb the enormity of it. 'But . . . the way I wrote it, Mike's pa ain't been dead but two months.'

'I know. Shocking, isn't it?'

'Shocking? It's damned indecent is what it is.'

'Of course.' Bowater lowered his voice. 'You think people want to read about decency? Why don't you write a book about a cloistered nun, see how many people buy that?'

'You got a point . . .'

'Just think about it,' Bowater encouraged. 'That's all I ask.'

'All right . . .' Mike muttered. He wandered off, his eyes on the deck. His lips were moving, but Bowater could not hear what he was saying, and he guessed – he hoped – he had bought himself a few hours of peace.

As it turned out, the notion that frailty's name might be woman so rattled Mississippi Mike that Bowater had little discourse with him for the rest of the afternoon and evening, until he was safely ensconced in his cabin with the door bolted. The next morning he stepped onto the side deck carefully, looked fore and aft to see the way clear.

130

'Captain Bowater!' Mike's voice was like a thunderclap, and like a thunderclap it came from overhead. Bowater turned and looked up. Mike was standing on top of the wheel box, leaning on the rail, looking down. 'Come on up to the wheelhouse! Take your breakfast up here! This is your big day, Captain!'

Bowater trudged wearily, grudgingly, up to the hurricane deck and across to the wheelhouse. Mississippi Mike was outside the wheelhouse, grinning, shouting, flying back and forth. It was not the Mississippi Mike who sheepishly asked Bowater's advice on writing. It was hard drivin, hard drinkin, most dangerous son of a whore riverboat man on the Western Waters Sullivan, the preliterary Mississippi Mike.

'Good morning, Captain,' Bowater said. His every cell was crying out for coffee, hot and black.

'Coffee, Captain?' Sullivan said, and without waiting for a reply turned to the deckhand polishing the bell and said, 'Berry, light along to the galley and get the captain here some coffee!'

Berry took off, returned, and Sullivan had the decency not to speak until Bowater had taken at least two good sips.

'Outskirts of Memphis here, Captain,' Sullivan said, nodding toward the shore. It was a gray morning, overcast and humid. Bowater could see that the shoreline was more crowded than it had been downriver: docks, warehouses, clusters of dilapidated shacks. Riverboats were tied up at various angles to wharves and to the shore itself. He could see wagons moving along like tiny models in a diorama.

Memphis . . . The voyage had been so wild he had almost lost sight of the destination. Life like the chapters of a book – one ends, move on to the next.

The Adventures of Samuel Bowater, Naval Officer.

Chapter the Thirty-fourth, In which our hero is shed of Mississippi Mike Sullivan at last, and sees his new command for the first time, and comes to understand into what new nightmare he has been plunged . . .

Bowater stared over the brown water and played with the idea.

'Just a couple miles or so upriver's the yard where your ship's a'buildin, Captain. Mr John T. Shirley's yard. That fella's a whirlwind, don't get in his way. Got a wharf there, we can drop you and your men off right at the shipyard.'

'Oh . . .' Bowater had not thought that far ahead. 'That would be marvelous, Captain Sullivan.'

'Least I can do.'

Bowater was silent for a moment, finished his coffee, felt much restored. 'I'll go and alert my men to be ready to disembark,' he said.

'No, no need, Captain,' Sullivan said, then leaned into the wheelhouse, shouted, 'Come right, you stupid son of a whore! Do you see that raft? Are you blind, you dumb bastard?' and from inside the wheelhouse, unseen by Bowater, the helmsman replied, 'I see the raft. Shut your mouth, you fat bastard!'

The *General Page* swung slightly to starboard, and Sullivan grinned as if the helmsman's reply had been part of some witty repartee. 'No need, Captain, I'll have one of my boys do it,' and with a shout, Sullivan dispatched the put-upon Berry to gather Bowater's men.

'Nothin like gettin the first sight of a new command, huh, Captain Bowater?' Sullivan said. 'I

would be honored to share that moment with you.'
It wasn't sincerity in his voice, but something meant
to sound like it.

'Yes, indeed . . .'

They steamed on, the shipping and the buildings,
the wharves and the traffic growing thicker as
Memphis opened up around them, and the *General
Page* inched her way toward the eastern bank of the
Mississippi River.

They were less than two hundred yards off when
Sullivan shouted, 'Here we are, Baxter, come right,
now!'

The *General Page* swung across the river, her bow
pointing at a makeshift shipyard sprawling along a
landing near a desultory-looking fort that Bowater
had been told was Fort Pickering. A great brown
earthen plot of land, scattered with stacks of blond,
fresh-cut wood, piles of iron with a patina of rust
turning them ruddy brown, carts and men and huffing steam engines. There were two sawmills spitting
out clouds of dust, several buildings that might be
ironworks, black smoke roiling from forge chimneys,
a dock with a small tug tied alongside.

There were two ships on the stocks, sister ships,
around one hundred and seventy feet in length,
thirty-five feet on the beam, and perhaps twelve feet
in depth. Bowater could see elegant curved fantail
sterns, a shallow deadrise, a nice run fore and aft. The
casemates rose straight up from the sides, nearly
vertical like the sides of a house. Only the fore and aft
ends of the casemates were slanted, the way he had
come to think an ironclad's casemate should be.

They were good-looking vessels, identical in pro-
portion, very different in their state of completion.

133

One of them was finished in her planking, her casemate covered in thick oak, pierced for guns, two aft and three on the broadside that Bowater could see. The shafts of her twin screws were in place, parallel to her waterline, the big propellers already mounted on either side of the barn door rudder. She had her first few runs of iron on as well, the plating covering her sides nearly to the level of the main deck.

She was far from complete, but she was well on her way, and a month or so of diligent effort might see her launched and commissioned, an operational man-of-war.

The other ship was not nearly so far along. She was no more than a wooden frame, the skeleton of a ship, with the first few runs of planking along her bottom. The stacks of wood on either side of her would no doubt become the rest of her planking, but as it was they were just stacks of wood. Through the space between frames Bowater could see there were no engines, no shafts, no boilers.

'There she is, Captain, the ironclad *Tennessee*!' Sullivan made a wide gesture, taking in the entire yard.

'I see two vessels, Sullivan. Which is the *Tennessee*?' As if he had to ask.

'It's the one with the good ventilation.' He pointed to the ship in frame. 'You're a lucky man, Captain. Ventilation's real important in a hot climate like we got here!'

Sullivan was enjoying himself. He turned, shouted orders at the helmsman, grinned, and stuffed a cigar in his mouth as the helmsman cursed him and spun the wheel. Sullivan rang up *turns astern* and with a creaking protest the paddle wheels stopped, then thrashed astern, and the *General Page* settled against the dock, the barge of coal trailing away downstream at the end of the towrope.

The brow had just gone over the side when the horseman rode up, hard pounding across the ship-yard, making the yard workers pause and look up. He dismounted in a flourish, ran the length of the dock, and leaped aboard. A minute later he was standing, breathless, on the hurricane deck.

'Captain Sullivan, a good job you come now,' the man said when his breath returned. A young man, he had the look of the river on him.

'What's up?' Sullivan asked, cigar in mouth.

'Captain Montgomery says best get your hide upriver! Council of war for the captains tonight. Most of 'em are hot to go after the Yankees at dawn!'

'Well, damn! That's some damned good news!' Mississippi Mike was wearing his dime-novel grin. 'What say you, Captain Bowater? You and your men want to join us in the fun?' His eyes flickered toward Shirley's yard. 'Or do you want to take your own boat to the fight?'

CHAPTER 9

May 8. – Meridian to 3 P.M.: Steamed up abreast of Sewell's Point batteries, preceded by the Naugatuck, Monitor, Seminole, *and* Susquehanna. *The squadron then opened fire. President Lincoln passed us in a steam tug. At 5:45 mustered at quarters. The* Merrimack *returned to her anchorage off Craney Island.*

Log of the USS *Dacotah*

Wendy Atkins had been in a play once. She had played Ophelia in a production of *Hamlet* staged by the Culpepper Community Players. Her performance had not been so bad, she believed, fending off the melancholy Dane's lewd suggestions, staggering around with a wild-eyed look, strumming her lute. There had always been a little extra burst of applause as she stepped onstage for her curtain call.

Of course, there were always a number of suitors in the audience who had wanted to make love to her, and they no doubt accounted for some of the enthusiasm. That was before she had alienated half the eligible young men in town, and frightened off the remainder. Still, she was not bad.

She recalled the many sensations that had come with her time onstage. The sick fright, waiting for her moment to step from behind the curtain and into the light, where all eyes would be on her, every ear listening to her speak her speech.

'Do you doubt that?'

It was the first line Ophelia spoke, and as the line passed from her lips, it carried with it all that fear and doubt, as if the emotions had been shackled to the words, and, bound together, they were all expelled at once. After the first words were out, she became the master of her domain. The stage was her home, as comfortable as her sitting room, and she moved about it with ease, spoke her lines with confidence, and even on occasion stepped in and helped one of her fellow players find their way when they had lost the thread of their speech.

She thought of that as she mounted the side of the tug, the young lieutenant taking her hand, because that was how she felt now. With those first words, her step onto the stage of deception, she had felt the fear melt away, and with it, a new confidence arise, a feeling that she was as much the person she pretended to be as she was Wendy Atkins.

Lincoln's presence had thrown her off her game, and how could it not have? The most famous man in the Western hemisphere, the most reviled man in her new nation, the man whose policies had led to the bloody conflict in which they were engaged, leaning on the rail of the deck and drawling as if he were leaning on one of his split-rail fences back home, making idle talk about the weather.

137

How could she not have been taken aback? But she recovered quickly, and her surprise was well in keeping with her character. Anyone, even the woman she was pretending to be, would have been surprised.

She stepped down on the deck and turned to assist Molly – Ingrid Nielsen – in negotiating the step up. Her eyes brushed over Lieutenant Batchelor. He wore a gun in a holster and Wendy had to imagine he considered going for it, but the dozen rifles pointing at his chest would have dissuaded him. Instead he was sitting with arms folded, hands in plain view, an amused look on his face. Wendy looked quickly away. She did not want to seem too interested.

Molly came up over the side with an ease that befitted a seasoned traveler, stepped on the deck with a huff. She was, by all appearances, still mad as a wet hen. The boatmen handed up their bags.

There was a bustle on the side deck, men moving quickly aside, and Abraham Lincoln stepped through, like Moses through the Red Sea.

'Ma'am.' Lincoln made a short bow to Wendy.

'Mr President.' Wendy curtsied. 'This is indeed an honor, and a pleasant surprise.'

'A surprise, anyway, I shouldn't wonder. I am flattered that you recognize me.'

'Oh, sir, how could one not?'

'But you've only just arrived here, after several years abroad.'

'Oh, sir . . .' Wendy said, alert to a trap, despite Lincoln's innocuous tone. 'Perhaps, Mr President, you are not aware, with all due respect, of how well known your likeness is in Europe.'

'Perhaps not. They always have had queer taste, on that side of the ocean.' He turned to Molly, and this time bowed deeply, took her hand, and kissed it in a courtly fashion.

'Miss . . .?' Lincoln looked at Wendy.

'Atkins, sir. Wendy Atkins.' It was as good a name as any, Molly had explained. Less chance of a slip of the tongue.

'Miss Atkins, please introduce me and tell your aunt that I am dreadfully sorry for what you two have suffered, and that we will endeavor to see you both properly accommodated until her husband's ship arrives.'

Wendy turned to Molly, introduced her to the President of the United States, and repeated Lincoln's words in French. Molly's harsh expression softened, and when she looked back at Lincoln it was with the face of one who understands power and appreciates those who have it. A woman used to spinning in that orbit. She bowed deeply, turned back to Wendy.

'Please tell the President that I am honored to be in his presence, and greatly relieved to at last be under the protection of such gentlemen, after the rough usage we have received. My husband's government will hear of Mr Lincoln's courtesy.'

Wendy translated, and as she did she wondered if the President could speak French. She searched her memory for any mention she might have read concerning that fact, but she could recall none. The Southern papers were not big on listing Lincoln's accomplishments.

The lieutenant who commanded the tug was issuing orders now, for chairs and a table and lemonade and an awning on the boat deck. Through the bustle Wendy saw Batchelor nod to the oarsman holding on to the line that had been passed from the tug. The oarsman dropped the line, gave a push off from the boat.

'Whoa! Hold her there, Reb!' a petty officer called out. Everyone on deck turned to the boat. The hammer of a rifle clicked back to the firing position.

'We've discharged our cargo,' Batchelor said, hands up. 'Reckon we'll head back to home port.'

'Not so fast.'

The lieutenant stepped over to Lincoln, carried on a whispered conversation that Wendy could not hear, try though she might, all the while staring vacantly around. Lincoln himself spoke to Batchelor.

'I'm sorry, son, but I'm afraid we have to ask you to come aboard.'

'What? We came under flag of truce! This is an outrage, sir, contrary to all—'

'I understand, sir, depend on it. You are not prisoners, don't think of yourselves as prisoners. You are . . . guests. We will set you free in due time, but for now it would not be convenient for it to be generally known that I'm aboard. You will agree, I'm sure,' Lincoln added, and the sad and amused face was back, 'that there are some over there who might wish me harm.'

Batchelor frowned and said nothing. A sailor tossed the line back to the boat and pulled it alongside. Grudgingly, slowly, Batchelor and the two men climbed aboard. They were led away, courteously, but at gunpoint. Wendy made a point of not watching them go.

The lieutenant of the tug and his petty officers were swarming now, eager to extend any consideration to the two women whom their commander-in-chief had deigned worthy of courtesy. They escorted first Molly, then Wendy, up the steep ladder to the roof of the deckhouse, which formed the boat deck.

That place had undergone an amazing transformation in the several minutes since Wendy had seen it from the water. A table and chairs were set up halfway between the wheelhouse and boats hanging from their davits aft, and on the table a jug of some liquid so cold the porcelain was covered in condensation. Four glasses stood around the jug. A gang of sailors were pulling tight the corners of an awning that cast a blessed shade over the deck. It was only nine in the morning, but already hot.

'Please, ma'am, won't you sit?' The lieutenant held a chair for Molly, it being understood all around which of the two women was the most important. Molly nodded imperiously and sat, and then the courtesy was extended to Wendy.

A moment later Lincoln appeared on the boat deck, and trailing behind, another man, also a civilian, but with the air of one close to power. The deference he showed the President was subtle, a man used to Lincoln's company. Not an equal, perhaps, but close.

'Madam' – Lincoln made a shallow bow to Molly – 'is there anything more you might need?'

Wendy translated. '*Merci, non,*' Molly replied.

From the wheelhouse a bell rang out and the tug gathered way. Lincoln said, 'May I present Mr Edwin Stanton, Secretary of War for the United States?'

Wendy translated. Molly made some reply that was polite but not fawning, the remarks of a woman to whom Secretaries of War were common enough.

Stanton made a bow, and to Wendy's surprise

141

replied in perfect French, 'It is an honor to meet you, ma'am, and I look forward to the honor of meeting your husband as well.'

Molly, if she was surprised, did not show it in any way. 'That is very kind, sir,' she said, then, gesturing at the chairs, said, 'Won't you join us?' She was already treating the tug as if it were hers, and Lincoln and Stanton her guests. Her self-confidence was so overwhelming that it carried all before her, like a cannonball blowing through a wooden palisade.

'Thank you,' Lincoln said, taking his seat, and Stanton sat as well. Wendy, least significant in that crowd, poured the lemonade.

'Tell me, Mr President,' Molly said, 'is it common for Presidents of the United States to be found sailing about in such small ships?' This time Stanton translated.

Lincoln smiled at the question. 'No, ma'am, not generally. This President in particular tries to avoid floating conveyance of any kind. Didn't have so good a time at supper the other night, did we, Stanton?'

'No, sir,' Stanton agreed. Wendy translated.

'America is so vast,' Molly said. 'You may live a thousand miles from the sea, never have any connection to it. There is no place in Norway that is more than one hundred miles from saltwater. We Norwegians cannot help but be bred to the sea.'

Wendy translated. She wondered if that was true, about no place in Norway being more than one hundred miles from the sea.

'I was bred to rivers, ma'am, and was a fair hand once at driving a river raft, out west, but that's the sum total of my knowledge of boats.'

'So what brings you out now?' Molly asked. 'Not a

yachting holiday, surely, in the middle of a war? Or am I impertinent to ask such a thing?' Her attitude was softening. She was no longer the angry, mistreated woman who had come on board. She was gracious, disarming, and Wendy was embarrassed to think that she had considered her own performance masterful. Molly was the real thing.

'Please, Mr President,' Molly continued, 'I am sometimes far too curious. My husband has often said as much. Please tell me to mind my own business.'

'No, no,' Lincoln said, after listening to Wendy's translation. 'No harm in my telling you what we're about. Stanton and I came down here to start a little fire under our admirals and generals. The American President is Commander-in-Chief of the armed forces, did you know that?'

'I did.'

'And sometimes, I find, I have to be a little more active in that role than I might wish. My officers seem to think all the legions of hell are arrayed against them, and not some ragtag bunch of Rebels. McClellan's over there in Williamsburg with more than one hundred thousand men and he tells me he can't take a step forward unless he has twenty thousand more. Now General Wool at Fortress Monroe, over there' – Lincoln pointed to the fortress several miles across the water – 'seems ready to let the Rebels stay in Norfolk for as long as it pleases them. Yesterday I had some of the navy's ships bombard Sewell's Point to see if there were still troops there.'

'We heard that,' Wendy offered. 'A terrific firing.'

'Where were you, ma'am, if I might ask?' Stanton asked.

'We were in Norfolk, sir, trying to find a way to get to the flagship.'

'We have heard that Norfolk is being abandoned. A tug deserted to us yesterday and reported as much. Did you see that?'

'Well, sir, there is great confusion. It seemed as if any number of civilians were trying to leave town. Whether the army was leaving or not, I could not say. I do not recall seeing any soldiers on the roads, or at the train station.'

'Hmm,' Stanton said. He and Lincoln exchanged looks. Wendy felt a shot of panic. *Damn it! Did I say something they know is a lie?*

'It is hard sometimes, in such circumstances, to know what is going on, even when it is right under your eyes,' Lincoln said, and his tone was friendly and reassuring. He reached out a hand, long bony fingers, and wrapped them around his glass and took a drink, and Wendy could not help but contemplate the extraordinary circumstances. How utterly bizarre the events of a life could be.

She saw the reticule in Molly's lap, felt the weight of the pistol still strapped to her thigh. The nearest sailors were thirty feet away in the wheelhouse, and they were not armed. She had it within her power, with one simple motion, to alter forever the tide of history. A clandestine move of her hand under the table, the squeeze of a trigger, and she could, at the cost of her own life, change entirely the fortunes of her new nation. She remembered the feel of the little gun's recoil, jerking her arm back as it discharged, the sense of lethal potential that the loaded weapon embodied.

She reached out her hand and picked up her glass

and savored the secret knowledge that the hand that held the glass might just as easily have picked up a gun, that it was her decision whether Abraham Lincoln lived or died, and he did not even know it.

Oh, God, save me from such hubris!

She glanced at Molly, but her aunt was staring like a sightseer at the shore beyond and did not appear to have assassination on her mind. Molly looked back at Lincoln. 'But today you take a boating holiday?' she asked. Stanton translated.

'No, ma'am. Today I am looking for a suitable place to land troops.'

Molly nodded, as if the news was only of vague interest to her, like hearing a story about someone you do not know. Wendy took a long drink of her lemonade because it seemed to her the best way to disguise her elation.

Looking for a suitable place to land troops! She and Molly had managed to land in exactly the right place. Had they been on board the flagship they could not have uncovered nearly as much information as they would in the next hour, their source the most unimpeachable of informants.

They would return to Captain Tucker with just the information he needed to make the best use of the ironclad *Virginia*. Tucker would be grateful, and beholden to them.

Wendy felt a pride, a sense of accomplishment, unlike any she had felt before. For the first time, she was not just supporting the cause of the Confederate States, she was fighting for it.

Lincoln is a fool, she thought, *to be so free with his information. One never knows to whom one is talking.*

And then she remembered, and her elation

collapsed like a bonfire burned through. Lincoln was not a fool. He knew perfectly well that even if she and Molly were Confederates, there was nothing they could do with the information. He had seen to it. They had no way to get off the tug.

CHAPTER 10

U.S. Flag-steamer Benton
Off Fort Pillow, May 11, 1862
SIR: I have the honor to inform the Department
that yesterday morning, a little after 7 o'clock, the
rebel squadron, consisting of eight ironclad
steamers, four of them, I believe, fitted as rams,
came around the point at the bend above Fort
Pillow and steamed gallantly up the river, fully
prepared for a regular engagement.

Captain C. H. Davis,
Commanding Mississippi Flotilla,
to Gideon Welles

Second Master Thomas B. Gregory, United States
Navy, in command of Mortar Boat Number Sixteen,
was not entirely at ease. The early morning was lovely,
the air cool and just a little damp, the sky clear blue.
The birds had resumed, in a tentative way, their chirp-
ing in the trees, protesting the intrusion of the second
master and his ilk. Perfect, the stretch of the
Mississippi River at Plum Point Bend, idyllic, like a bit
of Eden.

It seemed, somehow, disloyal to Second Master Gregory that he should find such beauty and tranquillity in Tennessee. Coming from Amesbury, Massachusetts, he had expected to find the depravity of Southern rural poverty, squalid slave quarters stuck behind grand plantation houses, barefoot people sharing dilapidated cabins with their pigs in the Mississippi mud. He had not expected to find the South as lovely as it was, as peaceful. He had to remind himself of why, and how much, he hated the Rebs.

He was standing on a wooden crate marked FUSES and looking over the casemate wall of Mortar Boat Number Sixteen, tied by a half-dozen lines to trees on the shore. Number Sixteen, like all its brethren, was an odd-looking thing. Its hull was no more than a barge, twenty feet wide and sixty feet long. On top of the barge was built an iron casemate, the sides angled slightly inward to deflect shot, so that the whole affair looked mostly like a small iron-clad without a roof or any means of self-propulsion.

The area within the walls of the casemate was mostly empty, save for the short, thick mortar mounted in the center of the deck. With its muzzle tilted straight up, it looked like a stew pot with fifteen-inch-thick sides. It sat on a low, heavy carriage. No wheels, there was no need of them. The gun was moved by boat, and when it fired, the water absorbed the recoil.

Aft of the mortar, a tent was set up, the kind of tent used by soldiers in the field, but here it was used to keep the powder for the mortar dry. Mounted on the sides of the casemate were the various implements for loading and servicing the gun. Arranged on racks along the edge of the deck sat the round shells, thirty-nine inches in circumference, that the mortar would lob a mile or so into the air, and that would, through the judicious application of science, experience, trial, and luck, land amid the Confederate troops holed up at Fort Pillow, out of sight on the other side of Plum Point.

The gun was the center of the mortar boat, literally and spiritually, and the men were there to service its needs. They did so that morning, slowly, lethargically, but Second Master Gregory did not mind. It was early morning, a morning that seemed to resist any effort to move quickly, and the men were moving fast enough that he could not call them beats.

The gun captain clipped the lanyard to the friction primer and stretched it out. Gregory automatically clapped a hand over the ear nearest the gun. The captain jerked the lanyard. The birds, the river, the sky, everything was obliterated by the gut-pounding roar of the mortar going off. The deck shuddered, the mortar boat was pushed down into the water, the air was filled with smoke and a noise that was like a physical presence, that seemed to go on and on long after the gun had fired.

Gregory's eyes traced the upward flight of the shell, a black dot against the blue sky. Up, up, up it went, hanging at the zenith of its flight, and then down, to drop beyond Plum Point. He listened for the detonation, though he knew there was no chance of hearing it. The first and second shell of the day he could hear explode, sometimes the third. But that was number five for the morning, and by then his hearing was so numb that even the men's voices a dozen yards away were muted and dull-sounding.

The gun crew set about swabbing the gun and preparing for the next shell, a slow, steady rhythm they would keep up all the daylight hours. The morning breeze carried the smoke away, and soon, one by one, the birds would set in again until the next blast silenced them. It seemed like a lazy, lethargic sort of warfare to Second Master Gregory, not at all the kind of dashing naval action he had envisioned when he volunteered.

He looked away from the mortar – there was no need for him to oversee the loading, the men knew the drill as well as he did – and looked off downstream, down the nearly mile-wide, brown, lazy water of the Mississippi, to where it was lost from sight around Plum Point. Mortar Boat Number Sixteen represented the southernmost point of Union control of the northern part of the Mississippi. Everything downriver from them was Confederate country, clear down to Vicksburg.

As he stared south, Gregory saw plumes of black smoke rise up over the wooded point like a line of campfires and his first thought was that the mortar had managed to set Fort Pillow on fire. But the smoke did not look like smoke from a fire, more like smoke from a smokestack, or a number of smokestacks. The dark columns were not stationary, but moving steadily toward them. *One, two, three, four,* Gregory counted. *Hallo, now what in the world could this be?*

Fifty yards upriver, also made fast to the trees on shore, lay the United States gunboat *Cincinnati*. She was one of the seven City Class gunboats, also known as 'Pook Turtles': 'Pook' for their constructor,

Samuel Pook, and 'Turtle' for their undeniable resemblance to that creature. A thin trail of smoke rose from her twin funnels, the output of fires that were banked and nearly out. Most of her crew were on hands and knees, holystoning the wooden deck that formed the roof of her iron casement. A lazy morning, playing nursemaid to the mortar boat downstream as it lobbed its shells at the invisible Confederates beyond the point.

In his cabin below, in his shirtsleeves, sitting behind his desk, Commander Roger Stembel fretted over his paperwork and dreamed of commanding a seventy-four-gun ship of the line, going toe-to-toe with two French first-rates at Trafalgar. Hand-to-hand combat across the massive decks of line-of-battle ships, a beautiful thing, lost to history, killed, like so many things, by the steam engine and rifled ordnance.

He sighed, perfectly aware of how juvenile his day-dreams were, on a par with dime novels read by boys who dreamed of the romance of war. Stembel was at least beyond that. There was nothing romantic in the ugly war in which he was now engaged. The romance of naval combat belonged to an earlier age.

Downriver the mortar boat fired, and Stembel felt the concussion of the blast and the recoil against the sides of his ship, like sitting inside a drum while some-one beats it. Then quiet, and above his head the steady *scrape, scrape, scrape* of holystones on decks. It was the same sound that Nelson would have heard above his great cabin, the morning of Trafalgar. Some things had not changed, but it was mostly the mundane things. Paperwork. Holystones.

Then the sound of footsteps, and Stembel sat

upright. He could hear the urgency in the steps as if they were speaking in some familiar, rhythmic code. He heard the steps on the ladder and he felt his heart race, heard the steps outside his cabin door stop, the fist banging the door, the voice of a midshipman calling, 'Captain Stembel, sir!' and all he could think was, *Oh, dear God, why do I not have steam up?*

The River Defense Fleet came on in line ahead, just as they had planned the night before. The *General Bragg*, long and lean, her walking beam engine driving her with a bone in her teeth, the *General Sumter* next in line, a side-wheeler like *Bragg* but smaller. Next came the *General Sterling Price*, big and boxy, awkward-looking compared with the ships in the van. In the *Price*'s wake came the *General Joseph Page* and the *General Earl Van Dorn*, almost side by side, as if in a race, and behind them, more or less in line, the rest of the fleet, the flagship *Little Rebel* and the others.

To Samuel Bowater, standing beside the wheelhouse, it seemed clear that one of them, the *Page* or the *Van Dorn*, was getting out of line, trying to charge ahead of her assigned position. Since he was not privy to the battle instructions, Bowater did not know which of the ships was breaking formation. But he could guess.

'Yeeeeehaaa!' Mississippi Mike screamed with the sheer thrill of the thing. Plum Point seemed to fall back and the river opened up in front of them, and there, tied to the bank, with no steam up that Bowater could see, one of the despised Union gunboats; just below it, one of the floating mortars, which, with virtual impunity, inflicted such misery on troops huddled in the river forts. They were alone. The rest of the fleet was farther up the river, tied to the bank, pants around their ankles.

'Yeeeehaaaa! Son of a bitch!' Mike grabbed the engine room bell and rang it again, though to Bowater's certain knowledge he had already rung up *full speed* five minutes before. Bowater could all but hear Guthrie cursing from three decks down.

The black smoke poured from the *Page*'s twin stacks, the walking beam worked itself up and down as if it was possessed. Bowater grinned. It was infectious.

In the past year Bowater had felt the touch of this wild recklessness more than once, blasting away at the Union fleet in Hampton Roads, defending Elizabeth City against the Yankee invaders until the ammunition was gone, then ramming and boarding. Incredible, but it was only a little more than two weeks before that he had driven the ironclad *Yazoo River* into the night battle below New Orleans.

There was a wild abandon to such a brawl, a release unlike any other, an extreme of emotion that could not be had by imitation, and Bowater could see how a man could become addicted.

Samuel Bowater and his men had no business being where they were. Their orders were to report to Shirley's yard, to assist in getting the *Tennessee* ready to launch. But Samuel had found the sight of the half-built hull greatly discouraging. And when Sullivan had learned of the coming fight on the river, and asked Bowater to come along to augment the *Page*'s crew with his own, Bowater found he could not resist. The thought of fiddling around in a ship-yard while a real fight was going on upriver was intolerable.

So here he was. And he felt guilty, exhilarated, wary, and ready to fight, all at once.

'You're right, Captain, devil take me, you are right!' Sullivan shouted over the cumulative noise of the racing side-wheelers.

'About what?'

'Mississippi Mike's mother! You know, Mississippi Mike in the book? She marries Mike's uncle – damn me to hell, that's gonna get 'em talkin! Just hope the boys in New York'll go for it!'

'They might not be so shocked in New York. They see a lot of that sort of thing.'

'Reckon you're right! Oh, look, that old peckerwood ironclad's getting under way! Ha ha ha! Too late for you, boys!'

The ironclad was drifting away from the bank. Thick black smoke was rolling from her twin funnels. They had caught the Yankee with no steam up, and now her engineers were throwing whatever they had on the fires – pitch pine, turpentine, oil-soaked rags – to get head up steam.

That was a mistake, Bowater thought. *Should have stayed tied to the bank.* A ship captain's first instinct was always to get under way, to get sea room to fight. But in this case the iron ship was better off with one side pressed against the shore, protected, while they fought the enemy off with their broadside. Now they were drifting and helpless.

Well, not helpless, entirely. As the *Bragg* raced for the Yankee ship, water creaming around the riverboat's submerged ram, the ironclad fired. From ten feet away she blasted the Rebel with her starboard broadside guns, four thirty-two-pounders, from what Bowater could see. The impact was lost from sight behind the deckhouse, but Bowater saw the shot come out the other side, blowing sections out of the superstructure, sending planks and splinters and heaps of cotton into the air in a cloud of flying debris.

But the gunfire did not slow the *Bragg* in the least. She slammed bow-first into the Yankee ironclad, which, fortunately for the Yankees, had slewed around at the last moment, leaving the *Bragg* with only a glancing blow.

'Did she hole the bastard, ya reckon?' Sullivan shouted the question. He was in a frenzy, dancing in place, leaning forward on the rail, like a dog straining at the leash. Bowater half expected Mike's tongue to come lolling out of his mouth.

'I think so. See, they're locked together.'

The *Bragg* and the ironclad seemed to embrace one another as they spun in the stream, and it was clear that the *Bragg*'s ram was stuck in the ironclad's side. If the ironclad went down, she could take the Confederate ship with her.

The ironclad fired again, with the *Bragg* pressed against her so close that she could not even run her guns out. The heavy balls ripped through the riverboat's fragile upper works, but the blast seemed to shake the *Bragg* loose. She backed away, turning sideways in the stream, seemingly out of control, as the *Price* charged past, putting every ounce of steam she had behind her wild run at the listing Yankee.

'Come left, come left!' Sullivan shouted into the wheelhouse, then charged in and grabbed the wheel himself, helped Baxter spin it over. The *Bragg* was drifting down on them, not under command, for what reason they could not see.

'Did her boiler blow?' Sullivan asked.

'I don't think so,' Bowater said. There was no evidence of that. It might have been a rudder gone, or tiller ropes.

The *General Page* did a wild turn clear of the drifting riverboat, and as she did the *Van Dorn* came charging past, making for the ironclad.

'Oh, you son of a bitch!' Sullivan roared, hurling more abuse on the River Defense boat than Bowater had ever heard him shout at the enemy. 'Son of a bitch is goin for our meat!'

But Bowater's eyes were on the *General Sterling Price,* racing to take the place of the *Bragg,* steaming into the storm of iron the Yankee was firing at her. She slammed into the ironclad aft, twisting her around in the river. The *Price* shuddered her full length, as if she had struck a reef. The ironclad rolled away under the impact, firing her guns into the *Price* as the riverboat hit and kept on going. The sound of rending wood, the screech of structural members ripped clean away were audible even over the gunfire, the shouting, the huffing of engines, and the slap of paddle wheels.

The fight was building, the ironclads from upstream having dropped down, their iron-encased central paddle wheels turning enough now to give them steerage. They were firing bow guns and broadside guns at the Confederates, crushing the flimsy upper works of riverboats never designed for that kind of abuse. But still the River Defense Fleet came on.

The once blue sky was hazy, the belching clouds of smoke hanging like fog over the river, giving everything a soft and milky look, the air choking, the water and the shoreline gray-looking through the haze. The mortar boat was firing fast, lobbing shells above the river that came screaming down from overhead and burst at water level, throwing their whistling fragments of iron in every direction, and Bowater had to wonder if there wasn't just as good a chance of hitting friend as foe.

It was a battle now, a genuine naval battle, a fleet action, played out on the twisting Mississippi River.

The *Van Dorn* charged past the *General Page,* past the *Price* and the ironclad, firing away at the mortar boat tied to the bank. Her eight-inch bow gun ripped a shell through the thin side of the mortar boat's casemate, left a neat hole as it passed on, and the *Van Dorn* fired again.

Bowater pulled his eyes from the sight, concentrated on what his ship was doing. The ironclad, the one that had been tied to the shore, was still in front of them. But it was listing, dragging itself toward shallow water, looking for a place to die. The *Price* had left it astern and was charging upriver toward the rest of the Yankee fleet.

'Baxter!' Bowater shouted in to the helmsman. 'Come right! Shave the stern of that ironclad and make for the big one coming down on the right side of the river!'

Baxter turned and looked at Bowater, the cheroot hanging from his lips, his expression somewhere between amused and aghast. Bowater felt his face flush red. He had entirely forgotten himself.

Then from the edge of the hurricane deck, the booming laugh of Mississippi Mike Sullivan. Bowater caught a movement from the corner of his eye, and before he could brace for it the arm came around in a great arc, the good-natured slap on the back like being hit with a club, and he staggered forward.

'You listen to him, Baxter!' Sullivan shouted. 'Do just like he said. Remember, Captain Bowater here went to the *Navy School*!'

Baxter grinned around his cheroot, spun the wheel. Down below, on the *Page*'s bow, behind the bulwark of pine boards and compressed cotton that earned the ship the designation of cotton clad, the gunners opened up on the crippled Yankee. The *Page*'s rifle gun roared, smoke and flame shooting out ahead of the riverboat. Bowater felt the recoil in his feet, the entire boat shuddering under the weight of the gun slamming back on her breeching.

Then it was the ironclad's turn. From the stern guns poking out of her sloped casement and the aftermost broadside guns that would bear, the Yankees lashed out at the passing riverboat. The crash of gun, the crush of wood, the shudder underfoot as the round shot and rifled shells hit, it was all familiar to Bowater, a part of the whole, along with the smoke and the noise and the controlled chaos.

They were up with the ironclad, not more than ten yards off her stern, and Samuel had his first real look at the despised Yankee gunboats, and what he saw was a nearly perfect weapon for the war they were fighting. Around one hundred and eighty feet long, about fifty on the beam, there was no effort made here to create a sleek craft, and there was no need for one.

Underfoot, the deck shuddered from the impact of iron that struck the *General Page*'s deckhouse and went right on through. All along the boiler deck below, the *Page*'s sharpshooters fired away with their rifles at the ironclad as they passed, the sound of the small arms puny under the roar of the big guns. Sparks like fireflies flashed on the Yankee's iron casemate as minié balls ricocheted off, the gunmen searching out the Yankees through the gun ports.

Bowater watched in awe as the ironclad slipped past. The Yankee gunboats drew around six feet, three feet less than the *Price* and nine feet less than the *General Bragg*. A centerline paddle wheel encased in iron, heavy guns bristling from every quarter, she was one of the most frightening things Bowater had seen, representative of the kind of industrial superiority the Yankees could bring to bear.

And yet she was sinking. Brought down by the most ancient of naval weapons, the ram.

'Yeeehaaa!' Mississippi Mike shouted. 'There, that one!' He pointed upriver to another of the ironclads dropping down, guns lashing out in every direction, black smoke rolling from her funnels. 'That's our meat! Right into her!'

The crippled ironclad fired again, her stern guns blowing holes clean through the deckhouse. Bowater doubted that the guns, at that short range, could be depressed enough to hit the engines or boilers, or elevated enough to hit the wheelhouse. As long as they missed the walking beam's A-frame and the steering gear, there wasn't much they could do.

Bowater pulled his eyes from the ironclad and looked upriver. No time for reflection. No time for philosophizing. That was the beauty of a fight such as this. It focused the mind wonderfully.

In the *Cincinnati*'s conical pilothouse, Commander Stembel was trying to focus, but it was not working very well. The smoke from the gun deck rolled up the companionway and was sucked out of the square viewing ports, choking and blinding. The noise was tremendous, the sounds of the great guns firing again and again, the shudder of the vessel from the recoil of her own guns and the impact of the enemy's guns on her iron-plated sides.

He had given up ringing the engine room. There was not steam enough to maneuver, and ringing for more would not make it appear. He stared out the view port. The first ship to ram them, and hole them, was drifting downstream, out of the fight. He hoped his gunners had blown out her boilers, killed every one of them, but he doubted it.

Another one was coming at them now, a big, boxy Confederate ram, charging like a bull, seemingly oblivious to the furious gunfire the *Cincinnati* was hurling at her. Stembel shouted a warning, grabbed a stanchion, and braced for the impact. There was nothing more he could do.

The Rebel struck aft with a terrible wrenching sound, rolling the *Cincinnati* away to starboard. The helmsman made a grunting sound and nearly fell as the wheel spun out of control and then stopped, a dead thing. Stembel met the man's eyes, wide with surprise. 'Rudder must be gone, sir. Done for!'

Stembel turned away, craned his neck to see out the view port. The Rebel was steaming on, forging upstream into the teeth of the rest of the Union fleet. Leaving the *Cincinnati* for dead.

We are not dead, goddamn it! Stembel clenched his teeth. Footsteps on the iron ladder. Lt. William Hoel was there. His cap was gone, his face smudged black, his hair matted down with perspiration.

'Sir? We're taking on water, sir, pretty bad. That last ram knocked a good hole aft!'

'Yes.' Stembel looked through the view port. 'It seems to have done for our steering gear as well.' He turned back. 'Lieutenant, take over here. Keep her headed for the shallow water. I have to see for myself.'

Hoel's 'Aye, aye, sir' came as Stembel was already dropping down the ladder, into the gloom and smoke of the gun deck. At each of the big guns, men stripped to the waist and gleaming with sweat hauled, swabbed, loaded, ran out, cursed. The officers behind them, in blue frock coats, with caps on heads, shouted orders and encouragement, and Stembel was proud of what he saw. The men were drilled, disciplined; they did not think, they just acted – loaded and fired as if nothing existed beyond their guns, as if they were not in a deadly fight on board a sinking ironclad.

Stembel made his way aft, called out encouragement, accepted the cheers of the men. He gagged on the smoke, relished the odd swirl of fresh air from a gun port. The casemate shuddered and rang from the crash of enemy shot against it, and in counterpoint the sharp pinging of the small-arms fire bouncing harmlessly away.

He reached the ladder to the engine room and climbed down, into the nearly unbearable heat and noise of the clanging pipes and hiss of steam and the working of the two big engines. He paused on the ladder, looked down into the half-light, the lanterns illuminating the space in parts here and there, and he tried to make sense of what he saw. There was something not right about the deck. The deck did not

161

seem to be where it was supposed to be, did not seem to be the solid thing he recalled.

And then he realized that the deck was underwater, and as he did he saw Chief Engineer McFarland come hurrying over – wading over – the water up to his knees. He moved with the exaggerated swing of the arms and push of the legs that people do when their movement is impeded in that way.

'Captain, the pumps can't keep up, sir!' the chief yelled and Stembel nodded. 'Water'll be up to the boilers soon, just when we're getting head up steam! Son of a bitch!'

'Yes, Chief,' Stembel shouted over the noise, the unrelenting noise. 'We'll beach her!'

The chief nodded, turned back to his work. Stembel climbed back to the gun deck, and suddenly he could not stand to be there, down below, blind. He could not go back to the pilothouse with its little view ports. He had to see, had to be able to look around and understand the way things lay. Like Nelson on his quarterdeck.

He climbed another ladder onto the hurricane deck and stepped out into the morning, blinking and squinting. The smoke from the battle was swirling around the river, blinding and choking, but still it was considerably more bright and cool on the hurricane deck than it was below.

The *Cincinnati* was sinking, his ship was going down. He could feel the list in her as he crossed the hurricane deck to the pilothouse. Time to get her on the mud. But here was another Rebel, coming up fast, her bow gun firing, steaming up on the port quarter where only one of the *Cincinnati*'s guns could reach her.

Fifty yards away, and someone from the Rebel boat shouted, 'Haul down your flag and we will save you!'

The words were like a slap. Stembel did not know what to say. *Haul down our flag?* But then from somewhere aboard the *Cincinnati*, someone shouted back, 'Our flag will go down when we do!'

Yes, yes, Stembel thought. He turned and hurried forward. He would direct the ship from outside the pilothouse, to the extent that he could direct a sinking ship that had no steering gear. Minié balls thudded into the wooden deck below his feet.

Then the Confederate ram struck, right on the port quarter. Stembel stumbled and fell forward as the *Cincinnati*'s bow was driven under by the force of the impact. The Rebel went full astern, drawing its ram from the hole it had punched, and none of the ironclad's guns would bear.

Stembel pulled himself to his feet and drew his side arm. He pulled the hammer back with his thumb, found a Rebel sharpshooter over the barrel, pulled the trigger. The gun jumped in his hand. He thumbed the trigger back again. He could feel his ship settling under him, wondered how much water they were in. He fired, thought of Nelson, so recklessly exposing himself. He wondered how different this moment was from Nelson's. The smoke, the gunfire, the despair at the thought of defeat.

He fired again. He wondered if perhaps Nelson also felt that the romance of war belonged to an earlier age.

He felt a punch in his shoulder, a straight line of burning pain running right through his shoulder, right through his neck, right through his throat. He gasped, staggered, dropped the pistol, grabbed at his neck. It was hot and wet with blood. He could feel the ragged skin under his hand where the ball had exited, passed clean through him. The pistol clattered on the deck. Stembel fell to his knees. Everything seemed hazy, indistinct, but it might have been the smoke. He fell prone, laid out on the warm deck planks, and did not move.

CHAPTER 11

*We started at the commodore's signal at 6 A.M.
and steamed round the point in front of Fort
Pillow. The boat guarding the mortar boat
immediately started into the current and ran for
the shoal water on Plum Point. The* General
Bragg, *Captain Leonard, which had the lead, ran
rapidly at her, striking her a glancing blow on the
starboard bow and receiving a broadside at 10
feet distance.*

Brigadier General M. Jeff Thompson
to General G. T. Beauregard

*When your sanctuary becomes your hell, there's no
damned place left to run. . . .*

Hieronymus Taylor pushed the insidious thought
aside. Too much to consider, when he wanted to
consider nothing.

He was sweating hard. Well over one hundred
degrees in the engine room. The boiler doors were
open and the lean bodies of the firemen and stokers
stood out in silhouette against the glowing white and
orange banks of coal. On the floor plates were piled

steep hillocks of coal into which the firemen drove their shovels with a grating sound, flinging more and more coal into the insatiable fire, all to raise the beast steam from the waters, to keep it moving.

The coal bunkers to starboard and larboard were no more than half full, which was bad, since they were the only real protection the boilers had from rifled shells that could pierce the riverboat's side as if it was wet paper. Taylor thought about the bargeful of coal that Sullivan had stolen in Vicksburg. They had left it tied to the dock at Fort Pillow. There had been no time to load it into the bunkers. All that potential protection, left behind.

Cottonclad . . . Taylor had laughed the first time he heard the term. *Cottonclad* . . . armor the ship with the softest, most flammable substance found in nature. Goddamned stupid peckerwoods. But he wasn't laughing anymore. Iron in any form was not to be had in the Confederacy, for all practical purposes, while the Yankees spit out so much of it they might be paving the roads with gunboat plating, for all he knew.

But we got cotton down here, oh boy, yes, do we have cotton . . .

Taylor's eyes moved to the top of the boilers. The lever arms of the safety valves were lashed down with white cotton rope that stood out in the dim light, and he wondered if Guthrie had done that on purpose, so it would be obvious to everyone that he had lashed the valves, and done so without permission from the wheelhouse. If he had, it was a wasted effort, because Sullivan would not mind if the valves were lashed now. He would probably insist on it. Safety was not much of an issue that morning.

Taylor was at the throttle, one hand on the reversing lever. It was Guthrie's station, of course, but Taylor had offered to take it, to free the engineer up so that he could run around like a windup toy, issuing unnecessary orders and generally annoying the engine room. Watching him as he flew from boilers to crankshaft to crossheads and back, Taylor realized that Guthrie was, at the heart of it, a smaller, shriller, quicker Mississippi Mike Sullivan. Mississippi Mike's alabaster pard.

The sweat was slick under Taylor's hand. He let go of the throttle, wiped his hand on his shirt. His appetite had been good in the early morning. He'd eaten a big breakfast – eggs, grits with syrup, soft tack, bacon – but now it sat like a rock in his stomach. He was afraid he might puke.

The wheelhouse bells rang again, *full speed,* the third time that horse's ass peckerwood Sullivan had rung for full speed. Taylor might have cursed out loud, but Guthrie beat him to it, cursing enough for both of them, enough for every engineer in the River Defense Fleet, for every engineer who had ever suffered the unforgivable torment of an idiot with his hand on the bell rope.

The *General Page* was going as fast as she was going to go upstream. Her steam pressure gauges were toying with fifteen pounds' pressure. A lantern hung near the front of the boilers seemed to cast its light directly on the gauges, as if it was making a special point of letting Taylor know how close to the edge they were running things.

His breath was coming shallow and his head was feeling light. He closed his eyes and breathed deeply and he seemed to pull the anger further into him with every breath.

He heard the muffled bang of a heavy gun. Not the *Page*'s gun, a gun from another ship. The Yankees, no doubt. He wondered if they were up with the enemy, how many Yankees there were.

In all his seagoing career he had never been much interested in what went on above the main deck. All the nonsensical blather of captains and pilots about snags and chutes and shifting bars was of no interest to him. His world was valves and crossheads and connecting rods, and that was how he preferred it.

That had changed with his first fight. When they started shooting at Yankees, suddenly his interest in what took place topsides had taken an exponential leap. He had even found himself laying the bow gun in the fight at Hampton Roads. But for all that, it was always a relief to get back to the confines of his engine room, to stand amid the perfect organization and pure logic of the machine.

Another gun went off, and immediately another, and a shell ripped through the superstructure above, blowing a hole through the fidley, missing the walking beam's A-frame by a few feet, no more.

'*Shit!*' Taylor shouted the word so loud that a few heads turned. 'Son of a bitch . . .' he said, lower. He could feel his heart in his chest, banging away at twenty times the speed of the engine behind him. His breath was coming shallowly again.

Guthrie was hovering in front of him, grinning. 'That there is what you call a Yankee forced air ventilator! Forced it right through the goddamn fidley! Sum bitch, them kangaroos nearly took out the walking beam! Reason a walking beam got no place on a fighting ship. You all right, Taylor?'

Taylor gulped air. 'Yeah, yeah, I'm all right.'

'Really? You look like a pile of horseshit.'

Another shell hit, farther forward, boiler deck level, Taylor guessed. Some low grunting noise escaped his lips. Guthrie turned back to him.

'Think I ate something for breakfast didn't agree with me.'

'Didn't agree with you? Hell, it looks like it hated your goddamned immortal soul!'

'Look, Guthrie,' Taylor was talking without thinking, 'I got to get topside, get some air, or I swear I'll puke all over the fuckin floor plates.'

'Yeah, yeah, go on,' Guthrie said, taking Taylor's place at the throttles as Taylor stood awkwardly, bent partway over. There was a note in Guthrie's voice that Taylor did not like, as if, in Guthrie's opinion, going on deck was not much different from going over to the Yankees. Taylor knew Guthrie felt that way because he would have felt the same.

He tucked that worry away, knew it would bother him later, but he did not care at the moment. Now that he had stood, had made his excuse, he could think of nothing but getting out of that engine room, away from the boilers and the gauges and the damned white rope on the safety valves.

He climbed up the ladder, moving faster with every rung, threw open the door to the fidley, and stepped out onto the main deck, starboard side. He put two hands on the rail, looked out over the river. The *Van Dorn* was blowing holes in the side of a mortar boat tied to the bank, while the mortar boat was lobbing shells over the top of the *Van Dorn* to drop on the River Defense boats farther out. But Taylor did not really care.

He had thought, going up the ladder, that his first

act on deck would be to puke over the side, and he hoped someone would see him, since that would lend credence to the idea that he had got hold of a bad side of bacon. But once he stepped through the door, into the relative fresh and cool air, he felt suddenly renewed, newborn, strong and able. His stomach pains eased, he felt the light breeze cool the sweat on his forehead and his drenched shirt. He breathed deeply for the first time in an hour.

He was angry now. His body and his mind were betraying him, his unmanageable fear stripping him of the very thing that he was. The engine room was where he should be, but his traitorous self had driven him out. There was nothing more unforgivable than betrayal. What did you do when you caught yourself betraying yourself?

Great God almighty, I'm scared, he thought. There, the word was out at last, free floating in his mind, at least, and probably in Guthrie's mind too, and that son of a bitch Bowater's. Bowater, he was certain, would never comprehend such a thing as what Taylor was suffering. You had to be a human being with human feeling to get yourself in the position Taylor was in, and he doubted Bowater qualified on either count. *Ice cold son of a bitch . . .*

Taylor was getting more angry, now that he was no longer standing in the presence of the beast, the beast that had seared the skin clean off of James Burgess and left him a horrible writhing thing on the deck plates, screaming for death to take him, and Hieronymus Taylor appointed the angel of mercy with a double-barrelled shotgun.

In the engine room he did not feel anger, because the other thing was so powerful, but up on the main deck, in the sunshine, it was only anger. He made his way forward, stepped around the forward end of the deckhouse just as the *Page*'s bow gun was going off. He watched the gun slam back, the river and the shore and the Yankees lost behind the gray cloud of smoke from the muzzle.

The *General Page* steamed straight into the cloud, the smoke whipped aft and engulfed Taylor, and then the ship broke out into the blue sky and Taylor could see the lay of things.

The Yankees were coming downriver, casting off from the bank, steaming to the aid of the mortar boat. The closest of the ironclad gunboats was just a few hundred yards upriver, down-bound, stern first, and firing like mad, guns going off from her broadside and stern gun ports. She was directly ahead, and Sullivan seemed to be making to ram her. Taylor pressed his lips together. He wanted Sullivan to slam the ship into the bastard, really hit her good.

He heard gunfire to larboard, and in the same instant the side of the deckhouse seemed to explode, a shower of splinters and shattered wood blown out over the water. Taylor shielded his face with his arm as sundry bits of debris bounced off of him. He raced forward, looked off the larboard side. There was a Yankee gunboat, one hundred feet off; he had not even known it. She was lashing out in her death throes. Taylor could see she was listing, limping for shallow water, the crew spilling out of the casement onto the hurricane deck as their vessel sank under them.

'Die, you son of a whore!' Taylor shouted at the gunboat. He ran forward to the bow where the gun crew were running the big gun out again. Buford

171

Tarbox was captain of the gun, the crew made up of the riverboat men, but also the former Yazoo Rivers, his shipmates, joining in with the General Pages. Ruffin Tanner was handling the swab, and he and Taylor nodded their greeting. Tanner's face was smeared black with powder smoke and his shirt was torn, a bloody gash visible though the rent cloth, but not enough to slow him down, apparently.

They were closing fast with the ironclad, but not as fast as the *Van Dorn*, which had turned its attention from the mortar boat to the new Yankee threat coming downriver. The *Van Dorn* was crossing over from the eastern shore, crossing the *Page*'s bow, making a ramming run at the iron gunboat.

'Get clear, you bastard!' Taylor shouted. 'Stand off!' He waved his arm frantically, trying to get the *Van Dorn* to clear the way for them. He felt a need like great hunger to have the *Page* drive her ram into the Yankee. He wanted to get right up with the blue-belly sons of bitches and start killing them, kill them as fast as he could.

'Get clear, for the love of God!'

There was no chance he could be heard aboard the *Van Dorn*, and no chance he would be obeyed if he were. He knew it. He could not keep from yelling. Some of the gun crew took up the shouting, yelling with him, waving their arms. Some shook their heads at the display.

'Run out!' Tarbox yelled. In place of his slouch hat he now wore a gray kepi he had picked up somewhere.

The men at the gun tackles leaned into the pull, the awkward gun carriage rolled forward. The ironclad was filling the air with shot, shells screaming past.

Taylor could feel the concussion of her cannon in the air and in the *Page*'s deck. He saw a respectable section of the *Van Dorn*'s deckhouse torn clean away, but she did not pause in her headlong rush to be the first to impale the Yankee.

'Stand clear!' Tarbox yanked the lanyard. The gun went off with a terrific blast, hurling inboard, blanketing everything in the cloud of smoke. Taylor felt the deck jerk under him, shudder as if they had hit a rock. It felt good, revitalizing. He relished the nearness of death, Yankee death, his death perhaps, a clean death from a bullet. He was not afraid.

The *Page* plowed through her own gun smoke and the scene opened up again, though now the haze hung so thick it was like steaming in a light fog. Visibility was perhaps two hundred yards through the smoke.

The Yankee was still under their bow, the distance closing fast, but now the *Van Dorn* was on her, churning up the last fifty feet. The Yankee gunboat turned hard, swinging her bow away from the ram, and an instant later the *Van Dorn* struck. Taylor could see the ironclad roll and twist with the impact, he saw the *Van Dorn* shudder and pause as her submerged iron ram pierced the wooden hull of the ironclad and kept on going. But the Confederates had struck at an angle, only a glancing blow, and not the bone-crunching right-angle impact they had hoped for.

The *Van Dorn* continued on upriver, past the ironclad she had just struck, right into the withering fire from the Yankees farther upstream, but Taylor had no more interest in her. The way was open now for them to hit, a clear stretch of water between the *General Page* and the Yankee gunboat.

Taylor stepped forward, the madness on him like he had never felt before. He looked up at the wheelhouse. Bowater was there, hand on the rail in his yachting holiday manner. Sullivan was bouncing back and forth.

'Ram that bastard!' Taylor shouted, pointing at the ironclad. 'Run that son of a bitch down!'

Bowater looked down at him, an odd expression on his face – part surprise, perhaps, part concern. Odd. Sullivan shouted, 'What do ya think I'm gonna do, you stupid bastard?'

Taylor turned and faced forward again. He had no time for Sullivan and his idiocy.

The ironclad was hammering them good, tearing apart the deckhouse above Taylor's head. The gun crew were ducking now, behind the bulwark of pine boards and compressed cotton that made a shield on the otherwise unprotected bow. Taylor wanted to tell them to get up, stand like men, load the gun, but he kept his mouth shut, kept his own council.

He glanced over at the *Van Dorn*. She appeared to be aground and was taking a beating from the ironclad and the others upriver and coming down. Taylor had a sudden sick fear that Sullivan would give up, turn and run, decide they were too outnumbered. He looked up at the wheelhouse again, but Sullivan was standing like a brick wall now, hands on the rail, ready for impact.

The ironclad was fifty feet ahead, no more. Black smoke was rolling from the *Page*'s chimneys. Guthrie was really pouring it on. Taylor could see the steam gauges in his mind and the thought made him stop, like remembering something terrible that you had managed to momentarily forget.

Twenty feet, ten feet, Taylor could see faces in the Yankee's gun ports, bare-chested men huddled in the shadows around the barrels of the big guns. A jet of smoke, the roar of a gun, and Taylor was knocked sideways. For an instant he was certain he was a dead man and he was not sure how he felt about it.

Then the *General Joseph Page* hit the ironclad, hit it square with every ounce of power the walking beam engine could muster. Already off balance from the force of the passing round shot, Taylor sprawled out on the deck, hitting hands first and sliding forward. He lay still, but just for an instant. As he made certain he was all in one piece, he scrambled to his feet.

The impact of the *Van Dorn* had swiveled the ironclad around, and the *Page* struck right on the corner of the casemate, just aft of the bow. And though it owed more to luck than strategy, it was a perfect hit. The Yankee's broadside guns could not train around forward enough, and the bow guns could not train aft to hit the *Page*. As long as she stayed where she was, the *Page* was safe from the ironclad's cannon.

Taylor raced up to the pine board bulwark and looked over the bow. The *Page*'s ram had pierced the ironclad's vulnerable wooden hull below the waterline. For the moment, the two ships were locked together. He heard the *Page*'s paddle wheels stop, heard them begin the slow turns in reverse.

'No, no, no!' he shouted. Didn't they see the chance here? Taylor could not stand the idea of backing away, out of danger. There, in the white-hot fire of combat, he could be burned clean, his manhood unassailable.

'Come on, y'all!' he shouted to the men crouched

behind the bulwark. 'Let's board the son of a bitch! Come on!'

Eyes met him, unmoving men, uncomprehending. They did not see what he did – the small, half-round foredeck of the ironclad, an easy jump from the *General Page*'s bow, the gun ports open wide.

'Come on!' No one moved, and Taylor did not have a weapon. He grabbed one of the riverboat men by the collar, jerked him to his feet. Taylor was stronger than most men even when not in a berserker rage, and the man was like a rag doll as Taylor pulled him up and jerked the pistols from the holsters on his belt.

The riverboat man got off a curse, a protest, the beginnings of a roundhouse punch to Taylor's head before Taylor shoved him back to the deck.

Two steps and Taylor was at the pine board bulwark, vaulting over it, a pistol in each hand. He landed on the small part of the *Page*'s deck forward of the bulwark, leaped without breaking stride across the four feet of water to the deck of the ironclad.

He came down hard, stumbled, straightened, was aware enough to marvel at the fact that he was now standing on the deck of a Yankee man-of-war. He heard screaming, shouting behind him, and the wild, bearded riverboat men came pouring over the bulwark. It was just their kind of madness.

Taylor ran up to the first gun port, pistols held straight out. His thumbs pulled back the hammers. Even over all the noise of the fight he could hear that clean, satisfying click of the action. He looked through the gun port but could see little in the gloomy interior. He fired at motion, something moving, saw another thing that looked like a blue coat and fired the left-hand pistol, cocking the right.

The riverboat men were there, crowding behind him. A pistol went off right in his ear, like a punch to the head. The riverboat men were shouting and storming the other gun ports. The deepwater men were with them.

Taylor stepped forward, pistol out, right up to the gun port. A face appeared and Taylor aimed, and suddenly the man thrust a rammer out, drove it like a lance into Taylor's chest. Taylor stumbled, the gun went off, the bullet pinged against the casemate.

'Son of a bitch!' Taylor shouted, thumbed the pistol's hammer again, drove at the gun port, thrust the pistol into the gloom inside. Something hit his arm – a ram or a club, something – but Taylor did not drop the gun. He swung it around, fired in the general direction of the blow.

The others were crowding the gun ports like dogs around a treed coon, shouting, firing, cursing. But the only way into the casemate was an awkward climb around the big guns, so awkward that the Yankees would have killed with ease any man who tried. Here was the Ark, and they, poor sinners, could only pound on the outside. They could not get in.

Taylor fired again into the darkness. It was no use – the gun crews were shying away from the ports, he could not hit anyone. But a ladder ran up the sloping front face of the casemate to the hurricane deck above. There, perhaps, was a way in.

'Come on! Come on, you bastards, follow me!' Taylor shouted. He had no control anymore. He felt as if his body was barely held together, as if he might fly off in a thousand pieces at any second, blown apart by the rage. He ran for the ladder, raced up, did not see or care if anyone was following. Over the edge of the casemate, and right in front of him, like an eight-foot-high anthill, was the conical pilothouse, pierced all around with small square ports. There, Taylor knew, were the officers.

He stopped, ten feet short, looked over the top of the Navy Colt .36, lined up the notch in the hammer, the brass sight at the end of the barrel, and the face peering out of the port. He pulled the trigger. The hammer snapped dead. He looked at the cylinder. All the percussion caps mangled, all the bullets gone. He threw the gun away, switched the pistol from left hand to right, and with a shout stepped forward, gun extended.

A puff of smoke shot from the pilothouse like the fire from a miniature broadside and a bullet whipped past Taylor's head. *Sons of whores are shooting at me,* Taylor thought, though they might have been waving a greeting for all the impression the bullets made on him. He took another step, gun level, pulled the trigger. The bullet went through the port as if it was a paper target, but if it hit anyone, Taylor could not tell.

An arm appeared through another port, pistol in hand. Taylor adjusted his aim, squeezed the trigger, and then the air was ripped apart by the *General Page*'s steam whistle, a strident scream, a demand for attention. Taylor turned, looked up at the *Page*'s wheelhouse. There were Bowater and Sullivan, waving like lunatics, gesturing for him and the others to return. The paddle wheels were turning, backing down, the gunboat trying to disengage from the ironclad.

Over the whistle came the sharp crack of a pistol

and Taylor felt a burn in his left leg, midcalf, and a sharp pain. He looked down, thinking that someone had snuck up, slashed him with a knife. That was what it felt like. He had been slashed before, he knew the sensation.

His pants leg was ripped, he could see bloody flesh through the torn cloth, and as he looked at it he realized he could not stand on that leg anymore. He tried to shift his weight to his other foot, but too late. His left leg buckled under him and he fell, hands down on the warm planks of the deck. The pistol clattered away, out of reach.

'Oh, son of a bitch!' he shouted. A bullet plowed into the wood a few feet in front of him and he drew back, then pulled himself forward, reached out for the gun. The pain was starting to come now, rippling up from his left calf where the bullet had done God knew what damage. He wrapped his fingers around the walnut grip, rolled over, thumbed the hammer, and fired defiantly at the pilothouse. He heard the bullet ping against the iron and spin uselessly away.

The *General Page* was still blowing her steam whistle and Taylor wished they would stop. He pushed himself up on his elbow, looked over the edge of the casemate. The men from the *Page* were scrambling over the bulwark as the riverboat pulled away, drawing its iron ram free, the gap between Confederate and Yankee growing wider.

Aw, damn ... last damn train to Memphis and I missed her ...

No matter. That was as good a place to end it as any, sprawled out on the deck of a Yankee ironclad. He held the revolver close to his face. Two intact percussion caps that he could see, perhaps a third

hidden from view. Two or three bullets if none mis-
fired. He could take three Yankees with him, as long
as the abolitionist bastards had the good grace to kill
him in turn. He would not be a prisoner.

He pushed himself up until he was kneeling,
clenched his teeth against the pain in his calf, aimed
and fired at the pilothouse. His shooting was getting
wild, and he cursed himself, told himself to concentrate, concentrate.

Behind him, he heard feet pounding deck, banging
up the ladder. *Here they come*, he thought, tried to
turn and face the attackers. A gun fired from the
pilothouse, the bullet ripped through Taylor's shirt,
grazed his skin, knocked him off balance. He fell forward, hands out, rolled on his back, gun up, aimed
forward.

A voice, 'It's us! It's us!' A hand wrapped around
the barrel of the gun and pushed it aside as Taylor
pulled the trigger. There was gunfire all around now,
small arms peppering the pilothouse, and Taylor
looked up into Samuel Bowater's face.

'Tanner!' Bowater shouted. 'Bear a hand!'

Here was salvation, and Taylor was white hot with
rage. 'Get out of here!' he shouted. 'Leave me be!'

Bowater slipped an arm under Taylor's arm and
Taylor felt Ruffin Tanner do the same and they hoisted
him up, and he – exhausted, in agony – could do
nothing about it but scream defiance.

'You fuckin peckerwood bastards! Let me be!' But
they would not.

Now Taylor could see the men who had come up
the ladder, his shipmates, ten or so, armed with
pistols and the .58-caliber Mississippi rifles from
the *General Page*'s arsenal. They fired away at the

pilothouse, filling the air with the crack of percussion cap, the bang of the rifles, the metal-on-metal sound of minié balls bouncing off iron. The viewing ports in the pilothouse were empty – no one dared show his face to that fusillade.

Bowater and Tanner were dragging him along now, his one leg useless, his arms draped over their shoulders, held fast, and he could not pull them away. Someone had taken the pistol from his hand. He was shouting, cursing, struggling, but it did no good.

Underfoot the ironclad's guns went off, three of the broadside guns, and the deck shook like an earthquake. Bowater and Tanner stumbled but kept their footing. The *General Page* was twenty feet off, backing away, taking a pounding from the Yankees as she drew back.

'Son of a bitch, where is that mick bastard going!' Taylor shouted but no one answered. They dragged him along, dragged him aft, past the pilothouse, with Tanner actually stepping up on the edge of the pilot-house, since there was no room otherwise for three abreast to pass. And even through the anger and the pain Taylor had a chance to wonder where they were taking him, leading him down the ironclad's deck.

They moved past the chimneys, under an awning stretched over a ridgepole that ran the length of the ship. Something about the deck did not seem right, something about the way it looked against the shore and the river. Taylor thought he was going mad, and then he realized the ironclad was listing. She was sinking under them.

He wanted to curse again, then order them to lay him down, and he shouted, 'Leave me here, you bastards,' but now the strength was out of him and

181

the words came out as little more than a whisper, and halfway through the ironclad fired again and smothered every sound on the river.

At last they came to the big, half-round iron casemate over the centerline paddle wheels, and Taylor saw what they were going for. One of the ship's boats, hung from davits, bumped against a short wooden bulwark that surrounded the hurricane deck. With no order given, Bowater's men swarmed over the boat, peeling the canvas cover off, casting off the painter made fast to a stanchion, casting off the falls.

'Get him in!' Bowater shouted, relinquishing his grip on Taylor's arm as four sailors took him up and hoisted him into the boat.

'Get in, get in!' Bowater continued. Yankees were coming up out of the hatches, onto the hurricane deck, but they were there to escape the rising water below, and they shouted in surprise at the sight of the Rebels stealing their boat, and their shouts were met with small-arms fire.

The men piled in, Bowater last. The boat was swung outboard on the davits, the falls were slacked away smartly in a barely controlled plunge. The aftermost broadside gun went off, no more than five feet forward of the boat's bow, the concussion and smoke and noise like the end of the world.

The boat slammed down on the water with a jar that made Taylor howl and curse, but no one paid him any attention. The oars came up with expert precision. Tanner in the bow shoved off, and the oars came down and the men on the thwarts pulled, pulled hard, bent into it like Taylor had never seen men bend into it, and they needed no encouragement from Bowater, who sat in the stern sheets, hand on the tiller.

Fifteen feet from the ironclad and they heard the crack of small-arms fire. A bullet smacked into a thwart by Bayard Quayle's right thigh, causing him to jump and shout, but he did not miss his stroke. Another whipped by and Ruffin Tanner shouted and dropped his gun and clapped a hand over his left upper arm and an instant later the hand was red with blood.

Taylor was slumped on the bottom of the boat, looking aft. He saw Bowater reach to his belt, pull out his pistol. A silver, engraved Colt that Bowater kept in a polished wooden box when he was not carrying it, a weapon of the high-born, a gun of the gentry, and he hated the gun and he hated Captain Samuel Bowater and he hated all of them, all of the slave-owning, mint-julep-sucking aristocracy who had got them into this horseshit war, hated them as much as he hated the Yankees, and he wondered where that left him now.

Bowater turned, leveled the gun at the ironclad, fired away, working the hammer with his thumb. Those who did not have oars joined in, firing off the Mississippi rifles at the crowd of Yankees on the hurricane deck.

The Yankees were still working the broadside guns, even with the ironclad sinking around them, and Taylor saw one of the big forty-two pounders run out, the muzzle aimed generally at them, and he thought, *If those kangaroos are loaded with grape or cannister, that's it for us.*

The gun fired. Round shot, it passed close enough to the boat that they could feel the wind of its passing, but it did not hit them.

Taylor looked to his left. The *General Page* was steaming up, her paddle wheels slapping the water, as if she meant to cut the boat in two. The men at the oars bent into it again. The boat shot ahead and the *Page* passed just astern, tossing the boat with her wake, her wheels stopping dead, then slowing, grinding, for turns astern. Sullivan had interposed his ship between the boat and the Yankee ironclad.

Bowater pushed the tiller over. The men pulled again and Bowater ordered, 'Toss oars,' as the pilfered Yankee boat came up alongside the *General Page*, a dozen men there to haul Bowater and his men aboard.

In the quiet as the boat came alongside, Taylor looked up into Bowater's face and Bowater looked down at him. And Taylor said, 'Don't you think I'm gonna thank you for this, you patrician son of a bitch.'

Bowater smiled. '*Patrician?* That's a hell of a word for an ignorant New Orleans peckerwood like you.'

Hands grabbed Taylor's shoulders and he was lifted up to the deck, and the rest of the men scrambled up after him. Mississippi Mike Sullivan was there, grinning wide. He shook his head. 'That was the stupidest goddamn thing I ever seen.'

CHAPTER 12

*Also by direction of the President, our vessels
shelled Sewell's Point yesterday mainly with the
view of ascertaining the practicability of landing
a body of troops thereabouts. The* Merrimack *came
out, but was even more cautious than ever.*

Flag Officer L. M. Goldsborough
to Gideon Welles

The tug rolled along under a perfect blue sky, the
black smoke from her funnel standing out bold
against that background until it was pulled apart by
the breeze, the bow cutting a neat wake through the
water of Hampton Roads. They were closer now to
Confederate country than Union.

'Mr President,' said Molly in her accented French,
'I think you are single-handedly invading the South.'
Stanton translated. Lincoln smiled.

'No, ma'am. I am simply borrowing the army and
navy for a little while, to see if I can make the dog hunt.'

Stanton translated, stumbling over the idiom,
making an awkward translation. Wendy stepped in
and explained.

'You Americans!' Molly said. 'Is it any wonder we find you all so charming?'

They closed with the shore and Lincoln picked up a pair of field glasses, ran them along east to west. A man stepped out of the wheelhouse, thin with a lined face and round spectacles, a well-worn derby pushed down on his head, a scroll of paper like an old royal pronouncement held under his arm. He approached, in a deferential way. Not a man who was close to the President, not one who was comfortable in the presence of power, like the Secretary of War or the wife of the Norwegian minister.

'Captain, set that right here,' Lincoln said, pushing the lemonade glasses out of the way, begging the ladies' forgiveness. The man with the derby unrolled the paper on the table. Wendy looked as close as she dared. It was a map of Hampton Roads and the shoreline. *A chart,* she corrected herself.

Lincoln weighted the edges with glasses and the pitcher. The man in the derby studied it, embarrassed by the company.

'Forgive my manners, ladies, my mind is elsewhere,' Lincoln said. 'Mrs Nielsen, Miss Atkins, this is Captain Robin Walbridge, the finest pilot in Hampton Roads. He is assisting me in finding a suitable place to land troops.'

Wendy translated. Molly just nodded. 'We are pleased to make your acquaintance, sir,' Wendy said. Captain Walbridge mumbled, nodded, studied the chart.

'Right here, sir,' Walbridge said, speaking very low, whether out of a concern for security or shyness Wendy could not tell. He pointed a thick finger at a place on the chart. Wendy let her eyes wander over

186

the paper, trying to appear bored and disinterested. 'This point is the point you see right yonder, sir.' He turned and pointed at the shoreline. Lincoln looked from chart to shore and back, nodded his big head.

Now Lincoln ran a finger over the chart. 'It would appear that there is water enough here for *Merrimack* to sail,' he said.

'Aye, sir. They say she draws around twenty-three foot of water, so yes, she could certainly get within range of her guns.'

Lincoln nodded. 'Very well. Let's keep looking.'

They cruised along the shore, poking in and out of Willoughby Bay, rounding the sand spit that made up the bay's northern shore. Beyond the bow, the Chesapeake Bay opened up, north to south, and beyond that, the open ocean. Wendy felt a thrill at the sight of it, a thrill that carried her beyond the tension of her circumstance. 'Oh, such beauty!' she said.

Lincoln looked up. 'What might that be, Miss Atkins? I know you're not speaking in reference to me.'

'Oh, sir . . .' Wendy felt herself blush. 'The ocean, Mr President. It is so beautiful, and it is so rare that I see it.'

Oh, Lord, we're supposed to have just completed a sea voyage!

Wendy felt herself tense from the gaffe, and she waited for Lincoln to point it out, but all he said was, 'I see it rarely myself, though I can't say I miss it. I miss the rivers of the West more. Tell me, miss, where is it you are from?'

'Culpepper, Virginia, sir.' Off balance, Wendy blurted it out, and even as the words left her mouth she tried to check them, which made the blunder even worse. She met Lincoln's eyes, his expressionless face, and she felt her cheeks burn. Her stomach twisted up, her palms felt wet. She wanted to explain, to pour out more lies on top of what she had said, but her judgment had not abandoned her completely and she kept her mouth shut.

Lincoln nodded. For a moment he did not say a word. 'I've never been,' he said at last. 'I hear it's nice.'

'Nice, sir, but far from the sea. And now in enemy hands, I fear. I am happier in Maryland, where I can at least enjoy the bay.'

Lincoln nodded again. His face was unreadable. 'Forgive me,' he said, and picked up the field glasses once more and trained them on the shoreline.

They steamed in silence for five minutes or so, five horrible minutes while Wendy replayed in her head every word, every nuance of her fifty-second conversation with the President. Finally Captain Walbridge, who had been standing as far away as he could and still remain one of the party at the table, gave a low cough, a signal he was about to speak.

'Mr President . . . the beach you see yonder? Good landing beach, sir. Surf generally ain't too much. Sandy shore, easy on the boats, sir. And there's not a devil of a chance of that *Merrimack* getting out here. Beg pardon, ladies.'

Wendy smiled and nodded. Molly looked as if she neither understood nor cared. Lincoln looked through the field glasses at the shore. Stanton stood up, planted a hand on the table, looked down at the chart.

'Captain Walbridge,' Lincoln said, never taking the field glasses from his eyes, 'please ask the lieutenant to get in as close as he can to the shore.'

'Aye, sir,' Walbridge said, and strode off quickly to the wheelhouse. The tug turned, ran inshore at an oblique angle, the surf rolling white, the tall dune grass, the yellow sand beach all becoming more discernible as they closed with the land.

Stanton picked up another pair of field glasses. 'Look at those dogs, following us on horseback!' he exclaimed. Wendy could see the horsemen, riding along the beach, gray-clad on brown mounts. If only they knew who was looking on them now! How desperate they would be to spread the word!

'Shall I have the lieutenant give them a round or two?' Stanton asked. 'Load of grape? Get them all in one shot.'

'No, Mr Stanton, I think not,' Lincoln said.

'There's a chance they'll divine what we're about, Mr President. Could give the Rebels time to organize a defense against our landing.'

'I imagine they'll be more suspicious if we start shooting at them.' Lincoln stood and looked down at Walbridge, returning from the wheelhouse. The pilot was a good head shorter than the President. 'Captain, I do believe we have found the place to land our troops. Do you agree?'

'Oh, yes, sir. Reckon it'll answer. Good landing place, no chance of *Merrimack* interfering.'

'Very well. Stanton, let's get back to Fortress Monroe and see Wool is motivated to move his men.' Lincoln turned to the women. 'Miss Atkins, pray tell Mrs Nielsen that we will soon have her off this disagreeable tug and quartered in more comfortable surroundings.'

Wendy translated. Molly nodded. 'Please tell Mr Lincoln that I require the use of the facilities,' she said.

'Oh . . .' Wendy felt herself blush. 'Ah, sir, my aunt wishes to use . . . ah . . . the facilities.'

Lincoln smiled. 'Of course. Captain, do you know if the facilities are presentable to a lady?'

'Aye, sir, I reckon. Lieutenant had the heads scrubbed out good, sir, on account of you and Mr Stanton being aboard.'

'I am pleased to hear it.' A midshipman was summoned, and blushing, stuttering, he led Wendy and Molly down a ladder and a narrow companion-way, then along the side deck to a polished wooden door.

'Ah, ma'am, this here's . . . ah . . .'

'Thank you, young man,' Wendy said. 'We can find our way back. You may leave us.'

'Yes, ma'am,' the clearly relieved midshipman said. He began to salute, hesitated, turned, and practically ran back down the side deck, disappearing around the front of the deckhouse.

Molly opened the door, looked inside. Two seats of ease with a freshly built bulkhead between and doors to each, improvements rendered for a President and his cabinet. Wendy could smell the fresh wood. The renovation was no more than a few hours old.

The two women stepped inside and Molly closed the door. 'I had no idea we would be in such company as the President,' Molly said. She spoke low, just a whisper, and she spoke in French, her Norwegian accent intact.

'Nor I,' Wendy said, also in French, the barest whisper. With the engine working just below and the slap of the water on the hull, the hum of the shaft and propeller, it was difficult even to hear one another, inches apart.

'Will you . . . are we to . . . do something . . . regarding the man?' Wendy stumbled through the question. Her eyes flickered down at Molly's reticule.

'Do you mean murder him? No, I think not. I am in no mood for suicide today. Besides, Lincoln is such a fool, the Confederacy is better off with him in command.'

Wendy nodded, embarrassed that she could have harbored such a thought as murder. But Molly had dismissed the idea only on practical grounds. She did not seem to think it outrageous.

'What of poor Lieutenant Batchelor?' Wendy asked.

'The lieutenant will be fine. They will set him free once the Yankees have taken Norfolk. I do not believe Lincoln will make him a prisoner, not when he came out under a flag of truce. Not when he was escorting the wife of the Norwegian minister.'

'Oh, Aunt, do you think we're discovered? I am so sorry for my stupid tongue.'

'Please, don't fret. You covered admirably, and you did not explain too much, which is certain death.' She paused for a moment, listened, considered. 'I do not know if we are discovered. I know quite a few Union naval officers, but thankfully none aboard this boat. Lincoln may suspect, but he cannot be certain enough to act.'

Wendy nodded.

'However,' Molly added, 'if we *are* discovered, we'll hang as spies for sure. Or assassins.'

'Oh . . .' That part had never occurred to her. Somehow Wendy had the idea that if they were caught they would be put ashore somewhere. Admonished and sent away. Even as she had toyed with the idea of putting a bullet in Lincoln's head, she had never really considered the reality of their situation.

But at the same time, the possibility of being hanged buoyed her spirits and gave her a renewed vigor. It was not so trivial a thing they were doing. It was life and death, literally.

'So we must not be discovered,' Molly went on. 'We have what we came for. We know where the Yankees will land. Now we must get back to Norfolk.'

The two women were quiet for a moment. Wendy waited for Molly to go on. When she did not, Wendy asked, 'How?'

'I don't know.'

Molly was starting to irritate, and that at least gave Wendy some relief from her newfound fears. 'We will have to see what happens in the next few hours. At the very worst, assuming we are not found out, we will most likely be deposited at Fortress Monroe, and from there we can talk our way to Washington. After that, who knows?'

Wendy nodded. That did not sound so bad. Molly put a hand on Wendy's shoulder. 'Don't you worry, dear. You'll see your beloved Samuel soon enough.'

'Oh . . .' Wendy flushed. This had all been about getting west to be with Samuel Bowater. She had entirely forgotten that fact.

Molly reached down and grabbed a handful of her skirts. 'Now, if you do not mind, I truly do need to use the jakes.'

By the time they returned to the boat deck and the company of Lincoln, Stanton, and Walbridge, the tug had come about and was retracing her wake back into Hampton Roads. Wendy watched the last glimpse of the ocean disappear around the sand spit. She turned at the sound of heavy guns, a mile or so away.

A scattering of ships swarmed like water bugs off Sewell's Point. Puffs of gray smoke erupted from their guns, lifted up into the air, and then, with the smoke beginning to dissipate, the flat bang of the ordnance reached their ears.

Molly leaned on the boat deck rail, watching the action, bored and disinterested as ever. Wendy joined her, and Lincoln approached the women.

'We are firing on the fort at Sewell's Point, which is that point of land there,' Lincoln explained, pointing a bony finger like a short sword at the shoreline. 'Do you see the odd-looking ship, farthest to the left? That is the *Monitor,* the savior of the Union.' There was a hint, just a hint, of irony in the President's voice.

'Indeed?' Wendy said, and stared at the ship with morbid curiosity as she translated to Molly. The Southern papers had been full of *Virginia*'s tremendous victory over the ill-conceived Union battery.

'You are familiar with her, then?' Lincoln asked.

'News of the great battle had just reached Europe when we sailed, sir,' Wendy explained. 'And while we were with the Confederates, they spoke of little else.'

'Indeed. And what did they say, if I might ask?'

'Well, they said that the *Virginia* was victorious, sir.'

Lincoln nodded.

'Might I ask . . .' Wendy continued, 'I do not wish to be forward . . . but did the *Virginia* win, sir?'

Lincoln smiled. 'I suspect that one will be the fodder for another two centuries of argument, at least. I can't answer, if I'm going to be honest. They both survived, they are both still fighting today. Hard to say how either was the winner.'

Wendy nodded. Lincoln held out the field glasses. 'Would you care to have a closer look?'

'Oh, yes, sir, thank you!' Wendy took the field glasses. She translated Lincoln's words to Molly, offered her aunt the first use of the field glasses. Molly took them, looked through them for a few seconds, the gesture of a woman who genuinely did not care about such things, handed them back to Wendy.

Wendy held them up to her eyes and adjusted them until the distant ships were in sharp focus. She swept them back and forth until the *Monitor* came into view and she kept her there.

Incredible . . . A round turret with a flat deck nearly awash. It was unlike any vessel Wendy had ever seen, and she had made a point of seeing as many ships as she could, since her first childhood passion for such things.

She was having a hard time reconciling what she saw with what she knew. The savior of the Union looked so utterly insubstantial, particularly in comparison with the mighty *Virginia*, which she knew well, having watched her steam in and out of the navy yard and up the Elizabeth River. How could that silly little Yankee notion have stood up to the *Virginia* even for five minutes, let alone battled her to a draw after four hours of combat?

'She is a singular vessel, sir,' Wendy said.

'She is that. And yonder comes her old friend.'

Wendy took the field glasses from her eyes and looked where Lincoln indicated. A black plume of smoke was moving up from the direction of the Elizabeth River, beneath the smoke a ship that appeared as no more than a dark slash on the water. Wendy lowered the field glasses. 'Is that . . . ?'

'That is the *Merrimack*,' Lincoln said. 'Or the *Virginia*, as the Rebels choose to call her.'

Wendy flushed again. 'Forgive me, I have never quite known what to call her. The European newspapers call her *Merrimack*, the Rebels called her *Virginia* . . .'

'It's no matter,' Lincoln said, his tone good-natured. 'She is an unwieldy tub by any name.'

'Will they fight?' Wendy asked. '*Monitor* and *Merrimack*?'

'I shouldn't think so. *Merrimack* comes out in the afternoons like an old bear looking for supper, but she will not fight.'

Wendy nodded, thinking of Batchelor's report to Tucker, to the effect that it was *Monitor* that was afraid to fight *Virginia*. Each side hanging back and swearing the other did not dare combat. *Hold me back, boys, or I'm a'gonna kill someone!*

Wendy put the field glasses back to her eyes and watched *Virginia* as she appeared from around Sewell's Point. She was too far off to make out any details, but with Lincoln's critique still in her head, Wendy had to admit that the ironclad did move in a plodding, ponderous way, like one of those dinosaurs that were all the rage among the scientists and bone collectors. Could this awkward thing, and the silly-looking hatbox on a raft, really be the end of the graceful and fleet sailing men-of-war?

'Sir?' The lieutenant commanding the tug stepped aft, saluted.

'Yes, son?' Lincoln said.

'*Merrimack* is coming out, sir, just around the point.'

'Thank you, Lieutenant, we have seen her.'

'Yes, sir. Also, there is a man-of-war coming to anchor by Fortress Monroe. I believe her to be the *Norvier*, sir, the Norwegian corvette.'

'Indeed?' Lincoln said. He turned to Wendy. 'Do you hear that?'

'Oh, yes, sir!' Wendy said, trying very hard to sound relieved. She translated to Molly, and Molly looked very relieved indeed, looked every inch the woman who saw her suffering coming to an end. 'Please thank the President for his hospitality, and ask if we might be transported to our ship,' she said, and Wendy translated.

'Of course,' Lincoln said, giving a shallow bow. There was a playful quality in his voice. A man in on the game. 'Of course. We'll get this all straightened out directly.'

From three miles away, from a height of eye of sixteen feet above the water, seen with aging eyes and the aid of field glasses, the Union fleet firing on Sewell's Point looked frail and insubstantial, like toy boats made out of sticks.

Flag officer Josiah Tattnall lowered the field glasses, rubbed his eyes. He placed one foot on the sloping side of the CSS *Virginia*'s squat, conical pilothouse to relieve the strain on his back. The ship underfoot was carving a straight wake through the upper reaches of the Elizabeth River. They had left Craney Island astern, their bow pointed straight north toward Sewell's Point. And the enemy. *Now, if only they will fight.*

Tattnall's eyes moved down to the ironclad's bow. The actual bow of the ship was below the waterline, but a false bow, like a triangular seawall, was built up on the deck to form a dry place for the men to cast the lead and work the anchor. It looked like a triangular hole in the water, with the bow wave boiling around it. Very odd. Tattnall still was not used to it.

On the front of the casemate, the heavy iron shutters were closed over the forward gun ports. They were made in two pieces and closed like a pair of shears over the port, worked by chains from the inside. *Virginia* had steamed into her first fight with only the bow and stern shutters in place. Buchanan, captain then, had been too impatient to wait for the broadside shutters to be installed. One shot from *Congress,* fired even as the ship was dying on *Virginia*'s ram, shot right through the open port and, ripping through the gun crew, had convinced them all that the shutters were worth having.

'Sir, I see *Monitor* now.' The speaker was Catesby ap R. Jones, first officer, standing beside Tattnall, still staring through his own field glasses.

Tattnall raised his field glasses again and looked at the fleet in the distance. He could hear the soft thud of the gunfire now, lagging far behind the puffs of gray smoke.

'Just to the east of the ship-rigged one, sir,' Jones added. Tattnall grunted. He wondered how long Jones had been watching the *Monitor,* waiting for his captain to see it before he had to bring it to his attention. But Tattnall's eyes could not match those of Jones, who was many years his junior.

'Yes, yes, I see her now, Mr Jones,' Tattnall said,

realizing that he never would have seen her if Jones had not pointed her out. With virtually no freeboard and a single turret only twenty feet in diameter, she was not easy to spot from a distance.

For a moment he just stared at her. *Monitor*. He had never been any closer than this to her, because she steamed away every time the *Virginia* drew too close. But she was not steaming away now, and they certainly had seen *Virginia* coming. Perhaps this was the day. The day when he would finish the work so ably begun by Admiral James Buchanan.

'Mr Jones, please see the guns loaded, but do not run out.'

'Aye, sir!' Jones said and disappeared down one of the hatches to the gun deck below.

Tattnall continued to stare, transfixed by the sight of the Union ironclad. God, how he wanted to come to grips with her! Buchanan had had his moment, ripping through the Union fleet on *Virginia*'s very first day under way. What a sea trial! He had been shot down, severely wounded by the treacherous Yankees. The next day it was Lieutenant Jones's moment, a historic, unprecedented battle, the first fight between ironclads. Anyone with any sense of naval history knew that that fight would be remembered for as long as men remembered ships and the sea.

He would not begrudge Jones his glory, and certainly not Buchanan, who had been a dear friend for decades. They were known in the service as 'Old Tat' and 'Old Buck.' And they were that. Old. Tattnall had joined the navy in 1812, Buchanan a few years later. Lord, they had been so young then, so full of the possibility of it all! What a way to end a lifetime of serving the United States Navy, firing on the flag they had defended, risking their lives to see the Union dissolved.

But Tattnall was ready to fight. Such an opportunity as this would not occur again in what was left of his life. He wanted to take the *Virginia* into battle. He wanted to fight *Monitor*. He wanted to beat her.

He lowered the field glasses and continued to regard the Union fleet as the *Virginia* steamed ahead. The other ships did not concern him. Their guns could do *Virginia* no harm, and their weak scantlings would be torn apart by the nine-inch Dahlgrens in *Virginia*'s broadside. He doubted they would even stay around for a fight.

No, it was *Monitor* he wanted. But every time he came close, the cheese box steamed away. He imagined the Yankees did not dare risk their invention in another fight with *Virginia*. They had tried to lure *Virginia* into a trap, tried to get her to steam into narrow channels where they could use fast rams on her. But Tattnall would have none of that. He wanted a straight fight, like the one Jones had had, gun to gun, ironclad to ironclad.

Let us finish this thing, and see whose ship and men are the finer.

Jones came back, reported the guns ready. Tattnall felt the old excitement build, such as he had not felt in years. The sun was warm on his head and the breeze felt good ruffling his white hair and he was going into battle.

He enjoyed four minutes of that pleasure and then he heard Jones shuffle and make a little coughing sound.

'Lieutenant?'

'Looks as if the Yankee fleet is getting under way, sir.'

In his excitement, Tattnall misinterpreted Jones's statement, thought the luff meant the Yankees were coming to meet *Virginia*, and he felt his excitement rise. And then he realized what Jones meant. The Yankees were steaming off. Heading for the protection of Fortress Monroe's guns.

Tattnall held the field glasses to his eyes. Sure enough. The ships were stern-to the *Virginia*. Heading northeast. Running away.

'Goddamn their cowardly hides!' Tattnall said out loud, all but shouting. He wanted to stamp in frustration. For some time, he and Jones just watched them go.

'I'm sorry, sir,' Jones said. 'We'll have another chance at them.'

'Yes, yes, of course,' Tattnall said, trying to hide his disappointment. *Damn them . . .*

Jones did not sound as disappointed. That was because Jones was a young man. Jones would have a second chance, or a third, or a fourth.

If there was anything Tattnall envied Jones, it was the luff's youth. Young men trusted in second chances. Old men like Tattnall knew that sometimes they never came.

CHAPTER 13

I avail myself of the occasion to thank you for your courtesy and all your conduct, so far as known to me, during my brief visit here.
Yours, very truly,

A. Lincoln
to Flag Officer L. M. Goldsborough

The Union fleet was getting under way, but Wendy and Molly, still in the company of their hosts, were waiting.

They stood in a knot on the tug's starboard side deck, an uncomfortable group, waiting for the dispatch boat. Molly, imperious as always as the aristocratic Ingrid Nielsen, Wendy, quiet and deferential to her overbearing aunt, a bit awed by the august company. Lincoln, who was hard to read. Polite and solicitous, still there was a quality in his manner that suggested he was not entirely on board with the idea that the women were who they said they were.

Wendy marveled at the many layers of suspicion and deception playing out in that little space of deck, tempered by the demands of diplomatic protocol. Lincoln, whatever he thought, clearly was not confident enough in his suspicions to challenge their story. Nor did he have to, because the *Norvier*'s arrival meant that within the next hour, the truth would be revealed with absolute certainty.

The tug's commanding officer, hovering around, eager to help, was completely unaware of the silent tragicomedy being performed right before his eyes.

A quarter mile off, and steaming toward them under a black plume, with a white pile of water under her bow, came the dispatch boat that had been summoned by means of signal flag.

'Please, Miss Atkins,' Lincoln said, 'tell Mrs Nielsen that I greatly regret that I cannot bring her myself to her husband's ship. The precarious nature of our military situation leaves me not a moment to spare, and I would not be able to do her husband the honor he deserves. Pray tell her I will send an invitation for them to join me at the White House as soon as is convenient.'

'Yes, sir,' Wendy said and translated to Molly.

'Tell the President I understand entirely,' Molly said and Wendy translated again.

They waited in uncomfortable silence another five minutes until the dispatch boat – another tug, but smaller than the one they were aboard – made her slow approach and bumped gently against the thick rope fenders that had been let over the side. Sailors passed lines back and forth, the two vessels made fast to one another.

An officer appeared on the boat deck of the dispatch boat, a man in his late twenties or early thirties, a neatly trimmed beard, blue uniform coat as if it had just left the tailor's that morning. He saluted the way one would demonstrate saluting to a new recruit. He might have been addressing himself to the lieutenant who stood at Lincoln's side, but the performance was for the President.

'Acting Master Newcomb,' the lieutenant said, giving back a much more lax salute, 'the President requires that you give these ladies transport.'

'Aye, aye, sir!' snapped Newcomb. He pulled a watch from his vest pocket, the silver case sparkling in the sun. He snapped it open, glanced at the face, snapped it shut, and replaced it with the ease of a familiar gesture.

A gang of sailors pushed their way past, wrestling with a wooden brow that had stanchions along its length and rope handrails adorned with fancy rope-work. They laid the brow across the rails of the two vessels. Two more sailors appeared bearing the women's scant luggage and they carried it over the brow and set it on the deck of the dispatch boat.

Lincoln muttered something in the lieutenant's ear. 'Mr Newcomb, please come aboard. The President wishes to discuss this matter.'

Wendy took a half step back, hoping to escape notice, to eavesdrop on the President's instructions, but Lincoln was not going to let that happen.

'Ladies,' he said as he led the way to the brow, even as Newcomb was crossing his boat deck to the ladder down. 'I fear this is where we part company. I cannot tell you what a delight it was for Stanton and me to have you aboard, even if it was such a trying circumstance for yourselves.'

Wendy translated. Molly replied to the effect that the President was courtesy itself. She turned to

Lincoln, gave a shallow curtsey, smiled, and said in heavily accented English, 'Tank you.'

Lincoln nodded his head. 'You are most welcome,' he said, then added, 'Who's to know, perhaps we shall see one another again shortly.' There was again that devilish undertone in his words, that suggestion that he was going along but he was not being played for a fool. Was he covering all bets, so that regardless of how it turned out, he would look as if he knew the truth all along? Perhaps.

With a helpful hand on their backs, Lincoln guided Molly and then Wendy to the brow, where sailors reached out to aid them in their crossing, though it seemed to Wendy as if the sailors were more interested in touching than helping.

Acting Master Newcomb was coming around the front of the deckhouse as Molly stepped aboard and strode aft, leaving Wendy alone to greet him.

'Ma'am,' Newcomb bowed. 'I am Acting Master Roger Newcomb, at your service.'

'Miss Wendy Atkins.' Wendy gave a dip. 'My aunt, Mrs Ingrid Nielsen,' she said, indicating Molly's back. 'She has had a very trying time.'

'We will do everything we can to accommodate you both,' Newcomb said in a solicitous and patronizing tone that gave Wendy an instant dislike for the man. He pulled his watch from his vest pocket, snapped it open, glanced down, as if to see if he was late for his appointment with the President. He snapped it shut, replaced it as he bowed to Wendy, then crossed the brow to present himself to Lincoln. Wendy stood looking idly around, looking at anything but the President, straining to catch any word of what he was saying, but Lincoln was careful that she did not.

Molly was sitting down on the boat's rail, her face in her hand. Wendy stepped over to her, suddenly concerned.

'Aunt,' she began in English, caught herself, and continued in French, 'are you all right?'

'My head is hurting terribly, I am sure it is from the sun, and too little sleep. Please ask the captain, when he returns, if there is a private place aboard to which I might retire until we reach the *Norvier.*'

'Of course,' Wendy said. She was concerned, but her concern was tempered with uncertainty. Was Molly really feeling ill? Or was this part of the play?

It does not matter, Wendy thought. *It all must be played as real.* That was why Molly had given no indication if her pain was real or feigned.

'Mr Newcomb?' Wendy said as she hurried back up the deck. Newcomb replaced the watch in his vest as he stepped on board, and the sailors whisked the brow away and cast off the lines.

'Yes, Miss Atkins?' His attitude was different now. Guarded, not so eager to please. Wendy could well guess the subject of his talk with Lincoln.

'My aunt, Mrs Nielsen, has a terrible headache. She is not at all used to such hardships as we have encountered. Is there a private place she might rest, until we reach her husband's ship?'

'Yesss,' Newcomb said, drawing the word out, as if he was not entirely certain. He glanced over at Molly, sitting on the rail. 'Yes, certainly.' His eyebrows came together. 'I will escort you there myself.'

'Oh, thank you, sir.'

Newcomb stepped past Wendy and Wendy trailed behind.

'Ma'am' – Newcomb gave Molly a quick bow – 'I wish you would do me the honor of using my cabin, until we reach the *Norvier*.'

Molly made a small sound that suggested her lack of understanding. She did not look up, so Newcomb found himself addressing her straw hat.

Wendy translated. 'My aunt does not speak English,' she explained. 'French is our only common language.'

'*Pas d'un problème,*' Newcomb said. *That is no problem.* 'I happen to be fluent in French.' The grammar was perfect, though he spoke with a stiff Yankee accent, and his generally pompous tone sounded twice again as pompous in French.

Molly still had not looked up save for a slight tilting of her head in acknowledgment of Newcomb's words. She did not say anything, so after a moment's silence, Newcomb said, 'Please, won't you follow me?'

'*Oui, oui,*' Molly said wearily. 'Wendy, help me up.'

With an arm around Molly's waist, Wendy helped her to her feet. Newcomb remained at a safe distance, several feet away, watching. He led them forward and around the front of the deckhouse to a brightly varnished door below the wheelhouse.

'My quarters are at your disposal. They are small, but accommodating.' In the dark interior, Wendy could see oak paneling and white-painted wainscoting, a bunk with rails to keep its occupant from rolling out, a small desk and chair, another larger wing chair, a sink, pitcher, and chamber pot. Small, but accommodating.

Molly did not say a thing, simply stepped into the cabin as if it were her birthright, head down.

Wendy said, 'Thank you, Captain, this is most gracious.'

Newcomb gave a nod of his head. 'Certainly. I shall send word when we are approaching the *Norvier*. I don't think it will take us above half an hour to close with her.'

Newcomb stopped, but he did not leave, and his eyes were on Molly, whose hat was tipped over her face. When the silence became too much to bear, Wendy said again, 'Thank you, Captain.'

'Certainly. Please forgive me, I must get my ship under way.' He pulled his watch, opened it with a click, looked down at the face, shut it with a snap, bowed, and left, closing the door behind him. A minute later the women felt the dispatch boat get under way, her wallowing motion changing to a more deliberate headway, the thump of the engine below coming faster.

In the half-dark of the cabin, Molly pulled off her hat and she smiled. She stood, leaned close to Wendy. 'So far so good,' she whispered, and then crawled into Newcomb's bunk and stretched out.

Wendy knelt beside the bunk. 'Have you any idea of what we'll do when we reach the *Norvier*?' she asked. She spoke softly, and in French.

'I do not know. Convince the minister that I am his wife? But I think if we can get the Yankees to leave us aboard, we should be all right.'

'I do not think those were Lincoln's instructions to Newcomb.'

'Nor do I.' Molly paused, as if uncertain whether or not she should say what she was thinking. 'There may be another problem.'

'What?'

'Well, it's like this, dear. If you lay enough eggs, eventually one will grow up to be a chicken that comes home to roost.'

'Whatever does that mean?'

'I don't know. I just fear we may have trouble from a different quarter.'

They heard footsteps now, coming down the side deck, walking with purpose. Molly lay back in the bunk, her arm draped dramatically over her eyes, her back to the room. Wendy turned and looked at the door, waited for the knock she was sure would come.

But it did not. Rather, the door was flung open and Acting Master Newcomb stepped in. Wendy leaped to her feet, gasped in genuine surprise. 'Mr Newcomb! How dare you . . . without so much as a knock—' But Newcomb was not listening.

'All right, Cathy, the jig is up,' he barked, as if commanding a stubborn sailor. 'You may leave off with the French and all your airs.' His lips continued to move even after he was done speaking. In the dim light the whites of his eyes stood out unnaturally bright.

Wendy stared, wide-eyed. She could not have been more surprised if Newcomb had doused her with a bucket of seawater. But Molly sat up slowly, swung her legs over the side of the cot. '*Pardon?*' she asked.

Newcomb smiled, and it was not a friendly smile. More in the nature of a leer. '*Par votre malheur vous se trouvez sur mon bateau,*' he said. *As your bad luck would have it, you find yourself on my ship.*

'Bad luck?' Molly said, and it gave Wendy a little stab of panic to hear her speak in English, so conditioned had she become to Molly's French. 'Not bad luck at all, Roger. It is the very best luck for me to find myself under the protection of a dear old friend.'

Newcomb was silent for a moment. His hand reached for his pocket watch, pulled it free, snapped it open. He glanced at it, replaced it. 'Humph,' he said at last. 'Miss Atkins, sit there, please,' he ordered, indicating the desk chair, and Wendy sat. Newcomb stepped quickly across the cabin, three strides and he was in front of Molly. He reached past her, snatched up her reticule from the bunk.

'Mm-hmm,' he said. He pulled the pepperbox pistol out of the silk bag. 'You always preferred this to the derringer.'

'These are dangerous times, Roger. A girl has to protect herself.'

'Indeed.' Newcomb slipped the pepperbox into his coat pocket. He looked around, saw Wendy's purse sitting on top of their carpetbags. He snatched that up as well, opened the clasp, looked inside.

'Captain, how dare you?' Wendy nearly shouted, her outrage genuine. To look in a woman's purse! It was the most extravagant liberty.

Newcomb closed the purse and put it down. 'It's nice to find a woman who's not armed,' he said dryly.

'It would be nice to find a gentleman, armed or otherwise,' Wendy retorted, but even as she spoke she felt the panic come to life.

Armed! She had become so acclimated to the weight of the gun on her thigh that she had forgotten it was there, but now she was reminded and she became sharply conscious of it.

Oh, God, is it bulging my skirts? She wanted to look, to adjust her petticoat, but she fought the urge, and sat with hands folded in her lap.

'Roger, come now,' Molly said, her voice like honey.

'No, no. None of that. You won't play me for a fool. I want to know what your game is.' His voice sounded to Wendy a few notes higher than it had been.

'It is very complicated,' Molly continued, soothing. 'It involves the Norwegian minister, nothing to do with the United States.'

'Don't lie to me!' Newcomb was on the edge of shouting. He seemed awfully upset about Molly's pretending to be the Norwegian minister's wife. Wendy wondered what their history was.

'The President,' Newcomb said, struggling to keep his tone under control, '*the President*, told me that you came to his ship under a Confederate flag of truce. He even had the Rebels still on board, and don't imagine they are not being asked a few questions. Cathy . . . how could you? A Confederate spy? It's so . . . it's so clichéd.'

Molly shrugged. 'These are trying times, Roger, dear. Sometimes we must improvise. But look here, if I were a Confederate spy, do you think I would have let Mr Lincoln live? I had my reticule in hand the whole time I was aboard.'

'I am not sure you would be willing to lose your own life for any cause. Do you really care about anything other than Cathy Luce?' But his voice had lost some of its conviction.

'I care, Roger.' She paused, looking into Newcomb's eyes. *God, she is a beautiful woman!* Wendy thought. 'I care about you.'

'Oh, Cathy, if only I could believe you—'

'You can believe me, Roger. I have never wanted to hurt you. The others I didn't care about, but you are different.'

210

Wendy watched, fascinated, as if she were watching a magic show. Which she was, in a way. Molly was a spell-caster, a conjurer who brought to life any number of people, such as this Cathy Luce, whoever she might be, all housed in her slight frame.

'Help me, Roger,' Molly said, softly, pleading. Newcomb nodded his head, as if mesmerized, and took a step forward.

And then the spell collapsed, broken under the weight of an ancient wrong, a remembered resolve, Wendy did not know what, but it was gone. Newcomb spun around on his heel. 'Oh, damnation!' He punched the bulkhead with his fist. He spun back. 'No, Cathy. Not this time. You will *not* charm your way out of this! The President of the United States himself ordered I get to the bottom of this!'

'Oh, Roger! You recognized me right off. If you felt nothing for me, why did you not tell the President then? Come now, you can't deny it. I need you, Roger. Help me.'

Roger stared at her, tight-lipped, standing very straight. 'Yes, I had feelings for you. I might even have loved you. I don't deny it. But after Fortress Monroe, that is over. I have my duty. No more.'

Molly turned to Wendy. 'When this is over, we'll talk,' she said.

'It will be over soon,' Newcomb said, crossing back to the door. The watch came out, was consulted and replaced. 'I will take you to the flagship and explain the situation to the admiral and President Lincoln.'

'Wait!' Molly said. Newcomb stopped, hand on the doorknob. He did not move. Finally he turned back. 'Yes?'

'There is nothing I can do to stop you,' Molly said. 'I do not even have a gun.'

Newcomb nodded.

'*I* don't have a gun,' Molly repeated.

'Oh!' Wendy said as she understood Molly's meaning. 'Oh!' The room swam in front of her. All her daydreams of pulling the pistol strapped to her thigh, and here was the moment to do it. She snatched up the hem of her skirt and petticoat, not caring in her panic if Newcomb saw her legs or drawers. Her hand reached for the butt of the gun, her fingers slick with sweat.

'Oh, son of a bitch!' Newcomb shouted. Wendy looked up. The officer had a panicked look, eyes on the gun. He lunged forward, hand out, to snatch the derringer away. Molly's leg came up in front of him and Wendy saw him go down, arm outstretched, fingers brushing her skirts as he hit the deck.

Wendy leaped up, pulling the little gun as she did. Newcomb was sprawled out at her feet, still reaching for her. She pointed the gun at his face, looking over the short barrel into his startled eyes. Her thumb pulled the hammer back, her finger was slick on the trigger.

'Don't shoot him!' Molly cried out. 'For God's sake, don't shoot him.'

Wendy took a step back. Her hands began to tremble and the gun shook with jerky little spasms. If Molly had not spoken, she would have put a bullet right between Newcomb's eyes. Without even thinking about it, she knew that in her panic, that was what she would have done. Her breath was coming fast and shallow.

Molly was on her knees beside Newcomb. 'Don't

212

move, Roger, dear, or I *will* have Wendy shoot you, and the Lord knows I do not want to.' As she spoke she rifled Newcomb's pockets, extracted the pepper-box and the Navy .36 from his holster. She stepped back, both guns trained on the Yankee.

'Very well, Wendy, you may put up your gun.'

Wendy did not move. She heard the words, but they meant nothing. She was still stunned by how very close she had come – an insignificant twitch of her trigger finger – to killing a human being.

'Wendy, sit down and put your gun away,' Molly said, more sternly this time, and Wendy obeyed. She took another step back, flopped down in the desk chair, stared at the gun in her hand. Everything seemed to have a weird light around it. The shocking events of the last few minutes, coupled with her profound exhaustion, were warping her perspective.

'Now, Roger, let's discuss this situation,' she heard Molly saying, but she was still looking at the gun. The hammer was cocked, and she knew she could not put it back in its holster that way, but how to get the hammer down again? Molly had never explained that. She tried pushing it with her thumb, but it would not move. She frowned. Perhaps pulling the trigger, just a bit.

She squeezed the trigger, very gently. The hammer snapped and the percussion cap flashed and the gun leaped in her hand with a sound like a cannon blast in that little room.

'Oh!' Wendy jumped, the gun slipped from her hand. Newcomb leaped to his feet, going for Molly, but Molly, quick as a snake, whipped up the .36, thumbed the hammer back with a crisp click, and aimed it right at Newcomb's chest, three feet away.

The pistol looked huge in her little hand, as if a child were holding her father's gun, but the aim was steady and unflinching.

'Sit, Roger,' she said, softly, as if she were offering him tea, and Roger sat. 'Are you all right, Wendy, dear?' Molly said next. Wendy nodded, too shocked to speak. There was a bright, roughly circular spot of light on the cabin side, daylight shining in through the hole the bullet had made.

The sound of the gunshot was just fading in Wendy's ears when she heard the footsteps on the deck, running. They stopped by the cabin door, and were followed with a knocking, and a voice. 'Sir? Are you all right? Is everything all right, sir?'

Molly raised the .36 a little higher. She and Newcomb held one another's eyes. Molly nodded her head.

'We're fine, Mr Pembrook. A bit of an accident,' he said. His voice was stiff, but convincing enough.

There was a pause beyond the door. 'Very well, sir,' Pembrook replied, though he did not sound altogether certain. 'I'll be in the wheelhouse if I am needed, sir.'

'Very well.'

They listened while Pembrook's footsteps disappeared, and then they sat in silence for a moment. Then Molly and Newcomb began at once, trampling one another's words, both stopping at the same instant.

'Roger, dear,' Molly said, 'I get to speak first because I have the guns. Now here's what is going to happen. When we get to the *Norvier*—'

'Under no circumstances,' Newcomb cut her short, 'will I cooperate with you. Never. I'll die first.' His voice sounded strained and unnatural.

Molly smiled her coquettish smile. 'You may yet, but actually you will listen first. Now, it is entirely possible that what Wendy and I have done could be construed as spying. And you know what the punishment is for that. Hanging. By the neck. Until dead. So really, Wendy and I have nothing to lose in shooting you, if need be, to help our escape.

'Here are your choices. Take us to the *Norvier* and leave us, tell them you were ordered to deliver us to a neutral, steam off before they can ask questions. Tell Lincoln I really was the minister's wife, and that will be an end to it. All will be fine.

'Or, you can resist, and I will shoot you.' The timbre of Molly's voice changed as she spoke, the volume lower, more menacing, a voice with no compassion. 'I'll shoot you, and your legacy will be that you were shot in your own cabin, with your own gun, by a woman who had disarmed you first. I'll see they find you with your trousers around your ankles. Is that how you wish to be remembered? Your death will at least be a source of unending amusement for generations of naval officers.'

That, Wendy could see, had struck home, as deadly a shot as the one she nearly put through his forehead. A man only had one opportunity to die well. A proud fool like Newcomb might go willingly to an honorable death, but to leave a legacy of such dishonor, to be laughed at in death, that was another thing entirely.

'You wouldn't,' Newcomb said. 'I know you too well, Cathy. I know you couldn't do such a thing.'

'No? Then why don't you go for the gun?' Molly raised the pistol, pointed it right at Newcomb's face.

'Go ahead, Roger. See if you can grab it before I pull the trigger.' There was not a single note of compassion in her words, and she spoke in the voice of a woman who could, in fact, do such a thing, and would, if forced to.

'What –' Newcomb began, the confidence drained from him. He grabbed at his watch, feeling for it, pulled it out and looked at it. He held it in his palm as he continued. 'What happens when Lincoln has the minister to the White House? Meets his real wife, if he has one?'

Molly shook her head. 'Roger, do you think the President of the United States really cares a fig about any of this? Do you think a man who is fighting a war will lie awake wondering about some tart he knew for a couple of hours? He has forgotten it already. It's dead. Let it rest in peace.'

Wendy watched the two of them, felt the palpable tension like some invisible energy move between them. Hieronymus Taylor had once told her that pure steam was absolutely invisible. That was what they were making, the heat of their passions turning the air between them to pure steam.

And then, almost imperceptible in the dim light, a tear rolled down Newcomb's cheek. He did not move, made no effort to brush it aside. It disappeared into his close-cropped beard.

Something in him had broken, some bulwark of resolve collapsed. Wendy wondered if sitting there he had seen in his mind the image of his own dead body laid out on the deck of the cabin, pants pulled down, revealing white, spindly, hairy legs. The sailors exchanging knowing grins as they lifted his stiff corpse onto a litter. He snapped his watch shut and slowly replaced it in the pocket of his vest.

It was another ten minutes of sitting there before Pembrook once again knocked on the door and announced their approach to the *Norvier*. Molly removed the percussion caps from Newcomb's pistol and handed it back to him. She kept the pepperbox in her hand, with her shawl draped over it. The three of them made their way to the wheelhouse.

Newcomb hailed the Norwegian man-of-war and asked permission to come alongside. After some confusion, which involved finding an English speaker aboard the Norwegian vessel, permission was granted.

Ten minutes later, Wendy and Molly stood on the *Norvier*'s white and perfectly ordered deck, in front of her gracious and flustered captain, while the dispatch boat, with smoke rolling from her stack, plowed a straight wake back toward Sewell's Point. Wendy was surprised to see that the small former tug could move so fast.

'Forgive me, sir,' Molly said, speaking French again, but this time with a French accent. 'We have had a terrible time, and wish to beg the assistance of a gentleman.'

CHAPTER 14

Where all acted so handsomely it would be invidious to discriminate, and I will simply state that the captains and crews of this [River Defense] fleet deserve the confidence which has been reposed in them, and my officers and men acted, as they always have, bravely and obediently.
Brigadier General M. Jeff Thompson
to General G. T. Beauregard

By the time they dragged Hieronymus Taylor back on board the *General Page*, the Battle of Plum Point was over. Thirty minutes after the River Defense Fleet had steamed around the bend and into the startled faces of the Yankees, Captain James Montgomery, aboard the screw ram *Little Rebel*, ordered the recall flag run aloft, and reiterated the order with a series of blasts from his steam whistle.

Some of the Defense Fleet did not need recalling. The *General Bragg*, first of the fleet into the brawl, had had her tiller ropes cut by a lucky Yankee shell, and thus disabled she had drifted downstream and out of the fight. The *General Price* was thoroughly torn up, and though most of the damage had been to her superstructure, one shot to the supply pipes in the engine room had knocked her out as well.

The other vessels of the fleet, the *Sumter, Van Dorn, General Page, Jeff Thompson, General Lovell, Beauregard,* and *Little Rebel,* all suffered damage to greater or lesser degrees, mostly lesser. For all the extraordinary amount of metal flying around, the casualties were light: the steward on the *Van Dorn,* W. W. Andrews, killed; third cook on the *Bragg* mortally wounded, and eight or ten more slightly wounded.

They left behind them a Yankee fleet that was much worse off than they were.

As Bowater helped lay Taylor easy on the side deck, someone up in the wheelhouse was spinning the *General Page* around, heading her downstream. Taylor cursed anyone who came into his line of sight, and Bowater guessed that cradling the engineer in his arms and cooing soothing words in his ear would be pointless, so he ignored the wounded man and looked out over the rail.

The river swept past like a panorama painting. The Union ironclads were still coming down, firing like mad, like some kind of prehistoric herd, wreathed in their own smoke as they steamed downriver. Bowater recalled reading how Blackbeard the Pirate used to do that – burn a slow match in his beard to make himself look like some demon from hell. Well, here they were, Satan's war machines, the genuine article, but they were too late.

You'd think Satan would know to keep his steam up, Bowater thought.

The ironclad they had struck, the one from which

they had rescued Taylor, was nearly sunk. She sat at an odd angle, her bow near the shore, the water lapping over the bottom edge of her casement, and Bowater was certain she was sitting in the mud. A perfectly designed machine for river combat, but the River Defense Fleet had found her Achilles' heel, her unarmored wooden hull, four feet below the waterline.

The *Page* continued her left wheel, and the western side of Plum Point Bend came into view. From aft, the thirty-two-pound stern gun fired. Bowater felt the deck shudder underfoot. The paddle wheeler had never been intended to absorb that kind of shock.

'Ahhh!' Taylor shouted. He was writhing a bit now, and his hand was gripping his thigh, as close as he could get, or dared get, to grabbing at his wounded calf. The bone was broken, Bowater was sure. The leg was not quite straight.

'All right, stand aside, you sons of whores! Shove!' The cook, Doc, pushed his way through. A short man, with a thick yellow beard and blond hair tied back, he looked like an ill-tempered elf. He was carrying lengths of wood and bandages. He was still wearing his apron.

He knelt beside Taylor, chewed his plug, looked over the leg while Taylor glared up at him.

'Leave me alone, you filthy son of a bitch!' Taylor shouted, but Doc did not acknowledge him.

'I said leave me alone!' Taylor reached up, grabbed a handful of Doc's apron, but the former cook, now surgeon, plucked his hand off as if it were a child's. 'Aw, shut up,' he said. He nodded to some of the riverboat men standing over them. The river rats knelt down, grabbed hold of Taylor's arms, and held them through a storm of obscenity, while Doc went to work setting and splinting the leg.

Ruffin Tanner was sitting on a crate a ways aft, leaning against the deckhouse side. Bowater went over to him. 'Is the arm bad?'

Tanner looked up. 'Naw. Torn up the meat some, but I don't reckon it hit bone. Bullet went clean on through.'

'That's lucky. Comparatively speaking.' Bowater helped him off with his coat, fetched some bandages from Doc, who gave them grudgingly, and bound Tanner's arm. He left him there, went forward to check on Taylor.

He stepped up to the group of men watching Doc do his work, and Mississippi Mike's big arm swung around and gave Bowater the breathtaking *bonhomie* smack. 'Come on, Captain, let's get back to the wheelhouse!'

Bowater did not care to follow Sullivan to the wheelhouse, but neither did he care to listen to Taylor curse and shout in pain, and he certainly did not care to have anyone think that the job they were doing on Taylor set his teeth on edge – which it did – so he followed Sullivan up the ladder to the hurricane deck.

Buford Tarbox was in the wheelhouse, and he nodded and spat in the direction of the spittoon when Sullivan and Bowater came in. 'Lookee here,' he said, nodding toward the starboard bow.

They were just passing the first of the ironclads, the one that had been so savagely mauled by the *Bragg* and the *Price*. She had crawled away from the fight and found a mudbank on which to die, sinking into the brown river.

She was motionless, dead, no smoke coming from her chimneys, her boilers ten feet underwater. The water was well up over her casement and lapping over her hurricane deck. The chimneys seemed to rise straight up out of the river, along with her three tall flagstaffs, forward, amidships, and aft. The wheelhouse and the centerline paddle-wheel box, rising above the hurricane deck, formed two small iron islands onto which the shipwrecked sailors had scrambled – dozens of blue-clad river sailors perched on those two dry places above the river. It was a ridiculous sight, and Bowater smiled.

Mississippi Mike roared. 'Look at them stupid Yankees! Damn me if they don't look like a bunch of damned turkeys on a damn corncrib!' He laughed until he doubled over, a laugh that Bowater was certain carried across the water to the miserable men on the sunken ironclad, and it must have been salt in their wounds.

Rub it in, Sullivan, rub it in, Bowater thought with delight, and he wondered when he had become so uncharitable. Was it the river, the war? Age? There had been a decency about him once, a magnanimous spirit that extended to friend and enemy alike. An officer and a gentleman. It was the spirit embodied in that phrase, a phrase he had once held as close and dear as his belief in a benevolent God.

But he was changing, he felt it. This was a different kind of war they were fighting, an all-out war. Just a month before, at Pittsburg Landing on the Tennessee River, the Confederates had attacked and overwhelmed the Yankees, only to be pushed back again, at a staggering cost to both sides. The bloodshed that day – such unprecedented bloodshed – changed everything. This was not knights of old on proud steeds. This was slaughter.

Gentlemen of honor, fighting in honorable fashion, Bowater thought. *Perhaps that very idea is as dead as the knights themselves.* This war seemed to bring with it a kind of savagery that he had never known, certainly not on the ordered quarterdecks of the old navy, showing the flag around the world.

Perhaps I have never really known war. Certainly the Mexican War had never been anything like this, not in the naval line.

Useless thought. He pushed his damned philosophizing aside and looked astern. The gunners aft were still firing away with the thirty-two pounder, but they were leaving the Yankees upstream, and the Yankees were making no effort to pursue. Astern of the *Page,* last in the Confederate line, came the *Van Dorn,* her superstructure badly torn up, her upper works showing a dozen great gaping holes fringed with shattered wood, but the black smoke pouring from her chimneys showed that her engines and boilers were unharmed. The sound of her stern gun, giving the Yankees one last farewell, was proof that the fight was not out of her.

They steamed around Plum Point Bend, steamed under the guns of Fort Pillow, came to an anchor. From the flagship *Little Rebel,* one hundred yards away, they heard, clear as a gunshot, the sound of cheering, and one after another, the crews on board all the River Defense Fleet ships took it up, shouting with abandon, letting the tension of the morning, the exhilaration, the fear, the excess of energy, pour out of their throats and up to the heavens.

Bowater did not cheer, of course. He had not abandoned so much of his dignity or sense of decorum that he would yell like, say, Mississippi Mike Sullivan, who was whooping like a Red Indian, throwing his hat in the air, pounding one and all on the back, firing his pistol at the sky, and generally behaving in an appalling manner.

Bowater stood with his back to the texan so that Sullivan would not have the clearance to give him another of his backslaps. He watched the celebration with the same mixture of horror and amusement with which he might view a minstrel show or some other crass entertainment. But it was all right. It was good. Good for the men to get that energy out. They deserved it. They had done damned good work that morning. Like the fight at Elizabeth City the previous February, it was one of the only battles so far in that war that could be called a fleet action. Unlike Elizabeth City, this time the Confederates won.

'Captain Bowater!' a breathless Mike Sullivan said as he staggered over, 'I surely do hope you and your boys will join us river rats in a little celebration when we gets back to Memphis. Oh, we're gonna tear it up good, you can depend on it!'

Bowater nodded. It was a scene he could happily miss, and one he would prefer his men to miss as well. But that, he realized, might be asking too much. His men had fought as hard as the riverboat men, and they would enjoy the bacchanal as much, and it would do morale no good for him to impose his sense of propriety on them.

'My men will join you, I've no doubt. But I have other business to attend to.'

'What-all you got to do that takes precedence over our celebrations?'

'I must get to Shirley's yard,' Bowater said, and he allowed the irony in his voice free reign. 'I must inspect my ironclad.'

The *Tennessee* was an ironclad in the same way that an assemblage of giant bones was an iguanodon. The basic structure was there, complete enough to suggest the final form of the awesome and powerful beast, but the chances of ever fleshing it out complete and bringing it to life were pretty slim.

Bowater stood at the gate, surveyed the shipyard. The *General Page* and the other ships of the River Defense Fleet that had suffered damage in the fight the day before had returned to Memphis for repairs. Bowater had walked to the yard from the hospital, after having personally seen to Hieronymus Taylor's admission, and watching the doctor drip laudanum on his tongue, though by then the engineer was pretty well played out.

There had not been much activity in the shipyard the first time Bowater saw it, but that had changed in the three days he had been gone. There were a hundred men at least, swarming over the yard and over the *Arkansas,* the more complete ship. Men running hawsers from the ironclad to the shore, men greasing the ways, men pounding wedges under the launching cradle. It was like the preparations for a wedding, and the *Arkansas* was the bride, and poor *Tennessee* the bridesmaid, shoved to the background and ignored.

Bowater hefted his seabag up on his shoulder, lifted his carpetbag, stepped across the trampled earth of the shipyard.

He set his gear on a pile of fresh-cut oak beams and, ignoring the chaos surrounding the *Arkansas,* walked slowly around his own ship, running a professional eye over her, and mostly liking what he saw. She was framed in oak, her planking yellow pine, her scantlings a respectable thickness. With twin screws and her relatively small size she would be nimble, by ironclad standards. He envisioned the iron ram bolted to her bow, the great damage he could do with that weapon, the heavy nine-inch guns sending their shells through the Yankees' wooden walls.

He walked around her bow, looked at the run of her hull, and liked the shape of her wetted surface. He liked the low profile of her hull, the elegant round fantail, reminiscent of a tugboat.

And then a voice, louder than the rest, broke through Bowater's reverie, a strident order: 'Hurry it along there, you lazy bastards, the goddamn Yankees'll be here, time you get that hawser rigged!'

The goddamned Yankees'll be here ... Bowater looked up, right up through the unplanked frames of his ship, right up at the blue sky above. They were working like mad to save the one ship that could be saved, and that was not the *Tennessee.* They might have beaten the Yankees at Plum Point Bend, but they could not hold them back forever. Here he was getting all moony about a ship he might never command, like falling in love with a woman in the last stages of consumption.

A quiet seemed to settle over the yard, which Bowater took to presage some new turn of events. He took his eyes off his own ship, stepped around her stern, stood in the shade of her partially planked-up fantail. The *Arkansas* was ready to go.

Men were standing on the foredeck and fantail, preparing for the ride down. More men were clustered around the launch cradle, sledgehammers in hand. A small man with a long black beard and a stovepipe hat that added six inches to his otherwise unimpressive height was flying from one place to another, seeing that all was in readiness, like a little girl setting up her dolls for a tea party.

John Shirley, Bowater thought, the ironclads' builder. He seemed to know it intuitively, though he had never seen the man.

When all hands were at their stations, the man in the stovepipe climbed aboard as well. From the foredeck he shouted, 'All right, let her go!'

The sledgehammers fell on the wedges, the air was filled with their pounding. And then the ironclad gave a little jerk and the hammers stopped and the men stood clear, and silent as a winter morning, the one-hundred-and-sixty-five-foot ship slid down the ways. She moved slowly at first, no faster than a man might walk on a casual stroll, but her speed built, faster and faster, an exponential climb with each foot she slid, until she was moving at a frightening speed when she parted the river with her rudder and sternpost, and floated free.

The *Arkansas* entered her native element with never a sound, from the last ringing hammer blow to the first swoosh of water closing around her hull.

No one cheered. No band broke into patriotic airs. For several moments no one even spoke. A ship launching, like a wedding or a birth, was supposed to be a time of optimism, a moment when the vessel's full potential lay before her, when she was all newness and perfection and had yet to be tried in combat or at sea, before there was an opportunity for her to be found wanting.

But this launching was not like that, because *Arkansas* was launched in desperation, launched before her time.

Despair thy charm, Bowater thought, *and let the angel whom thou still hast served tell thee,* Arkansas *was from her mother's womb untimely ripped.* Her builders had slid her into the water not because she was nearly ready to go forth and fulfill her destiny, but because they had to get her the hell away in the face of an encroaching enemy. She would not steam proudly from the dock to fight the Yankees, she would be towed away to a place where she would be safe from them, followed by barges loaded with the rest of her, the parts they had not had time to assemble.

The solemn launch put Bowater in mind of another he had seen, less than four months earlier, in Portsmouth. Then it had been the Confederate iron-clad *Virginia,* built on the burned-out hull of the old *Merrimack.* She had not slid into the water, rather the water had been let into the dry dock while the silent watching navy men waited to see if she would flip over from the weight of her casemate. That had been a launch like this; not celebratory, but quiet, intro-spective, the kind of event staged by men who understood the terrible odds against which they fought.

Thoughts of Norfolk inevitably brought Bowater's mind around to thoughts of Wendy Atkins and her little carriage house behind her aunt's home, and he felt a rush of longing, a sting of guilt that he had not thought of her more, had not written in two weeks. Wendy. She seemed part of a different life, a life he longed to get back to, and especially to her.

For more than a month they had been hearing of the Yankees' big push on the Peninsula, more than one hundred thousand strong, or so it was reported, though Bowater was certain that was something of an exaggeration. But no matter what the size of the army, it was bigger than that of the Confederates defending the place. Richmond was supposed to be in a panic.

If the York Peninsula falls, Norfolk cannot be far behind, Bowater thought. *What will Wendy do?* Bowater knew enough Yankees from the old navy to know they were unlikely to rape and pillage, that Wendy and her aunt would be safe enough, even in an occupied city.

Still, he wondered if she would try to get out. Where would she go? Culpepper would be the likely answer. For a moment he toyed with the idea of asking her to come west, to join him, but that was absurd. He had no idea where he would be next week, let alone where he would be by the time she managed to get out to Memphis on the crowded and unreliable railway.

He shook his head, as if trying to jar loose his own pointless musings. Wendy was safe, out of harm's way, and that was the best place for her. No doubt she was busy at the naval hospital. He could not speculate on when he would see her again; such thoughts would make him crazy.

'Sir?'

Bowater, his eyes on the *Arkansas*, watching her without really looking at her, had not noticed the approach of the short man with the stovepipe. 'Sir?' the man said again, and this time Bowater looked over. The man extended a hand. 'Lieutenant, I am

John Shirley, constructor here. May I be of some assistance?'

'Mr Shirley, an honor.' Bowater took the hand and shook. Shirley's palms were rough and calloused, like a seaman's, or a shipbuilder's. 'You have done a fine job on the *Arkansas*.'

'Thank you, Lieutenant. I am proud of her, I don't mind saying it. Worth three regiments of soldiers when she's done. If I could have got the men and the material, why, we could have had two boats launched today, but it weren't to be. Had to choose one, get her along, at the expense of another. But Lordy, let me tell you, it's akin to having to choose one child to live over t'other.'

Bowater nodded and the two men fell silent, contemplating the injustice of it all. Then Shirley said, 'Forgive me, Lieutenant, I didn't catch your name.'

'Abraham.'

'Abraham?'

'Abraham, father of the child sacrifice.'

Shirley wrinkled his brow. Not a man of great imagination, Bowater decided.

'I am Lieutenant Samuel Bowater,' he said. 'I have been assigned to take command of the ironclad *Tennessee*.'

'Ahhh . . .' Shirley said as his confusion turned to embarrassment. 'Well, it weren't quite right, what I said, about one over t'other. The old *Tennessee* ain't burned yet, we might still get her in the water.'

Bowater nodded. 'I am glad to hear it.'

'We've had a power of trouble getting men. General Polk, this whole thing was nearly his idea, but will he send me any men from his army to help in constructing? No, not a blessed one. And him a

230

bishop – a bishop! Did you know that? Goddamned Episcopalian bishop. Now how's that for Christian charity? And I gave him the names of a hundred men under his command who are qualified shipwrights.'

Shirley was an energetic man, Bowater could see that. He spoke in the same frenetic way that he moved, racing around, getting the *Arkansas* ready to launch, his thoughts all over the place.

'I've brought about thirty men with me,' Bowater said, 'not shipwrights, regrettably, but good, hardworking men. I see you have timber for completing the *Tennessee*.' Bowater nodded toward the stacks of wood positioned around the ship. 'What of her iron plating?'

'Most of her iron's here . . . well, not here, exactly. Across the river, Arkansas side, but it's there. Just needs paid for and we pick her up.'

Bowater nodded. 'You have the funds to pay for her?'

'Not exactly. But Secretary Mallory, he's been a real gentleman about advancing money, as needed. Wouldn't have got half done on the *Arkansas* if it weren't for that.'

Bowater nodded. 'And her machinery? Engines?'

'Oh, yes, sir, we got all the machinery in order. Right over there, on the second barge, there's *Tennessee*'s engines.' Shirley pointed enthusiastically.

'I see,' said Bowater. 'And why, pray, are her engines on a barge?'

'Oh' – Shirley hemmed a bit, threw in a few ha's – 'Well, we reckoned it would be best to get them away, you understand. Engine's a damned hard thing to get these days, worth its weight in gold. More than that. You can't make an engine out of gold, can you? So the provost, he said, get the

231

engines out of town with the *Arkansas*. It's a minor thing, no cause for worry. Come time to drop them engines in, why, we'll just tow her back upriver.'

Bowater shook his head. Lost causes were becoming something of a specialty of his, and, romantic though they might be, he was not sure that he cared for them so very much.

He spent another hour with Shirley, during which time the contractor tried to bolster his spirits with regard to the possibility of getting *Tennessee* in the water. The more he talked, the more Bowater felt the blue devils torturing him. By the time he bid farewell to John T. Shirley, Samuel Bowater was thoroughly depressed.

'Lieutenant!' Shirley called just as Bowater was stepping through the gate. He turned, and Shirley hurried up. 'Almost forgot. This come for you yesterday. Didn't know who the hell "Samuel Bowater, Esq." was, so it went plumb out of my mind.'

Bowater put down his seabag and took the package, wrapped in brown paper. It was heavy, the box inside hard – a wooden box, not cardboard. Addressed to him at Yazoo City, but somehow, miraculously, it had been correctly rerouted.

Bowater's first thought was that it was from Wendy, but he looked at the return address and saw that it was from his father. So, it would not be anything of an uplifting or sentimental bent, but that was all right. He was wandering in the wilderness, and any contact with his former life was welcome.

Thanking Shirley, he made his way to a nearby hotel, which the contractor had suggested. He secured a room and, key in hand, stumbled up the narrow stairs, fiddled with the lock on the door until he managed to open it.

The room, with its sagging bed, faded curtains, patchy rug, and faint smell of mildew did not lift his spirits. He dropped his carpetbag, seabag, and the package from his father, shed his frock coat and vest, flung his cap away, and sprawled on the bed.

He lay there for some time, drifting in a place between wakefulness and sleep, a place that offered no rest or peace. At last, with a sigh, he rolled over and sat up.

The first thing to catch his eye was the packet from his father, but he was not in the mood to read William Bowater's stoic reports of wartime Charleston. A little humanity would have suited him, and he knew he would not find it in his father's correspondence.

Instead he fished around in his carpetbag and pulled out a package that Mississippi Mike Sullivan had given him, saying only, 'Here's what I done. Have a gander, would you?' as Bowater left with Taylor for the hospital. The bundle was wrapped in brown paper and bound with tarred marlin, but there was no question as to what it was. The latest adventures of Mississippi Mike Sullivan, the Melancholy River Rat.

Without thinking, Bowater ripped the paper off and read the note on top, written in Sullivan's barely legible scrawl.

Dear Captain Bowater,
    This here's the latest chapter I writ and I wood be honored wood you read it and tell me what you thik and don't go easy on me neither. Like always, I follered yer ideas and they was damned good

ones to. I still reckon some of them names you come up with is a bit queer, but you know best on such things.

Yer frend,
Mississippi Mike Sullivan

Bowater smiled as he read it, remembering the look on Sullivan's face as he handed the pages over. What was it? Sheepishness? Yes, it was that, but something more.

Vulnerability. That was what it was. Mike Sullivan, human mountain, was vulnerable and he knew it. Bowater found himself wondering at the courage it took for Sullivan to expose himself to the possibility of devastating ridicule. No wonder he was so very secretive about their literary endeavors.

But Bowater had to be in the right mood to stomach Sullivan's 'lit-rit-ur,' and at the moment he most certainly was not. He set the manuscript aside, picked up the package from his father, and tore off the paper.

Inside was a wooden box, which Bowater suspected contained a bottle of wine. He slid the cover off. Inside, an 1853 Château Pétrus, a merlot from the Bordeaux region. And while Bowater the Younger generally eschewed merlot as inferior black-strap, he was aware that a few of the French vintners were doing some astounding things. And if William Bowater had gone to the effort of sending this wine halfway across the country, there had to be a damned good reason.

Samuel uncorked it, examined the cork, poured a bit in the glass he carried with him, wrapped in cotton and silk. He swirled it under his nose. *Excellent.* He sipped. A complex but subtle wine, fruity but not obnoxiously so. He could taste the French oak from the cask in which it was aged. It gave the wine a somewhat more manly palette. He held the wine in his mouth a moment, then swallowed. The merlot was fabulously deep and beautifully textured with a lasting finish. He smiled. Held the bottle up and examined the label. A touch of civilization, here in the wilderness.

He sat on the bed and tore open his father's letter, angling it toward the candle burning in the holder on the nightstand.

My Dear Son, he read and he frowned and squinted at the page. His father always began a letter *Dear Samuel:*. Always a colon. The comma was a new degree of intimacy.

I trust this finds you well and safe. I pray that it does. You have seen hard fighting in the fourteen months since you took that difficult step of resigning your commission and joining the Confederate States Navy, and I have feared for your safety every minute. Those naval officers who remained with the Union sit fat and idle on board their big men-of-war, which every day I can see on close blockade off our harbor, taking no greater risk than chasing unarmed runners, while you and all the brave men of the Confederate Navy, like David of old, go into battle with little more than slingshots and ships in sinking condition. No one has ever praised Goliath for his courage in facing David, and why should they? There is no courage needed when your force is overwhelming.

Bowater studied the handwriting to see if there was any sign that his father had been drinking. There was nothing in the letter so far that sounded like the William Bowater, Esquire, who had raised his son to be a man of honor and discipline, and not some libertine sentimentalist. He wondered what the old man would say if he knew that most of his son's fighting of late had consisted of brawling with river men.

By now you are thinking that the old man is getting soft in the head, and perhaps I am. Perhaps the war is wearing me down. Lord, it has been just over a year, not so much time, but how dreadfully sick I am of the death! Young men who march off so full of promise, and all that is ever heard again is a letter describing what minor skirmish or what camp disease has laid him in his grave. And despite the great setbacks our cause has suffered, I do not believe the conflict will soon end. I find myself both proud of our new nation's determination, and frightened by the terrible toll it will exact.

You will remember Donald Wood, I have no doubt. An affable young man, very capable and with much promise. I do believe he had hopes of courting your sister. In any event, he is the latest of our young men to die, shot down in some minor and already forgotten skirmish on the Peninsula around Yorktown. I fear for his mother's health, with the grief she has suffered.

Bowater looked away from the letter, let his eyes settle on the dancing flame of the candle.

Donny Wood . . . ?

The name brought back a rush of images.

236

Catching frogs in creeks, watching the big ships warp against the Charleston docks, fishing from leaky rowboats. All those things that boys will do. Playing at soldiers. Running wild with Donny Wood was how the young Samuel Bowater had coped with the rigidity of the Bowater home. He did not understand that then, of course, but he saw it now.

And now Donny was dead and no doubt buried in a shallow and unmarked grave. Samuel had urged him to apply to the Navy School, but Donny wished to follow his father into business, just the thing Samuel wished to avoid, and so they had parted ways, and saw one another only infrequently over the intervening years. And now Donny was dead.

Donny must have made a good soldier. *Esprit de corps* came naturally to him, which it did not to Samuel. Samuel had envied him that, his easy ways, but he could not emulate them, because that was not how he was raised. Donny had been, as his father said, affable, capable, tough when he had to be. He would not have been one of these malingerers, whiners, and grumblers. A great, great loss. A loss to the Confederate Army, to Charleston, to Samuel Bowater. He felt as if his own childhood had been cut down by a Yankee bullet.

Bowater read through the rest of the letter, but quickly, because his head was still full of Donny Wood. He read about his sister's grief and made some vague promise to himself to write to her.

He set the first page aside. Between the first and second was a bank draft for the amount of five hundred dollars. Confederate money, but still it was a significant sum. This too was utterly unprecedented. His father had never done the like before.

I have enclosed a bank draft for a certain sum,
Bowater read, the last paragraph of the letter.

Perhaps funds will buy you some small comfort,
replace what you have lost in the destruction of
your last ship. I don't know. I wish there were
more I could do. I wish I could come there and
shield you from harm, as I did when you were a
boy, but God help me I do not know what to do
so I send money. It is a hollow thing, Samuel, and
made more hollow still as money does us little
good in Charleston these days. There is precious
little to buy, with the blockade squeezing us
tighter.

I am proud of you, son, and love you dearly.

Your affectionate father,
Wm. Bowater, Esq.

Affectionate father ... He had never been that.
Over the past year, Samuel Bowater's well-ordered
life had been twisted around and spun off in so many
directions, he felt sometimes as if there was nothing
left that was certain and solid. And here was another
surprise. Donny dead, William now his 'affectionate
father.' Battered, exhausted, depressed, grieving, and
confused, Samuel Bowater lay down, fully dressed,
and slept.

CHAPTER 15

The great craft building in Memphis has been taken up the Yazoo to be finished, and a mechanic from there says it will be fifteen days before she will be ready. We must catch her there before she can be fitted out

LIEUTENANT Samuel L. Phelps
to Flag Officer A. H. Foote

The next morning, Samuel Bowater went to Shirley's yard and saw that things were moving apace. With the *Arkansas* already towed off downriver, Shirley could dedicate what men he had to work on *Tennessee*. A dozen shipwrights, house carpenters, and day laborers were climbing over her hull, planking up, port and starboard.

After he had satisfied himself with the work taking place, and moved by his father's newfound spirit, Bowater went shopping. It was near noon when, cardboard box in hand, he stepped through the big front door of the military hospital and let an orderly guide him to the ward in which Hieronymus Taylor lay.

He stood beside the bed for a moment, looking at Taylor, whose eyes were closed and who was apparently asleep. The engineer was propped up with pillows to a near sitting position. He looked bad, with a week's growth of salt-and-pepper beard, face paler than usual, with a waxy look to it and a sheen of sweat. He had lost quite a bit of weight, Bowater realized. Taylor seemed to be suffering in his own personal hell, and Bowater did not know what it was.

At last Taylor opened his eyes, slowly, and let his head loll over until he was looking at Bowater. 'Cap'n.' He spoke slowly and his voice was weak. 'I heard all the celebratin goin on last night, on account of our great victory. You lookin pretty smart for a fella been drinkin, whorin, and brawlin all night.'

'Just drinking and brawling, actually. And it's the whoring that really takes it out of one.'

Taylor managed a thin smile. After a pause he said, 'Ain't this where you tell me how good I look?'

'It would be, if you didn't look like absolute hell. Chief, you got to try and get some rest, do you understand?'

'Yeah, yeah . . . been hearin that from the damn doctors all mornin. Well, if it's any comfort, reckon I'd drop like a rock was I to try standin up, so it looks like I ain't goin anywhere for a while.'

'Good. Good.'

They were quiet for a moment and Taylor closed his eyes. He opened them again. ' "Mississippi Mike" don't look too good this mornin.'

'You've seen him?'

'He was by, hour or so past. Brought me a nice little flask, some cigars.'

'Just what the doctor ordered.'

Taylor smiled again. 'Sullivan's lookin to get rid of Guthrie, I reckon. He's tryin to scout himself up a new engineer.'

Son of a bitch, Bowater thought. 'He's made a few veiled references to having my men sail aboard his boat. Laying the groundwork for stealing my crew, I suspect. Now he's after my engineer?'

'He and Guthrie never did see eye to eye, and from the sounds of it, it ain't gettin better. Never thought much of ol Sullivan, but I gots to say, Guthrie is one royal pain in the ass.'

'Certainly. But so are you, Chief.'

'Course I am.' Taylor closed his eyes for a moment, rallied his strength. 'But I'm a damned good engineer, which fact compensates for me bein a pain in the ass. Guthrie ain't even a good engineer. They like to go to fisticuffs here any day, Guthrie and Sullivan. Sullivan'll cut him loose, soon as he finds a new man.'

Bowater was suddenly afraid that Taylor would take Sullivan up on the offer. They were river rats of a feather, after all. As a warrant officer, Taylor could resign anytime he wished and join the army, which had authority over the River Defense Fleet. And while Bowater certainly would have been pleased to swap Taylor for a more agreeable man, or at least one who kept to himself, he did not care to find himself without any engineer at all.

'So what did you tell him?'

Taylor closed his eyes again and chuckled. 'As if I'd sail with a damn peckerwood calls hisself "Mississippi Mike." Hell, I'd rather be engineer on board the *Tennessee*, with the damn engine a hundred miles downriver, than sail on that ol *General Page*.'

Bowater nodded, oddly relieved. For a long moment they were silent. 'Chief,' Bowater said, and felt himself flush with embarrassment even as he approached his prepared speech. Taylor opened his eyes and looked up. 'I happen to see this on sale for an absurd price, so I picked it up for you.'

Bowater held up the box, two feet long and a foot wide. Taylor shuffled himself to a sitting position, frowned at the box as if he had never seen the like. At last Bowater had to thrust it at him just to get the engineer to take it.

Taylor set the box on his lap and opened the cover. Inside lay a violin and bow and a little bag of rosin and spare strings. In the daylight streaming in through the big windows the varnish on the dark wood gleamed as if it were wet.

Taylor said nothing. He just stared at the instrument.

'I don't know a thing about violins, and the price was so good I fear it may be a very inferior instrument,' Bowater lied. He actually knew a fair amount about violins, though he did not play himself, and at two hundred and forty dollars he expected this one to be reasonably good. 'In any event, I know you lost your old one with the *Yazoo River* and I imagined it would help pass the time if you could play. And I suppose . . .'

Bowater was rambling but Taylor was not listening. He reached slowly into the box and with his left hand lifted the instrument by the neck, gently, as if he was lifting something of unknown fragility. Bowater stopped talking.

Taylor tucked the violin under his chin and plucked at the G string. Bowater had insisted that the shopkeeper tune the instrument before he took it, but Taylor was not satisfied. He gave the tuning peg the slightest twist and there was a barely perceptible rise in the note coming from the vibrating string. He did the same to the D, A, and E strings, tweaking them ever so slightly. He listened with eyes closed to the last dying note, then his right hand reached for the bow.

Bowater smiled. Whatever torment Taylor was suffering, it was made worse by not having the release that music gave him. He understood that, because he found the same release in painting, an emotional blowdown, pouring his unconscious self out onto the canvas.

If William Bowater had found in his heart a new degree of empathy and concern for his brethren, then Samuel guessed he could as well. And what better use to put his father's money to?

Samuel waited for Taylor to say something, but he did not. Instead he lifted the bow and brought it down on the strings and drew a long note. Bowater looked around, embarrassed, considered suggesting that perhaps Taylor should not play in the hospital ward. Several of the patients were looking over, their expressions ranging from curiosity to annoyance.

Hieronymus Taylor, eyes closed, was utterly unaware of the stares of his fellow sufferers. He seemed unaware of anything. Bowater had seen men in such a state before, sailors in port after long months at sea, looking at the taverns or whores on shore, completely mesmerized by desire. He had never seen such a reaction to a classical instrument.

Taylor tried the bow on each of the strings, listening to their notes, and then he set in. Bowater had expected 'Camptown Races' or 'Roll the Old Chariot Along' or 'Shenandoah'' – the best he could hope for

– or any of the various crude, barbaric popular ditties with which Taylor had once amused the men and driven Bowater nearly to distraction.

But he did not play any of those. Instead it was Mozart, Mozart's Quintet in G Minor, one of Bowater's personal favorites. He looked at Taylor to see if this was for his benefit, or if the engineer was mocking him, but Taylor's eyes were closed and his lips moved a bit and he was oblivious to everything but the instrument.

He played as if the music had been dammed up inside of him and now, finally, the dam had burst and the notes were flooding out. The music filled the ward, which Bowater noticed had surprisingly good acoustics. Those who could sat up in bed. Nurses and doctors filtered in, stood off to the sides, watching and listening. Bowater, caught up in the beauty of the sound, did not even register the fact that he was as much the center of their collective gaze as was Taylor, not until the last few measures played out and Bowater looked around and flushed with embarrassment.

Taylor let the bow bounce off the strings and the patients and the hospital staff applauded, but the engineer did not seem to notice any more than he had noticed anything since he had lifted the instrument from the box. He leaned back on his pillow and smiled, a sort of tired yet sated smile. He ran his eyes over the violin, shook his head. At last he looked up at Bowater.

'I thank you, Cap'n. I surely do. I can't recall a greater kindness done me.'

Bowater shrugged, even more embarrassed. 'It's not much of an instrument, I fear.'

'It's fine, fine. Just lovely.'

'Yet I perceive it does not have quite the depth and timbre of your old one.' And that was true; Bowater had noticed as much midway through the piece.

Now Taylor shrugged, a dismissive gesture. 'The old one was a Guarneri, been around since the 1650s. We ain't gonna see its like on the Mississippi agin.'

Bowater's eyes went wide, despite himself. 'A Guarneri?' Some people held the Guarneri family to be superior even to the Stradivari in violin-making. 'Dear God, and you took it to sea? Into battle?'

'Only fiddle I had.'

Bowater was speechless. His head was filled with images of that exquisite instrument being blown to splinters by a Yankee shell. 'How did you happen to come by a Guarneri?'

Taylor smiled. 'Gift from my pa.'

'This would be the pa you told me spent his whole life loading freight on the docks of New Orleans?'

Taylor smiled, a smile of shared and unspoken understanding. 'It was somethin like that,' Taylor said.

'What a terrible waste,' Bowater said.

'Lost a lot worse'n a fiddle that night, Cap'n,' Taylor said, and there was a catch in his voice, as if a word had caught momentarily, blocking the rest in his throat, just for an instant. He choked it out, looked down at the violin, coughed as if trying to clear the source of his discomfort.

So that is it, Bowater thought. 'In any event, I had best be running along,' he said, trying to breeze through the awkwardness of the moment.

'Yeah, yeah . . . and thanks, Cap'n, again, for the fiddle.' Taylor met his eyes. There was sincerity there. It was an unusual look for Hieronymus Taylor.

'You're welcome. I'll come again.' The men shook hands and Bowater took his leave.

In the lobby of the hospital he paused, stared out one of the windows. Was it the nightmare of death on board the *Yazoo City,* in that last desperate hour below New Orleans, that had so affected Taylor's mind as to set him on this path of self-destruction? It was certainly possible.

And what, Bowater wondered, *does that say about me*? Taylor's reaction was perfectly understandable, but what kind of a person became more upset over the destruction of a rare violin than over the deaths of ordinary men?

Bowater shook his head. He had seen death before, of course, more than Taylor, he imagined. He had seen the casualties of the Mexican War, the men blown apart by naval gunnery at the bombardment of Veracruz. Men died all the time at sea, from falls or disease or any of a countless number of shipboard accidents, circumstances unknown on riverboats.

Death was a constant, as much as foul weather or rocks and shoals. Bowater had seen more men go over the standing part of the foresheet than he could remember. He had been aboard the captured slavers during cruises off the African coast, had seen the horrors of the lower decks. Was he beyond feeling now?

He thought of Thadeous Harwell, first officer aboard his first command, shot down at the Battle of Elizabeth City. Young, enthusiastic Harwell, and the memory gave him a sharp knife thrust of sadness, and with it came genuine relief that he could still feel such an emotion.

CHAPTER 16

*On the next day, at 10 o'clock A.M., we observed
from the* Virginia *that the flag was not flying on
the Sewell's Point battery and that it appeared to
have been abandoned.*

Flag Officer Josiah Tattnall
to Stephen R. Mallory

The Norwegians were kindness itself to the pair of
exhausted-looking, disheveled, French-speaking
American women who had appeared on their deck,
transported there by a United States dispatch boat
and requesting they be returned to the Confederacy.

The crew of the *Norvier* acted with such dispatch,
in fact, that Wendy had the clear impression that the
Norwegians were eager to be rid of them. Molly
began with her usual sort of explanation – believable,
detailed, but not overly so, spoken in a fluent French
that oozed sincerity and vulnerability. She explained
how the Federals refused to take them to a
Confederate port, despite their being citizens of
the Confederate States, after the ship they were on
was captured by Yankees off Cape Hatteras.

She had got no further than that when the officer to whom they were speaking, who Wendy assumed to be the captain, cut her off with an apology, hands held up to ward off further explanation. He turned to another man, who had approached them in mid-conversation, a man in finely made civilian clothing who, though having just completed a trans-Atlantic voyage, looked as if he was ready for an evening at the opera. This Wendy took to be the Norwegian minister. If he had a wife, she was not in evidence.

The two men spoke in rapid Norwegian and the women could do no more than listen and try to deduce, from the tone and the hand motions, what was being said. Wendy worked out her best-guess translation:

CAPTAIN: Your Honor, I don't know what these lunatic women are talking about. Something about the Federals not allowing them to go home.
MINISTER: What do they want from us?
CAPTAIN: Apparently they want us to take them over there. (The captain at that point gestured toward the south.)
MINISTER: Very well, let us get them the hell off this ship and have no more to do with this. Lord, we don't want to start an incident an hour after the anchor has dropped!

That was just Wendy's guess, but she would have wagered all the money pressed against her breasts that she was within a biscuit toss of being right. Before Molly could begin again, the captain informed her that they would be taken ashore, and he turned and shouted for a boat to be cleared away, shouting orders over the two women's attempts to thank him.

An hour later, with the sun just lost in the west, they fetched the beach at the foot of the battery at Sewell's Point, the very spot from which they had left that morning in the first light of day. Lincoln's boat and the other Federal vessels that had been shelling the fort were long gone, the *Virginia*, hulking and dark, riding on her mooring half a mile away.

The *Norvier*'s launch was crewed by twenty young Norwegian sailors, tricked out in blue-and-white-striped shirts and flat-topped hats that they wore at a jaunty angle, bound around with a strip of black ribbon embroidered with the name of their ship. They were handsome, blond, smiling men who seemed to appreciate the women in the stern sheets. They took every opportunity to meet their passengers' eyes and smile, while Molly smiled coquettishly back and Wendy blushed and the officer sitting beside them scowled at his men in disapproval.

The boat ground up on the gravel shore and the oarsmen hopped out one by one and dragged the boat up on the beach, until at last they were able to assist Wendy and Molly out onto the dry ground. Molly thanked them all in French, and though it was clear they did not understand the words, her meaning was obvious, and they smiled and gave their welcomes in Norwegian. The humorless officer ordered the boat to be pushed back into the water and hustled the sailors back aboard, and soon they were pulling for the *Norvier*, a gray and indistinct object, half lost in the gloom.

'Lord, I would sign aboard that ship in a minute if they would promise to put me in the fo'c'sle!'

Molly said. Wendy was too exhausted to be scandalized.

'Now what, Aunt?' Wendy said. She sat with a thump on a knee-high rock. The gentle surf pulsed against the shore and the saltwater washed over Wendy's shoes but she did not have the energy to move them. Whatever spirit had been driving her along through the chaotic day was now entirely drained from her. Her body seemed to know it was safe to collapse now, with her feet back on Southern soil, her neck apparently free from the hangman's noose, and the question of whether or not she should blow out the brains of the President of the United States decided for her. She felt like a chicken, beheaded, hung by its feet, all the life juices drained from her.

'That's quite an image,' Molly said.

'What?'

'A beheaded chicken. You don't look as bad as all that.'

Did I say that out loud? Wendy thought. She must have, or else Molly was reading her mind. The soldiers that were moving down the beach were marching with an astounding symmetry, thousands and thousands of them, and the orange light streaming from the rifles they held over their shoulders lit the sky like sunset.

'Come on, dear,' Molly said, and Wendy woke to find herself still sitting on the rock, Molly's protective arm around her shoulders to keep her from falling onto the beach. 'Do you think you can stand? Lieutenant Batchelor is here to help us find some transportation back to Norfolk.'

Wendy looked around. In the fading light of sunset

she could see Lieutenant Batchelor standing a few feet away, pristine in his frock coat. 'Lieutenant . . . how good to see you! How . . . ?'

'The Yankees let me go, just as they said they would. Spent a fair amount of time questioning me, but they got nothing that I didn't tell them when we first pulled alongside. To hear me, you would have thought I was the most ignorant man in the Confederacy.'

Wendy smiled, genuinely pleased. 'I am so happy to see you safe, sir. I would not have you hurt, or a prisoner, for our sake.'

Batchelor gave a shallow bow. 'I thank you for your concern, but it is duty, ma'am.'

Actually, Wendy thought, *it is because I am trying to meet up with my lover in Yazoo City.* She wondered how sanguine the lieutenant would be if he understood the true genesis of their wild mission.

Molly slipped her arm under Wendy's and helped her to her feet. Her muscles ached and she had some difficulty in standing straight. *Lord, this must be what it is like to be eighty years old.*

They walked toward the fort, and as Wendy's muscles warmed and stretched she was able to walk more easily, until finally the limp and cautious step were gone and she moved like herself again. They entered the fort through the small door from which they had exited that morning, stepping into a place very different from the one where they had spent the night.

Wendy remembered the garrison as a small band of generally bored soldiers. They were a small band still, but they were not bored. Men were rushing in and out of the casemates, carrying loads of whatever they could – boxes of fuses, shells, small arms – and loading them into the backs of wagons, while restless horses, tapped into the frantic mood of the place, shifted in their traces and snorted their displeasure.

'They are abandoning the fort,' Batchelor explained, leading the women past the batteries and hastily built barracks. 'Yankees were shelling them again today. You must have seen them. No one has any doubt they'll be coming ashore soon.' He stopped and looked at Molly. 'I hope you know where.'

Molly smiled. 'I do.'

'Good,' said Batchelor. 'Let's get you to someone who can use that information.'

The carriage in which they had come from Norfolk had, by Batchelor's orders, remained there, waiting on them. They climbed in and the coachman cracked his whip and they rattled and shook their way out of the fort and down the moonlit road. Soon Wendy was asleep again. She dreamed strange dreams of her mother and Samuel Bowater and Abraham Lincoln, of ships sinking under her and guns firing. Molly shook her awake as they rolled through the gates of the Gosport Naval Shipyard. Night was fully on them, the blackness through the carriage windows broken only by certain points of light, lanterns and larger fires. Wendy did not feel particularly refreshed.

They stepped out of the carriage into a scene much like that at the fort at Sewell's Point, but on a considerably grander scale. More wagons, hundreds more men shifting every conceivable article that might be found in a shipyard and moved by hand and by wagon. Barrels of powder, barrels of shot, round and conical shells, metalworking machinery, coils of rope, brass deck howitzers, boxes and boxes of paperwork, it was all being hustled across the yard, loaded in wagons, bound for Richmond by train or wagon or foot. For the past year the Confederate Navy had enjoyed the considerable windfall of Yankee resources that had come to them with the taking of the naval shipyard. Now all that could be moved was being moved, before it became Yankee property once more.

'They're taking everything,' Molly observed as she crossed the cobbled yard to Tucker's office. 'Will you take the buildings too?'

'Don't need buildings, ma'am,' Batchelor said. 'Wish to hell we could take the dry dock, though. I'd trade all of it for the dry dock.'

They found Captain John Tucker in his office, which was considerably more empty than it had been twenty-four hours before. The desk and chairs were there, the file cabinets as well, but the piles of papers were gone, the crates half stuffed with documents all absent. There was an orderly look about the place, the kind of orderliness you can only get in an unoccupied room.

Handsome Jack sat at his desk, a few charts scattered around, the only paperwork left.

'I'm pleased to see you have tidied up a bit,' Molly announced as she swept into the room. 'I was going to suggest that you need a woman around the place.'

Tucker looked up, gave as much of a smile as his weary face would allow. 'Do you know one who is available?'

'Available women? I know plenty of available women. I just don't know any ladies. Save for my dear Wendy, but you can't have her. Her heart belongs to another sailor.'

'Ah, well . . .' Tucker stood, gestured to the chairs, and Wendy sat, gratefully. 'What have you found out?'

'The Yankees will land at Ocean View near Willoughby's Point. Tomorrow, I reckon,' Molly said.

'Tomorrow?' Tucker said. He pulled out a watch and snapped it open in a gesture so reminiscent of Newcomb that it made Wendy flinch. 'It is twelve forty-eight now. May tenth. Do you mean they will land on the eleventh?'

'No,' Molly said. 'I did not know it was past midnight. They will come today.'

Tucker nodded. He seemed neither surprised nor alarmed. 'Ocean View? You have it on good authority?'

'Quite good.' Molly told him the story, from the tug's intercepting them on the way to the flagship, through the shock of Lincoln's presence, to their being allowed to join him on the boat deck for the bulk of his scouting expedition. Batchelor nodded his confirmation of their story. There was nothing for him to add. Molly's recollection was flawless.

She went to great lengths to describe what a gentleman the President was, how well-mannered and droll and quick-witted, and Wendy was sure her aunt was needling Tucker, trying to get some rise out of him, but in that she failed. Tucker simply listened, did not react.

'The Norwegians were very kind to bring us back to Sewell's Point,' Molly finished. 'I don't think they wished to have a dog in our fight.' She did not mention Newcomb or the incident in the cabin.

Tucker leaned back, tossed the dividers he was holding on to the chart. 'Good work, Molly. As ever.

Excellent. There had been some concern that the Yankees would push down the Elizabeth River, bottle us in.'

'I would be very surprised,' Molly said. 'They are deathly afraid of the *Virginia*.'

'They should be. So, if they are coming overland, we have half a day at least to complete our evacuation. After they get their troops ashore. By noon today, we must be gone.'

'And Wendy and I with you?' Molly prompted. 'I do believe we have fulfilled our half of the bargain.'

'Admirably, my dear Molly, most admirably. I will be aboard the last boat out of here, and you and Wendy will be with me. I will certainly be up for the remainder of the night making preparations, but there is no cause for you to be as well. Your house is not too far from here?'

'No, and my bed calls with an irresistible siren's song,' Molly said. Wendy, though she thought herself acclimated to her aunt's outrageous proclamations, still was mortified to hear Molly mention her bed to this man.

'You must go to it, then. I will have the good Lieutenant Batchelor take you home and collect you in the morning, say, nine o'clock?'

Molly stood. 'Two bells in the forenoon watch,' she said. 'And if the lieutenant is even ten minutes late, we will come hunting for him. And you.'

'I understand,' said Tucker, also standing. 'It is why I have chosen my most punctual officer.'

The carriage in which they had arrived had already gone off on some other duty, but after some time Batchelor managed to locate a buckboard, half loaded with galley fixtures, that he commandeered for the time it would take to drive the women home. He climbed up onto the seat and took the reins, and Molly and Wendy shuffled in beside him.

They rode in silence back through the streets to Molly's home, streets that were mostly deserted, and Wendy wondered if that was because the bulk of the people had already fled town, or if they had given up and gone to ground in their homes, waiting for the Yankees.

They arrived at last at the dark house they had left the day before. There was something anticlimactic to their return, Wendy thought, a step back after the extraordinary measures they had taken to leave that place. But it was only for a single night's sleep, she knew, and indeed, the thought of a soft bed absolutely trumped any other consideration.

She climbed with difficulty down from the seat, and Molly after her, and she noticed that even her aunt was not moving as spryly as she had. Batchelor took their bags from among the galley stores and led the way through the white picket fence and up the flagstone path to the front door.

He stepped aside and Molly pulled a key from her reticule, unlocked the door, and swung it open. The moonlight and the illumination from distant gas lamps came in through the door and through the gauzy curtains and dimly lit the room in patches of dark blue and gray. Batchelor stepped in and Molly behind him and then Wendy. In the faint light she could see the shadowy shapes of chairs and love seat in their familiar places. She knew the room so well, dark or light.

Then something in the blackness shifted, something moved, something scraped on the floor. Wendy gasped, heard Molly shout, 'Damn!' saw Lieutenant Batchelor take a step into the room. And then from the dark place, a pistol fired, a great flash of orange and yellow in a horizontal column, and Wendy saw Batchelor flung back, arms up, crashing to the floor, knocking Molly aside like a bowling pin.

She heard herself scream and she staggered back, hands on her mouth. The echo of the shot died away. And then, through the dullness and ringing in her ears, Wendy heard, clear as the gunshot, the sound of a pocket watch snapping open, snapping shut.

CHAPTER 17

*I then dispatched [Jones] to Norfolk to confer with
General Huger and Captain Lee. He found the
navy yard in flames, and that all its officers had
left by railroad . . . the enemy were within half a
mile of the city. . . .*

Flag Officer Josiah Tattnall
to Stephen Mallory

In the dark, Wendy saw Molly make her move for the
door. Off balance, Molly lunged to her right, but
stumbled over Batchelor's body. She grabbed Wendy's
arm, hard, and pulled, trying to drag her along out the
door.

'Stand still!' Newcomb's voice was hoarse and
shrill. The pistol fired again, the sharp crack of
percussion cap, the explosive sound of the cartridge
going off. The room was lit up in the lightning flash
of orange and yellow and red. Something on the wall
shattered. *Mirror,* Wendy thought, *ridiculous to think
of that, of all things.*

'Don't move, or God help me, Cathy, I'll blow your
brains out!'

Molly froze and Wendy froze, and for a moment Wendy could hear nothing but her own breath.

Finally, Newcomb broke the silence. 'Close the door and light a lamp. Now.'

'I can't close the door,' Molly said. 'This poor man you murdered is in the way.'

Wendy's eyes were beginning to recover from the muzzle flash. She could see Newcomb now, the dark outline of his body, on the far side of the room, standing in shadow. She could see Molly, tense and tight-lipped beside her, could just make out the features of her face. She heard Newcomb sigh in exasperation.

'Drag him out of the way and close the door. And by God if one of you tries to run, I will kill the other.'

Molly nodded toward Wendy and they stooped down and each grabbed one of Batchelor's legs and pulled him inside. Wendy thought perhaps the man was only wounded, hoped desperately that that was the case, but now she knew he was not. There was no response, no life at all in the body they were dragging.

Then Batchelor's body gave a sigh, a gasp, as if it was struggling to draw breath, and Wendy screamed and dropped the leg. Newcomb screamed, 'Don't move!' and the pistol fired again, the muzzle flash lighting Newcomb's startled face. The bullet whizzed by, thudded into the half-closed door. The gunsmoke tasted bitter in Wendy's throat.

'Goddamn it, Roger, take your goddamned finger off the trigger!' Molly said.

Quiet again, in the wake of that order, and in a voice that sounded as if it was struggling for calm, Newcomb said, 'Close the door and light a lamp.'

Molly stepped around the body and shut the door. It clicked with a finality like a tomb being sealed, and half of what light there was in the room was gone, and it was hard to see even the shapes of things. Wendy could hear Molly's hand patting the side table, looking for the box of matches. She found them at last and with a scraping sound struck a light, and suddenly Molly's face was illuminated, her lips taut, her eyebrows together – angry, frightened, her mind working, her mouth shut.

She lifted the chimney off the lamp on the table, lit the wick, and turned it up. Now the yellow light fell on the dark shapes and gave them color – the floral patterns in the upholstery, the stripes in the curtains, the intricate pattern of the oriental rug.

Wendy looked down at Batchelor. The bullet had hit him dead center in his chest. There was a bloom of dark red around the wound, soaked into the gray cloth of his frock coat. A puddle was forming beneath him, a swatch of red on the floor and carpet where they had dragged him. His eyes were open, his skin was white like candle wax. His expression was one of surprise. Wendy felt her gorge rise and she looked away, quickly.

Now they could see Newcomb as well, and he was not a lovely sight. He was wearing his uniform pants and a white shirt, splotched with great patches of perspiration and stained and smudged in various places. Over that was a civilian vest and on his head a slouch hat. His eyes seemed wider than Wendy remembered. He held his navy .36 at waist height, held it in his left hand. With his right he pulled his watch, snapped it open, looked at it, returned it to the pocket.

'Roger, this will not end well—' Molly began.

'Shut your mouth.'

'You are a dead man, Roger, either way. If the Confederates get you, they will hang you for a spy in your civilian clothes. If your people get you, they will hang you for a deserter.'

'Hah! Deserter! See here, you . . . I know who you are. I know! So we wait here, and when the Union takes Norfolk again, I present them with a Confederate spy and assassin.'

'Oh, come now—'

'Yes, damn you, assassin! Worming your way into the President's confidence, getting close to him, so at a later date you can come back and kill him. Oh, don't think I haven't worked this all out! Hang for a deserter? No, I think not. Promotion would be more like.'

Molly shook her head, an expression that implied pity. 'Roger, Roger . . . what are you going to say? You had me on board your boat, let me escape to the Norwegians, then deserted in order to capture me again? I think—'

'Enough!' Newcomb roared, so loudly that Wendy started. He raised the gun and, straight-armed, advanced on Molly until the wicked octagonal barrel was just inches from her face. 'Enough of your *lies*! You have played me, lied to me, tricked me into falling in love with you, made me think you loved me . . . enough! I'll turn you in and you will be tried and you will be hanged and may God damn me if I am not right in the front row to watch it.'

Molly stared at him, right over the black steel of the gun. She did not flinch. For a long moment they remained that way, eyes locked, pure loathing in the air between them.

Finally Molly sighed, turned, and stepped away, as if she were simply done with Roger Newcomb. 'I am too tired for this nonsense, Roger. I am going to bed.'

'Wait,' Newcomb said, following her with the gun as she walked away. He paused, unsure what to say. It seemed to Wendy as if he wanted to object but could find no reason for it. 'You stay here. You can sleep on the couch if you want, but you stay where I can see you.' He walked sideways toward the door, eyes on Molly, and picked up the reticule she had dropped in her surprise.

He shifted his gaze toward Wendy, the first time he had looked at her. With the .36 Colt he gestured toward her leg. 'And you, give me the gun you have hidden there.'

Wendy felt herself flush. She tried to think of some way out, something to say, some clever thing that Molly might come up with, but there was nothing. 'Very well. Turn around.'

'Do you think I'm stupid?'

'You don't think I'll lift my skirt in front of you?'

'Give me the gun, you slut, or I'll get the goddamn thing myself!'

Wendy felt her lips press tight, her eyebrows come together. *You son of a bitch,* she thought, an expression that she had never in her life spoken and only rarely thought. She reached under her skirts, ran her hand up her leg to the gun, exposing as little of herself as she was able, flushing with humiliation and fury.

'Slowly, slowly,' Newcomb said, the .36 aimed at

her now. Wendy slipped the gun from the holster, held it by the butt between thumb and forefinger, handed it to Newcomb. Newcomb took it, looked to see it was not loaded, then tossed it aside. With the barrel of his gun he waved Wendy over toward Molly.

'All right, Cathy,' he said, 'let's see what you're hiding under *your* skirts.'

'Roger, you must be joking.'

'Do it! God knows I won't be the first you've lifted your skirts for, you filthy barracks hack.'

Wendy could see the rage, unfiltered, on Molly's face. Slowly, deliberately, she lifted her skirts to reveal the frilled pantaloons she wore underneath. Newcomb stepped closer, cautiously, the gun held ready but beyond Molly's reach. He ran his left hand over her legs, feeling for weapons hidden beneath the cotton. Molly kicked his hand away.

'That's all you get, you pathetic bastard,' she hissed. 'It's all you'll ever get.'

Wendy felt the sweat stand out on her forehead. Molly was frightening, more frightening at that moment than mad Newcomb and his pistol.

'You don't frighten me, Cathy Luce,' Newcomb said, stepping back. He did not sound so sure.

Molly smoothed her skirts. 'Stop calling me Cathy Luce,' she said. 'My name is Molly Atkins.'

Newcomb squinted in surprise, as if he was trying to get a better look.

'Molly Atkins,' Molly said again. 'You have no idea what you are into here.' With that she stepped over to the love seat, sat, then reclined and closed her eyes.

Newcomb stared at her, pulled his watch, consulted it. He looked at Wendy, looked at Molly.

263

'Well,' Wendy said, 'if we are all just waiting on the Yankees, I guess I'll get some sleep as well.'

'You—' Newcomb began and stopped. Whatever he had been expecting from his prisoners, this was not it, and it seemed to unnerve him, which Wendy imagined was to their advantage. She crossed over to a big wing chair and curled up as best as she could and closed her eyes. She waited for Newcomb to do something, say something, but there was only silence.

She was more exhausted than she could recall ever having been. If he was going to kill them or rape them, then their sleeping now would not change that. A bullet through the head, she imagined, was better taken while asleep anyway. She sat with eyes closed and prayed, preparing her soul in case she woke up on the other side of mortality. And as she made her peace, she fell asleep.

She woke sometime later, how much later she did not know. Still motionless, she opened her eyes and surveyed the room. Through the drawn curtains it appeared to be full daylight, so she imagined it was seven o'clock in the morning, at least.

Batchelor's body had been dragged aside and lay near the piano, a quilt that her grandmother – Molly's mother – had made years before draped over him. Newcomb was on the move, pacing, rifling drawers, reading correspondence, crushing it in his hand. He did not see her watching him. The watch went in and out. Whatever madness had been urging him on the night before now seemed to have complete control.

He spun around and Wendy shut her eyes quickly, then opened them again, just a crack, to peer out through her lashes. Newcomb was leaning into the window, curtains pulled back, looking out, first left, then right, craning around to increase the arc of his vision. The sunlight fell on his lined face, made his wild hair look even more out of control. He straightened, tugged at his clothes. He spun around again, stamped over to the love seat where Molly slept with her back to the room. He shook her, hard.

Molly rolled over slowly, sat up, as if awakened from the untroubled sleep of the innocent and safe. It had to be an act, Wendy imagined, even cool-as-a-cucumber Molly could not be entirely unruffled.

She stretched, arched her back, yawned, which made Newcomb jerk in agitation. With some difficulty he pulled his watch, his hand full of crushed papers, old correspondence by the look of it.

'What is this?' Newcomb demanded, holding the paper in Molly's face as if it was evidence of some betrayal.

Molly glanced quickly at the papers, then met Newcomb's eyes and held them. 'Letters, it looks like,' she said.

'Letters! Letters, yes, letters addressed to Molly Atkins.' He threw a letter on the floor. 'Molly Atkins, Molly Atkins, Molly Atkins!' With each accusatory repetition of the name he flung a letter to the floor.

'Molly Atkins,' Molly said. 'That is my name. I told you that last night. Whomever you think you fell in love with, she does not exist.'

Newcomb stood straight, spun around, flung out his arms. He muttered something; Wendy could not make it out.

'Wendy, dear,' Molly said, as if Newcomb were not there, 'I am sure they will send troops to look for poor Lieutenant Batchelor. Have you heard any yet?'

Newcomb stopped his agitated fidgeting, glared down at Molly. *She has gone too far,* Wendy thought.

'Shut your mouth, you bitch!' Newcomb said, his volume building with each word. His arm drew back across his chest and before Molly could raise an arm to ward off the blow, he whipped the gun across her face. Molly spun round, sprawled out on the love seat. Wendy could see the bright red line of blood across her white cheek, her expression of fury and fear.

'You cowardly little puke!' Molly hissed. 'I'll kill you for that!'

'Kill me . . .' Newcomb advanced on her and for the first time Wendy saw the shadow of fear on Molly's face, and then Newcomb hit her, right in the face, hit her with his balled fist and sent her flying to the floor.

'You bastard!' Wendy shouted and flew at him, lashing out with her fists, but her punches were nothing to him. He hit her with the back of his hand, made her stagger back. Behind her, Molly was pulling herself to her feet.

'Keep away from me, you bitch,' Newcomb growled.

'You dirty little coward!' Wendy shouted, backing away.

Newcomb turned on her, advanced on her, the gun held at waist height, pointing at Wendy's heart.

'Coward!'

'Shut up!' he shrieked. 'Shut your mouth!'

'I will not shut up, you bastard!' Wendy screamed back. The control was gone now, the pistol pointed at her chest meant nothing. 'You little chicken-hearted—'

'Shut your mouth, damn you!'

Molly was getting on her feet. In her hand she clutched the poker from the parlor stove. *Keep looking at me,* Wendy thought.

Newcomb's jaw was working hard. With his left hand he jerked the watch from his pocket, opened it, stared at it.

'Stop that, you damned lunatic!' Wendy shouted and her hand lashed out and snatched the watch from Newcomb's hand, tore the fob clean out of his vest. She threw the watch down on the floor as hard as she could, but it only bounced on the carpet, so she brought her heel down on it with all the force she could bring to bear. She felt it crush underfoot, heard the satisfying sound of glass and metal fracturing.

'You . . . bitch . . .' Newcomb said, looking at the remains of the watch at his feet. The words came out in a whisper, and they carried far more menace than did his shrieks. He looked up, raised the gun. Over his shoulder Wendy could see Molly flying across the room, a fury of petticoats and blond hair, arms drawn back as if she were chopping wood with an ax.

Newcomb sensed her there, swung around just as Molly swung the poker. He raised his hand to deflect the blow. The poker hit the gun, knocked it free from his hand with a dull clanging sound. The pistol dropped to the carpet and the poker bounced off Newcomb's shoulder. Newcomb slammed his fist into Molly's stomach, doubled her over. Wendy saw her eyes go wide as she fell to her knees and Newcomb hit her in the face, backhand, and she was flung to the floor once again.

Wendy screamed, screamed from her gut. She had never imagined such violence, not by a man against a

267

woman. She flailed out at Newcomb, as ineffectually as before. Wendy saw his fist draw back, saw it come around at her face. It seemed to come slowly, as if he were moving underwater, but yet she could not avoid it, there was nothing she could do.

And then he hit her, right on the side of the head, and she saw her whole world burst into a flash of light, a roaring noise, and she was twisting and going down. She put her hands out and felt the carpet and then her whole body thudded against the floor and then it was all blackness.

When she came to, she did not know where she was, how she got there, how long she had been down. She opened her eyes, saw the wainscoting, the leg of a chair. Her head ached horribly. She heard screaming, shuffling, fighting, and she remembered. She turned her head, saw Newcomb lifting Molly to her feet, a handful of hair in his fist, saw him hit her again and Molly go down with a grunt.

Seconds ... a few seconds ... Wendy realized she had not passed out for more than that.

Get up ... get up ... but she seemed to have no control over her legs, her arms. She could not move, she could only watch.

Watch, as Newcomb kicked Molly hard. Watch as he dropped to his knees and flung her skirts aside, ripped her pantaloons off her legs. Watch as he fumbled with his belt, shouting, 'You bitch, you bitch, you bitch!' like some kind of mantra.

Molly was screaming, but groggy, slurred, shouting, 'No, no!'

Get up ... get up ... and Wendy thought she felt some life in her arms, as if they were coming to now, as if she were coming awake from the head down. She reached out an arm, reached it toward Molly, as if she could help, saw the tips of her fingers extending uselessly out.

Get up . . . She put her hand flat on the carpet, put pressure on it, found she could lift herself, an inch, two inches. She felt a tingling in her legs, as if they were coming to life now, life returning to all her body. She pushed herself higher, got the other arm under her.

Molly was groaning in pain and despair, punching feebly at Newcomb who was on top of her now. Wendy pushed herself to her knees, her head pounding, the room whirling in front of her, and she fell forward onto her hands and knew she would fall if she stood up. Instead she crawled, crawled toward Molly and Newcomb, crawled to where she could impose herself into his violence. Her hand came down on something hard and cold. She looked down. The pistol.

Wendy picked the gun up, surprised by how heavy it was. She pushed herself up onto her knees and this time it was better, this time the room remained fairly motionless. With two hands she held the gun straight out, saw Newcomb's head over the barrel and pulled the trigger.

Nothing happened. She pulled harder. Still nothing. *Hammer* . . . She remembered, from deep down, Molly's brief lesson. Her right thumb caught the knurled top of the hammer and pulled it back, and even over the sound of the violence the *click, click, click-click* was loud and ominous.

Newcomb came upright on his knees, twisted to look behind him. Over the barrel Wendy saw the look of shock on his face and then she pulled the trigger.

The gun flew back, knocked her to the floor, wrenching her arm. The room was lost in the flash and smoke and noise. Wendy lifted herself with both arms, got a knee on the floor, pushed herself to her feet. She stood for a second, the gun limp at her side.

Aim the gun, aim the gun . . . She knew she had to be ready in case she had missed but she could not make the room stand still long enough for her to concentrate on anything but her own balance.

At last the room ceased its spinning and she half lifted the gun. She took a step forward. There was no need to aim. Newcomb lay sprawled out on the carpet, half on his side, half on his back, his face covered with blood. Blood dripped from his nose and made black, wet pools on the carpet. He did not move.

'Aunt . . .' Wendy dropped the gun, knelt beside Molly, who had lifted herself up on her arms, brushed her skirts down around her legs. 'Aunt . . .'

Wendy looked into Molly's eyes and saw a coldness and a deadness that she had never seen before. Her aunt's lip was swollen and blood ran down her chin and there was a long bloody gash from the pistol-whipping. Her eye was puffy and red, the top of her dress around her neck ripped.

'Here, Aunt, let me help you up,' Wendy said. She stood, offered a hand, helped pull Molly to her feet. She could not think of anything else to do, did not know what to do next.

Molly looked down at Newcomb's body, stretched out on the floor. 'Bastard,' she said, softly, then louder. 'Bastard! Bastard!' She kicked Newcomb and he rolled over on his back and she kicked him again and again and Wendy did not know what to do, did not know if it was better to let her go or to stop her. So she did nothing, and finally Molly staggered back, hurt and exhausted, staggered back and fell into the wing chair and closed her eyes.

Wendy looked around the room, saw the quilt-draped body of Lieutenant Batchelor, and she remembered. She remembered the promise of transportation out of that horrible place, of passage to Richmond and safety and civilization. They had to get to the shipyard and soon, because the Yankees were coming, and the yard would be abandoned and they would be left behind.

'Molly, we have to go,' Wendy announced, but Molly just looked at her as if she were speaking a foreign language. Norwegian.

'We have to get to the shipyard before Tucker sails and leaves us behind. Come on.' Molly did not respond, so Wendy grabbed her hand and pulled her to her feet. 'We have to go, Molly, come on!'

Wendy picked up Molly's bag and thrust it into her hand and Molly held it, automatically, her hand acting on its own. Wendy picked up her derringer from where Newcomb had tossed it and replaced it in the holster on her leg. She grabbed her bag and Molly's reticule and headed for the door. She stopped when she realized that Molly was not following. She turned. Molly was staring at Newcomb's body. She was not moving.

'Come along, Aunt!' Wendy ordered. She took Molly's hand and pulled her across the room and out the door.

Together they stepped out into the yard. The sun was well up, it had to be late morning. There was no one in sight, no movement on the streets. In the

271

distance Wendy could hear the occasional shout, the odd bang and clash, sounds of desperation and flight, but nothing that gave any indication of how things sat in Portsmouth or Norfolk.

They hurried down the path, Wendy still half towing Molly, and out the gate, not bothering to close it. They walked down the narrow cobbled street to where it met with Water Street, running along the edge of the Elizabeth River to the Gosport Naval Shipyard. They stopped. Great plumes of black smoke rolled up from the very place where the shipyard stood.

'This is not a good thing,' Wendy said, but Molly did not reply. 'Come along.' They stepped out, quickened their pace, hurrying on the verge of a run. Wendy's breath was coming faster through the twin exertions of running and pulling Molly behind. Her bag was banging painfully against her thigh, but her sense of urgency did not allow her to slow. She could smell the smoke now, it grew more overwhelming with each step they took toward the navy yard. She could see flames reaching up, even in the brilliant sunlight. She could hear the crackle of fire consuming wood.

When they reached the wall of the shipyard they slowed their pace to a quick walk, tried to regain their breath as they hurried for the gate. Wendy wanted to ask Molly if they were too late, but she did not, because Molly did not seem to be with her anymore.

At last they came to the big iron gate, and there they stopped and dropped their bags and panted for breath, coughing with the smoke swirling around them.

The gate was hanging open, there was no guard

there. The big ship houses were in flames, as were the timber sheds, storehouses, mast houses, and rope-walks. A great mass of black smoke roiled up from the buildings, the red and yellow flames reached up out of the windows and grabbed at the roofs. It was a scene of complete destruction. There was not one other human being in sight.

CHAPTER 18

HAMLET: . . . *I have heard,*
That guilty creatures sitting at a play
Have by the very cunning of the scene
Been struck so to the soul that presently
They have proclaimed their malefactions.
Shakespeare, *Hamlet,*
Act II, Scene 2

Samuel Bowater felt like Noah's less-enlightened neighbor.

It came to him as he stood contemplating the ship ways on which the *Arkansas* had once stood. *Arkansas . . . Ark . . .*

The *Arkansas* was long gone, towed away downriver, like Noah's boat carried off on the flood. And here he was, with an ark of his own, half built. He was desperately trying to finish her up, but the water was rising fast.

The River Defense Fleet's victory at Plum Point Bend had electrified Memphis. The sailors of the fleet were lauded as heroes, eulogized to the heavens, lionized in the press, boozed up for free in the taverns. Some of the better-known brothels even offered attractive discounts to veterans of that fight.

And there were a lot of veterans. It seemed to Bowater that suddenly every third man in town was a sailor in the River Defense Fleet. The ships themselves would have sunk under the weight of all the swaggering ersatz river men who claimed association with that special branch of the army. He just hoped that all these fellows with their newfound enthusiasm for the war would be there when it came time to confront the Yankees again – and that time would come – but he suspected they would not. He suspected that when the iron was flying again they would all go back to being blacksmiths and barbers and bottle washers.

Samuel Bowater always found the praise of civilians tiresome, and he found the adulation in Memphis more tiresome than most. He blamed his poor attitude on the frustration of having his new command still in frame, her iron on the Arkansas side of the river, her engines towed away to God knows where, and the still-powerful Yankee fleet just a few miles upriver.

The bluebellies were weaker by two ironclads, that was true, but it would not be true for long. The first ship that the River Defense Fleet had struck, which turned out to be the USS *Cincinnati*, was still in the mud. Reconnaissance north of Plum Point Bend revealed that she had not moved from the place where she sank in water up to her casemate roof. But the Yankees were making prodigious efforts to raise her, and there was little doubt they would succeed, and then the *Cincinnati* would be towed away to Cairo, Illinois, for repair, and soon she would be fighting again.

The second ship that the Confederates had rammed, which the papers were saying was the *Mound City,* had been raised already and was off to Cairo. And so the sinking of two ships, which, had they been Confederate, might have been the ruin of the fleet, was to the Yankees with all their extraordinary resources just a big inconvenience, no permanent setback.

The Yankees were weaker for the moment, but they were still there, and they still had powerful gunboats, and they would not be caught a second time with their pants around their ankles. And without surprise working for them, the River Defense Fleet would be murdered by those iron monsters. What was needed was a Confederate ironclad.

And that was the very thing that Bowater was driving himself to distraction trying to build.

He had allowed his men forty-eight hours to revel in the adulation of an adoring Memphis, and then back to work. On the morning the grace period was over, Bowater walked briskly the half mile from his hotel to the waterfront. The spring morning was warm, the walk invigorating, and he arrived at John Shirley's yard at 7:50 with a glow of optimism, which was snuffed out as soon as he found that he was alone. He had ordered his men to report to the yard at eight o'clock, not a minute after. By 8:05 not one was there.

The former Yazoo Citys were quartered in various places around town. Bowater considered sending a boy to fetch them, but realized that would be pointless. They were not likely to be at their assigned quarters. More likely they were scattered like chaff through the bars, whorehouses, fetid back alleys, and jails of the town.

Bowater was just working up a good head of profanity when John Shirley stepped out of his office and over to the gate to greet him. 'Captain, Captain, good to see you. Congratulations on your victory. You know I had not yet heard of it when we spoke the other day, and you didn't say a thing about it, did you? Humility, it's a damned important trait, I say, and I reckon you got it in spades. A man should take a power of pride in that kind of humility. Where are your men?'

'I was just asking myself the same.'

'Well, I should expect they're a bit under the weather this morning. Whole town was celebrating last night. Good to have something to celebrate, ain't been much good news of late.'

Ruffin Tanner appeared at ten minutes past, his tongue thick, his eyes bleary, one hand pressed tenderly to his temple, apologizing for his tardiness. His arm was in a sling and the sling was dirty and stained. The first of his men to show up, and he was *hors de combat*, useless in the shipyard. Bowater gave him a sharp order to see things laid along for setting the next plank in place, as best as he could with one arm. He was not in a charitable mood.

One by one the others straggled in, Bowater's men and the dozen or so that Shirley had scraped up. They set to work under the constructor's careful eye, shaping and steaming planks, fitting the square beams of the casemate, pounding drifts and trunnels, turning the pile of lumber on the ground into the ironclad *Tennessee*.

Bowater spent some time watching them, but there was little he could do, because he was no shipwright. So once he was satisfied that Shirley and his foremen knew their business and would keep the men at it, he commandeered a desk in Shirley's office and began to write. Requisitions for ordnance and powder, requests that more sailors be transferred to his command, requests to recruit river men from the armies stationed nearby, payroll information, submissions for reimbursement for the men's housing expenses, it was all terribly depressing.

After some time of that, Bowater was distracted by a sound like a footstep on the two wooden stairs leading up to the office door, a sound like a footstep but more sharp, wood knocking on wood. He looked up. The door swung open and Hieronymus Taylor made his way through, walking with a crutch, his leg bound up in a heavy wooden splint. Bowater watched the engineer hobble across the floor, struggling with the splint and the unfamiliar crutches. He did not offer to help. He knew Taylor better than that.

Taylor flopped down in a chair beside Bowater's desk. 'You could at least offer some goddamned help,' he said. The body was worse off, but the attitude was Hieronymus Taylor of old. They would not mention the violin. That was mutually understood.

'I am forgetting myself,' Bowater said. 'And you the hero of Plum Point Bend. I've heard some mighty tall versions of your exploits.'

'Hell . . .' Taylor put a cigar in his mouth, then spit out a fleck of tobacco. His hands were trembling. Beads of sweat stood out on his forehead.

'I cannot imagine that you are discharged from the hospital by your doctor's orders,' Bowater said. 'And from the looks of you, you would be best to be in bed.'

'Bed. If I stay abed they'll find me agin.'

'Who?'

'All of them. The ol ladies with their proclamations and presentations, the damn schoolchil'n comin to cheer the wounded sailors up, the damn mayor and his claptrap. Like to make a body shoot himself rather than listen to all that horseshit.' He scraped a match on the desk, lit his cigar.

'I wonder if every attempted suicide gets that much attention.'

'Suicide?' Taylor took a big puff of his cigar. 'That what you reckon I was doin?'

Bowater held up his hands in a gesture that said 'I don't know.'

'Suicide, hell. I'm a big hero, Cap'n.'

'You're going to be a dead hero, you keep on the way you are, and that is the one and only thing the Confederacy has enough of already. And while I might be entirely indifferent to the possibility of your death, I would not care to try and find another engineer.'

'Cap'n, I'm touched. But what the hell you need an engineer for? You got no engine.'

'We'll get it back.'

'Well, you best hurry. Boilers and shaftin, too. You gonna feel mighty damn foolish, you get that casemate built and realize you forgot to put the engines and such in first.' The perspiration was still building on Taylor's forehead and Bowater wondered if he was feverish. His casual act was taking it out of him.

'How did you manage—' Bowater was cut short by a booming voice just outside his door. His heart sank as he heard Mississippi Mike Sullivan shouting, 'You

279

doin good work, boys, damn good work! Y'all keep her up, now!'

Sullivan flung open the door, his massive frame filling the space. Like Taylor, he had a cigar clenched in his teeth. Unlike Taylor, who hobbled sick and wounded, Sullivan was a typhoon, as always. 'Cap'n Bowater! What the hell you doin to that fine ship? I told you ya needs ventilation in this part of the world! Now if you go and put planks on the whole damned thing, she's gonna be hot as Beelzebub's barbecue down below. Next thing you gonna do some damn fool thing like coverin her up with iron plating!'

'Fear not, Sullivan, I think she is in little danger of being plated with iron anytime soon.'

'I'm happy to hear that! Now, Captain, it occurred to me, you ain't got what I would call an ideal situation, your men housed all over the damn town. You know how sailors can be, let 'em run wild like that. Just look at ol Hieronymus Taylor, here. One night on the town and he looks like somethin the devil brought in in his carpetbag. So I thought I could do you a friendly turn, let your boys bunk on board the *General Page*. Plenty of room, good quarters. Keep 'em all together. Free of charge. What do ya say?' Sullivan withdrew his cigar and held it in meaty fingers, grinning wide.

'That's very kind of you, Captain, and I certainly would feel better knowing my men were under the vigilant eye of the hardest drinking, hardest driving, most dangerous son of a whore riverboat man on the Western Waters. But I thought the River Defense Fleet was remaining at Fort Pillow, a good hundred miles upriver from here.'

'We go up and down. Here and there. Not a

problem at all, get your boys to work of a morning.'

Bowater nodded. Sullivan was clearly hoping that once Bowater's men were aboard the *Page*, he could begin to incorporate them into his own crew. Give him a month and every one of them would be assigned to the *Page*, and Bowater would have not a man left.

'Unfortunately, Sullivan, since you are an army outfit, and we are navy, I fear the paperwork would be a nightmare.'

'Ah, paperwork, hell, paperwork don't stand no show 'round here. We don't need no paperwork. Just send your boys over.'

'Forgive me, but you know how we professional military types are. Has to be by the book. It's what makes us so damned insufferable. But thanks.'

'You think on her, anyhow.' Sullivan puffed his cigar. 'Say, here's another thing. I seen a notice for some fancy playactors, thought you might be interested. You bein a man of letters and all.' He fished around in the pocket of his sack coat, pulled out a crumbled handbill. 'Here she is.' Sullivan unfolded it, squinted at it.

' "The Theatre Troupe of the South," ' he read, ' "just recently returned from their triumphant tour of England and the Continent of Europe, where they were lauded by the crowned heads for which they performed, are pleased to announce an encore performance of Mr William Shakespeare's *The Tragedy of Hamlet, Prince of Denmark.*" '

Sullivan looked up. 'Now I wasn't so sure about this. This ain't one of them things where they got them fat gals all singin in some foreign language, is it?'

'I don't reckon,' said Taylor. 'Way I hear it, she's a play, just talkin and such, plus a whole deal of sword fightin and double-crossin and murder and the like.'

'Well, hell, that sounds just grand! Cap'n Bowater, you ever heard of this here *Tragedy of Hamlet*?'

'Yes, something, I believe.' He glared at Taylor, wondered what the man knew.

'So what do ya say?' Sullivan asked. 'We should go see this here! Go tonight!'

'I'm not sure,' Bowater said. 'I have an awful lot of work to finish up.'

'You need some diversion, Cap'n,' Taylor said, a smile playing on his lips. 'Been workin too damn hard. We all were kickin out the jams after the battle, an you just carryin on with work, like a busy little beaver.'

'Perhaps. But you, Mr Taylor, are far too ill to attend. I must insist you go immediately back to the hospital and remain there until your strength returns.'

'Maybe tomorrow I will. But now I'm all worked up to see this here play. Heard some good things about it. Wouldn't miss her for worlds.'

'Then she's settled!' Sullivan said. 'The three of us, we're gonna see us some *Hamlet*.'

Sullivan made his exit, stage right, in the same whirlwind of energy in which he had entered. Bowater could hear him in the shipyard, yelling at the men working on the *Tennessee*. He turned and glared at Taylor.

Bowater nodded. 'Funny that an uneducated mudsill like you should recommend *Hamlet*, of all things, for Sullivan to see.'

'Why's that?' Taylor was all innocence, but he

could not keep the devil out of his voice, and the bit of a grin that formed around his cigar.

'It would almost suggest some familiarity with the play, which I would not expect from a simple salt-of-the-earth kind of fellow such as yourself.'

'I done heard of the play before. Always thought it was about a little pig.'

Bowater sighed. 'Taylor, you are a great pretender, but I happen to know the truth of you.'

'That a fact? What would the truth of me be?'

'That you're just acting at being a semiliterate river rat. That you are actually an educated man, a man of arts and letters.'

Taylor continued to grin, but Bowater was sure he saw a hint of uneasiness there. 'Now ain't that the biggest load a crap I ever heard. You tell me, Cap'n, if that was true, why would a fellow with an education pretend to be a low-down dirty pecker-wood like me?'

'That is a good question,' Bowater said. 'That is one hell of a good question.'

CHAPTER 19

HORATIO: . . . *So shall you hear*
Of carnal, bloody, and unnatural acts,
Of accidental judgments, casual slaughters,
Of deaths put on by cunning and forced cause,
And, in this upshot, purposes mistook
Fallen on the inventors' needs.

Shakespeare, *Hamlet,*
Act V, Scene 2

Samuel Bowater had seen his share of theaters and opera houses. During fourteen years as an officer in the United States Navy, on the European Station, the Mediterranean Station, and the South American Station, Bowater had indulged in some of the finest performances, in the most sumptuous theaters, that the civilized world had to offer. The opportunity to see such performances, along with the chance to take in the museums of England and the Continent, the Sistine Chapel, Venice, Florence, the Parthenon, all the glory that was Greece and the grandeur that was Rome, were the singular benefits of belonging to a service that offered little chance of promotion, and even less of action.

As far as his own country was concerned, his notion of a theater was the stately, elegant, but not ostentatious Charleston Theater on Meeting Street in his native Charleston, South Carolina.

Along with the Charleston Theater, Charleston was home to the Dock Street Theater, or was until it burned down. The Dock Street Theater was believed by many to be the first theater built specifically for the purpose in the United States. When the Dock Street burned, any number of other theaters – houses of culture, venues for the great works – sprang up to take its place. Fire and decay had claimed most of them. But the Charleston Theater still stood as a monument to Southern culture.

That was, to Bowater's thinking, further proof that Charleston was indeed the hub of all that was worthy and good in both the Confederate States and the United States, and that the farther one moved from that shining core of civilization, the more dark and barbaric things became, until, at last, you found your-selves among Mexicans in California.

And so the Tilton Theater of Memphis, a good six hundred miles distant from Charleston on a rhumb line, nearly a third of the way to California, was about what Bowater expected. With its peculiar smell and peeling flocked wallpaper, dirty, cramped box office, worn carpet in the lobby, and pools of an unidentified viscous substance on the floors to which his shoes stuck, it was a place best suited to minstrel shows or burlesque. Bowater imagined its boards saw more of that sort of thing than they did the Bard.

With some apprehension Bowater accompanied Mississippi Mike Sullivan through the lobby and into the house. The theater was crowded, a rough-looking bunch, and Bowater wondered if they knew what kind of entertainment was in store for them.

Sullivan moved like a *Wabash*-class frigate through the crowd, shouldering it aside, and Bowater followed along in his wake. Behind Bowater, Hieronymus Taylor thumped after them, panting in his effort to keep up.

Sullivan did not stop until he was at the front row, where he found three seats together, once he had ejected two people who were already there. He was grinning widely, enjoying himself. Having discovered the pleasures of being a man of letters, Mississippi Mike was now eager to scarf down the other fruits of civilization.

'Here, right up front, where we can see this *Hamlet* good and proper,' he announced, and Bowater and Taylor took their seats. Taylor pulled a handkerchief from his pocket, wiped his forehead. He looked pale and his hand shook.

'Now, Sullivan,' Bowater explained, 'you should understand, with Shakespeare, sometimes the language can be a little hard to follow.' Bowater's chief hope was that Shakespeare's language would be so foreign to Sullivan that he would not notice the striking similarities between *Hamlet* and the plot of *Mississippi Mike, Melancholy Prince of the River,* that Bowater had been feeding him.

'Aw, hell, Cap'n, language ain't no problem. You should hear how some a these dumb-asses along the river talks. If I can understand them ignorant cusses, reckon I'll have no problem with this here burlesque.'

Bowater was going to point out that *Hamlet* was not exactly burlesque, but he realized that any interpretation was possible with the Theatre Troupe of the South, so he kept his mouth shut.

They were ten minutes in restless anticipation before the house lights dimmed and the footlights came up and the sentinels Bernardo and Francisco came from stage right and left. They were wearing costumes reminiscent of Roman soldiers, which Bowater guessed were left over from an Easter pageant. Horatio and Marcellus soon joined them onstage, and hard on their heels, and moving like a somnambulist, the ghost of Hamlet's father.

The white greasepaint on his face made him look like the inverse of a minstrel, and it occurred to Bowater that it would have been funny to cast a black man in the role, for just that reason. A black man in whiteface. But clearly the Theatre Troupe saw nothing amusing in their production of *Hamlet*.

Mississippi Mike jabbed Bowater in the ribs. 'You was right, about the ghost,' he said in a loud whisper.

'What?'

'About the ghost. You said folks loves to see ghosts in things, and I reckon you was right. See, they got a ghost too.'

The ghost drifted around the stage, wide-eyed, looking more confused than vengeful, and then drifted off at the sound of a stagehand doing a rooster call, stage right.

Claudius, Polonius, Laertes, Gertrude, and Hamlet came and went upon the stage. Mississippi Mike squinted up at them, shook his head every once in a while, trying to follow the story line. Hamlet, with great moans of dismay, sawing the air with his arms, expressed the wish that his too, too solid flesh would melt, and Bowater wished it would too, and soon. He

287

decided that the Theatre Troupe of the South was creating as grand a parody of *Hamlet* as Mississippi Mike's.

From back in the darkened house came a low buzz from the audience, a general restlessness, the occasional loud voice or shout of derision. As Bowater had guessed, the entertainment was not what that crowd had expected. The mood was growing volatile as it dawned on the audience that the play contained no burlesque and that the next act would not be a minstrel show, just more of the same, men in stockings and big hats.

Horatio entered, stage left, and said, 'Hail to your lordship,' to which Hamlet, exhausted from his ennui, said, 'I am glad to see you well, Horatio! or I do forget myself.'

Mississippi Mike's elbow struck again. 'They gots a Horatio too, 'cept he ain't a darky. I guess when you come up with some good ideas like we done, you ain't gonna be the only one's gonna think of it.'

'No doubt. It wouldn't surprise me if there were even more things in common with our book. It's perfectly normal.'

Mike listened for a minute more, then asked, 'What in hell are they all talkin about?'

'I'm not sure,' Bowater said. 'Something about a king.'

Mississippi Mike nodded and turned his big face back to the stage. He squinted and shook his head through the next few scenes, and Bowater was beginning to think the big man might just sit through the whole show and never have a notion of what was taking place on stage.

It was around Act I, Scene 5 that things began to

go sour. Bowater, finding the ghost no longer amusing, stole a glance at Sullivan as Sullivan stared and
frowned at the stage. Sullivan turned and looked at
Bowater, too fast for Bowater to avert his eyes, and
Sullivan said, 'If I ain't mistaken, that there ghost was
goin on about some murder and poison and some
such, and I could just swear I heard somethin about
incest and marryin a queen what was that Hamlet's
mother. You thinkin the same as I'm thinkin?'

'I am thinking nothing,' Bowater assured him.

'Hmm. All right, you just let me do the thinkin,
then.'

Sullivan turned back to the play, and Bowater could
see he was judging it in a different light now,
scrutinizing it for similarities to his own literary
efforts. He heard Taylor whisper, 'So how you likin
her so far, Sullivan?' and Sullivan say, 'I ain't sure,
Chief, I ain't so sure.'

Act I gave way to Act II and Rosencrantz and
Guildenstern made their appearance. Sullivan shifted
uncomfortably, frowned, opened his mouth to speak
but closed it before he did. Act III rolled around and
Bowater was not certain he could stomach much
more of the Theatre Troupe of the South, but he was
kept firm in his seat by Mississippi Mike Sullivan, who
looked more and more as if he was about to explode.
Hamlet ran his sword through a hidden Polonius and
Mike turned to Bowater and said, 'Goddamn! Do
you see what's goin on here?' He did not whisper.

'There do seem to be some similarities, but you
know, Sullivan, there are classic plots that are often
resurrected—'

'Classic, my Royal Bengal.' He turned back to the
stage, just as Claudius was instructing Rosencrantz

289

and Guildenstern to escort Hamlet to England, and that was the last straw. Sullivan leaped to his feet, pointed an accusatory finger at the stage, shouted, 'You dirty dogs! Where the hell you get your hands on that? You answer me!'

The confusion on Hamlet's face was well worth the price of admission. The generally loquacious Dane was at a loss for words. His mouth opened and closed like a dying fish.

'You give me some answers, now!' Sullivan advanced on the stage. Bowater glanced over and met Taylor's eyes and Taylor smiled as if this were the most amusing thing he had ever seen, which it might have been.

Bowater leaped to his feet. 'Sullivan, let's forget this and—'

'Forget it? Forget it, hell!' Sullivan roared. 'It's your damned ideas they's stealin, Cap'n, and I won't stand fer it!'

Someone farther back in the house, lost in the dark, shouted, 'Sit down, you dumb bastard, and shut your trap!'

'I'll shut *your* trap for you!' Sullivan shouted back.

The shouter replied, 'I'd truly like to see you try!' but Sullivan was not paying attention to him. In a surprisingly graceful leap he mounted the stage and advanced on Hamlet, grabbing him by the big round frilly collar around his neck and jerking him close. 'You got yer hands on my book, you dirty lyin dog, and I want to know how!'

'Sullivan, get the hell down here!' Bowater shouted, but his voice was lost in the chorus of boos and shouts from the already restless audience.

'I swear,' Sullivan said, drawing back a fist, 'I'm

gonna beat your brains out if you don't start talkin.'

Hamlet held up his hands to ward off the blow, shook his head in silent pleading. Bowater wondered if the Theatre Troupe of the South had received such treatment at the hands of the crowned heads of Europe. Most likely, if the crowned heads were at all discriminating.

'Get off the stage, you fat ox!' shouted a man just behind Bowater.

Hieronymus Taylor turned on him. Taylor was on his feet, as were most of the audience now. 'You want him off, you go get him off!' Taylor shouted. 'If you got the grit!'

'Grit? I'll show you grit!' The man bounded over the seats and clambered up onstage. The friends he left behind urged him on as if he were a fighting cock in a ring.

Bowater glared at Taylor. 'Just tryin to be helpful,' the engineer said, grinning.

'You're going to see the result of your helpfulness here any second!' The mood was ugly, explosive, the audience filling the dark theater with taunts, curses, orders for Sullivan to get the hell offstage. The cast of the play had spilled out from behind the curtain, but now they were backing away as they gauged the atmosphere in the place.

The man from behind Bowater gained the stage and charged at Sullivan and Sullivan punched him in the face with his right hand even as he maintained his grip on Hamlet's frilly collar with the left. The man hit the stage and his friends howled and jeered. He bounded up and flung himself at Sullivan again.

Bowater sensed a shifting in the crowd, the mob closing in, pulled by the action on the stage, which they were enjoying much more than they had the previous performance.

Sullivan let go of Hamlet, who quickly retreated, stage right, and turned to the man flailing him with his fists. The attacker was sinewy and tough, but a fraction of Sullivan's size. Sullivan grabbed him by the crotch with one hand, the shirt collar with the other, and with apparently little difficulty hoisted him aloft, charged for the edge of the stage, and flung him clean over Bowater's head and into the outraged faces of his cronies.

That was the moment when the whole place erupted. Like an army crazed for blood and ordered to charge, the audience swept forward, climbing over seats, charging down the aisles. Bowater raced to the stage with Taylor thumping after him. They turned, backs to the raised platform, ready to meet the onslaught.

One of the men from the seats behind them charged and Taylor caught him in the midriff with his crutch and doubled him up, then dropped him with a roundhouse. Bowater ducked a wild swing, shoved the man back, thought, *We're dead men . . . two hundred against three . . .*

From behind and up onstage came a wild shout, a kind of prolonged crazy yelp, a hair-raising battle cry, and three hundred pounds of Mississippi Mike Sullivan sailed overhead as he flung himself bodily onto the massed and charging crowd. A dozen men went down with Sullivan on top of them, a heap of flailing arms and legs, flying slouch hats, and cracked boots kicking the air and one another.

Bowater took a painful punch in the chest but managed to work an elbow to his assailant's jaw before the follow-up landed.

Taylor wielded his crutch like a quarterstaff and his expression was maniacal. 'Come on, come on, you bastards!' he shouted to the crowd at large, jabbing and swinging, felling a teamster with a blow to the side of the head, taking a fist in the jaw. Grinning and cursing, he worked the crutch with surprising efficiency, deflecting arms and legs, striking with quick jabs and sweeping blows.

Sullivan was roaring like a bull, knocking men right and left, but even as he shouted Bowater could see the smile working on his face.

There were knots of fighting men all over the theater, and Bowater realized as he fended off a punch with his left, jabbed with his right, that it was not hundreds against three, it was a free-for-all, all hands in, a chance to settle old scores or beat up on someone new or just release some tension in a debauchery of violence.

He saw someone balance on the back of a chair, above the mob, then launch himself into the air. He hit Sullivan square in the chest, and the two went down in a heap, taking half a dozen with them. To his right Bowater heard a strangled voice. 'You . . . son . . . of . . . a . . .'

He turned. Some scraggly-looking peckerwood had climbed up on the stage, got an arm around Taylor's neck, was choking the life out of him, even as he tried to fend off all comers with his crutch.

'Damn you!' Bowater vaulted up onstage, the tails of his gray frock coat swirling around his legs. The man choking Taylor was kneeling down, and Bowater gave him a brogan in the ribs that sent him sprawling. Upstage he could see Claudius and Laertes kicking the hell out of Hamlet, who lay curled on the boards

293

with his arms over his head, while Gertrude screamed at them to stop.

Bowater was wondering if he should interfere, for the sake of art, or let them go for the same reason, when he was hit with a flying tackle, waist high, and went down hard on the stage. He kicked his way free, taking several blows as he did, sent his unknown assailant flying with a well-placed foot to the chest.

The shouting seemed to build, there was a new quality to it, and Bowater looked out toward the house but he could see nothing beyond the footlights. He could hear feet pounding, men running in or out or both. He heard the word 'Cops!' shouted above the tumult, and then there was someone else trying to take a jab at him and he could think of nothing but self-defense.

He was a dirty-looking fellow with only a few teeth, and they were not much to talk about, a slouch hat that had somehow remained on his head, filthy dungarees. He was small and scrappy, looked mean. He caught Bowater in the stomach and doubled him up. Bowater crossed his forearms in front of his face and they caught the uppercut that he knew was coming. The arms saved Bowater's teeth, but still the force of the blow flung him to the stage.

He rolled stage right. The man kicked at where he had been but his foot found only air. Bowater kicked out at the leg he stood on and dropped him like a bail of cotton.

At his right hand, Bowater saw a sword – Claudius's sword, by the looks of it, which must have been ripped from the actor's belt. He wrapped his fingers around the grip, flicked his wrist, and the scabbard flew off, revealing a dull, tarnished, rust-splotched blade, but a blade nonetheless.

Bowater scrambled to his feet, came on guard just as his attacker was ready to charge. The man stopped, eyes on the still-sharp point that hovered inches from his face. The man grinned and drew a bowie knife a foot and a half long, with a hand guard, like the men aboard the *General Page* carried.

'Is there some reason you feel the need to fight me?' Bowater asked. 'Isn't this a bit absurd?'

The man shrugged, as if the question were too weighty, and lunged with the knife. But there was no way he was getting past Bowater's defense, because now they were fighting in the manner to which Bowater was born.

He parried, knocked the big knife aside, brought the blade up so the assailant, wide-eyed, was staring at the point mere inches from his throat. Bowater need only straighten his arm and the man was dead.

The man backed away, took a new grip on the bowie knife, tried to see how he could get past that snakelike blade. Shoes pounded across the stage but Bowater did not dare take his eyes from the man. And then a voice shouted, 'Put up your weapons, put them up! That's a police order!'

Without even a beat the man with the bowie knife turned and fled backstage, a blue-clad officer chasing behind. Bowater tossed the sword to the stage and it clattered at the feet of another policeman, who was pointing a gun at him. The policeman looked him up and down and said, in a tone of pure contempt, 'Look at you, an officer, brawling like a regular plug-ugly. You should be ashamed.'

CHAPTER 20

I have also desired Captain Lee to abandon the navy yard ... destroying, if practicable, what he can not save. I beg that the Virginia *may cover these operations ...*

General Joseph E. Johnston
to Flag officer JOSIAH Tattnall

They stepped tentatively through the iron gates of the shipyard, Wendy leading, Molly following. They entered the way one might enter a stranger's house where the front door was left open. Wendy's first impulse was to call out 'Hallo?' but she resisted, understanding that that was absurd.

They walked farther in, over gray cobblestones flecked with black soot. Molly said nothing, but she followed now without being begged or pulled along, and Wendy hoped some of the shock of Newcomb's assault was dissipating, that her aunt's senses were returning.

They could feel the heat of the flames, though the nearest burning building was several hundred yards away. The fires rose three and four stories high, brilliant even in the direct sun, and in the heart of the flames, black and half caved in, Wendy could just make out the huge A-frame ship houses, the buildings that housed ropewalks and storehouses and the various shops.

One year and twenty days before, the retreating Yankees had set fire to the shipyard in what the Confederacy regarded as an unprecedented act of vandalism. Now the retreating Confederates had done the same.

'Dear God . . .' Wendy said, looking wide-eyed at the destruction. Molly said nothing. They walked on, walked toward the only part of the shipyard where there were no burning buildings, the wide area where the dry dock opened onto the river, the only direction in which they did not meet a wall of flames.

'Molly, they might have sailed,' Wendy said, hoping to dull the blow to Molly if the fleet had gone, if Tucker had abandoned them. But her voice did not carry over the low-pitched furnace-roar of the flames, a dull, constant, near-deafening growl, punctuated with cracks and snaps and the shudder of something big collapsing in the inferno. Wendy shouted, 'They might have sailed without us!'

Molly nodded but said nothing, and Wendy was not certain she heard, or if she understood.

They plunged deeper into the dockyard. They were surrounded by burning buildings now, to the right and left, the closest less than fifty yards away. The heat was sharp on Wendy's hands and face; the black smoke rolled around them, engulfing them and then lifting on the breeze to give them a moment's fresh air before falling on them again. They coughed and staggered on.

Wendy wondered if she had made a mistake, if she

should not have tried to lead them across the burning yard. Surely the men who had fired the buildings were long gone. She felt the near approach of panic, wished above all things that there were someone to whom she could defer. She did not want to make these decisions. But there was only Molly, and Molly was like a sleep-walker now.

Wendy turned and looked back, wondering if they should go back the way they had come, leave the yard through the main gate before the flames closed around them and blocked that route. But she could no longer see the gate or the low brick wall that surrounded the shipyard. It was lost in the smoke and clouds of ash, in the orange and red flames. She was no longer certain of what direction they would walk to find the gate. *Press on,* she thought. What more could they do?

Then through the roar of the flames came an explosion, deafening even through the layers of noise, jarring like thunder right overhead. The ground trembled beneath their feet, and to their left one of the massive walls of flame lifted off, flame shooting skyward like a giant cannon pointed straight up.

Wendy staggered and dropped to the ground, pulling Molly down with her. She lay with her cheek pressed to the hot stone, hands clapped over her head. Debris fell around them, bits of flaming wood bouncing on the ground like rain. Wendy felt some-thing hit her back, like a punch, but a weak punch. She looked up. A brass doorknob lay beside her, dented and smoking, rolling back and forth in a semicircle.

She glanced over at Molly. A shattered bit of lathe, burning like kindling, was lying across her back and the skirts of her dress. Her skirts were on fire, and in the heat and the noise and the shock Molly did not even know it.

'Oh! Aunt!' Wendy shouted. She pushed herself onto her knees, began beating Molly's skirt with her hand, then snatched up her carpetbag and began beating the cloth with that until it was extinguished. Where the flowing skirts had been there was now a great charred hole, through which Wendy could see Molly's chemise, dotted with black holes of various sizes, and through the larger holes, her bare legs.

Wendy struggled to her feet, checked Molly's dress to make certain the fire was out, then offered her aunt a hand. Molly took it and Wendy pulled her to her feet.

'Must have been a powder store,' Wendy shouted. They looked around. There were flaming bits everywhere, most small but some the size of desks. Two of them actually were desks, or what was left of them. They had been lucky to have been hit by nothing worse than doorknobs and lathe. Wendy did not think they would be lucky again.

Together they turned and looked back the way they had come. The smoke was thicker now, the direction of the gate even more uncertain. 'Let's go on,' Wendy said. The words came out with more resignation in her voice than determination.

They collected their bags and staggered on through the smoke, through the heat that now felt like a thing of substance, like a massive tangle of spiderwebs through which they had to fight their way. Wendy's head was swimming and she was coughing uncontrollably, holding her handkerchief to her mouth, but it seemed to do no good. She stumbled, recovered before she fell. Her eyes ached and tears streamed down her cheeks. She thought her sleeve was on fire and she batted at it, but it was only the heat from the flames.

She began to wonder if they would wander through that hellish place until they were overcome by smoke, if the flames would sweep over their unconscious bodies and reduce them to ash and smoke and extinguish everything that they were. No one would ever know what had become of them.

Then, as if stepping from one world into another, they were past the nightmare of flames and smoke. Before them, through clear air, lay the Elizabeth River. It was wondrous, like a miracle, like how it must be to die in violence and awake in heaven. They were upwind of the burning buildings now, and the wind that just a moment before had held them engulfed in smoke and killing heat now kept them free of it.

Molly looked at Wendy and Wendy at Molly. Molly's face was smudged black, with whitish lines running down her cheeks where tears had carried the soot away. Even through the soot Wendy could see the awful bruises on her face, the dried blood, the swelling around her eye. Her hat was gone and her snood half off, so her long blond hair hung partway down her back, while the other half remained contained. Her eyes were red, her dress flecked with black soot and charred, torn, and burned through. Molly looked bad, and Wendy knew she did not look much better.

'We've reached the promised land,' Wendy said, but Molly did not respond.

In her relief at being free from the smoke and

flames, Wendy had lost sight of why they were there, and it was only after she had sated herself with fresh air that she remembered. Tucker had promised them passage out of there, a place aboard a Confederate ship bound upriver to Richmond, ahead of the invading Yankees. They were here to catch a boat. But there were no boats to be seen.

'Damn it,' Wendy said softly. She walked fast toward the dry dock, where the USS *Merrimack* had become the CSS *Virginia*. At the edge of the river she stopped and looked right and left, south to the end of the shipyard where the brick wall ended at the water's edge, north to where the dockyard ended in a mountain of flame that was once a ship house. Nothing.

'Oh, damn it!' Wendy shouted now and flung her carpetbag to the ground. For Molly's sake she was trying to be optimistic, but she was running short. She wanted to scream. She wanted to cry. She wanted to shoot someone – Newcomb, Tucker, Abraham Lincoln – some damn one whose death would give vent to her rage.

She turned to Molly. Looked for something there, anything, a suggestion, some encouragement. But Molly was sitting on one of the low capstans alongside the dry dock and staring out over the water toward Norfolk to the east. No emotion registered on her face or in her eyes. It was a blank, dead stare, the look of someone waiting her turn at the gallows. She said nothing.

Wendy felt the tears welling up, overflowing, running down her cheeks. After all this, all the hell they had endured, and now they were left behind by the man who had promised to save them, a man of supposed honor, who had abandoned them.

They could not go back through the flames, and the river in front of them was impassable. There was nothing now but to wait for the Yankees, wait to be taken up as spies and hanged. The Yankees would find Newcomb's body, and if she and Molly were not hanged for spies then they certainly would be hanged as murderers. All their efforts had done nothing but make their situation worse.

Wendy swore, clenched her fists, let the tears come. And that was when she saw the boat.

It was not a boat like a tugboat or a gunboat, but a boat like the kind carried on board a ship, the kind of boat that plied between ship and shore, ubiquitous and unremarkable. About twenty feet long, wide and deep, painted a smudged and dirty white with dark blue trim along the gunnel, it floated against the seawall, tied fore and aft to bollards on the shore.

Wendy could see only a part of it, but, intrigued, she left her aunt and walked to the edge of the seawall and looked down. There were several inches of water in the bottom, but that did not seem very unusual – Wendy had seen supposedly seaworthy boats with more. The oars were there, and the thole pins to hold them in place, and lying across the thwarts, long canvas-wrapped poles. There did not seem to be anything particularly wrong with the boat. Inadvertently left behind, Wendy guessed, in the frantic rush to abandon the place.

'Aunt, Aunt, see here!' she called excitedly, waving Molly over. Molly turned her head and looked, but she did not stand.

'Look, Molly, a boat! We can go after Tucker and the others with the boat.' Molly's eyes flickered down to the seawall, then back up at Wendy. She made no response.

Wendy was not deterred, because here was a tiny flash of hope in the darkness. They could do this, the two of them, they could get in the boat and row it away to where the Confederate fleet had disappeared. Hell, they could row all the way to Richmond if need be.

Wendy grabbed up their bags and dropped them down into the boat where they landed with a small splash in the bottom. She was making the decisions now for the both of them, but she told herself that was all right, she was doing the right thing.

'Come on, Aunt Molly,' Wendy said. She stepped over to the capstan and held out her hand. Molly looked at her for a second, the dull, dead look, then reached out and took the offered hand, let Wendy pull her to her feet. Together, hand in hand, they walked over to the seawall. The boat was a few feet below the edge of the stone wall.

'Here, Molly, just sit on the edge of the wall and you should be able to slide down into the boat. Here, let me help.' Wendy eased her aunt down until Molly was sitting on the edge of the wall, legs dangling down. Slowly she slid forward, her feet searching for the thwarts, until they found something solid and she slid the rest of the way. She stood on the thwart, then, wordless, turned and sat.

Wendy followed, sliding into the boat in the same manner. She cast off the lines holding the boat against the seawall and gave a strong push. The boat bobbed and moved slowly out into the stream until at last there were twenty feet of water between them and the shore.

She looked back at the shipyard, the buildings in flames, the great column of smoke. On the edge of the seawall was something bright and red and Wendy realized it was Molly's reticule. They had left it behind.

Damn. She was sorry to lose the pepperbox, but there was nothing for it now. There was no going back.

Motionless, exhausted, Wendy watched the seawall slip by as the river slowly swept the boat along. She stared at the wall for a full minute before it occurred to her that the boat was moving upstream, heading away from, rather than toward, Hampton Roads and the Confederate fleet.

She frowned, looked around as if she might see what was causing this phenomenon. How could they drift upstream? And then she thought, *The tide!* The tide, she concluded, must be flooding, rushing in with enough force to make the Elizabeth River run backward.

'Aunt, we have to row now,' Wendy said. She struggled with one of the long oars lying across the thwarts. It was terribly heavy and awkward, and she was just able to wrestle it over the side of the boat and between the two thole pins, the way she had seen sailors do it. Balanced there, it was not too bad.

She turned to Molly. Her aunt had not moved. She just stared aft, and Wendy felt the tears of frustration coming. 'Oh, Molly, please, please, you have to row with me!' she pleaded.

Molly turned her head slowly and looked at Wendy, and Wendy said, 'Please, Molly, I know it is horrible what you have suffered, but if you don't row now, then we'll both die. Please, Molly . . .'

A tear rolled down Molly's cheek, a single tear, glinting in the sun. Then Molly leaned forward and picked up an oar and she too wrestled it over the side of the boat and between the thwarts.

The tears were still running down Wendy's cheeks, but she smiled. 'Good, Molly, that's good. Now, together, let's pull.'

They leaned forward, pushing the looms of the oars forward and down, then they brought the blades down until they felt them bite water, then leaned back, fighting the resistance. The boat slewed around a bit, its drifting slowed. Forward, oars down and then back, they pulled again, and this time the boat made headway against the flooding tide. Then once more, together, they pulled.

Roger Newcomb thought he was dead.

He lay there, motionless, eyes closed, but aware, conscious, alert. His head pounded as if it were being physically hammered, his body ached all over, his mind was a turmoil, a nightmare chaos of rage and fear and half-remembered violence. The only clear, rational thought that managed to work itself through that jumble was that he was dead, and suffering the torments of hell. It was the only thing that made sense.

He did not move and did not try to move. He just lay there, eyes closed, but the longer he lay, the more his thoughts began to organize themselves and the more he began to suspect that he was actually still alive. Nonetheless, it was some time before he dared open his eyes, mostly for fear of what doing so might reveal.

At last he did it. Slowly, both eyes together. The

pain in his head redoubled. He blinked but kept his eyes open, trying to puzzle out what he was looking at.

Not hell, he did not think. Whiteness. A white field. He looked at it for a full minute. *Ceiling ... I'm looking at a ceiling ...*

He allowed his head to loll over to one side and he saw crown molding and the top of a wall. Farther, and he looked directly at a window with the sunlight streaming in, and he groaned and shut his eyes and let the pounding settle.

I am not dead. .... He lay there with that new understanding, and slowly it came back. Hunting down the bitch spy, holding her until the Union troops could arrive, confronting her with her mendacity. He remembered the rage. He remembered what he had done and he was glad of it. But he did not remember anything else. He did not know how he had come to be lying on the floor.

He wondered if the women were still there. For all he knew they were sitting right behind him, ready to kill him. He wondered if the Union forces had arrived yet. His pants were around his knees. *God, they can't find me like this.* It was just how that bitch had threatened to leave him. He was beginning to panic.

With a deep moan he opened his eyes and sat up, pushing himself up slowly, inch by agonizing inch. When he was sitting up he stopped and waited for the pain to settle some, then slowly, torturously, he stood.

He was alone in the room. He did not know where the women were, but they were not here. There were blood splatters all over the carpet, and his .36 Colt lay at his feet. Slowly, carefully, trying not to fall or pass out, he pulled up his pants and buttoned them. He turned around. The body of the secesh officer he had shot lay by the piano. His eyes moved to the mantel over the fireplace. The clock said 11:10. He had been out for hours. His face felt sticky and encrusted.

He took a faltering step toward the door and the shattered remnants of the mirror that was mounted there. He peered into a jagged shard of glass still hanging in the frame, but he did not recognize at first the terrible image that looked back. Smeared with dried and crusted blood, hair standing up and sticking out at odd angles, eyes bloodshot red.

He reached a tentative hand up and probed at his scalp. He could feel a ridge of torn skin, hard with dried blood. An image swam in his head of that other woman aiming his gun at him. Had she shot him? The bullet must have grazed his scalp, knocked him senseless. Blood had poured from the head wound. They must have left him for dead.

But he was not dead. He was alive and he could feel his strength returning, and with it a renewed sense of purpose, and a newfound fear.

It had set in only a few moments after he let them board the Norwegian ship. *What have I done? What sort of a coward am I?*

He fended off the tentative inquiries of Master's Mate Pembrook. *Sir, are you quite certain everything is all right? Sir, are you sure that was the President's orders?* But he was not certain that Pembrook was mollified. There was no telling what that little bastard would do, to whom he would talk, and what he would say.

Cathy! Oh, God! They had met at an officers' ball at Fortress Monroe soon after the fall of Fort Sumter.

She was so beautiful, the center of attention, and she had picked him to escort her! She had lived in Portsmouth, but since the horrible Rebels had taken the place, she was afraid to remain. Or so she told him. Even told him which street she lived on, and he had never forgotten it.

Beautiful, intelligent, vivacious. Insatiably curious about the United States Navy. She had a thousand questions and he, fool that he was, had answered them all, had shown her lists of the fleet dispositions, extolled the virtues of this secret plan, the shortcomings of that.

Oh, he had impressed her, all right, with his encyclopedic knowledge. Knowledge that he had labored so intently to acquire, that he might impress his superiors, only to give it away to a damned secesh spy!

Cathy Luce! They had seen one another for five months, on and off, and Newcomb had been ready with a marriage proposal when suddenly, one day, she was not there anymore. He had been frantic, heartsick, confused, but he had his duty, and that took precedence over everything, even love. He was never able to find out what had become of her.

And now he knew. Now he knew it was all a lie, even her name, and he knew he had to stop her. He had packed his haversack, dressed in civilian clothes, told Pembrook he had secret orders from Admiral Goldsborough himself. *Tell no one of my absence, do you understand?* He had the boat land him at night north of Portsmouth.

He wondered how many other Union officers there were who had willingly told her every military secret they held, in order to get a kiss on a front porch. Or more. She had allowed him a few liberties. He wondered what she might have done for a captain, or an admiral.

The thought made the pressure rise again, like a boiler pushed well beyond its limits. He knew what she was now. Passion, honor, and duty all demanded the same action. Take her. Bring her in. Expose her. See her hung.

The Union troops were slated to land at Willoughby's Point at ten o'clock and now it was 11:15 and they would be there soon. Before, he had looked forward to their arrival, eagerly anticipated handing over the assassin to General Wool and accepting the thanks and accolades of both the army and navy, not to mention that of the President of the United States. There would be no talk of desertion.

But now? He had nothing. He was out of uniform, behind enemy lines, gone from his post without permission.

God, what if they find me like this? He pulled his eyes from the horrible sight in the mirror, looked around the room. On the floor, lying amid a scattering of its own broken parts, lay his pocket watch. He walked over slowly, stooped, and picked up the remains. The hands had stopped at 9:34, which must have been when the bitch had crushed it.

'Goddamn her . . .' Newcomb spoke aloud for the first time since coming to. The sound of his voice seemed to make everything more real and more urgent. He had to get out of that house. He had to do something. When the Union troops found him, he had to have some reason for being where he was, doing what he was doing.

He slipped the remains of his watch into his vest

pocket. On the fainting couch, where he had left it, he found his haversack. He pulled it open, peered inside. Telescope, loaf of bread, coil of half-inch rope, cartridges and percussion caps, some gold coins, his small Bible, it was all there, all the things he had packed for his mission.

He slung the haversack over his shoulder, picked up his pistol, and headed for the door. The bright sunlight was agony on his head and made his eyes water but he did not slow as he walked down the path to the picket fence and the road. He stepped out into the street. There was nothing going on, nothing moving, as if the town were holding its breath, waiting for the invaders to do what they would.

Newcomb looked around. To the south he could see a great column of smoke rising black above the roofs of the houses and he wondered if Union troops were burning property as they took it. It took him a moment to orient himself, a moment to realize that he was looking in the direction of the Gosport Naval Shipyard.

'Oh, those bastards,' he said. The secesh must have torched the place before abandoning it. 'Oh, those vandalous bastards.'

He wondered if there was anything he might do to save the yard. Judging from the smoke, the fire was pretty well established and covered a lot of ground. But perhaps there was something he might do, something of importance he might save. If they found him there, when they came, heroically fighting the flames to save something vital for the Union, then perhaps there would not be so many awkward questions, even if he did not have the secesh spy in his custody.

He started to walk and then he started to run.

Soon he could see the low brick wall that surrounded the shipyard, a place he knew well from its time as a United States Navy facility. He was nearly to the gate when it occurred to him that perhaps it was not yet abandoned, that he might be running right into a trap.

He slowed to a walk, approached the gate carefully. He stopped at the edge of the wall, peered around it. The gate was hanging open, no guards. He stepped around the corner of the wall. No one inside the yard that he could see. It looked entirely abandoned, the only movement the waving and leaping of the fires that were still consuming the buildings scattered around the yard.

Newcomb stepped through the gate, moving cautiously, looking around for secesh, and for some opportunity, something he might do.

He was too late, as far as he could see. Half the buildings had collapsed into charred rubble, and those that had not were too far gone to be saved. Not that he alone could have done anything in any event.

He walked on. Through the smoke he could catch glimpses of the river, and that made him think of the dry dock. When the navy had abandoned the shipyard the year before they had mined the dock and tried to blow it to kingdom come. If they had succeeded, then the Rebs would never have been able to bring that Frankenstein's monster *Merrimack* back to life. Newcomb wondered if perhaps the Rebs had also mined the dry dock, to deny it to the Union.

He began to run, despite the agony in his head from each jarring footfall. If he could prevent the dry dock from being destroyed he would be a hero for certain. As he raced through the smoke he decided that even if the dock was not mined, he would try to round up barrels of powder and mine it himself, just so he could be discovered in the act of saving it.

He broke through the curtain of black smoke, out into the open place where the cobbled dockyard ran down to the river, with the dry dock just ahead. He hurried on, hoping against hope that the secesh had filled the thing with gunpowder.

He was near the edge of the dry dock when he saw a red bag of some sort lying on the ground. A reticule. He knelt beside it, reached out a hand and lifted it. It was heavy. He looked inside. Half covered by a handkerchief he could see the pepperbox pistol.

Newcomb looked up, looked around. He was the only human being in the dockyard, that he could see. On a bollard nearby he could see dock fasts for a ship's boat trailing over the edge of the seawall. He squinted upriver. He forgot entirely about the dry dock.

CHAPTER ONE

The enemy's boats above Fort Pillow are now moored in narrow channels behind sand bars, where we can not attack them again, but we will wait and watch for another opportunity.
Brigadier General M. Jeff Thompson
to General G. T. Beauregard

Samuel Bowater walked stiffly uphill to the hospital. He was sore in several places from the beating he had taken at the Tilton Theater, the most violent theater-going experience of his life.

In performances past, when the final curtain fell on *The Tragedy of Hamlet,* it had been the stage that was littered with bodies, while the audience remained largely intact. But that wasn't how it played out in Memphis.

After the police managed to bring the brawling to a stop, and the only ones left in the theater were those who had not tried to run, or could not, Bowater had looked out over a scene much like the aftermath of battle. Men were sprawled on the floor or draped over seats or leaning against walls nursing wounds.

313

Mississippi Mike Sullivan had a cut lip and a laceration over his eye that had smeared his face with blood and made his grin look even more maniacal. Bowater found Taylor propped up against the stage. He was sweating, barely conscious. His frock coat was torn and his hands were bloody, but the splint on his leg seemed to have held. His crutch was broken in two, and he still clutched the short end in his hand.

The police had tried to arrest Bowater and Sullivan and Taylor, but Bowater would have none of it. Instead, he ordered the police officers to fetch a litter and take Taylor to a hospital. And because Bowater was a Confederate officer, and because he was so well practiced at issuing orders in a voice that did not admit of argument, and because he approached the situation with an entirely unfeigned attitude of moral, social, and military superiority, the police officers obeyed. They called him 'sir.' They did not mention arresting him a second time.

Once Bowater had Taylor secured in the hospital with another healthy dose of laudanum in his stomach, he staggered back to his hotel, stumbled into his room. He picked up the bottle of merlot that his father had sent, pulled the cork, and slugged it right out of the bottle. He drained it, and did not even care that he had degenerated to the point where he could do such a thing. To complete his descent into barbarism, he wiped his mouth on his sleeve, then shuffled out of his frock coat and let it fall to the floor.

The next morning, aching, sore, he crawled out of bed. He did not bother going to the shipyard. He could not endure it. Instead he went to check on Taylor. It was not at all unheard of that someone should die from a broken bone, especially someone who had behaved as stupidly as Taylor. He wondered, as he humped his weary body uphill, what he would find.

He found the chief engineer asleep and looking bad, damned bad. His face had a grayish pallor, his eyes had dark circles around them. There was a sheen of perspiration on his skin. Bowater did not wake him, but sought out his doctor to get the prognosis.

The doctor frowned and shrugged his shoulders. 'Fifty-fifty chance that the fever will break, and there's no mortification. That's if he stays put. He wanders off again and starts brawling, he's a dead man for certain.'

Bowater returned to the engineer's bed, and now Taylor was stirring. He looked up at Bowater through half-closed lids and managed a weak smile. 'Cap'n . . . you gettin to be quite a hand at brawlin . . . make a river rat outta you . . .'

'My highest ambition.'

They remained silent for a moment. Taylor closed his eyes and Bowater thought he was asleep again, but a moment later Taylor said, 'I know that performance weren't worth horseshit, but why'd Sullivan git s'all-fired mad?'

'I don't know.'

Another long silence, and then Taylor said, 'Well, it made fer a pleasant evenin, anyhow.'

Bowater did not respond, and soon Taylor was breathing deeply and rhythmically, so Bowater walked silently away. He paused just inside the front door, stared out through the heavy glass, tried to make up his mind what to do.

Duty called him to the shipyard, but only because

that was where his men and ship were. There was no work for him to do, not while the men were laboring under Shirley's frantic oversight. And for all their hard work, neither he nor Shirley nor any of the men really believed they would get the ship finished. But of course they could not say that, and they could not give up trying. He found the whole thing so futile and depressing, he did not think he could drag himself down to the yard.

Coming up the walkway he saw Mississippi Mike Sullivan, stepping quickly, his lips pursed so Bowater guessed he was whistling, though he could not hear. Sullivan held something shaped very much like a whiskey jug in a crocker sack, a weak attempt at discretion. As usual, Sullivan did not look much worse for the beating he'd taken the night before. His lip was swollen with a nasty cut, and the gash over his eye was now a jagged line of dried blood, but beyond that he seemed quite robust.

That clay-eating peckerwood, Bowater thought.

Sullivan did not see Bowater there as he burst through the door and strode across the tiled floor, and Bowater considered letting him go. He was never enthusiastic for Sullivan's company, even less so at that moment, with the blue devils tormenting him. But neither did he care to allow Sullivan to continue his recruitment efforts.

'Sullivan!' he called out, and Mississippi Mike whirled, paused, stammered, a guilty stammer.

'Damn, Brother Bowater! How the hell are you?'

'Fine, fine. What have you there?'

'Oh, this?' Sullivan looked at the burlap-wrapped jug as if he were surprised to see it. 'Medicine, Cap'n, medicine for our beat-up engineer.'

316

'My engineer, Sullivan. Not "our" engineer.'

'Did I say "our"? Well, of course, the man's like a brother to me, always was. Known each other better'n ten years now.'

'In any event, Chief Taylor is sound asleep and he needs to stay that way. The doctor said something about having to keep him from drinking himself to death.'

'Doctor, hell . . . This here's the finest Tennessee corn red-eye, aged in tin buckets fer the time it takes to get her from the still to the jug. Ain't nothin sets a man up better.'

'An absolute panacea, I'm sure. Now let's get out of here before the contents of that jug explodes and kills us all.' Bowater half led, half pushed Mississippi Mike out the door and down the path.

'It's a fortunate thing, Cap'n, I ran into you,' Sullivan said. 'I was gonna hunt you down, after I gave old Taylor the cure. I'm headin upriver on a little scoutin expedition, reckoned you might want to come along.'

'I think not.'

'Aw, hell, Cap'n, what better thing you got to do? Sit on your ass an watch yer men work? You ain't no shipwright. Ol' Shirley's got them at it, and he'll keep 'em at it.'

'Still, I cannot leave my command.'

'Look here, Cap'n. Whole reason you're workin so damn hard is to get your ship ready to fight them Yankees. Am I right? You know you're gonna have to fight 'em. So what's a better way to spend yer time betwixt now and then, watchin a bunch of pecker-woods plank a boat up, or steamin upriver and seein what the enemy's fixin to do?'

Bowater frowned. *Damn Sullivan and his damned backwood, white-trash logic*. There was an ulterior motive here, Bowater was certain of it. Sullivan had all but finished his draft of *Mississippi Mike, Melancholy Prince of the River*. Bowater suspected that Sullivan wanted to trap him on board the *General Page* for the hundred miles between Memphis and Fort Pillow so that they could put the finishing touches on the book.

'Very well,' Bowater said, sighing as he spoke. Sullivan was not wrong, it would be a great help to get a sense of the enemy's force and disposition, and it was true that there was little he could do in Memphis. He had already come to that conclusion.

He could put up with Sullivan, he could put up with the damned penny dreadful, if it would get him closer to the enemy and allow him to feel, just a bit, that he was actually doing something of worth.

Wendy and Molly Atkins sat on the boat's thwarts and pulled oar for as long as they were physically able. They worked the long looms fore and aft until their muscles burned with the effort, until their palms were slick with blood from hands rubbed raw, until their throats were parched. It was a big boat and would have been a handful for two experienced seamen to row. For the women, unused to such labor and unfamiliar with the art of rowing, it was torment.

It took ten minutes just to establish a rhythm, so that they were able to pull together and make the boat move forward, and not jerk side to side as first one, then the other, pulled her oar. They had managed to leave the Gosport Naval Shipyard astern, but just barely. They could still see it.

An hour of rowing, and then for the eighth time Wendy crabbed her oar – failed to raise it high enough on the forward sweep, so the blade caught the water and was pinned back against the boat – and she could do no more. She slumped forward on the handle of the oar, buried her head in her arms, let her aching hands dangle. 'Forgive me, Aunt, but I must rest,' she muttered, eyes closed, face toward the bottom of the boat.

Molly said nothing. After a moment Wendy looked up. Molly was staring south, toward the navy yard, but now her face showed something more than just apathy and despondence. There was something else there. A spark. And if she was still not the Molly Atkins of yesterday, neither was she the nearly dead thing that Wendy had pulled from the house.

Molly shifted her eyes from the shipyard and met Wendy's. 'I think I saw an anchor,' she said. She pulled her oar in, laid it on the thwarts, and climbed forward. The tide was carrying them upriver again, sweeping them back over the distance they had so laboriously covered.

Wendy half turned to see what Molly was doing. Her aunt had found an anchor, like a small grappling hook, up in the bow. She threw it over, let the thin anchor line run through her hands. She took a turn around a cleat, the line came taut, and the boat snubbed to a stop.

'There,' Molly said. 'Now we can pause to think, without having all our labor undone by the tide.' The punishing work at the oars seemed to have done much to restore her.

The wind was steady from the west. Wendy turned her face into it, let the cool breeze sweep over her flushed skin. 'The tide has to turn sometime,' she suggested.

'Humph,' Molly said. 'Yes, well, it had better hurry the hell up. The Yankees'll add murder to our list of crimes, if they catch us.'

'They cannot catch us. We must get clear of here.'

They were quiet for a moment, then Molly said, 'Goddamn that John Tucker and his goddamned promises! Where the hell was he? How could he leave us?'

Wendy let the question pass. She was looking at a wooden bucket stuck under the stern sheets, a thing she had not noticed before. It had a checked cloth over it that looked very much like a napkin. With some effort she pulled her oar in and laid it on the thwarts, then stood awkwardly, her legs protesting after being cramped in a sitting position and subjected to the effort of rowing.

The heavy boat was stable enough for her to stand with confidence. She made her way aft, picked up the bucket, and looked inside. She saw four fresh ship's biscuits, a chunk of ham, two apples, a knife, and a folded paper. She unfolded the paper, read the note.

'Molly, listen to this!' she said, then read out loud.

Dear Molly,

I write this note in haste. We have been ordered to sail immediately. The yard is already burning, and the fires spreading fast. Lt. Batchelor has not returned and I have made every effort to await your return, but I can delay no longer. I will leave you this boat with food and water aboard. You will not be able to row it, I do not think, but the sailing rig is complete and you are a resourceful woman. We are ordered up the James River, look for us there.

Godspeed,
Cpt. Jn. Tucker

Molly looked down at the poles and folded canvas that lay across the thwarts. 'Sailing rig,' she muttered. 'Of course, that is what it is . . .'

Wendy was too busy tearing off a chunk of bread and attacking the ham with the knife to look at the mast and sail. She stuffed her mouth full, struggling to chew. She recalled her manners, cut a more sensible piece for Molly, and handed it over.

The two women, famished, sat on the thwarts and ate in silence, bobbing on the Elizabeth River. Upstream of them, the black columns of smoke from the burning yard rolled away to the east, partially obscuring the town of Norfolk off their starboard side. But overhead the skies were blue, the day warm, and the water just slightly ruffled by the wind. The weather seemed too pleasant for their world to be collapsing around them.

They ate all there was to eat and found the water butt and drank and then Wendy stood. 'Very well, let us get the mast stepped and the sail set.'

Molly looked up at her as if she were speaking nonsense. 'Stepped?'

'That is what you call putting a mast in place.'

'Did you learn all this from your sailor boy?'

Wendy flushed, waiting for some ribald comment to follow, but Molly said no more. 'I have read stories of the sea since I was a girl,' Wendy said, 'and have picked up a thing or two.'

Her tone was more confident than she was. She had never actually sailed a boat herself, and had only been aboard small boats under sail three or four times. As she unfolded the canvas and looked with dismay at the tangle of ropes and the various varnished spars, she chastised herself for having reveled in the beauty and romance of the thing without paying strict attention to how it was done.

'Well, the longest one must be the mast,' she said. She looked around. There was a hole through one of the thwarts and a block of wood with a matching hole in the bottom of the boat. 'And this must be where it goes,' she added. 'Here, Aunt, bear a hand.'

The mast had been laid down in the proper orientation for stepping, which Wendy thought was fortunate until it occurred to her that it was probably put like that on purpose. They maneuvered the heel of the mast in place, and then hauling, straining, cursing, they lifted the pole, eighteen feet long, and worked the heel into the hole. At last the mast came straight up and then dropped in place with a thump that made the boat quiver underfoot.

Wendy looked up with satisfaction. They had 'stepped the mast,' a thing she had often read about and now had accomplished. But that was only part of the job. There were half a dozen or so lines coming down from the masthead and pooling at her feet. She pulled them apart, followed them up the pole with her eyes, trying to divine their purpose.

'This one' – she gave it a little tug – 'raises the sail. I forget what it is called. Here, hold this.' She handed the line to Molly. 'These' – she untwisted the lines; they ran from the top of the mast, with a small block and tackle at the lower end – 'are . . .' She was not certain.

The lower block had a hook on it. *All right . . . the hook must go somewhere . . .*

She looked around. On the outboard edge of the thwart aft of the one through which the mast stepped were eyebolts, port and starboard, that looked very much as if they would accept the hooks, so Wendy tried one.

'Oh!' The lines were some kind of rigging to support the mast. She pulled on the end of the rope and hauled the line taut. And there, as further proof of the correctness of her hypothesis, was a cleat on which to make the line fast. She set up the other supporting rope on the starboard side. She looked up. All the lines were now accounted for.

'I think that is it, Aunt!' Wendy smiled. 'Let's hoist the sail now.'

The line that Molly held ran from her hand, up through a hole in the mast and down again. It was attached to a light gaff to which the head of the sail was laced. Wendy stepped around until she and Molly were side by side. She reached up and took hold of the rope and together they pulled. The gaff and sail lifted off the thwart. They pulled again and again. The sail unfolded, fluttered in the breeze as they pulled it up.

The manila line was agony on blistered and bleeding hands, but they hauled together, and soon the gaff was as high as it would go. The boat began to heel to starboard and the foot of the sail flogged gently in the breeze.

'We have to pull up the anchor,' Molly said, as much a question as a statement. They went forward and tugged on the anchor line, but they could not move it. They could not pull against the pressure of the wind and the tide on the boat. The anchor line was like a solid thing.

'Just untie it and let it go,' Wendy said. 'Wait for my word.' She went aft, sat on the stern sheets, and took the tiller. She held it amidships. It was the third time in her life she had held a boat's tiller, having been allowed brief and closely supervised turns at steering on two of her previous outings.

'All right, untie it!' she called. Molly unwrapped the line from the cleat. It leaped from her hands, spun overboard, and suddenly the boat was free, swinging away to starboard, lively with motion. Wendy pushed the tiller to starboard to bring the boat back on course. It turned, farther and farther, and the sail began to flap, so she turned it the other way.

Steer small, steer small . . . That was what she had been told, over and over, but she had been too proud to ask what the hell that meant. At last, in context, it had made sense, and that was when she really began to get a feel for the boat. And that was when she had been made to relinquish the tiller.

So now she concentrated on steering small and on how the sail was setting. It looked right, except that the bottom corner nearest her was too far out. 'Molly, could you pull on this rope.' Wendy pointed with her left hand. 'I think the sail is too loose.'

Molly worked her way aft. The rope ran through a block on the lower corner of the sail and then back into the boat. Molly pulled and the corner of the sail came more inboard and Wendy made the line fast on a cleat. The boat heeled farther over and a gurgling sound came from its waterline as it raced along. The wind blew fresh on Wendy's face and she could see the shoreline moving swiftly past. And for all the horror of the past twenty-four hours, she was thrilled.

CHAPTER 22

*The abandonment of the peninsula will, of course,
involve the loss of all our batteries on the north
shore of James River. The effect of this upon our
holding Norfolk and our ships you will readily
perceive. Captain Tucker's command covers our
right flank. I am much pleased with his
intelligence and zeal.*

General Joseph E. Johnston
to Flag officer Josiah Tattnall

Flag Officer Josiah Tattnall stared through field
glasses at the absence of a flag.

He stood just aft of the low conical pilothouse at
the forward end of CSS *Virginia*'s ironclad casemate.
The gentle westerly wind ruffled his thick white hair,
made the tails of his gray frock coat tap against his
legs. The heavy ship hardly moved at all, even as it
tugged on its moorings off Sewell's Point. It felt
more like standing on a rock than any vessel Tattnall
had ever been aboard.

But at that moment, Tattnall's focus was on shore.
He was examining the Confederate batteries on

Sewell's Point. There was no flag.

Tattnall lowered the glasses, rubbed his tired eyes. He raised the field glasses again, this time swept them along the earthen redoubts. No guards paced with glinting bayonets, no men lounged on the thick walls, no Negroes filled sandbags. No one. Deserted. By the looks of it, the battery was abandoned.

'Sir, you called for me?' The voice of Flag Lieutenant John Pembroke Jones.

'Yes, Lieutenant, yes. Here, have a look. Is it my tired old eyes, or is there no flag flying at Sewell's Point battery?'

Jones took the field glasses and studied the fortifications, which just the day before had been pounded by Union ships, including the *Monitor*. 'I do not believe there is a flag flying, sir,' he said at last. 'I can't see a soul stirring there.'

Tattnall frowned. *Damn Huger was supposed to notify me if he was abandoning his position* . . . The *Virginia* had been kept at Sewell's Point to protect Norfolk from the Union Navy, and she had been damned effective in that job. Every time she showed up, the Yankees skedaddled. She had fired only one shot since the great battle with *Monitor*, and that had been a parting shot in disgust at the Union fleet that would not close and fight. She was the undisputed queen of Hampton Roads.

But if the Yankees took Norfolk and Portsmouth, and once again had possession of the naval yard, then *Virginia*'s position there was untenable. She ate coal at a prodigious rate, and her engines were too unreliable for her to be without a dockyard nearby.

But where would he go? There was no ship afloat with guns heavy enough to penetrate *Virginia*'s ironclad hide, but Tattnall was not so certain about the big guns at Fortress Monroe. He was not enthusiastic about steaming past that place during the daylight hours, through tricky shallows and the crossfire of Monroe and the Rip Raps, and the pilots would not take her through at night.

Richmond was where the *Virginia* belonged, up the James River to the capital, fight the Yankees as they tried to use their gunboats to cover McClellan's flanks. But the James River was tricky, and shallow, and *Virginia* was clumsy and deep.

Tattnall took the field glasses back from Jones, trained them to the south, toward Craney Island. The island was four miles away, but he thought he could make out the Stars and Bars still flying in the breeze. Jones's considerably younger eyes confirmed it.

'Lieutenant, take a boat down to Craney Island and see what's happening there. We have to know if the Yankees have landed, and what Huger is doing with his damned army.'

'Aye, aye, sir!' Jones saluted.

'And send up Parrish and Wright.'

'Parrish and Wright, aye, sir.' The lieutenant disappeared down the hatch, and Tattnall was able to enjoy the agreeable quiet once again. From inside the casemate he could hear a dull pounding, someone fixing something, it never stopped. At the far end of the hurricane deck a gang of sailors were overhauling boat falls. But where he stood, it was quiet. Hard to believe they were surrounded on all sides by warring parties, great armies struggling over the fate of two nations.

Tattnall frowned and paced.

'Sir?' It was the pilot, Mr Parrish, and his chief

assistant, Wright. Tattnall did not care for them, did not think them bold enough in assuming risk. *Virginia* was a man-of-war, she could not be safe all the time. But that was the nature of the breed, with pilots.

'Mr Wright. It appears the battery at Sewell's Point has been abandoned. If the Yankees take Norfolk we will have to sail up the James River to Richmond. I wish to confirm with you that we can do so.' They had been over this before. But Tattnall had to know that it could be done.

'Well, sir,' Parrish said patiently, 'we can get her to within forty miles of Richmond. If the ship can be lightened to a draft of eighteen feet.'

Tattnall nodded. *Virginia* drew twenty-two feet. To raise her by four feet would require throwing nearly everything overboard, save guns and powder. It would raise the iron shield out of the water and expose her vulnerable wooden hull. It would render her indefensible. But it would be worth it, to get her upriver. If he could not do that, then he would blast his way into the Union fleet, rip them apart until he was run down by Yankee rams, until the ironclad sank under him with guns blazing and flags flying. That was how a ship like *Virginia*, and an old sailor like Josiah Tattnall, should die.

'Very well,' Tattnall said. His eyes were following Jones's boat, which was just leaving *Virginia*'s side, heading southwest toward Craney Island. Four men were pulling oars, two were stepping the mast amidships. Jones sat in the stern sheets, a hand on the tiller.

Suddenly, Tattnall felt very unwell. His stomach churned. A headache was building like storm clouds.

'Thank you, pilot,' he said and Parrish and Wright disappeared. Tattnall leaned heavily on the rail that ran around the hurricane deck. *I am old*, he thought, *old, old, old*.

Roger Newcomb tried to see upriver through the drifting smoke of the navy yard. He stood near the end of the great granite dry dock, coughing, wiping his eyes, trying to focus his telescope on the northern reaches of the Elizabeth River.

There was no telling how far ahead those two bitches were. They might have left two hours before him, or twenty minutes. They might be alone in a skiff, or they might be in a longboat with twenty secesh sailors. He just did not know.

He snapped the telescope shut – useless thing – and cursed out loud. There was only one thing he knew with certainty, and that was that he had to follow them, and run them to ground before they could reach the protective arms of the Confederacy. He needed a boat.

That realization spurred him. He put the telescope back in the haversack and began to work his way north across the navy yard, but he was met with fire that made the way impassable, or with the charred remains of buildings, a few blackened brick walls standing here and there, empty window casements like eye sockets in skulls. It was pointless. Anything worth having there had been taken by the secesh or burned in their wake. He would not find a boat.

Cursing, he ran back across the navy yard, through the smoke and the heat, out the iron gate in the low brick wall. The streets were deserted, the people either hiding or fled. He raced for the north end of the shipyard and the docks he knew lined the waterfront.

His head was a riot of pain, made worse with each footfall, and that only fueled his fury. He had been shot with his own gun, he knew it, but he would not let the words form in his head because the humiliation was too great. Instead he focused on the treachery, the lies, the unfathomable viciousness of that bitch. Both of them. Because the dark-haired one was a part of this too, as guilty as the Luce whore.

He came to the north end of the wall, the northern boundary of the shipyard. Beyond that, the town of Portsmouth consisted of wood frame houses and various businesses tucked into red brick buildings. Trolley tracks cut parallel lines down the hard-packed dirt streets.

He crossed the road at an angle, heading for the water. With the breeze blowing the smoke from the burning yard off toward Norfolk, he could smell the fish and coal dust and brackish mud flats of the waterfront.

A Negro in a big slouch hat stepped from an alley to Newcomb's left. Newcomb rested a wary hand on the butt of his gun, but the man stopped short twenty feet away. Their eyes met, and the black man took a step back, his face registering fear and revulsion. He turned and fled back the way he had come.

Stupid nigger, what got into him? Newcomb thought as he hurried on. Then he recalled his own reflection in the mirror, the crusted blood, the hair wild and matted. He was a frightening thing to look at.

The waterfront consisted of wharf after wooden wharf, stretching north along the Elizabeth River and

331

piled with barrels and bales of sundry goods, cotton and hay and straw. Rising above them was a tangle of masts and smokestacks like a forest in winter – seagoing ships and brigs and schooners, fishing smacks, tugs, packet boats. They were all tied up and seemingly abandoned in the panicked town.

Newcomb paused, let his breath settle, looked around. There was nothing moving on the river. He waited for a minute, then another, to be certain he was not being watched. He took a step toward the docks, then stopped.

The river was not entirely deserted. He could see a boat now, about two hundred yards away, and coming up from somewhere downriver. The boat was driven by a dipping lug sail, a crew of seamen leaning on the weather rail to steady it. It had to be a man-of-war's boat, it could be nothing else.

Newcomb sucked in his breath. He felt the sweat stand out on his forehead, though he was not certain why. *Is it them?* If so, why would they be coming upriver? They should be heading to Richmond, or to hell, or wherever secesh trash went.

He pulled his telescope and focused it on the boat. Six men that he could see. They seemed to be wearing the bibbed frocks of navy men, but there was no uniformity, and that, to Newcomb, meant Rebel. He swept the glass aft to the officer in the stern sheets. His coat might have been faded blue, but Newcomb did not think so. More likely the gray of the Confederate Navy.

Newcomb felt a tremor in his stomach, felt an impulse to run inland and hide. He lowered the glass, took a step back.

Wait, wait, wait, he thought. *I'm a civilian, aren't*

I? Nothing about him indicated that he was a Union naval officer. That fact might get him hung as a spy if the secesh caught him, but it also meant that the men in the boat, even if they did pay any attention to him, would not see him for what he was.

He lifted the glass again, pretended that he was entirely calm, and watched the boat approach. *All right, if they land anywhere near here I'll hide*, he decided at last, but the boat made no move to approach, and soon Newcomb realized they must be heading for the navy yard.

All right, all right, what does this tell me? The Federal forces have not yet taken Norfolk, or those bastards would not dare come sailing upriver like it was a holiday. Whoever those Rebs are, they do not know the yard is abandoned. Damned secesh, just what you'd expect . . . left hand doesn't know what the right is doing . . .

He continued to watch as the boat swept by, making good time with the sail set and the tide flooding. None of the boat crew even looked in his direction. Finally it was lost from sight behind a warehouse upriver of where Newcomb stood.

I need a boat . . .

He needed to find a boat that he could handle by himself. A fast boat, one that could outsail the Rebel boat that had just passed him, in case it came to that.

Through the maze of rigging and spars he saw a single thin mast, no more than twenty feet high. It looked like a possibility. He walked out along the wooden wharf to which it was tied.

The boat floated four feet below the level of the wharf, a long, lean thing, ketch rigged. It was what the people of the Chesapeake called a log canoe, with a hull that looked for all the world as if it were planked up, but was in fact burned and carved from a few big logs fastened together. They were generally used in the oyster fishery, as apparently this one was, judging from the dried mud, broken shells, and dark pool of fetid bilgewater in the bottom.

But that did not matter. The boat was simple to sail and fast and that made it ideal. Newcomb looked around to see if the owners were near, but the only people he could see were a hundred yards away and paying no attention to him. He climbed down into the boat, lowered the centerboard, cast off the dock fasts, and pushed away from the wharf.

He raised the jib and then the mainsail, which was an odd-looking thing. It had no gaff, but rather a triangular head and a loose foot, rather like the jib. The clew was cut off and a short spar was laced there and the sheet attached to that.

The sails flogged as they went up and the boat began to drift downwind. Newcomb took his place at the tiller, leading the sheets aft. He hauled both sheets taut, the sails hardened up, and the boat began to gather way, heeling over and moving so nimbly that Newcomb sucked in his breath in surprise. He rounded up a bit to slow her down, then fell off the wind, letting the lean boat gather way. In less than a minute he was cleaving the small chop at four knots, the tiller firm and responsive in his hand.

Soon the town of Portsmouth dropped away and the river opened up before him. He turned the bow more northerly. The quick and weatherly log canoe pointed so high he thought he might well fetch Hampton Roads on that one tack. Newcomb was well versed in small boat handling, had sailed nearly every kind of rig imaginable, but he could not recall any boat so nimble and fast.

He kept to the center of the river, well away from the tricky mud banks, equidistant from Portsmouth to the west and Norfolk to the east, since he did not know who was in control of either town. He scanned them with his telescope as best he could, but the glass revealed nothing beyond the fact that they both seemed deserted, that virtually no one and no vessels were moving along the waterfront.

The town of Norfolk yielded to the brown fields and clumps of trees to the north, and Newcomb had to tack once to stand more into the center of the river, then again to return to his northerly course. The low western shoreline dropped away where the southern and western branches of the river met, and four miles downriver the great expanse of Hampton Roads and the mouth of the James River opened up before him.

He picked up his telescope, twisted around, and looked astern. Nothing. Just empty river and a shoreline crowded with idle shipping. He looked forward, his pulse quickening. He made himself be calm, be methodical. Swept the glass west to east.

There was a boat. It was under sail, about a mile or so ahead. It was on a starboard tack, sailing roughly southwest, but as Newcomb watched, it turned up into the wind, tacking around. It seemed to stall, sail flogging, caught in irons for a moment. It was too far to see what was happening, but whoever was sailing the boat was apparently no expert.

Newcomb's hands were trembling. He was grinding his teeth together and he made himself stop.

You bitch . . .

CHAPTER 23

HAMLET: O it offends me to the soul to hear a robustious periwig-pated fellow tear a passion to tatters, to very rags, to split the ears of the groundlings, who for the most part are capable of nothing but inexplicable dumb-shows and noise.

Shakespeare, *Hamlet*,
Act III, Scene 2

Mississippi Mike steadfastly refused to allow his literary *doppelgänger* to die at the end of the book.

'I admire the knife fight, an the poison an all that,' he said to Bowater, sitting on the edge of a frail-looking chair in his cabin aboard the *General Joseph Page*. 'I surely do. But it don't make no sense to have Mike kilt off, an this the first book we done.' He stood, made an expansive gesture. 'Hell, Cap'n, when this here book goes like hotcakes, I reckon me an you'll be writin two, three of 'em a year, minny-mum! Can't kill the damned golden goose right off.'

'Very well.' It was pointless to argue. On artistic

grounds, Bowater could generally sway Sullivan to his way of thinking, but this was a commercial consideration, and Mike was intransigent. 'Let's see what we have.'

Sullivan sat again. Bowater picked up the manuscript and read. The fight scene, the very end of their opus.

Mike's ol pard Larry took a lucky stab at Mike with his big ol bowie nife and he cut him a good one, right acrost the arm, and Mike bled jest like a pigll do when his throtes cut.

'Tere warnt no call to do that,' Mike sed an he dropt his nife an put his hand over where he was cut. 'Warnt no call at all,' he sed an now he was getin some angry an he hit Larry right square in the jaw an hit him so hard ol Larry fell right down flat an dropped his nife to.

'Yer my meat now, Mississippi Mike,' Larry sed and gabbed up a nife but he grabed Mississippi Mike's nife by accident and Mike picked up Larrys nife. They went at her like a couple of ol bucks in ruttin season and next thing Mike cuts Larry a good one.

Jest then Mike's ma fell right out of her chair. 'Oh, Mike, they done poisoned me, I knows it!' she called and then she died, right then and there.

'Poisoned? What all's goin on here?' Mike demanded.

'Reckon Im done fer now, Mike,' Larry said, 'Same as you. On account of that nifes got poison on her. Same poison done fer yer ma.'

Mississippi Mike jest nodded his worried hed but he didnt say nothin on account of he knew there warnt no poison could kill him.

Bowater nodded his approval as he read. 'This is excellent, Sullivan,' he said and looked up at Mike's beaming face. 'You just wrote this?'

'Wrote her up last night. I'm awful careful now about who I lets see that. Keep her under lock and key when I ain't actually in my cabin. I don't know how them actor sons of bitches got their hands on her, but I got my ideas.' He leaned closer, said in a stage whisper, 'I reckon it's that little weasel Guthrie, down ta the engine room. He's got it in fer me, has fer a long damn time. I jest got plumb full up of his lazy damned careless ways and I started tellin him what's what and he don't care fer it. Damn engineers. Damn the whole breed of cat.'

Bowater raised the glass of brandy that Sullivan had provided. 'I'll second that.' Finally, he and Mississippi Mike had found common ground.

If there was one good thing about Spence Guthrie, the nervous, rodentlike malcontent in the Page's engine room, it was that he made Hieronymus Taylor seem like a reasonable and cooperative individual.

No sooner had Bowater and Sullivan come aboard than Guthrie had started in: the coal's no good, the new firemen didn't know their business, the condenser's shot and no spare parts to be had. 'Whole damn walking beam's shifting around, the bearings's so worn. I been with whores didn't move as much as that fucking walking beam.' All in that shrill voice, on and on, until even Bowater wanted to strangle him.

Not even Mississippi Mike Sullivan deserved Spence Guthrie.

They had got under way around noon, after listening to Guthrie explain why the boilers would probably blow up and kill them all, jest because some goddamn people think a damned army riverboat's their own private yacht, jest run her up and down the damn river hows'ever they please, an never mind about the engine room, they'll do jest fine on their own, thank you please, jest there to serve the lords and masters in the ruttin pilothouse anyhow . . .

Later, after their literary *salon*, during which they finalized the climactic end of *Mississippi Mike, Melancholy Prince of the River*, Sullivan relieved Tarbox in the wheelhouse for the evening watch and Bowater found a dark place on the fantail and sat. He watched the moonlit banks and the scattered lights on shore slip past, listened to the slap of the paddle-wheel buckets, the creak of the walking beam overhead, let his mind go away, far and away.

He wondered where Wendy was. The news he was getting from Norfolk was not good. With McClellan on the Peninsula, Norfolk could not stand for long. The shipyard would be lost, and Wendy, if she did not escape, would be in enemy-held territory. She would be behind the lines, and he would not see her again until the war was over, and he no longer believed that it would be over soon.

So Wendy Atkins was yet another thing that the Yankees had taken from him.

'No, no,' he said out loud. She would not allow herself to be trapped that way. She would get out, somehow, before the Yankees arrived. She and that aunt of hers, who seemed a resourceful woman. Off to Culpepper, where the Yankees could not reach her. There would be a letter, any day, he was certain. When he returned to Memphis there would be a letter.

He went to bed, woke to the sound of the anchor chain rattling out the hawsepipe. He stood and scratched, splashed water on his face, dressed, and stumbled out on deck. The sky was just taking on the suggestion of dawn. The earthworks of Fort Pillow loomed over the starboard side, hulking and black, and if Bowater had not seen it several times already he would never have been able to differentiate fort from shoreline.

He could make out a few other boats anchored around, but the majority of the River Defense Fleet was gathered downriver at the little town of Fulton.

One of the *Page*'s deckhands rounded the corner of the boiler deck. He stopped when he saw Bowater, jerked a thumb over his shoulder. 'Sullivan wants ya, ta the larboard gangway. Cap'n,' he growled and then left.

What, no tea and biscuits in bed? Bowater thought. *Reckon that's what passes for a courteous summons in the river-rat vernacular.*

He hit himself on the forehead with the heel of his palm several times, berating himself for even thinking the word *reckon* and trying to drive the vial colloquialism from his mind. That done, he settled his cap on his head, ran fingers through his goatee, and walked around the boiler deck to the steps forward. He took the ladder cautiously down to the main deck and walked around to the larboard gangway.

Mississippi Mike was already there, with four of his crew, the *General Page*'s gig floating alongside.

340

Sullivan held a haversack. It looked like a lady's reticule in his big hand.

'You ready fer a little scoutin, Cap'n?' Sullivan asked, smiling wide.

'I reck—' Bowater closed his eyes, let his irritation settle. 'I imagine so.'

'Good, good. Let's get under way.'

Wordless, the four river men climbed down into the boat and took up the oars. Sullivan climbed into the stern sheets. Bowater followed. Doc arrived at the gangway with two steaming bowls of burgoo and two mugs of coffee. He snarled as he handed them over.

'Thankee, Doc! Shove off!' Sullivan said. The men pushed off, the oars came down. Sullivan worked the tiller with his knee and handed Bowater a bowl and mug. 'Reckon we'll have our breakfast under way, Cap'n, if'n that's agreeable to you.'

'Thank you.' Bowater took the bowl, looked at the sloppy mess, wondered if Doc's resentment ran so deep that he might adulterate the mush in some way. But Sullivan was already shoveling it in, and Bowater, as a career navy man, was no stranger to horrid food.

Anyway, what the hell could he do to it that would make it worse than it is in its natural state? Bowater wondered as he took a spoonful.

It was a lovely morning, quiet and calm, with the promise of a perfect blue sky revealed by the growing light. The quiet dip of the oars was the least intrusive of sounds, and Bowater could hear the rustle of animals along the shore, the shrill and musical cry of birds. Little islands of fog hung over the water in isolated patches of gray. Thankfully, Sullivan kept his mouth shut, and Samuel was able to enjoy the slow, steady pull upriver to where the Yankees lay.

341

Bowater was just letting his mind drift away on the beauty of the place, so serene it seemed otherworldly, when Sullivan said, 'Jest around this here bend, an we'll see the first of them Yankees.'

Bowater was brought back to unpleasant reality. Far from taking an idyllic pull through a newfound Eden, they were rowing right under the guns of a powerful enemy.

That thought raised a few questions.

'Sullivan, are you intending to just row up to them and have a look around?'

Sullivan nodded. 'Pretty much how I see it. They ain't too alert, this time of the mornin. Yankees ain't used ta gittin up with the sun.'

Bowater frowned, scratched his goatee. He was skeptical. 'They could well have a picket boat,' he suggested.

'Doubt it. They had a picket boat, we wouldn'ta caught 'em with their pants down around their ankles at Plum Point, would we?'

Which is exactly why they are more likely to have a picket boat now, Bowater thought, but he kept his mouth shut because he did not want to appear overly cautious. There was his personal dignity at stake, as well as that of the Confederate States Navy.

They came around the bend, keeping close to the eastern shore where the trees cast deep shadows on the water. The sun was well up now, illuminating the western bank in brilliant orange, glinting off the brown water of the rolling Mississippi. And there was the enemy fleet.

The Yankee gunboats were tied to the banks, long and low and rusty brown, lit up bright in the morning sun. Awnings of light gray canvas were stretched over sections of their hurricane decks. Thin curls of black smoke lifted from their smokestacks, indicating banked fires that could be stoked up quickly in case of another Rebel attack.

One, two three, four, Bowater counted, vessels of what the Yankees called the 'City Class,' named for northern river towns. The two that had been sunk during the Battle of Plum Point had not returned. There was a fifth ironclad as well, bigger than the City Class boats, which Bowater imagined was the flagship. They were ugly things, but deadly, built for river fighting.

'Look there, how they got logs around them boats.' Sullivan nodded toward the ironclads. Booms of cyprus logs floated like low bastions around each ship. 'Reckon they don't care to get poked by our rams no more.'

Along with the gunboats, there was a smattering of steamers swinging at their anchors in the stream. Most of them Bowater recognized from the Battle at Plum Point. He had taken care to observe the fleet even as they rammed their way through, had jotted down notes concerning the enemy's strength.

But there were more steamers now, more than he had seen before. Not ironclads, but riverboats, sternwheelers, with the low freeboard and square, bulky deckhouses of their ilk, capped with pilothouses on top of that and sporting tall twin smokestacks at the forward end of the deckhouse. And, curiously, suspended between the smokestacks, each boat had a big cut-out letter – *M, Q, L,* and others – one letter per boat.

'These here boats are new to the fleet,' Sullivan said in a low voice. One of the oars squeaked in the tholes and Bowater wondered if they should not have muffled them. 'Whadda ya make of 'em?'

Bowater looked over the boat nearest them, riding at anchor two hundred feet away. The sides of the deckhouse had been planked over, and bales of cotton were stacked against the forward end to offer the boilers some protection against shot, and he could see where more work was still being done. On her tall wooden paddle-wheel box was painted the name *Monarch*. Between her stacks, the letter M.

Ahh, Bowater thought. When a cloud of gun smoke hung over the water during battle, and only the tall stacks were visible above it, the letters would allow each ship to identify the others of their fleet.

'Rams,' Bowater said. 'They must be rams. They are clearly set up for a fight, but there are no guns at all, no heavy ordnance mounted fore or aft.'

Sullivan nodded. 'Reckon you're right.'

Bowater ran his eyes along the anchored fleet. They would be very effective, if handled right, a seaborne cavalry and just as unstoppable. Then, from the far end of the anchored line, he saw a boat. It came around the stern of a ship sporting the letter Q between her chimneys. It was pulled by a dozen men wearing the white frocks of the United States Navy.

'Boat,' Bowater whispered, forcing the calm in his voice.

'Where?' Sullivan asked.

'Coming around the north end of the line of rams. There.'

The boat had turned bow-on to them, the oars rising and falling with that curious illusion of a rowed vessel seen head-on, as if the oars were simply going up and down and not fore and aft at all, as if the oarsmen were just slapping the water.

'Ah, hell,' Sullivan said. One of the oarsmen spat tobacco over the side, dripping on the gunnel. They pulled on.

Bowater remained silent, waiting for Sullivan to make some move, to issue some order. The Yankee boat was three hundred feet away and closing quickly. Their direct and unwavering approach suggested that they had seen the Rebel intruder.

'Ah, Sullivan . . . I don't wish to impinge on your unique style of command, but hadn't you better do something?'

Mississippi Mike sighed. 'Reckon so,' he said. He reached down into the bottom of the boat, pulled out a five-foot-long pole encased in a canvas sleeve. He pulled the sleeve off to reveal a white flag. He unrolled the flag and held it aloft, waving it slightly to make the cloth flutter in the still air.

Bowater's jaw and stomach dropped together. 'What the hell are you doing?' he hissed.

'Flag of truce,' Sullivan explained.

'Flag of . . . what are . . . are you out of your idiot mind?'

'Naw, naw, Cap'n, we got to go over, talk with these here Yankees.'

'Talk with the . . .'

'Sure. Jest a little par-lay, you know.'

Bowater looked wildly around, a trapped-animal gesture. The picket boat was closing fast. He could see rifles in the hands of the bowman and the officer in the stern sheets.

'What is this?' Bowater demanded, his voice full of accusation. Was Sullivan going over to the Yankees?

345

Bringing a Confederate officer prisoner to sweeten the deal?

'It ain't nothin, Cap'n, we jest need a little help from these fellas. Hell, after all the time you was in the U-nited States Navy, I reckon they figure you fer an honorary Yankee as it is.' Sullivan waved the flag back and forth. 'No offense,' he said.

Bowater was still sputtering when the picket boat came within hail. 'Toss your oars! Toss them! I want to see your goddamned hands!'

'Go ahead, boys,' Sullivan said to the oarsmen, who held their oars straight up. They looked not in the least bit concerned. The long-bearded Mississippian on stroke looked positively bored.

'Toss oars,' the Yankee officer called again and Bowater thought, *They're tossed, you dumb bastard*, and then realized the officer was talking to his own men. The picket boat drifted up alongside. The bowman had exchanged his rifle for a boat hook. He grabbed the gig and pulled the two boats together.

Sullenly, Bowater looked over at the Yankee boat. The men holding their oars straight up wore white cotton shirts with blue bibs across their shoulders and straw hats on their heads, a uniform as familiar to Bowater as anything in his life. The officer in the stern sheets wore a blue frock coat with the shoulder boards and cuff insignia of a lieutenant, identical to the one that he, Bowater, once wore. The rifles pointed at them, five in all, were British .577 Enfields.

'What's this about?' the Yankee officer demanded. He addressed the question to Bowater, naturally, since Bowater was the only uniformed man in the boat, with the insignia of an officer on his coat and hat.

'I have no idea, Lieutenant,' Bowater said. 'Ask the peckerwood with the flag.'

The Yankee's eyebrows came together. He opened his mouth, but Sullivan spoke first. 'Cap'n . . .' Sullivan began.

'Lieutenant,' the Yankee officer replied.

'Pardon. Lieutenant, we've come under flag of truce. Like to have a word with your commandin officer, if it ain't much bother.'

The Yankee officer seemed as stunned and speechless as Samuel Bowater, but he found his voice. 'You were not showing any flag of truce when we spotted you. Don't think you can come spying around here, and then go scot-free with a flag of truce.'

'Now, Lieutenant, you don't have to be like that. Jest want to have a word with whoever you gots in charge here.'

The lieutenant scowled at them. He looked at Bowater but Bowater just shrugged. 'I think we'll let Captain Davis sort this out,' he announced at last. 'You will proceed to the flagship, there' – he pointed over his transom at the larger of the ironclad gun-boats – 'and go aboard. We'll follow directly astern. If you alter course one degree, we'll fire into you.'

'You ain't even gonna offer us no coffee or biscuits? Now that there,' Sullivan addressed his men, 'is Yankee hospitality. Makes a man grateful to be a Southron, don't it? Ship oars! Give way!'

The gig crept past the picket boat and the picket boat turned and followed in her wake and together they pulled for the flagship.

'Sullivan . . . what the hell . . .' was all Bowater managed to get out through his clenched teeth, his jaw tight with rage. It was the coal barge all over

347

again, and once more he had let Sullivan play him for a sucker. But this time, for his stupidity, he would end up in a Yankee prison.

'Don't you fret, Cap'n. Hell, you gonna thank me for this, one day.'

They swept up alongside the flagship where a dozen sailors in white frocks aimed a dozen muskets at them, while a petty officer with a pistol gestured them aboard. They climbed the ladder built into the gunboat's steeply angled side, the iron plating still damp from the morning dew.

Bowater counted five gunports in her broadside, but he could not see the size of the ordnance hauled back into the dark of the interior. His eyes swept the hurricane deck as they stepped off the ladder and under an awning spread from the bow amidships. Two deck howitzers. Despite the anger and uncertainty he could not stop gathering intelligence.

The lieutenant from the picket boat followed behind. 'Mr Grimes,' he addressed the petty officer, 'hold these prisoners here while I see if the captain will see them.'

'Aye, sir,' said Grimes, waving the Confederates amidships.

'Come under a flag of truce! We ain't prisoners!' Sullivan shouted at the lieutenant's back, but the lieutenant did not respond.

'We're whatever the Yankees say we are, you stupid ape,' Bowater said in a loud whisper. 'Prisoners of war, spies, whatever the hell they want.'

'Now don't let the blue devils get ya, Cap'n. They may be Yankees, but they got some civ-li-zation, I'spect. Ain't gonna keep us prisoner when we come under a white flag.'

Bowater folded his arms and glared out over the water, too angry to reply. Soon the lieutenant was back and he ordered Bowater and Sullivan to follow him, with the rest of the crew to remain topside under guard.

They followed him forward and down through a small, square hatch to the gundeck below. It was dark, save for the patches of light that came in through the open gun ports and around the big guns hauled inboard. Bowater, his eyes not accustomed to the dark, could just make out the cavernous space on the beamy vessel, the rows of guns, much like the gundeck of a seagoing man-of-war. Forward, four bow guns leered out over the river. The ordnance seemed to be a mixed batch, thirty-two-pound smoothbores, forty-two-pound rifles, and a few others mixed in. A heterogeneous lot, but a powerful array of weapons.

They did not linger on the gundeck, to Bowater's disappointment. He would have liked to gain as much knowledge as he could about the ironclad, but the lieutenant, wanting no doubt to prevent that exact thing, led them down another ladder to the deck below.

They were under the waterline now, and Bowater imagined they must be very near the bottom of the shallow-draft vessel. They were in an alleyway lined with brightly varnished wood-panel doors. Behind them, a bulkhead separated this living space from the boilers and engine room aft. The space was illuminated by a series of lanterns mounted on the cabin sides.

'This way,' the lieutenant said tersely as he led them forward. He stopped at the penultimate door and knocked.

'Come.' A voice from within.

The lieutenant opened the door, waved his prisoners in, followed, and shut the door behind. They were in a wide cabin, a place that functioned, apparently, as the captain's office, day cabin, and dining room.

Seated behind a desk was a man in shirtsleeves and braces, a man in his mid-fifties or so, thinning dark hair combed over, a dark and very full moustache that covered his upper lip entirely, and a gray beard that ran just along his jawline, leaving his chin oddly exposed. On the desk was a scattering of papers and journals and a plate with remnants of egg and toast. The man leaned back and looked at the Confederates. He did not stand. He did not smile.

'Sir, these are the Rebel spies we apprehended,' the lieutenant announced.

'Spies?' Sullivan began but the officer behind the desk held up his hand and Mississippi Mike fell silent.

For a long and uncomfortable moment the officer just looked at Bowater and Sullivan. His eyes were dark and penetrating, but Bowater met them and did not look away. Finally, the Yankee spoke.

'I am Flag Officer Charles Davis, commanding United States naval forces on western waters.' He leaned forward for emphasis, elbows on his desk. 'Lieutenant Phelps here tells me you were scouting our forces under cover of the shoreline when he apprehended you.' He addressed his words to Bowater.

'We was flyin a flag of truce,' Sullivan began, but Davis held up his hand again.

'I was speaking to the officer,' Davis said. 'As he is in uniform, he is liable to be considered a prisoner of war. As you are not' – he looked at Sullivan for the first time – 'you are liable to be hung as a spy.'

'Oh, hell, Commodore, spy, my Royal Bengal. We come under a flag of truce 'cause we wanted to have a word with you. Got a thing to discuss, goes way beyond this here unfortunate hostility betwixt North and South.'

Davis shifted his gaze to Bowater, and Bowater wondered what in hell he was going to say. He himself had had no intention of approaching under flag of truce, had no idea of what Sullivan was up to. But he couldn't say that, because the flag of truce was the only hope they had to keep out of some stinking Yankee prison.

'My name is Lieutenant Samuel Bowater, Confederate States Navy,' he said, very formal. 'This gentleman is Captain Mike Sullivan' – Bowater came within an inch of saying Mississippi Mike – 'of the River Defense Fleet of the Confederate States Army. They are irregulars with no uniform, but they are legitimate combatants. Captain Sullivan asked me to accompany him on a parlay with the commodore under flag of truce, and I agreed.'

'Parlay? About what?'

Bowater stood for a second. He could not bring himself to say 'I don't know,' which was the only true answer.

Sullivan jumped in. 'Here she is, Captain.' He took a step forward, so that he was leaning over the captain's desk. 'Captain Bowater and me, we're what you might call men of letters. Been writin a book, hell of a book. An now we're done with her, and we have to get her off to New York, on account of that's where all them publisher fellas is.'

Davis's eyes narrowed. 'You . . . wish to send a book to New York?' He looked over at Bowater, but got no help from Bowater's incredulous expression.

'That's right. They's a place called Harper and Brothers, they done a whole mess of books, and we reckon they'd just be eager as can be to get their hands on this one.' He reached into the haversack, which Bowater had not even noticed in Sullivan's hand, and pulled out the familiar sheaf of papers, the manuscript of *Mississippi Mike, Melancholy Prince of the River*. He laid it on the commodore's desk as if it were a holy relic.

Davis looked warily down at it, as if it might not be safe to touch. 'Let me understand you . . . You came to us under flag of truce because you wish me to mail a book to a publisher in New York?'

'That's it exactly, sir,' Sullivan said, straightening and smiling wide. ' 'Cause some things, like art and such, well, they don't know the boundaries of war. Ya understand? Can't let a little thing like this here unpleasantness git in the way of havin lit-rit-ur get to the folks what would appreciate it. And hell, there ain't no other way I'm gonna get this to New York, without I gets a Yankee to send her. Here, I wrote the address down, right there.'

Bowater felt himself flush red. Before, he had been frightened by the possibility of becoming a prisoner of war. Now, he was simply humiliated to have this naval officer regard him as a part of Sullivan's idiocy. He closed his eyes. *Dear God, just let the damn Yankees shoot me, please, just let them shoot me now . . .*

He opened his eyes again. Davis was still staring at the manuscript and shaking his head, just slightly. Finally he looked up and addressed Mississippi Mike.

'You want me to do this thing for you. What do you have to offer me?'

Sullivan, unbidden, grabbed a straight-back chair that stood against the bulkhead, set it close to Davis, and sat. He leaned toward the commodore, spoke in a low voice. 'Reckon I could tell you a thing or two about the force we gots down ta Memphis.'

Bowater stiffened, felt his hands clench. *Sullivan, you traitorous bastard!* The whole manuscript thing was bad enough, but now Sullivan was making him an unwitting partner in treason.

Davis looked Sullivan up and down as if assessing the man, then looked up at Bowater. 'What do you say, Lieutenant?'

'I say . . . and I say this on my honor as a gentleman . . . that everything Captain Sullivan has told you so far is the truth. But I did not know that he intended to trade military secrets in order to get this manuscript posted. I will not be a party to that. Imprison me if you will, I'll not engage in such treachery.'

Davis considered that. 'Well spoken, Lieutenant. Mr Phelps, please see Lieutenant Bowater to the hurricane deck. I'll have a word with Captain Sullivan, here.'

Phelps led Bowater to the hurricane deck. The four men from the *General Page* were sitting, smoking and chewing. One was engaged in conversation with the bluejacket who held a rifle on him. Bowater stood apart, folded his arms, fumed.

The coal barge thing was bad enough, when he had been made a party to theft, but now he was a party to treason.

Never mind my own culpability, he decided. He had

to report Sullivan, had to see him tried and sentenced. Hung, preferably. Such treason could not go unpunished. If that meant that he, Bowater, was cashiered from the service, sent to prison, so be it. It was what honor demanded.

Some time later, Mississippi Mike reappeared on the hurricane deck. He was smiling widely. The haversack was bunched up in his hand. The manuscript was not inside.

'All right, boys, we done what we come to do. Let's git on home.'

The sailors with the rifles looked up at Phelps for instruction. 'Commodore says let the Rebs go,' he said, but the sailors still kept their weapons aimed at the Southrons as they climbed back down into the gig and pulled away.

They rowed in silence, save for Sullivan's soft whistling, which was like a knife working under Bowater's skin. Finally, as the Union fleet disappeared around the bend, Sullivan said, 'Well, Captain Bowater, I reckon that was one successful sum bitch of a mission.'

Bowater glared at him. 'You do, do you? By God, Sullivan, I'll see you hang for that.'

Mike Sullivan laughed, that full body laugh. 'Hell, Cap'n, I brung ya with me so's you could show that fancy uniform to the Yankees, let 'em know we ain't foolin, so's ta help yer own book along, and now you wanna hang me? Hell.' Then, a moment later added, 'Don't you even want to know what I told the commodore?'

Bowater did not reply.

'Figured you did. I told him how at Plum Point they near wrecked half our fleet. Boilers shot out, more'n a hundred men kilt, half them that was left over skedaddled. Most of our River Defense Fleet in a sinkin condition. Told him how the only ironclad we gots down there'll never git finished. Actually, that part's most likely true. Anyway, he bought my stretchers right up, was jest like a little kitty, jest lappin up milk, on account of that's what he wanted to believe.

'So now, when them Yankees do attack, and they will, now they ain't gonna be ready fer what's really waitin for them. An that's jest what I'm gonna tell Cap'n Montgomery when I reports to him.'

Sullivan put a cigar in his grinning mouth. He poked Bowater in the chest with his sausage finger. 'So we got our book off to that there Harper and Brothers in New York, an we got the Yankees all thinkin there ain't no threat to them, downriver. Now ain't that some good trick, Cap'n?'

Bowater glared at the finger and then up at Sullivan. 'Go to hell,' was all he said.

CHAPTER 24

*On returning to the ship, he [Lieutenant Jones]
found that Craney Island and all the other
batteries on the river had been abandoned. . . .
[T]his unexpected information rendered prompt
measures necessary for the safety of the* Virginia.
*The pilots had assured me that they could take the
ship, with a draft of 18 feet, to within 40 miles of
Richmond.*

Flag Officer Josiah Tattnall
to Stephen R. Mallory

Wendy could feel her confidence and her boat-
handling ability growing with every foot of their
course made good.

She concentrated first on steering small, on preventing the boat from taking wild swings to port and
starboard, on not turning so far to weather that the
sails flogged, then jamming the tiller over so they
swung far off to leeward. A little experimentation
showed her how little she had to nudge the tiller to
get a response, even with that heavy, beamy boat.

Steer small, steer small, she kept the words running

in her mind until soon the tiller was amidships, the boat tracking nicely. She lined up a point of land with the boat's stem and kept it there, correcting her course with minor adjustments of the helm as the boat tried to wander to one side of the river or the other.

'You're getting the feel of it,' Molly said. Even she could see the difference.

They cleared Portsmouth, leaving that town in their wake, with Norfolk under their bow. Sitting on the weather side of the boat, they kept their eyes forward as they stood on toward the waterfront.

'Um, Wendy,' Molly said at last, tentative in her ignorance of boats, 'we seem to be heading toward Norfolk. Shouldn't we turn to the left?'

Port, Wendy thought, but she did not correct her aunt. After a lifetime of trial and error she was finally learning not to embarrass herself with such pretension.

'Yes,' she said, 'perhap . . .' It was exactly the problem she had been considering. She understood the theory of tacking, of how a sailing vessel worked to windward. She tried to feel the wind on her face, but she could get only a rough sense of its direction. Now that the boat was moving along so well, she hated to change anything.

'Perhaps we won't have to tack,' Wendy said next. She was thinking out loud. She pushed the tiller to leeward, an inch, then another, watched carefully as the boat began to turn up into the wind. The town of Norfolk disappeared behind the sail. If she could turn just a bit more, then they could sail clear into Hampton Roads on that heading.

She gave the tiller another inch to leeward and the

elegant curve of the sail's forward edge collapsed, the canvas rippling and snapping and bulging out. Wendy jerked the tiller back and the boat swung quickly downwind, the sail filling, the Norfolk waterfront sweeping by.

Steer small, steer small! She eased the tiller the other way, brought the boat carefully back to its original heading.

'We'll have to tack,' Wendy announced.

'All right . . . what shall I do?'

Wendy was not sure. She tried to picture what would happen when they brought the bow of the boat through the wind. The line from the corner of the sail, which she believed was called the 'sheet,' ran through a block just in front of her and was fastened to a cleat. She did not think it would need adjustment.

'When we tack,' Wendy said, 'then the other side of the boat will become the higher side, and we'll have to shift over there.'

Molly nodded.

'All right, here we go,' Wendy said, trying to sound confident. She pushed the tiller over to the leeward side. The boat turned up into the wind, higher and higher. The sail began to flog, a distracting and unnerving sound, but Wendy kept the tiller over. The shoreline beyond swept by, the sail rippling as it passed through the wind.

Then they were on the other tack, the boat pointing almost downriver, the wind coming over the starboard bow. The sail was pressed flat against the mast by the wind, and Wendy thought, *That can't be right . . .*

Somehow the gaff and sail should have been

moved to the other side of the mast in order for it to set right on the opposite tack. But, unseamanlike as it looked, it was doing the job, driving the boat along, and Wendy played with the tiller until the bow was as high on the wind as it would go.

Molly did not look confident. She was looking at the sail, looking at the shore.

'We have to sail on this tack for a bit,' Wendy explained, 'so that when we tack again we can sail past Norfolk.'

Molly nodded. 'Because it does appear we are going back the way we came,' she said.

'I know. But not for long.'

For five minutes they held that course, crossing the Elizabeth River from east to west, and then they tacked again. It went smoother that time, and with the wind back over the port bow, the sail set correctly, which was a relief to Wendy. Seeing the sail pressed awkwardly against the mast made her very uncomfortable.

They cleared Norfolk, made Finner Point where the river opened its wide mouth to Hampton Roads. Craney Island was three miles ahead on the port bow, and beyond that, only the shimmering open water of the Roads, with the low blue-gray coast of Newport News a thin line on the northern horizon.

'I see a boat,' Molly said.

'Where?'

'There.' Wendy could hear the forced calm in Molly's voice, and in her own. She looked where Molly was pointing. A small boat, not unlike their own, coming upriver under sail.

No reason to be afraid, Wendy assured herself, but she was. 'What do you think we should do?'

Molly shook her head. 'Sail on. Hope they ignore us.'

Wendy nodded, ran an eye over the approaching boat. They had the wind a little astern and they were coming up fast.

'I wish we had a telescope,' Wendy said.

'I prefer guns,' Molly said. 'Where is the pepperbox?'

'We left it behind.'

Molly nodded. 'Do you have your gun?'

'Yes. I put it in my carpetbag.' Wendy wondered how much of that morning her aunt recalled.

Molly dug through the bag, pulled out the little gun, examined the chamber and the percussion cap. 'We have one shot. We had better make it a good one.'

Four minutes passed before the boat was up with them. From fifty feet away, the women could make out six men sitting on the weather side, and a man who appeared to be wearing an officer's frock coat at the tiller.

'I hope to God these aren't Yankees,' Molly said. She adjusted her skirts so they covered the gun in her right hand.

The strange boat turned up into the wind. Its sail came back and it stopped dead, like a carriage with the brake set. The officer called out, 'Heave to! Heave to in our lee!'

What does that mean? Wendy wondered. No doubt it involved stopping so the men could determine who they were. Wendy turned the boat slowly up into the wind. The sail began to flog and beat, and the boat lost way, until at last it drifted to a stop ten feet from the other.

360

'Ladies, I am Lieutenant John Jones, flag lieutenant, Confederate States Navy. May I ask your business?' the officer said. He spoke in the accent of the South. His coat was gray. Dark gray, but none-theless gray. Wendy felt relief spread like the warm glow from a shot of whiskey.

'We are leaving Norfolk, before the damned Yankees get there,' Molly said. 'I am a particular friend of Captain John Tucker, and we are attempting to reach him.'

The officer in the boat nodded. 'Tucker is with his squadron in the James. But there are Yankees every-where. You'd be better to land and go on foot.'

The women nodded.

'What news do you have of Norfolk?' Jones asked.

'The Yankees were not yet there when we left, about an hour or more past. The navy yard is in flames.'

That news seemed to take the officer by surprise. 'Are you certain?'

'Yes,' Wendy said. 'We were there ourselves. It is quite overcome.'

The officer nodded. 'Very well. I wish I could offer you more assistance, but I fear I have urgent business.'

'Sir, you are kindness itself, but we will be fine, I assure you,' Wendy said. She was feeling optimistic, for the first time in a long time. She was eager to be under way.

'Very good, ladies. Good day.' Jones tipped his hat as if they had met on the street, and not bobbing along in boats in the middle of a theater of war. The navy boat fell off and soon was under way, running upriver. Wendy and Molly fussed with the sail and the tiller until they were also under way again, downriver for Hampton Roads.

They did not see another sail for nearly an hour.

Craney Island was broad on the port bow and a mile off when Molly happened to notice it, astern of them, and coming downriver fast.

'Is it Lieutenant Jones again, do you think?' Molly asked.

Wendy glanced over her shoulder, then back at the sail overhead and the boat's heading, then back over her shoulder. 'I don't know . . .' She did not think so – the shape of the sail did not look right – but this new boat was nearly a mile away, and she could not be certain. 'I don't know,' she said again.

They tacked once more to gain sea room from the mud flats on the eastern shore of the river, then tacked back. It was an awkward maneuver as Wendy tried to shift the sail around to the other side of the mast, which she managed to do, but only after getting the boat in irons for a few confused moments. By the time they were back on the port tack, the boat coming up astern was much closer.

It was not the Confederate officer Jones.

They could see that now. This boat had a jib and a mainsail, whereas Jones's boat had only a single sail much like their own.

'Oysterman,' Molly pronounced, 'or someone fleeing the Yankees like we are.'

Wendy nodded. She felt as uncertain as Molly sounded.

But why would anyone care about us? she thought. *Even if they are Yankees, surely they have better things to do than come after us?* Whoever they were, she assured herself, they would not care about a couple of

362

harmless women in a boat. There was only one person she could think of who might want to hunt them down, but she had already put a bullet through his head.

She saw that whole nightmare scene again, played out in her mind as if she were seeing it for the first time. She tasted the revulsion and fear and wild fury all over, felt the kick of the big gun in her hand. She tried to summon up remorse for what she had done, but it was not there.

I feel not that deity on my bosom, she thought and wondered if that should concern her. She wanted to talk about what had happened, what she had done and felt, had a desperate need to verbalize it. She wanted to spill it all to Molly, but she could not broach the subject with her aunt. Not with Molly. She could not bring it up again.

She wished that Samuel were there. Samuel would understand. He would help her understand. These were things that he had faced as well. Men were supposed to perform such acts as killing with never a thought, but Samuel was more introspective than that. She knew he lacked nothing in courage, but not feeling fear was not the same as not feeling at all.

She missed Samuel desperately. It was ironic, but since the moment she had decided to make her way west, there had hardly been two consecutive minutes to think of him. At that moment, however, hand on the tiller, boat tracking north through the small chop at the river's mouth, quiet save for the water on the hull, she thought, and she recalled how much she loved him and how painfully she wanted to be near him.

'That boat seems to be making for us,' Molly said, soft and calm.

Wendy, pulled from her thoughts, looked over her shoulder. The boat was in their wake, directly astern, about half a mile away. The river was two miles wide at that point, and yet the boat was right there, right behind them.

'I doubt it. More likely my keen sense of seamanship has led me to choose exactly the best course downriver, which this fellow also knows.' Wendy could hear how hollow her efforts at being flip and unconcerned sounded.

She looked back again. It did seem that the boat was making an effort to close with them.

I'll tack . . . tack away and see what he does, she thought, then realized how pointless that was. The boat astern was clearly sailing much faster than they were. It might be chasing them, or it might not, but either way it would overtake them soon, and then they would know. And tacking would make no difference one way or another. They stood on.

And the boat astern of them did as well, coming up fast, coming right at them, unwavering in its attempt to overtake them. Twenty minutes later, they knew. The boat was chasing them.

'I can see only one person there,' Molly said. She was looking astern. The boat was a hundred yards behind them now, sailing at least two knots faster than the women's boat. 'Who could it be?'

The women looked at one another, and all the questions and fears passed between them, unspoken.

'No,' Wendy said. 'No. I blew his goddamned brains out.'

It was all so agonizingly slow, so painfully

364

inevitable, like a lingering death. One hundred yards, seventy-five yards, fifty yards.

'It's him,' Molly said, her voice dead.

'It can't be.' But Wendy was no longer so certain. Why had she not felt for a pulse, tied him up, slit his throat, something?

'It is him. I can see him clear enough now.'

'You have one bullet.'

No one spoke. Newcomb was twenty yards astern. They could see his horrible blood-caked face, his clothes filthy and torn, the hair wild on his hatless head. He looked like a statue, a gargoyle, motionless in the stern sheets, eyes locked on them. Wendy wished he would curse at them, scream at them, order them to heave to, anything but that silent, relentless approach.

'Goddamn him!' Wendy said out loud, all but shouting. Her nerves were played out, she had to act. Just standing on was tantamount to submitting to the lunatic bastard.

'Hold on, Molly! Don't shoot until we are on top of him!' Wendy bit down, pressed her lips together. Took one last look over her shoulder, then thrust the tiller hard to starboard.

The heavy boat spun up into the wind and kept on going. In the few seconds it took to turn one hundred and eighty degrees, Newcomb's boat covered the distance between them. Wendy watched the shoreline spin past as the boat came around again on the port tack, spinning a neat circle, and then Newcomb's boat was right under their bow.

They hit with a shock that sent Wendy tumbling forward. The boat rolled, dipped her rail under the water, and Wendy had an image of falling masts and crushing wood, Newcomb flying from his seat and water pouring in before she landed across the aftermost thwart. She heard a shout like a bull's bellow, knew it was the outraged cry of Roger Newcomb.

She struggled up. Their boat had stove in the bow of Newcomb's boat entirely, and the impact had sent Newcomb's mainmast by the board, though their own still stood. Molly was clawing her way up from the bottom, the gun still in her hand. Newcomb's boat was filling fast, going down.

'Where's Newcomb?' Molly shouted, gun held out. It was suddenly quiet. Wendy could hear her and Molly's breath, coming hard.

Then Newcomb was there, leaping up from behind the mass of shattered wood and torn canvas that had been his boat's rig. Bounding over the wreckage, his eyes wild, fresh blood running down his face. He had a pistol in one hand, a wooden bucket in the other

'Son of a bitch!' Molly shouted, held the gun out. Newcomb flung the bucket at her. She flinched and pulled the trigger.

The gunshot made a weak cracking sound, like a thin twig breaking underfoot. Wendy saw Newcomb jerk around, stumble, and fall. He came down hard, falling across the gunnel of the women's boat. But he was not dead.

He pushed himself up on one arm, his .36 Navy Colt held in front of him, a horrible leer on his face. Slowly, agonizingly, he pulled himself on board, the gun steady, the muzzle aimed always at Wendy or Molly, moving between them, as if trying to decide whom to kill first.

Newcomb got both legs aboard and sat down heavy on the thwart, leaning against the gunnel, mouth open, sucking air. The wreckage of his boat drifted off, half sunk, held up only by the buoyancy of the wood.

Newcomb's head flopped forward, as if he did not have the strength to hold it up. Wendy searched him for a bullet wound, hoping desperately that Molly had managed to hit him, that he would bleed to death before their eyes. But there was nothing. He had fallen while twisting out of the way of the bullet. She had missed.

'Ladies,' Newcomb said at last, guttural and ironic. 'How nice to see you again . . .'

Wendy could see Molly's jaws working, see her arms tense. She was afraid that Molly was going to launch herself at Newcomb, try to claw him to death. 'Molly . . .' she warned. The .36 was pointed at her aunt's chest. She would never make it across the boat before he shot her.

They sat in their silent world of hatred as Newcomb waited for his strength to return, for the pain to subside. Ten minutes they sat, then Newcomb stirred. His gun swung over to point at Wendy. His thumb pulled the hammer back. The click was loud in the quiet air.

'You bitch . . . you shot me.' His voice sounded stronger now, as if in the moments of quiet he had recovered some of his strength. 'I should just kill you now.'

Wendy looked at the gun and then at Newcomb's crazy eyes, and her hatred was so profound that it blotted out the fear she knew she should feel. 'Go ahead, you cowardly little puke,' she hissed.

Newcomb gave a half grin, eased the hammer back. 'No, no. I can wait for the pleasure of seeing you kicking and jerking at the end of a rope. Pissing yourself as you die. Be worth it.'

Wendy looked away in disgust, her eyes moving upriver, toward the column of smoke rising up from Portsmouth. Were the Yankees there yet? Would their navy come upriver soon, to rescue the wayward Acting Master Roger Newcomb?

There was a boat coming down from Norfolk, just coming into view as it rounded Finner Point at the confluence of the southern and western branches of the Elizabeth River. It was nearly two miles away, little more than a white square bobbing on the blue water. *Yankees?* If they were, it was quite possible that she and Molly would hang. But at least they would be saved from whatever more horrid plan Roger Newcomb had.

Then another thought came to her. *Is it Lieutenant Jones? The Confederate Navy?* She pulled her eyes away quickly, so that Newcomb would not follow her gaze. She tried not to think about the boat. It would play out the way it would. There seemed to be little that she could do now to influence her fate.

'So we wait . . .' Newcomb was saying. 'We wait, wait, for the Union to wipe out all the stinking secesh like the vermin they are, and then we go and take you two to the proper authorities, and I am made captain while you are hung.'

The women did not respond. They sat silent and glared at Newcomb, and that seemed to unnerve him a bit. 'Or maybe I'll have to kill you as you try to escape, I don't know, I shall see. We'll see.'

Wendy looked beyond Newcomb, out toward the eastern shore of the river. The tide had turned, the boat was slowly drifting downstream toward

Hampton Roads. She wondered how long Newcomb would just sit there.

Finally, with a grunt of effort, he stood, gun held loose at his side. He jerked his pocket watch from his vest, glanced down at it, put it away, seemed not to notice that the face was crushed, the case and the hands broken off. 'Perhaps we should be on our way,' he said.

Wendy glanced astern, involuntarily. She caught a glimpse of the boat, much closer now. She cursed herself and turned her head away. Heard Newcomb gasp. She looked up. He was glaring at her, the gun pointed at her face. 'You traitorous bitch!' he shouted. 'How long have you known they were there?'

Wendy looked astern, no point in pretending now. The boat had halved the distance between them. She still could make out no details, but by every appearance it seemed to be Jones's boat. She had stared long and hard at it when they met before; she recognized the shape of the sail.

She looked back at Newcomb, met his eye, held his gaze unwaveringly. 'How long have I known *who* was there?'

'Who? Who? I'll give you . . . get up in the bow. Both of you, get the hell up in the bow!' Newcomb gestured with the gun. Wendy stood, made her way forward, a hand on the gunnel, Molly in front of her. They came to the forwardmost thwart and sat, facing aft. Neither woman cared to have her back to the lunatic with the gun.

Newcomb sat with a grunt in the stern. He pushed the tiller over with the hand still holding the gun, sheeted in the sail with the other, and made it fast.

The boat fell off the wind and gathered way and Newcomb brought the tiller amidships. He was a very good boat handler, Wendy could see that, and it made her even more angry. She wondered if Jones's boat was the faster of the two. Or whether it would matter.

Newcomb's eyes were everywhere, looking at the set of the sail, looking aft at the approaching boat, looking past the bow and out to weather. The boat was moving fast, heeling in the westerly breeze. They were not sailing hard on the wind, as they had been before, the point of sail that Wendy had chosen to get them out of the river and into the Roads.

She turned and looked forward. Newcomb was making for an open place on the eastern shore, a wide marshy place called Tanner's Creek.

'Turn around,' Newcomb shouted and Wendy turned back. She settled her hands on her lap. She waited.

They moved fast on the beam reach, and the boat astern did not seem to be gaining anymore. Soon Wendy was aware of the shoreline close at hand. She looked to starboard. They were not more than a hundred yards off the reedy, wild riverbank. She looked to port, expecting Newcomb to shout at her, but he did not. She could see Tanner's Point fine on the port bow. Newcomb was going to duck out of sight behind the point.

Ten minutes later the land was all around them, the mosquitoes beginning their torment as the boat moved slowly through the shallow, muddy water. Newcomb brought the bow around to close with the shore, and Wendy thought for certain the boat would take the ground, but it did not, gliding along silently and nearly upright in the wind shadow of the land.

Finally the bow nudged into the sandy shore on the east side of Tanner's Point. Newcomb ordered the women to sit on the center thwart, then he climbed over the bow and pulled the boat as far up as he could. He tied the painter to a sapling at the edge of the tall grass.

'Get out.' Newcomb gestured with the gun, and Wendy, then Molly climbed awkwardly out of the boat. He made them turn their backs to him, and for a horrible moment Wendy thought he was going to put a bullet through their heads.

Instead he bound their hands behind their backs, tied them tight with thin, rough cordage. 'Wouldn't have to do this . . .' he muttered, a lunatic's monologue, 'if I thought I could trust you . . . give your word . . . *would* if you were civilized women and not damned Southern trash . . . secesh garbage . . .' He tied their wrists swiftly and securely, with the marlin-spike seamanship skills he had learned in the United States Navy. He pulled a pocket knife and cut a long strip from Wendy's skirt and gagged them.

'This way.' He shoved Wendy toward the shore and Molly after, prodded them along as they stumbled and made their way through the tall dune grass. The stiff vegetation whipped their faces and scratched their skin and with their bound hands they were not able to fend it off.

Tanner's Point was only one hundred yards wide, and soon they came to where it met up with the water of Hampton Roads. To the southwest, two miles away across the mouth of the Elizabeth River, was Craney Island. The horizon to the north and south was bordered by low shoreline, and straight across from them, open water marked the mouth of the James River.

'Wait here.' Newcomb pointed to the ground where they stood, ten feet from where the grass gave way to the riverbank. He went ahead by himself, peering through the grass, looking south.

They remained like that for some time. How long, Wendy did not know. The minutes crawled along. Finally, through the screen of grass, they could see the boat. It was Jones's boat, heading toward Hampton Roads. Wendy could see the gray-clad Jones in the stern sheets. He was making no effort to look for them, none that she could see. He was just sailing on.

The despair took Wendy by surprise, caught her unawares. She had invested all her hope in Lieutenant Jones and the Confederate Navy and she had not even realized it. But the sailors had passed by, had not even glanced in her and Molly's direction. Through the tall grass, she watched her last hope disappear from sight, heading north toward Sewell's Point.

Now they were alone, bound and gagged. There was nothing more they could do but await the pleasure of Roger Newcomb.

CHAPTER 25

Had the ship not been lifted, so as to render her unfit for action, a desperate contest must have ensued with a force against us too great to justify much hope of success; and as battle is not their occupation, they [the pilots] adopted this deceitful course to avoid it.

Flag Officer Josiah Tattnall
to Stephen R. Mallory

Midshipman Hardin Littlepage brought the news: Lieutenant Jones's boat was back.

Flag Officer Tattnall's health had not improved in the hours that Jones had been gone. The thought of the army summarily abandoning Norfolk did not help. The idea of the soldiers handing over to the Yankees the Gosport Naval Shipyard and everything it meant to the Confederate Navy, without so much as a shot fired, ground him down like a boot heel on his neck. He lay in his bunk. He felt sick to his stomach, and feverish.

If Norfolk was gone, then the *Virginia* was floating around untethered, like one of those damned hot air

373

balloons the Yankees were using to spy on Confederate lines, a balloon that had broken loose. And she couldn't operate that way for long. *We'll take her up the James River*, he thought, but that did little to mollify him. There was hardly room enough in Hampton Roads for the beastly ship to turn. What would she be able to do in the James River?

With a sigh, then a groan, Tattnall stood. His cabin, such as it was, was on the berthing deck and all the way forward. He made his way up the ladder to the gun deck, and then to the hurricane deck. He stepped into the open air just as Jones's boat was sliding alongside. A minute later the lieutenant was reporting.

'Sir, I went ashore at the naval yard, which was in flames. Everything was going up, sir, beyond saving. No one was there. No officers, anyway. One yard worker told me the officers had left by train for Richmond. From there I went to Norfolk, to confer with General Huger, as you instructed. I was told Huger and the army had also left by train. The enemy was within half a mile of the city; the mayor was treating for surrender.'

Tattnall nodded, felt more and more unwell. He wanted to sit but he made himself stand. He could see the concern in Jones's face. The lieutenant paused in his narrative, unsure if he should continue.

'Go on,' Tattnall said. He did not need the sympathy of a junior officer.

'On the way back upriver, I discovered that all the batteries on the river have been abandoned, including Craney Island. I encountered a boat with two women aboard, fleeing the city, and later saw another boat, which might have been the same, I couldn't tell. It put into Tanner's Creek and I didn't think it important enough to follow. Other than that, there was no traffic on the river.'

Tattnall nodded again and leaned on the rail. It was what he had feared, but also what he had expected. *Damn those army sons of bitches!* The thought of them piling on the trains and rumbling out of town for Richmond made Old Tat furious. *They've done for me, the bastards . . .*

'Very well, Mr Jones. Good work. Please pass the word for Lieutenant Jones.'

Two minutes later the executive officer, Lieutenant Catesby ap R. Jones, climbed up through a casemate hatch, saluted, nodded to Pembroke Jones. Tattnall had Lieutenant John Jones repeat his report to Lieutenant Catesby Jones.

'Gentlemen,' Tattnall said when Jones had finished, 'as you know, the pilots say we can get the ship up the James River, get her within forty miles of Richmond, if we lighten her by four feet. That will be a hell of a job, but it will be worth it, I think. We might be able to do some good in the James, take on the boats the Yankees have sent up there. Anyway, it is the course I would choose, but I would like your opinions as well.'

Both officers were nodding assent before Tattnall had even finished speaking. 'It is the most judicious course, sir,' Catesby Jones said.

'I agree,' John Jones said.

'Very well,' said Tattnall, 'assemble the men.'

Catesby Jones saluted and summoned the boatswain, who began piping the men topside. Soon they were all there, crowding on the casemate roof, over three hundred men: naval officers, blue-water sailors, landsmen, mechanics, dockworkers, laborers, soldiers, whoever they had been able to scrape up to haul a gun tackle or shovel coal into a furnace. But whatever they had been before, however disparate a group, they were now the crew of the *Virginia*, battle tested, and Flag Officer Tattnall loved them, just as he loved the ship under his feet.

'Men,' he said, speaking as loudly as his weak lungs would permit, 'here is the situation. I'll give it to you straight. The army has abandoned Norfolk. The navy yard is in flames.'

A murmur like a breeze through long grass swept through the men. When it subsided, Tattnall went on. 'We must get *Virginia* up the James River, as close up to Richmond as she will go. We can aid in the defense of the capital, maybe take some of the enemy's ships, or sink 'em. But that means we have to lighten her, toss over everything but the guns and powder. It will take a prodigious effort on your part, but it is the only way to save our ship. What say you?'

They replied with cheers – three loud, genuine, enthusiastic cheers – and Tattnall could see that these men would do everything that they were capable of doing to see the Virginia safe, just as he would.

'You make me proud,' he said over the dying cheers. 'Go to it.'

He watched the officers telling off the work parties, and he was grateful for their loyalty and their youth, their intelligence and energy, and he was jealous of it too. He wanted more than anything to be foremost in the effort to save the ship. He wanted to fling himself into the work with the kind of unfathomable energy he had known forty years ago. But he could not. He was old and sick. He made his way carefully back to his cabin, lay down on his bunk, and closed his eyes.

Wendy watched Roger Newcomb pace and stare out over the water and pull his shattered watch from his vest pocket and stare at it and she thought, *God alone will be able to save us from this madman.*

His grip on reality – apparently weak from the start – was getting weaker still. His muttering had increased in quantity while going down in volume, so that now what came out of his mouth was no more than an incoherent babble, like someone speaking in tongues. It was unnerving.

Wendy's wrists, like Molly's, were still bound, the skin rubbed agonizingly raw by the rough cordage that now grated on the sores it had opened. She could feel the occasional trickle of blood running down her fingers. She could not see Molly's hands, but she guessed they were just as bad.

The gags, at least, had been removed. Once the Confederate boat had passed well clear of them, beyond shouting range, Newcomb had removed the strips of skirt from their mouths and interrogated them as to the identity of the men in the boat. Since Wendy had drawn his attention to the boat, she bore the brunt of his questioning.

'Who are they? *Who are they?!*' He had kicked Wendy hard, sent her sprawling into the dirt. She spit out sand and blood.

'You little cowardly bastard!' she shouted. 'Strike a woman whose hands are tied?'

Newcomb grabbed a handful of Molly's hair, jerked it painfully so her head was back. He held the pistol to her temple. He did not speak and he did not have to.

'Confederate Navy. We met them when they were going upriver. The officer said his name was Jones. Lieutenant John Jones.'

'Lieutenant John Jones . . . What else did he say?'

'Nothing. He asked if we needed help. He was a gentleman.'

Newcomb ignored the implication, paced to the water, looked north and south. He came back again. 'What else?'

'Nothing.' Wendy could see the anger, driven by madness, and she thought she had better come up with something.

'He called himself a "flag lieutenant," ' she offered. It had meant nothing to her, but apparently it meant something to Newcomb. He stood straighter, regarded her as if trying to divine the truth, paced back to the water. Jerked his watch from his vest and replaced it without even looking at it.

It had been several hours since that questioning, and they had not moved from their place in the high grass on Tanner's Point. Once, Newcomb had said, 'We'll just wait here until the United States Navy comes upriver, and then we shall see.' The words had come out so lucid, so conversational that they took Wendy by surprise. But soon he was muttering again, and she could catch the words *flag officer* and *Virginia* and a few obscenities and other words that she thought she could understand, but she was not sure.

Madness . . . There was no method in it.

The sun went down, blazing red and orange right in their eyes as they faced west, and the moon rose in the deepening blue sky, until the land on the far side was no more than a dark shape in the moonlight and the ruffled surface of the water just visible.

Wendy's wrists were agony now, and she could hardly feel her hands. They seemed swollen and dull, dead things, and cool, like touching wet gutta-percha. She wondered how long her hands could remain tied like that before the damage was permanent. She wondered if she would live long enough for it to matter.

With the fading light, the insects swarmed. They attacked her bleeding wrists with vigor, biting the torn flesh. She flailed her arms to the extent that she could, but she could not rid herself of them. She shook her hair over her face to drive the biting flies and mosquitoes away, but they would not be thwarted. She wanted to scream. She looked over at Molly. Their eyes met; the mutual fear and misery passed between them. But there was fire there, too, in Molly's eyes, and Wendy was pleased to see it. Molly had not given up.

Roger Newcomb paced the shoreline, looking out over the water, as if he were waiting for a ship that would arrive at any moment. But nothing came. Nothing moved on the water.

The sharp edge of fear began to dull, misery began to overtake her, and despite the pain and the torment of the insects, Wendy felt her eyes begin to close. She lay down on her side, fell in the sandy dirt with a thump, unable to ease herself down with her hands. She closed her eyes. She thought of Newcomb putting a bullet through her head as she slept, and it no longer seemed the worst thing that could happen.

Some time later she woke, startled awake by something, but she did not know what. She had no notion of how long she had been asleep, but she was stiff and groggy and she guessed it had been a few hours at least. She looked over at Molly, who apparently had also been asleep, and who was also now awake. Molly was looking toward the shore.

The moon was higher now, casting more light on the land and the water. It fell on Roger Newcomb as he paced, waved his arms, stared up the shoreline, paced again. His movements were more frenetic than ever.

'He saw something on the water,' Molly said, speaking in a barely audible whisper. It was the first thing she had said since Newcomb had taken their boat, and Wendy felt an irrational sense of relief at the sound of her voice.

'What do you think?'

Molly shook her head. 'Yankee navy ship?'

They were quiet again, listening. The frogs and the buzz of the insects made a blanket of sound through which little else could be heard. But there *was* something else. Wendy could hear it, just hear it, far off. The occasional clanking sound, the huff, the rippling water of a bow wave. It sounded like a steamer. A steamship coming down from Hampton Roads. The Yankee navy.

The ten-foot path between where the women were lying in the grass and the open shoreline was pretty well trampled now, after hours of Newcomb's obsessive shifting between his prisoners and his vigil on the beach, and Wendy could see a good section of the water from where she lay. She struggled to her knees, pushing up with hands she could not feel. She looked as far north as she could.

At first there was nothing. Only the dark water, barely distinct from the land. But slowly, slowly, from the north, something came into view, something moving on the water. No masts that she could see, no paddle-wheel boxes, no high superstructure or sweeping sheer of gunnels. It did not seem to be a ship at all, just a dark menacing presence, some leviathan making its way toward Norfolk, something sent up from hell to punish them all, Yankee and Southerner alike.

She stared at it, puzzled, cocked her head. And then like a flash of inspiration it came to her. She looked at Molly and Molly nodded. '*Virginia*,' she whispered. The mighty Confederate ironclad.

It had been five hours before that when Josiah Tattnall returned to his cabin and stretched out in his bunk fully clothed – 'all standing,' as the sailors said – save for his shoes and sword belt. He lay for a while in the dark, listening to the wild sounds of the men lightening the ship, the drag and bang of the dismantling: galley, cabins, mess tables, fresh water, spirits, food, boatswain's stores, personal effects, all of it gathered up, wrenched free, carried up, tossed overboard. Gangs of men formed human chains to pass the tons of pig iron ballast up from the bilges.

Tattnall could envision the great mass of jetsam floating around *Virginia* and piling up on the bottom. He wondered if they would go aground on all the material they were throwing over the side.

He closed his eyes, enveloped by the din of the men struggling to save his ship. He had had command of her for less than two months, but he loved her as much as any ship he had ever sailed. She was the most powerful thing afloat in all the Americas. All the world, most likely. Proof of what the Confederate States of America could accomplish, even with so little.

His thoughts drifted off to ships past, to when he was young and strong and never fell ill, when it seemed his life would go on forever and nothing would ever slow him down. He fell asleep and dreamed disquieting dreams of ships and stormy seas and threatening coasts.

He awoke later with someone shaking his arm. He opened his eyes, came instantly awake, a thing bred into him from years of command, when a summons from dead sleep invariably meant he was needed to step in where disaster was imminent, when he had to rush topside and begin making decisions the instant his feet hit the quarterdeck.

'Yes?' In the feeble light of a single lantern he could see the troubled face of Catesby Jones.

'Sir, we have thrown over everything we can. We have raised the ship. She's drawing eighteen feet now, sir.'

'Very good.' Tattnall stood awkwardly. Jones made no effort to help, and Tattnall was glad of it. He felt feeble enough without receiving a patronizing hand. 'Let's get under way.'

'Ah, sir . . .' Jones equivocated, and the tone in his voice made Tattnall look sharp at him. 'There is a problem. The pilots now say they can't take the ship above the Jamestown Flats, even with an eighteen-foot draft.'

'They . . .' Tattnall did not know what to say. 'They say . . . they can't get the ship up the river?'

'No, sir.'

'Well . . . goddamn them, they have said any number of times they could, if we raised her to eighteen feet. You have heard them. Damn it, I asked them again just this evening!'

'Yes, sir.'

Tattnall took a deep breath. He had to hear it from the pilots. Before he went into the rage he felt building, he had to hear what the pilots had to say.

Without a word to Jones he stepped from his small cabin into the open space at the forward end of the berthing deck. The other cabins, he saw, had been disassembled, the bulkheads no doubt flung over the side, but his had been left untouched. In the light of the single lantern hanging from the overhead he found the ladder to the gun deck and climbed up, quicker than he had climbed a ladder in some years.

The gun deck was more brightly lit, with lanterns down the centerline of the ship. Most of the ship's company were there, within the one-hundred-and-fifty-foot casemate. Even with all those men the space looked empty now, with everything but guns gone by the board.

Tattnall looked around quickly, then snapped to Jones, 'Pass the word for the pilots.'

'Yes, sir.' Jones hurried off. Two minutes later he returned with the pilots, Parrish and Wright, miserably in tow.

'Sir,' Parrish said.

'Sir,' Wright said.

Tattnall glared at them. He meant to ask them what this was all about, but he could not make the words come out. He was paralyzed by fury. The two pilots looked sheepish, miserable, and guilty.

'Sir,' Parrish began again, 'we represented to you that we could get the *Virginia* to within forty miles of Richmond. But you must understand, that was in the event that we had an easterly wind. You see, an easterly will raise the level in the river enough to carry eighteen feet that far up. But as you know, sir, we have had westerlies, two days of westerlies, and they have had quite the opposite effect. We simply do not have the depth of water now to get the ship upriver.'

Tattnall was silent for a moment more. The pilots fidgeted like children. 'Sir, if you could raise the ship to fourteen feet draft, I do believe we could get upriver,' Wright said, as if trying to be helpful.

'She cannot be raised to fourteen feet,' Tattnall said.

'Yes, sir. We are very sorry, sir, but we cannot raise the level of the water above what it is.'

The whole thing seemed unreal, it was all too horrible. Tattnall had long seen the moment coming when Norfolk would fall to the Yankees. He had examined every option. There were only two that he would consider.

The first was to save the ship. Lighten her, get her up to Richmond. The option he had chosen. But if that could not be done, then his second choice would have been an all-out assault on the Union Navy. Fling himself and his ship at the wooden walls, plow through them, tear them up the way Old Buck had done. Eventually the *Virginia* would have been rammed and sunk – the Yankees had brought ships to Hampton Roads for just that purpose – but not before the ironclad had struck the Federals another serious and devastating blow. Perhaps even sunk that damned *Monitor* once and for all.

That second option had always held some appeal, suicidal though it was. Tattnall knew he would not live forever. Hell, he would be lucky to live through the war. To die with guns blazing, surrounded by the shattered fleet of an enemy, that was how an old man-of-war's man should go. Like Nelson. And the men would have followed, would have stood to their guns with the water rising around their ankles, because they were the men of the *Virginia*, and they were Southerners. If the pilots had told him about the effect of the westerly wind, his decision that evening would have been very different.

They had known all along, the bastards. They themselves pointed out that it had been blowing westerly for two days. They might have mentioned something.

But they did not, and now the pilots had robbed him of the attack option. With the *Virginia* raised by four feet, the bottom edge of her iron casement was out of the water, and two feet of her vulnerable wooden hull was exposed. A ship that hours before had been invulnerable to any shot fired by seagoing artillery now could be sent to the bottom by a tug-boat with a rifled gun in the bow.

It was one thing to attack the Union fleet in a mighty ironclad impervious to shot. Quite another to go into harm's way with an Achilles' heel two hundred and seventy-five feet long and two feet wide. He could not ask his men to do that. He could not. The pilots had stripped him of any choice.

Tattnall glared at the two men and they made a halfhearted attempt to meet his eyes. *Why did you do this?* Tattnall wondered. He did not think they were traitors. *Cowards . . . damned cowards . . .* That was the answer. They knew what Old Tat would do with the ship if he could not get her to Richmond.

They did not want to be part of such a desperate fight.

'Get out of my sight,' Tattnall growled and the pilots saluted and scurried away. The flag officer turned to the Lieutenants Jones.

'Those yellow bastards have sunk us,' he announced. 'Goddamn their miserable hides. Goddamn the whole race of 'em. We can't save the ship, and we can't let her fall into the Yankees' hands. We can save the crew. Sailors are near as scarce as ironclads. We'll put her on shore near Craney Island. Get the men off, then burn her. Let the powder in the magazine finish her off. March the men overland.'

The lieutenants were nodding. 'I concur, sir,' said Catesby Jones.

'I do as well,' said John Jones.

Tattnall nodded. He had not asked their opinion. 'Very well, let us get steam up as fast as we can. Not a minute to lose. Damn Yankees are so close I can smell them.'

He left the officers, climbed up into the small, conical wheelhouse, looked out at the moonlit water through the narrow eye slits in the iron casement. A view he knew and loved. He would not look through those slits at an enemy man-of-war again. The world's mightiest ship, brought down by cowards and slaves. He thought he might actually cry, and he was glad he was alone.

The deepwater channel down the Elizabeth River was less than a mile from where Roger Newcomb stood. In the moonlight, the massive shell-backed ironclad was perfectly visible, steaming upriver.

Merrimack . . . He stared in awe at the great beast,

pouring smoke from her single stack, black against the blue-black sky. The secesh called her something else now, but to Newcomb and every sailor in the United States Navy she would always be *Merrimack*.

Newcomb once again felt exposed, vulnerable. His instinct was to flee back into the tall grass, crouch down, and peer out from that cover. But he restrained himself. Even if anyone on board the Confederate flagship was looking, they would not see him there on that dark point of land. And even if they did, they would not be interested in him.

He held his ground, fished around in his haversack for his telescope. He had seen *Merrimack* in the distance on several occasions, but never this close. He pulled the glass out, focused on the passing ship.

There was something odd about her, something different, he was sure of it, even though he could barely make her out against the dark water and the land. She was right abreast of him, steaming past, and he followed her with the glass.

What is it? What is it?

He could see the full length of her hull. That was it. He could see bow and stern sections, usually submerged, and not just the casemate. The top of the two-bladed prop broke the water with every revolution and made it flash white. They had lightened her, raised her draft.

The only reason for raising her draft was to get her somewhere she could not go before. *Why? Where do they want to take her?*

He tried to divine motives. Were they hiding her from the Yankees? Springing some trap? If so, he had to find out.

The significance dawned on him slowly. This was

important, damned important, perhaps the most important bit of information in the whole theater of operations. The Union forces, army, navy, everyone in Washington, all of them were more worried about *Merrimack* than they were about all the other Confederate military forces in southern Virginia combined. McClellan had almost canceled his Peninsular campaign for fear of that one ship.

And here he was, Roger Newcomb, the only man in all the Union who knew for certain where the *Merrimack* was. If they were going to make him a captain for bringing in the two bitch assassins, what would they do when he also brought them word of the trap *Merrimack* was waiting to spring?

She was south of him now, and soon she would be lost from sight on the dark river, and he could not let that happen. He had to tail her, dog her, know where she went. The Union Navy would be there soon, and he would report from his secret mission with two dangerous assassins as prisoners, and the most crucial military information imaginable, all in his possession.

He put the telescope back in the haversack and raced up the beaten path. He felt as if he had been born again.

CHAPTER 26

The Virginia *no longer exists, but 300 brave and skillful officers and seamen are saved to the Confederacy.*

Flag Officer Josiah Tattnall
to Stephen R. Mallory

Wendy saw Newcomb running up the trail toward them. It was the first time she had seen him run. She did not know what it meant, but she was not optimistic.

The sight of the ironclad seemed to have done something to him. She braced herself to see what it might be. Any change, she imagined, would be for the worse.

He stopped, breathing hard, despite the short distance. 'Get up,' he said. There was a new look on his face. Not the cold fury she had seen before. Something different. He looked all on fire. Evangelical.

Awkwardly the women stood. Wendy's fear had been dulled after hours of waiting, but she felt it come fresh again. *Is this where he executes us? Does he think the Confederates are back?*

But once again, Newcomb failed to put bullets through their heads. Rather, he pulled his pocket knife out and cut the ropes binding their wrists. It was an extraordinary sensation, the constricting cordage falling away. Numb as they were, Wendy could feel pinpricks in her hands, sharp stabs of pain and a dull burn.

Slowly she brought her hands around to look at them in the dim light. She had thought they would be swollen to twice their size, but to her surprise they looked pretty much as they always had, save for the torn flesh on her wrists and the blood and the awful work of the insects.

Molly was gently rubbing her own mangled wrists.

Newcomb waved his gun down the trail. 'Go on, back to the boat.' Molly went first, and Wendy behind. They stumbled and searched for the trampled path, but this time they could keep the dune grass off their faces, and it made the going easier.

Soon they came out to the little strip of sand where they had left the boat. The tide had fallen and most of the boat was grounded, and it was only with a great deal of straining that Newcomb was able to get it floating again. He ordered the women aboard. They waded through soft mud that sucked at their shoes. They climbed in and took their places in the bow. Newcomb put an oar over the transom and in the light breeze sculled the boat out of Tanner's Creek.

Sitting in the bow, looking aft, Wendy could see the end of Tanner's Point disappearing astern. They were heading upriver, in the wake of the *Virginia*. She waited for Newcomb to turn north, to head for Yankee country, but he did not.

South. He stood on south, and when the first ruffle of breeze made the sail flutter, he pulled the oar in, laid it on the thwarts, and hauled the sheet until the sail was drawing. They made perhaps two knots in the light air, slicing silently through the water of the Elizabeth River. Sailing south.

Wendy wanted desperately to turn around, to see what she could see beyond their bow. At first she did not dare, certain that it would inflame Newcomb.

Still, she reasoned, so far he had done nothing but yell and threaten.

It had occurred to her, kneeling in the tall grass, waiting for Newcomb to kill them, that he needed them alive. She did not forget the violence at the house, the horrible thing he had done to Molly. But still, he needed to present them, captured Southern assassins, to his superior officers as justification for his absence. She knew that would not keep Molly and her alive forever – Newcomb was liable to go completely berserk at any moment – but for the time being it was some protection.

She swiveled around, looked ahead. She could make out the hump of Craney Island against the low shoreline beyond. *Virginia* was visible in the moonlight, the great column of smoke from her stack making a black cloud against the stars and the moonlit sky. She was a mile or so away. She did not seem to be moving much faster than they were.

'Turn around,' Newcomb growled, finally noticing her. She turned back. *What on earth is he planning?*

Lord, if they could just get aboard that Confederate ship, or attract the attention of her men. But they would have to get closer than a mile away. Much closer.

It took the better part of an hour for them to cross the river at a diagonal. Wendy watched the shoreline, trying to determine where they were going. She watched Newcomb's face, trying to gauge what he had in mind, following the ironclad.

She saw Newcomb squint into the dark, saw his eyebrows come together as he tried to puzzle something out. She turned and looked forward and Molly did as well. She braced for Newcomb's shout, but he was apparently too absorbed in what he was looking at to care about his prisoners.

The *Virginia* was a little south of Craney Island. After a moment or so, Wendy realized that the ship had stopped dead, no doubt run aground on the mud flats that extended a quarter mile out from the island.

Newcomb stood on, closing with the ironclad, until they were no more than half a mile away. He turned the boat up into the wind and let the sail come aback, pressed against the mast, then pushed the tiller over and tied it in place. The boat came to a stop, rocking slightly in the small chop, its only motion a slow drift downriver on the falling tide.

There was a whirl of activity around the Confederate ship. Lights like fireflies on a summer evening moved up and down the casemate and dotted the top of her turtle back. Lights moved across the water from ship to shore and back again.

After a while the tide and current had carried the boat far downriver, and Newcomb got them under way again, coming back to within a quarter mile of the *Virginia*.

They are abandoning ship, Wendy thought. It was the only explanation for what she was seeing. They

392

were conveying all of the crew to shore, and leaving the ironclad behind.

But they will not leave her for the Yankees, surely?

They watched for another twenty minutes, watched as three boats pulled for the shore, and then just one returned. They could see the lanterns held by men climbing up the side of the ship and then disappearing down inside. Through open gun ports they could catch glimpses of the lights moving around the interior of the casemate.

After a while the lanterns emerged on the top of the casemate and once more moved down the side of the ship and into the boat. One after another they were extinguished, until the boat was swallowed up in the dark, and the only light on the water was the moon's reflection and a soft glow that seemed to emanate from within the ironclad itself.

Newcomb did not move. He did not speak. He did not tell the women to turn around, and they did not.

There was a light of some sort within the ship's interior, Wendy was certain of it, and she was almost as certain that it was getting brighter. She wondered if dawn was coming, but a glance at the eastern sky told her it was still the dead of night, with dawn an hour or more away.

She looked back at the ship. The gun ports were clearly visible, oval points of light against the dark iron casement. And then Wendy understood. The ship was on fire. The Confederates had abandoned the *Virginia* and set her ablaze. They would not leave her for the Yankees. They would destroy her first.

She felt Newcomb shifting behind her. She turned. He was easing the tiller over, getting the boat under way. Once again she waited for him to turn the boat north, to head downriver, but he did not. He pointed the bow straight at the burning ship.

'You think I'm going to give up . . . you little secesh whores?' he said, speaking to himself, apparently. 'Think I can't save that ship now?'

'What are you talking about?' Wendy asked, disgusted, curious, frightened.

Newcomb pulled his eyes from the ship and looked at her. The zealous look she had seen on Tanner's Point was there, threefold. His eyes were wide and he was smiling, which made his face look even more horrible. 'Those traitors think they'll keep that ship out of Union hands by burning her. Well I'll be damned if they will. She's the *Merrimack*, pride of the Union Navy, and she will be again.'

Oh, Lord, he is going to try and save the ship!

She turned back and looked at *Virginia*, now only a hundred yards or so ahead, close enough for Wendy to get a sense of her massive scale. She could see flames through the gun ports, but could not tell the extent to which she was engulfed. Might Newcomb do this thing? By the look on his face, it was clear he would die trying, and see that his prisoners did as well.

They closed with the ship, the great casemate rising up overhead like a small, humpbacked mountain. Through the gun ports, around the muzzles of the heavy guns, they could see the flames on the gun deck. The men who had put her to the torch had done their job well, but Newcomb did not hesitate.

They came up with the *Virginia*'s bow. Newcomb brought the boat alongside, bumping it against the ship's side. The smell of burning wood and hot iron was sharp in their noses. They could hear the flames crackling and hissing inside the iron shell.

Newcomb stood with one hand resting on the *Virginia*'s deck. He aimed the .36 at the women. 'Get up there,' he said, gesturing with his head toward the ship. The women hesitated. Newcomb straightened the arm with the gun, sighted down the barrel. 'Get up!'

No choice. Newcomb was even more fixated on the ship than he was on them. It was not hard to imagine what a hero he would be if indeed he could save the ironclad for the Union. And that meant that the lives of his prisoners were of considerably less value than they had been even two hours before.

Wendy stood and grabbed onto a bollard on the edge of the *Virginia*'s deck. She stepped onto the gunnel of the boat, managed to get a leg on the ship's deck and pull herself up, a difficult and humiliating move. She looked up, still on hands and knees. A few feet inboard of the ship's side, a low wooden bulwark made a V-shaped false bow that would keep the area within the V dry even when the deck outside was submerged. Wendy grabbed hold of the top of the bulwark and pulled herself up.

She turned as Molly grabbed onto the bollard and hoisted herself up in the same manner. Wendy took hold of Molly's arm, helped pull her aboard, and helped her to her feet.

Newcomb stepped to the center of the boat, balancing with one hand on the *Virginia*'s deck, and grabbed the long painter that lay coiled on a thwart. He handed the coil of line up to Wendy.

'Tie that onto the bollard.'

Wendy took the rope, looked at it, looked at Newcomb standing below her. He was in the boat, and they were on the ship. A mistake. He had made a mistake. She and Molly were not likely to get a better chance.

'Tie the goddamned painter to the bollard, you bitch, I don't have time for your games!' Newcomb raised the gun and Wendy flung the rope in his face, side arm, as hard as she could, knocking him back into the boat, as much from his off-balance effort to shield his face as from the force of the blow. She turned and shoved Molly, pushed her right over the low bulwark and leaped after her, so they tumbled together onto the foredeck, screened from Newcomb by the wooden wall.

Wendy pushed herself up on her arms, looked around. They had only a few seconds before Newcomb found his feet and came after them, but where would they go?

Inside. Through the gun ports. There was no other place.

There were three gun ports at the forward end of the ship, one over the centerline and one on either of the rounded corners of the casemate. Each of the gun ports had a heavy iron shutter, built in two parts like the blades of scissors. The gun ports, thankfully, were open, the shutters swung out of the way and held off the gun port by a chain that ran through a hole in the casemate to the interior.

'There! Let's go!' Wendy shouted, nodding toward the far corner. They could hear Newcomb screaming, a high-pitched, horrible sound, 'Goddamn you! Goddamn you!' and Wendy was certain now that they would be killed immediately if they were caught. Newcomb had a bigger vision, and the assassins he had captured were only an impediment.

They kept low as they ran across the foredeck, waiting for the crack of Newcomb's pistol, the ball in their bent backs. There was a gun blocking the way through the center gun port, and in any event it was too high for them to reach. But they could get to the one on the far corner by standing on the bulwark where it met the casemate, and there was no gun there.

They reached the far bulwark, ran hard into it as they tried to stop, turned together to see if they were too late, but they could not see Newcomb. The boat must have drifted off as he flailed to regain his feet, and that bought them a few seconds more.

'Go, Molly, there!' Wendy pointed. Molly stepped up onto the bulwark, caught her foot in her filthy, tattered skirt, freed it, reached up for the opening. The gun port was higher than Wendy had realized. Molly was just able to get her head and shoulders through. Wendy put her hands on Molly's rear end and pushed, let Molly push her feet against her shoulders, and finally she was in.

Wendy climbed up onto the bulwark, reached up into the gun port. The interior of the casemate was brilliantly lit with the flames that were burning up the wooden sides on which the iron plating was fastened, burning in patches on the deck where flammable material had been spread. Halfway through the gun port she could see the chains holding up the heavy iron shutters where they came through the casemate and were held in place by a lever. She prayed the lever would not let go right then.

Molly grabbed her hands and pulled and Wendy kicked her way up.

She heard Newcomb shout. The pistol cracked, a

bullet struck the iron casemate near her flailing legs and whistled away, and then she was in, falling to the gun deck only two feet below the edge of the gun port.

She pulled herself to her feet, with Molly's help, and looked around. Flames everywhere, climbing up the sides of the casemate, roaring up through the hatches from the engine room below. Thick black smoke rolled in clouds along the overhead, was sucked out through the hatches above. The sound was nearly deafening. She felt as if her skin would blister in the heat. There was no chance that fire would be put out by Roger Newcomb acting on his own – but that truth would make no difference to him.

They were trapped on the burning ship, Newcomb, armed, furious, just behind them. He might die trying to save *Merrimack*, but he would see they went with him.

'God forgive me, Aunt, I've killed us both!' Wendy shouted above the flames.

Molly shook her head. A sharp roar like an explosion filled the casemate, made the deck shudder underfoot, and Wendy was certain the ship was blowing up. A scream built in her throat and she stifled it. Halfway down the gun deck, one of the big guns, engulfed in flame, leaped back as if trying to escape, half-flew across the deck, slammed with a clanging sound into the gun opposite, tilted, and fell with a crash that shook the deck again.

Fire made it go off, Wendy imagined. Breech ropes burned through.

'We have to hide!' Molly shouted.

Wendy nodded. To their right and above their heads was a semi-enclosed platform, a ladder leading up. 'There!' Wendy shouted. They raced to the ladder, took the steps fast, tumbled onto the small deck, dark and smoke-filled.

It was the pilothouse. They could see the flames playing off the spokes of the wheel, the smoke being sucked out of the narrow view slits. On hands and knees they crawled to the forward corner and huddled against the ship's side, lost in the shadows forward of the wheel box.

It was less than a minute later when they saw Newcomb.

From where they hid they could look right down the companionway of the pilothouse to the burning gun deck below. They saw Newcomb move past, slowly, pistol in front of him. A hunter. He was looking everywhere, stepping aft, peering into the few places where the ship was not engulfed in flame. They saw him double over as he coughed, put a handkerchief over his nose and mouth, push on. They pressed themselves against the side of the ship, sat silent. He could not go too far aft. The flames would stop him, and he would know they could not have gone there either. He would be back.

Thirty seconds, an excruciating, breathless thirty seconds, and they saw him again, stumbling forward, retching from the smoke. But still alert, still looking. He stopped, a few paces away. His eyes moved up the ladder, until he was looking at them, looking directly at them, as if he were engaging them in conversation. But there was no recognition on his face, nothing to indicate he had seen them. They were hidden in the shadows, partially obscured by the wheel box, invisible to eyes that had lost their sensitivity to the dark in the glare of the flames.

Newcomb stepped toward the ladder, slow and cautious. The pilothouse was an obvious choice for a hiding spot. There were not many options.

He reached the ladder and took a step up, then another, gun ready, hammer back. His eyes, his wild eyes, were everywhere. He would see them in a second, there was no way he could not, not from so close up. They were trapped. They would soon be dead.

Another step, and his chest was level with the deck of the pilothouse. His head was thrust forward, as if that would help him see. He scanned the space, beginning at the side opposite where the women were hiding, running his eyes slowly around the small stage.

Behind him, another gun discharged, a huge sound echoing around the interior, deafening even over the roar of the flames. The vessel shook as if it had been struck.

Newcomb wheeled around in surprise, twisted on the ladder to see aft.

With a flurry of skirts, a shriek like a banshee, Molly launched herself off the side of the ship and flew across the deck at Newcomb, so suddenly Wendy shouted in surprise.

Newcomb swung around, fired the gun, and Molly hit him square in the chest. The two of them flew down the ladder in a wild, chaotic tumble to the deck below.

Wendy leaped to her feet, raced for the ladder, all but jumped down to the gun deck. Newcomb was pulling himself away, trying to disengage himself from Molly, who was slashing at him with clawed hands, cursing and screaming, out of her mind with rage. Five feet from his right hand, the pistol lay on the deck.

'Oh!' Wendy shouted, ran for the gun. Newcomb cocked a leg, kicked Molly hard, knocked her free, lunged for the pistol. The smoke was coming thicker now, a dark cloud filling the forward end of the casement, obscuring objects even close up.

Wendy fell to her knees, grabbed at the gun, but Newcomb got there first. His hand wrapped around the butt, he swung the weapon around at Wendy's face. Wendy grabbed the barrel and shoved it away as he pulled the trigger.

The pistol fired six inches from her head. The barrel jerked from her fingers, the sound of the shot like a hammer blow, the bullet loud in her ear as it flew past. Newcomb's crazy eyes were a foot from hers. She screamed, raked his face, slashed at his eyes with her nails, slashed him again. He shrieked, rolled away, the gun still in his hand.

Wendy pushed herself up. Molly was standing, heaving for breath. Her left arm was hanging limp, blood running down her fingers, soaking the torn sleeve of her dress. She kicked Newcomb hard in the head, kicked him again.

Wendy grabbed her good arm, pulled her back, even as she was lashing out with her foot again, shouted, 'Go!' She pointed toward the gun port through which they had come. They had to get out. The ship was a death trap. Fire or bullet, they would die by one. 'Go! I'm right behind!'

Molly nodded, raced for the gun port. Newcomb was sitting up, blinking sight back into his eyes, looking around, pushing himself to his feet. Wendy raced after her aunt. The smoke roiled around them. Molly put a leg out the gun port, grabbed the sill with her uninjured arm, swung herself out of the casement.

'No, no, you bitch!' Newcomb roared. He was twenty feet aft, barely visible through the smoke, on his feet, stumbling forward. Wendy backed away, ducked under the pilothouse platform. Too late, she could not get out of the gun port without him seeing her. He would shoot her dead as she tried.

Newcomb limped, cursed, staggered forward, the gun in his hand. Wendy pressed back into the shadows. *Dear God, did he see me?* She was cornered now, she was dead if Newcomb had seen her crawl into that narrow space.

He staggered past, heading for the gun port, following Molly, thinking perhaps that Wendy had gone first. He fired the pistol, put a bullet right through the open gun port, shouted a stream of profanities.

He reached the open port, swung a leg through, straddling the opening, peering out. He reached up and grabbed the sill and began to hoist himself through. Halfway in, halfway out, and that was when Wendy saw the shutter's lever.

Oh God, oh God . . . She flew out of her hiding place, her eyes locked on the lever, her teeth clenched, waiting for the bullet. Five feet, four feet, three feet, her hands stretched out in front of her, she saw in the corner of her eye Newcomb turn, Newcomb scream, Newcomb raise the gun and fire. Felt the bullet pluck her skirt, and then her hands were on the lever and pulling.

For a second it would not budge and she heard Newcomb scream 'No!' and heard the click of the hammer and saw him try to claw his way back in, and

402

then the lever was free in her hands, no resistance. The chain flew through the hole with a wild rattling sound and the heavy shutters swung down and caught Roger Newcomb half in, half out, hundreds of pounds of iron jaws swinging on a single pivot; it caught him there and held him as surely as the hand of God.

The pistol fired, the bullet thumping into the deck. Wendy twisted sideways, waiting for the next shot that would kill her, praying that Newcomb was dead.

He was not. Newcomb's head, shoulder, and gun hand were inside the casement, his left hand and leg outside, the shutter pinning him vertically by the chest. The gun was on the deck where he had dropped it and he was flailing wildly around, his hand slamming against the shutter and grabbing at the edge and trying to pry it away. But the iron shield was built to resist the impact of solid shot at point-blank range, and there was no chance at all that he would move it.

Wendy backed away, eyes on the struggling man, just as Newcomb seemed to notice her. He looked up with bulging eyes, gaping mouth. Wendy wondered if he was being slowly crushed to death, like some barbaric death sentence from another age.

His eyes met hers, and she could see they were wild with pain and fear and fury. He reached out a hand to her, fingers spread, but whether he was looking for help or hoping to get hold of her, to take her to hell with him, she could not tell.

She pressed her hands over her face, overwhelmed by the horror of the scene. She thought of picking up the gun, finishing him off, more for mercy than vengeance, but she knew she could not do that.

Without rage or fear to drive her, she could not shoot a human being.

She stepped sideways, past Newcomb, five feet away, but she could not take her eyes from his, she was transfixed by those mad eyes. They were staring at her but they were seeing the face of certain death. He stretched his hand farther toward her. She sobbed, made a choking sound.

When Newcomb's voice came, it was strangled and cracked. 'Help me,' he said. A trickle of blood came out of the corner of his mouth.

'Oh, God!' Wendy cried, turned her back on the man, and fled. She ran across the deck, past the pilot-house ladder. She fell, felt the pain shoot through her arms as her damaged hands hit the deck, pushed herself right to her feet with hardly a break in her momentum. The smoke was thick and black and choking, she could hardly breathe, her eyes were streaming with tears from the acrid smoke and the horror of what she had just witnessed.

She was becoming disoriented. She stopped. Left or right? She had to get out of the casemate before the smoke overwhelmed her. She could feel her head growing light. She was getting dizzy. Her throat ached from coughing and she had no idea, left or right.

She turned right for no reason at all, other than that she had to turn in one direction. She stumbled forward, through the blackness. Her legs were shaking. She wanted to fall down. But she could see something in front of her, something moving, ghost-like in the smoke.

'Wendy! Wendy!' It was Molly, her voice like a dream. 'Wendy, here!' She could see her aunt's arms waving, her face just visible in the smoke-filled place.

Wendy stumbled on, felt Molly's hands on her, pulling her. The smoke seemed even thicker there, and she realized Molly was outside, standing on the bulwark, half in the gun port, and the smoke was getting sucked out around her.

'Come, dear, right out here!' Molly shouted, and Wendy put a leg through the gun port, grabbed the sill overhead, swung the other out. Molly leaped out of the way and Wendy slid down the side of the casement, slid just a few feet until her feet hit the top of the V-shaped bulwark. She felt herself stagger, thought she would fall, tried to recall what was below her. Then Molly's strong hands were on her arm, pulling her, and she fell inboard, onto the foredeck inside the bulwark.

She landed in a heap and lay there, breathing the air, blessed fresh air, as the smoke rolled away overhead.

She heard Molly's voice in her ear. 'Newcomb?'

Wendy shook her head. It was a few seconds before she could speak. 'Done for,' she said.

Molly let her lie still for a minute more, then said, 'We have to go. It's not safe here.' She helped Wendy to her feet, but Wendy was feeling stronger, the fresh air revitalizing her. Together they climbed over the bulwark and down into the boat, which thankfully Newcomb had tied alongside. They cast off. Wendy set the sail.

Toward the after end of the ship, another cannon discharged, blasting a column of flame over the water.

'We should land where the ship's crew landed, over there.' Wendy pointed toward the dark shoreline.

'Wait,' Molly said. 'I have to know about Newcomb.'

'He's dead. He was caught by the shutters on the gun port.' Wendy did not describe that final, hellish scene. She tried to exorcize it from her mind, but it would not go.

'We thought he was dead before, and he lived,' Molly said with a finality in her voice that Wendy had not heard in some time. 'So this time we wait, until we are certain.'

Wendy sailed the boat around the burning iron-clad. Port and starboard, guns went off, the shells screaming by overhead.

At last they could see Newcomb's arm and leg hanging out the gun port. They were not moving, and Wendy hoped that he was dead, hoped he had died quickly. For their sake she hoped he was dead. And for his, because she did not want to think of what he would be suffering if the fire were reaching him now. She did not need that on her soul.

They stood toward the shore, getting some distance from the ship, then Wendy hove the boat to, the way she had seen it done. They stayed more or less in place, watching the ship burn. Three more guns fired, and then no more. Flames were reaching out the gun ports, licking up the side of the case-ment, making the outline of the ship quite visible in the dark.

Then Wendy realized that it was not so dark. The sun was coming up in the east, a thin line of gray sky on the far horizon. A new day, and they were still alive.

'Very well,' Molly said, breaking the long silence. 'I am satisfied that Newcomb is dead.'

Wendy put the tiller over and the boat began to move. She headed toward shore, and in the gathering gray light could see the landing where the crew of the *Virginia* had set foot on shore, a weary old wooden dock leading up to the bitter end of sandy road.

Wendy brought the boat alongside and Molly tied the painter to a piling. They climbed up a slick wooden ladder to the dock. Silent, they turned and looked across the water at the burning ironclad. Acting Master Roger Newcomb's funeral pyre.

'Bastard,' Molly muttered. 'I wish I had killed him myself.'

And then the CSS *Virginia* exploded. The top of the casemate seemed to lift right up, as if a massive creature made of red and orange and yellow flame were standing up inside, tearing it apart as it stood. Black shards of iron and the long guns like exclamation points lifted up, up into the dawn sky. The entire explosion – the light, the noise, the concussion – was so massive that it melded all into one overwhelming sensation, hurling itself at the women standing dumbfounded on the dock.

They looked with wide eyes and open mouths, and then the shock wave rolled over them and knocked them clean off their feet, tossing them to the ground like children's dolls. They clutched the dirt for protection and felt the earth tremble, and that was the most frightening thing, feeling the only thing in life that is absolutely immovable quivering as if it had no substance at all.

They did not move. The explosion at the shipyard had been a nightmare, but it was a minor affair compared to this Armageddon. Wendy could feel the impact of ironclad parts falling around them. She pictured the huge sections of iron plate, the guns and carriages and shot and massive wooden beams hurling through the air and she wondered if any would drop on them, if Roger Newcomb had killed them after all.

When it was quiet they looked up. The sky was lighter overhead. Massive sections of casemate lay smoldering all around them. A falling cannon had shattered a small oak near the side of the road.

They got to their knees and then to their feet. The *Virginia* was a low dark spot on the water, still burning, like a barge on fire. The casemate was gone, the decks were gone, everything that had made her the invincible ship she was had been blown to the heavens, and now the parts that had once been the USS *Merrimack*, the hull and machinery that had lived already through one sinking and burning, were dying their final death.

The *Virginia* no longer existed.

Molly nodded. 'Now I am very satisfied that Newcomb is dead.'

The women turned and headed up the road. Behind them, the sun broke the horizon, sent its orange light down the road at their feet, threw long shadows ahead of them. A new day. They headed for Richmond.

CHAPTER 27

Our only hope is to make ourselves useful 'up-stream,' and we will keep the enemy at this point in check until they are largely reinforced. The enemy's boats above Fort Pillow are now moored in narrow channels behind sand bars, where we can not attack them again, but we will wait and watch for another opportunity.

Brigadier General M. Jeff Thompson
to General G. T. Beauregard

It was some time after the death of CSS *Virginia* when Samuel Bowater read the news. It saddened him, the way he would have been saddened by the death of someone he had known briefly in person, knew well by reputation, and had come to deeply respect.

Bowater had been there on the night the USS *Merrimack* had gone down, scuttled and burned by the men who had been sent to save her. He had helped raise the hulk of the ship and maneuver it into the dry dock at the Gosport Naval Shipyard. While he had been ferrying supplies around the Norfolk area, chafing at the tedium and flailing around for a way to get into the fight in a meaningful way, he had watched the ship's slow transformation. He had stood by the dry dock on that solemn day in February, just four months before, when she had without fanfare floated free of the blocks.

Four months . . . Bowater wondered if any ship in the history of naval warfare had done so much, had so influenced strategic thinking, had changed the very nature of shipbuilding as profoundly in a career that had lasted just four months. He did not think so.

Four months . . . It seemed more like four years, four times four years, since he had stood beside that granite dry dock in Virginia. Since he had been able to spend evenings with Wendy Atkins, enjoy the trappings of civilization, far from the barbaric shores of the Mississippi.

But no, it had only been four months since then, and less than a month since the Battle of New Orleans. Now the army under Ben Butler, whom they were calling 'Beast,' was in charge in the Crescent City, and Farragut was coming north.

And Bowater, by order of Secretary Mallory, was not concerned with what was happening downstream. It was the enemy upstream, pushing south, that he was there to help stop. Squeezed from both sides, and the pressure was becoming terrific.

He did not know how much fighting he would be doing with the *Tennessee*. They were planking her like mad, but the army would not send any shipwrights, and even house carpenters were getting scarce. The men Bowater had brought with him were good for heavy lifting but not much else.

Construction dragged its tedious way along. Two

lots of lumber for deck plank sat at the Memphis and Charleston Railroad depot, but the manpower was not there to transport it to the shipyard. The iron plate still sat on the Arkansas side of the river, finished but unpaid for, and despite all Bowater's prodding, Shirley could not be induced to take possession of it.

The shipbuilder had any number of excuses: he did not want to waste time before the iron was needed, he did not want to clutter up the yard, the boats were not available to bring it over. But Bowater had a good idea of the real and unstated reason for his reticence. Shirley did not want to pay for iron plate for a ship that he believed would never be launched.

And then there were the engine and shafting, sent downriver with the *Arkansas*. At some point soon it would be time to put them in, and all work would stop until that was done. They couldn't seal up the casemate without first installing the shaft, at least. And if it was not there, then what?

It was all very depressing, so Bowater made a point of not thinking about it.

Noah, he reflected, had built the whole damned ark by himself in less time than it was taking them to finish this gunboat. And just as Noah had his neighbors to taunt him, so Bowater had Mississippi Mike Sullivan.

The ships of the River Defense Fleet moved up and down the river, staying mostly under the guns of Fort Pillow but sometimes dropping down to Memphis. Sullivan did not miss a chance to come by the yard to inspect the half-built *Tennessee*, a look of barely suppressed amusement spread across his bearded face.

The River Defense Fleet was quite literally on the front lines of this fight. The fleet and Fort Pillow

411

formed the levee holding back the Yankee flood. That was it. Remove even one of them and the Yankees would be swarming over Memphis in a few days, and the Mississippi River would be in Federal hands from Cairo, Illinois, clear down to Vicksburg. The very fate of the Confederacy, perhaps, was being decided one hundred miles upriver, and Bowater could do nothing but struggle to finish a ship that no one, himself included, believed could be finished. It was intolerable.

Bowater understood – and he hated the fact – that if he hoped to get into the fast-approaching battle, it would have to be at Mississippi Mike's side.

And that was why, on that perfect morning on the third of June, Lieutenant Samuel Bowater, CSN, found himself just outside the now familiar wheelhouse of the *General Page*, half a mile upriver from Fort Pillow and a good hundred miles from where he was supposed to be.

He watched the sunlight play over the surface of the river and the scrubby vegetation on the bank, and his thoughts drifted off to how he might paint that scene, how desperately he missed painting, how the intense focus of rendering a scene on canvas gave him, for the time it took, a reprieve from the myriad other thoughts that plagued him. He had given Hieronymus Taylor his music back, and it had made a world of difference to the engineer's recovery. He could use a similar diversion.

He shook his head. The guilt over his jaunts upriver with Mississippi Mike was bad enough. He could never bring himself to open a paint set, not then. Such self-indulgence was not in his nature.

To the north, hidden by the humps of land and the

wild turns of the Mississippi River, the first Union mortar of the day fired with a faint, dull thud. Bowater watched the black streak of the shell against robin's-egg blue, watched it arc neatly into Fort Pillow just to the south and go off with a flash and a sharp crack. Just as they had done to the forts below New Orleans, the Union mortars were pounding away at Fort Pillow, and with equally indifferent results.

Fort Pillow was in grave danger, to be sure, but not from the Union mortars.

Nine days before, on the twenty-fifth of May, General P. G. T. Beauregard's seventy-thousand-man army, crippled by dysentery and typhoid and still recovering from their wounds at Shiloh, had abandoned Corinth, Mississippi, in the face of the Union forces creeping toward them. The Confederate line moved fifty miles south, to Tupelo. Fort Pillow, eighty miles west of Corinth, was left flapping in the breeze. The Union gunboats might not dare to face the fort's artillery, but the Union Army would have little difficulty in sweeping over their defenses in a land assault.

The Federals did not know it yet, but Fort Pillow would soon be theirs. And then it was only the River Defense Fleet between them and Memphis.

And Bowater and Sullivan continued their strange dance.

'Now, Cap'n,' Sullivan said, leaning on the rail, trying to meet Bowater's eyes as Bowater drank his coffee, stared out over the water, and tried to ignore him. 'Comes a time a fella gots to face the truth. Even if ya do git yer boat built, git her planked up and iron-clad an all, you ain't got no engines. If ya ain't got engines, ya don't need no engineer.'

This was the one point on which Mississippi Mike was persistent. He had given up his hope of snatching Bowater's men, but he was still agitating for Hieronymus Taylor, as if Taylor were a chattel slave for Bowater to dispose of as he pleased.

'Ask him yourself,' Bowater said. 'I have no authority over his warrant.' Taylor, much improved over the past weeks, had actually accompanied them on this trip. If Bowater took a few steps forward and leaned over the rail he would be able to see the engineer up at the bow, sitting on one of the bollards, his leg, bound in a lighter splint now, thrust out before him.

'Ah, come on now, Cap'n,' Sullivan said. 'I can't go poachin in another man's engine room, it ain't right. It'd be like me askin yer sister to marry, without I asked yer pa first.'

Bowater found that analogy particularly revolting. 'Oh, I see. That's why you don't ask him yourself. And here I thought it was because you know Taylor wouldn't sail with you even if the fate of the Confederacy depended on it.'

'Taylor's pleased to make like he don't care fer me. It's his way. Not like the kind of worshipfulness he shows you . . .'

Bowater ignored the irony. 'You have an engineer.'

'Call that little skunk an engineer? Know what he done this mornin? I ring down three bells, he tells me he ain't got the steam. Ain't got the steam, my Royal Bengal. So I jest goes right down to the engine room, jest to have a look-see. He got so much goddamned steam he's blowin it through. Load of horseshit. And you'd think I walked in on his weddin night, the way he's screamin about me goin down ta the engine room, like I ain't got no right to be down there. Come at me with a wrench and I laid him out good.'

Sullivan grew madder and madder as he told the story, his normal flip attitude deserting him, and Bowater felt a genuine spark of empathy. He had had run-ins enough with engineers over the course of his career. But always the strict discipline and order of the United States Navy had prevented the black gang from running amuck. The River Defense Fleet enjoyed no such discipline or order.

Taylor was a pain in the Royal Bengal, to be sure, but he was also an extraordinary engineer. Nothing in his engine room was ever in disrepair. And while Bowater suspected that Taylor had, in the past, flanked him with that 'ain't got enough steam' bit, the instances were few, and never at a critical time. None of that could be said of Spence Guthrie.

Bowater sympathized with Sullivan. But he would not give him Taylor.

'Cap'n, would you jest talk to Taylor, then? See if he don't want to sail with us? I'll put that pecker-wood Guthrie on the beach in a second.'

From below them, as if it were rising from the deck, came a sound – part shriek, part triumphant shout, part cry of wounded pride – a noise that could only come from the throat of Spence Guthrie.

'Sullivan, you bastard, I knew you was tryin to git me off this boat!'

They still could not see him – he was on the side deck right under their feet. Bowater wondered how long he had been standing there listening, if he had crept up there for just that purpose.

Now they could hear his feet clapping on the deck boards as he ran forward, raced up the stairs, made a fast walking charge across the hurricane deck to where they stood, his arm held out straight, an accusatory finger like a lance pointing at Sullivan.

'I knew you was plottin agin me, you fat son of a bitch, and now I gots my proof!' Guthrie's skin was very white and the black smudges of coal dust stood out vividly. His hair made his head look like a porcupine that had suffered some internal explosion, his scraggly beard like an afterthought. It was hard to imagine what color his shirt and pants had originally been.

'Git the hell off this deck, you little bastard, or I'll kick you clean down to the boiler room,' Sullivan growled. It was the first time Bowater could recall seeing Sullivan genuinely angry – red-faced, eye-bulging, fist-balled angry. He had seen Mississippi Mike get punched, kicked, threatened with knives, shot at, jumped by a mob, arrested, seen chairs broken over his head, but he had never, in all that, actually seen him get seriously angry. Until now. And it was not pretty.

But Guthrie was angry too, angry enough to be oblivious to the clear and present danger that a furious Mike Sullivan represented. 'You the one gonna leave this here boat, Sullivan. Gonna leave her in a pine box, you hear? Hit me when I ain't lookin, like you done this mornin, I'll teach you, you son of a bitch.'

'You will, huh?' Sullivan stepped away from the rail, made fighting room around himself, pushed up his sleeves. He towered over Spence Guthrie, weighed as much as two of him, but Guthrie was undeterred. He stepped back as well. A few more men appeared on the hurricane deck. Bowater saw Hieronymus Taylor

416

clomping awkwardly up the ladder at the forward end. Buford Tarbox stepped out of the pilothouse, leaned on the side, cheroot in mouth.

Bowater did not think this would provide much entertainment. How long did they think Guthrie could stand up to the ursine Mississippi Mike, going slug for slug?

And then the knives came out.

Charles Ellet Jr., steaming down the Mississippi River in the ram *Queen of the West*, felt like Agamemnon of old. Agamemnon, playing the utter fool at Troy.

Ellet, in his former life, was a civil engineer, and had been for many years. He was not a young man. Early in the war he had come up with an idea for fitting out fast steam vessels as rams that could dash at an enemy vessel and sink it faster than it could be sunk with gunfire.

He had been pushing the idea for almost as long as the war had been going on. He went first to the navy, but the navy showed no interest in his ideas, so he took them to the War Department. The War Department was not very enthusiastic either.

But then, on the eighth of March, 1862, the Confederate steamer *Virginia* demonstrated to a skeptical world just how effective a steam ram could be. Edwin Stanton, Secretary of War, was ready to listen to Charles Ellet Jr.

So now he was Colonel Charles Ellet, United States Army, in command of an odd assortment of nine army ram vessels, with little in common save for their strengthened bows, the wooden bulwarks protecting their boilers, and the built-up iron rams bolted to their stems. Urged on by Stanton, he had rushed his rams to Plum Point in the wake of the Confederate attack that had sunk two ironclads and, to Ellet's morbid satisfaction, proved the worth of the ram as a weapon of river warfare.

He personally had arrived on board the *Switzerland*, the last of the fleet, ten days earlier. He was brimming with plans for attacks, runs by Fort Pillow, fights with the Rebels. But Flag Officer Charles Davis showed no interest in his ideas. He would not join Ellet, would not offer one gunboat for the protection of the rams, or any naval officers to man them. He did not return Ellet's correspondence. He did not seem overeager to do much of anything.

Colonel Ellet could stand it no more. He was, after all, army, and not under Davis's command. He could do as he wished, by order of Secretary of War Edwin Stanton, as long as it did not interfere with Davis's plans. And Davis did not seem to have any plans.

Scout boats had reported a single Rebel ram tied up north of the guns at Fort Pillow. The night before, Ellet had determined to act.

He devised a ruse: steam within gunshot of the Rebel, and when the Rebel attacked, retreat upriver, where more of his ram fleet waited to spring the trap.

But, like Agamemnon at Troy, Ellet had decided that before going into battle he would put his crew's temper to the test.

He called the men together, told them his intentions. 'It's a dangerous thing we're doing here,' he said. 'Steaming right up to the Rebel fleet, right under the guns of Fort Pillow. I won't make a man of you go against your will. If any don't care for that kind of risk, he can just step over to the starboard side, and we'll see you put off on another boat.'

He had folded his arms, triumphant in his speech, but felt the triumph melt like ice as more than half his men, including the captain, two out of three of the pilots, the first mate, all the engineers, and nearly all the crew, shuffled to the starboard side and stared up at him with blank faces. A good part of the morning was lost as the unwilling men collected their gear and the second mate brought the *Queen* alongside a barge to let them off.

He was Agamemnon, old and foolish, but he had no Odysseus to correct his blunders. So instead he begged men from the rest of his fleet and got under way, the *Monarch* following in his wake.

He stood now in the wheelhouse, watching the banks of the Mississippi slide by. This was as personal as it could be. He had conceived the idea of the ram fleet and through undaunted will had pushed it through the bureaucracies of Washington, pushed and did not stop until it became a reality floating on the Mississippi River. His passion for the rams was so powerful that it had sucked a significant portion of his family into its vortex. Between brothers, nephews, and son, there were six Ellets sailing as part of the ram fleet.

Just ahead of them, but unseen around the river bend, the day's first mortar fired, arched its shell high into the air to drop unseen on Rebel heads. Ellet felt his muscles tighten. He tapped his fingernail on the sill of the wheelhouse window. The Rebel steamer would be not too far now, and Ellet prayed to God that it would still be there, tied to the bank, ready to show the same kind of grit the Confederate fleet had shown the month before.

He turned and caught a glimpse of *Monarch* before

a bend in the river hid her from sight. *Monarch* was commanded by his brother, Alfred W. Ellet. Alfred had also given his men the option of going ashore, but every one of them had elected to stay with the boat, and Charles wondered why that was, when his own men did not.

Glad to weed out that bad material, in any event, Ellet thought and then thought no more on the matter. He stepped out of the wheelhouse and looked fore and aft and saw that everything was in readiness. Not that there was much to do to prepare. The rams had not a single gun on them, beyond small arms. Ordnance was not what they were about.

'Sir?' An ensign called down the deck from the wheelhouse and Ellet hurried back.

The *Queen*'s new captain, standing by the big wheel, pointed downriver. 'There, sir.' Half a mile away, a Rebel steamer lay against the western bank, the thread of smoke creeping from her chimneys. To the east, and still out of sight, the water batteries of Fort Pillow, and climbing up the steep shore the higher gun emplacements that could drop plunging fire on them.

'Excellent. Let's slow to one bell and give them a chance to get under way.'

The captain grabbed the cord, rang one bell, got a jingle in response. The *Queen of the West* slowed as the engineer below let the steam pressure drop. Ellet looked astern. He could just see the *Monarch* farther upstream, which was as it should be. Alfred would be waiting, ready to dash out and hit the Rebel broadside as the *Queen* lured it upriver.

They stood on. Field glasses revealed little about the Rebel ship. Stern-wheeler, walking beam engine.

Some sort of bulwark on the bow with a gun there. That was about it. There were men on the hurricane deck, or so it seemed, but the appearance of the Queen seemed to generate no excitement.

'Rebels aren't too damned observant,' Ellet growled at the captain. 'I wonder if they're even awake.'

The captain was nodding his concurrence when the first of Fort Pillow's guns fired from one hundred and fifty yards away. The sudden blast in the still morning made Ellet start. The shell screamed past, missing the wheelhouse by no more then twenty feet.

'Reckon they're awake now,' the captain said.

It would not have been much of a fight with fists, but knives were something else entirely. With knives, Sullivan's bulk worked against him, while the quickness that Guthrie enjoyed with his wiry frame more than compensated for Mississippi Mike's greater reach.

They circled, crouching low, arms out, crablike. They each held in front of them one of the huge bowie knives with the full hand guard so beloved by the Westerners. They took tentative swipes at each other, feeling the other's distance, the speed of his reaction.

Bowater, watching, recalled when Sullivan and Tarbox had gone at it. Sullivan landed one good kick and it had been over, and Tarbox seemed to have forgotten it by the time he stood up. This brawl did not look as if it would be resolved so easily.

By the wheelhouse, money was moving from hand to hand. Tarbox was taking the bets.

Guthrie made the first move, stepping into the

421

circle of Sullivan's arms, his left arm blocking Sullivan's right, his knife flashing out and down. Had he made a proper lunge, Bowater noted, front foot out, back leg extended, arm straight, the way Bowater's fencing tutor, Monsieur Ouellette, had taught him, Guthrie would have run the knife into Sullivan's gut. But he did not. It was a quick slash and a jump back out of the way. Sullivan twisted clear of the attack and charged.

He came at Guthrie in a flurry of big arms and steel, knocking the smaller man's knife aside, slashing with his own blade. But Guthrie was as quick as he looked, and much stronger. He leaped back, recovered, met Sullivan's knife, hand guard to hand guard, and held it. Guthrie's foot darted up and caught Sullivan between the legs, and only Sullivan's lightning fast left hand blocked Guthrie from landing a kick that might have done for Mississippi Mike.

They both staggered back, reassessing, still circling. The men crowding the deck were getting vocal, and seemed pretty evenly divided as to who they wished would run a knife through whom.

Captain and engineer came at one another again. Sullivan feinted with his knife, connected with his brogan, right in Guthrie's stomach, doubling the engineer up. Sullivan stepped back to deliver another kick and Guthrie charged like a bull, head-butting Sullivan in the stomach. The breath came out of Sullivan's lungs like steam from an emergency valve but he still managed to bring both hands down on Guthrie's neck, which dropped the engineer to the deck.

Sullivan might have ended it there, if he had not been stumbling back, gasping, barely able to hold his blade. Guthrie rolled over, and willing hands pulled him to his feet, gave him a restorative shake, and pushed him forward.

By the time Guthrie staggered after him, Mississippi Mike had managed to catch his breath and resume his defensive stance, but halfhearted, heaving, as was Guthrie. They came at each other as if they were half asleep, or drunk, or both. Knives swept the air. Sullivan grabbed Guthrie's knife hand, and Guthrie did the same to Sullivan, and they stood there, each holding the other's wrist, forming a circle with their arms, like kids playing a game, teeth bared, faces red, each straining to break the other's grip.

Close upriver, perhaps two hundred yards, one of Fort Pillow's guns fired, a startling sound. Bowater jumped, wheeled around. There was a steamer coming downriver, a Yankee steamer. No one had noticed its approach.

Then from behind, a sound like a grunt and a muffled scream, like someone violently ill. Bowater turned back. In that instant of distraction, Spence Guthrie had managed to free his knife hand. Now his bowie knife was buried in Mississippi Mike Sullivan's gut, almost up to the hand guard. Blood was spilling fresh on the deck.

Sullivan grabbed Guthrie's hand, pulled the hand and the knife away, pulled the blade clean out of his gut. His right hand made a wide sweeping arc through the air and the hand guard of his knife hit the side of Guthrie's head with an impact like round shot, point-blank range.

Guthrie flew sideways, limp as a doll, a spray of blood flying off his face. He hit the deck and did not move, just as Sullivan fell to his knees, hand on his stomach. Blood ran between his fingers. His eyes were wide. He fell slowly onto his side and lay there, curled in a ball.

The fort fired again. Bowater pulled his eyes from the two men laid out on the deck, looked upriver. The Yankee was coming on through the water battery's fire, making right for them, the *General Page*, helpless, tied to the bank, the captain and chief engineer *hors de combat*.

Someone had better do some damn thing, he thought. He looked across the deck at Buford Tarbox, first mate, who was looking back at him.

'Cap'n Bowater, I reckon you're in charge now,' he said, the cheroot never leaving his mouth.

'Me?' Bowater argued. 'You're the first officer, damn it.'

'That's right. First officer. I ain't a cap'n of nothin.'

Bowater shook his head. This was absurd, the *Page* was an army vessel, but arguing was even more absurd. 'Quarters!' he shouted. 'Hands to quarters! Cast off the fasts! What steam do we have?'

He looked around. No one moved.

'Git, you som bitches!' Tarbox shouted and the men scrambled.

'What steam do we have?' Bowater asked again. There were only a few men left on the hurricane deck, and the only one who knew was out cold.

'Mr Taylor,' Bowater turned to Hieronymus Taylor, who was looking down at the groaning Mississippi Mike. 'Could I impose on you to take over in the engine room?'

Taylor looked up, met his eyes. Bowater had expected the half-amused, half-resigned look, a look he knew well, on Taylor's face. But that was not it.

There was something else. He could not place it. On another man it might have been trepidation, hesitation. But not on Taylor. Bowater did not know what it was.

Fort Pillow fired again, three guns in rapid succession. The battery was almost lost in its own gun smoke. And the Yankee stood on.

'Reckon I'll git below,' Taylor said, and hobbled off.

CHAPTER 28

If not already done, for God's sake order the River Defense Fleet to defend every bend and dispute every mile of river from [Fort] Pillow here.
Brigadier General M. Jeff Thompson
to General Daniel Ruggles,
Confederate States Army

For Bowater, stepping into command was like pulling on an old, worn coat. Once he began issuing orders, he forgot about how utterly absurd it was that he should be in that situation. His mind was entirely taken up with strategy.

Yankee, water battery, current, steam, bow gun. His world was reduced to those elements, the only ones that mattered.

He leaned into the speaking tube that communicated with the engine room. 'Mr Taylor, are you there?' he shouted. He waited a moment, opened his mouth to speak again, when Taylor's voice echoed back up the tube. 'I'm here, Cap'n.' That familiar tone of exasperation, it was good to hear it again.

'What do you have for steam?'

Another pause, a sigh of even deeper exasperation. 'Still below service gauge. I can give you one bell in five minutes.'

'Very well. As soon as you can.' Bowater straightened, looked out the wheelhouse window. They had no steam, but the current was with them. Worst case, they could cast off and drift down to the rest of the River Defense Fleet, anchored below Fort Pillow.

The guns of the fort were blasting away, the low water battery and now the guns higher up, sending a shower of metal across the river, but the Yankee was pressing on through it. *He's a cool one*, Bowater thought. It was one of the rams he and Sullivan had seen upriver. A big letter *Q* hung between the chimneys.

What to do, what to do . . . Bowater stepped out of the wheelhouse, looked down the boat's larboard side, the side pressed against the riverbank. The lines were all cast off, save for the bow and stern, and those were ready to slip. He turned to look where Sullivan and Guthrie had fallen. Their shipmates had carried them away, and all that remained of their fight was a pool of Mississippi Mike's blood, and a splatter of Guthrie's.

With his mind occupied, Bowater had not given them a second thought, but now he did. He recalled Guthrie's big knife thrust into Mike's gut. He had seen gut wounds before. There was not much hope for anything but a quick death, and even that was not likely.

Guthrie? Bowater could not tell. That hit he took to the side of the head might well have crushed his skull. Sullivan was strong enough to do it. In a day or two, they might both be dead.

What a God almighty waste, Bowater thought. The Confederacy could scarcely afford to have its own people killing each other. The Yankees were doing that fast enough.

He heard a creak, a groan behind him. The walking beam made its first agonizing move, up and down, with just steam enough to drive it. The paddle wheels began to turn, slowly, painfully, like an old man getting out of bed.

Good enough. Bowater strode back to the wheelhouse. 'Cast off, fore and aft,' he said to Tarbox.

Tarbox stepped quickly to the larboard side. 'Cast off, fore and aft!' he shouted and the bow and stern fasts, looped around trees ashore, came snaking through the low brush and whipped back aboard. The distance from boat to shore began to open up, a strip of muddy water between them. Bowater turned to the helmsman. 'You have steerage?'

The helmsman grunted, spun the wheel a half turn. 'A bit. Enough.'

'Very well. Make for the Yankee steamer.'

'Yankee steamer,' the helmsman repeated, gave a turn to starboard, steadied her up. The *General Page* could barely stem the current with the steam she had. They were a long way from having the momentum to ram, while the Yankee had a full head of steam and the current to boot. If she got a clean shot with her ram, it might be the end of the *Page* and Bowater's brief tenure with the River Defense Fleet.

He grabbed the engine room bell cord, rang up three bells, could well imagine the string of profanities Hieronymus Taylor was pouring on his name.

They were crossing the river diagonally, closing

with the Yankee. Fort Pillow was flinging shell and round shot across the water, but it seemed to have little effect on the intruder.

'Tell the bow gun to fire when ready,' Bowater said and Tarbox nodded, carried the order forward. In a minute the first mate was back. 'You gonna fight this son of a bitch?' he asked, disinterested, as if the decision did not involve him.

'Perhaps . . .' As he said it, a cat's-paw of wind enveloped the fort, lifted the smoke away, revealing the batteries, the turned earth of the redoubts climbing up the bank. And beyond that, another column of smoke, a double column, twisting together to form a single black line, rising from the river, upstream.

Oh, you tricky son of a bitch . . .

'It's a trap, Mr Tarbox,' Bowater said. 'There is at least one more of these Yankee rams waiting upstream for us. See the smoke?'

Tarbox looked in the direction that Bowater indicated. He puffed his cheroot, nodded his head.

'Reckon we best get the hell outta here,' Tarbox said.

Bowater nearly said, 'Reckon so,' but he stopped himself. 'Yes, indeed.'

Forward, the *Page*'s bow gun fired, adding to the din from the fort. 'Tell the men on the stern to fire when they bear,' Bowater said to Tarbox, then to the helmsman, 'Bring her around. We'll make for the rest of the fleet below the fort.'

The helmsman spun the wheel, and with the mounting steam and the current with them at last, the *General Page* seemed to fly downriver, leaving the Yankee in the hail of fire from Fort Pillow. The stern chaser, loaded and ready, fired upriver. They were almost up to their anchorage before the gun fired a second time.

Bowater conned the steamer to a place between the *Colonel Lovell* and the *Little Rebel* and ordered the anchor let go. The Yankee had turned on his heel and was steaming back upriver, with nothing to show for his efforts.

Doc appeared at the wheelhouse door. Dried blood formed a new layer of stains on his apron, on top of the rest of the filth. There was a smear of blood on his worried-looking face as well. 'Cap'n Bowater?' he asked with more deference than Bowater would have thought he had in him. 'Cap'n Sullivan, he's askin for ya.'

'Very well.' Bowater looked into the cook's blue eyes and saw trouble. 'Have you been ministering to him? How is he?'

'He ain't good. Well . . . hell, I don't know. Gut wound's a bad thing. Reckon you know that. Sullivan says he'll be fine, but hell, I don't see how.'

Bowater nodded. 'Guthrie?'

'Still out cold.'

'Very well.' He gestured toward the forward ladder and Doc led the way down to the boiler deck, then aft to Sullivan's cabin. Bowater stepped into the familiar room where he and Mississippi Mike had created their masterwork, then into the sleeping cabin beyond.

Sullivan was stretched out on his bunk, his shirt torn open, a pile of bloody bandage on his stomach. His skin looked white and waxy, and the dim lantern light shone on the film of perspiration that covered his body.

'Cap'n Bowater,' Sullivan said, his voice lacking the

drive and timbre that Bowater had come to expect. 'I would sure admire a drink of water.'

'No water!' Doc shrieked from behind Bowater's back. 'I done told you, no water!'

'Aw, hell, is he here?' Sullivan said. 'How's a fella supposed to live with no water?'

'I don't know,' Doc said, with more of the old cussedness back in his voice. 'I just know gut wound means no water.'

Sullivan let his head roll back in a way that implied resignation. 'Doc told me you took command up there. What happened, Cap'n? With the Yankee, an all?'

Samuel stepped closer. He felt himself growing solicitous, as if it was all right to be genuine and caring in this instance, since the man was going to die anyway. He told him about the trap upriver, and the firing from the fort and their escape below Fort Pillow's guns.

Sullivan nodded weakly. 'You done a good job, Cap'n,' he said, and though Bowater found that Sullivan's patronizing compliment rankled, he kept silent because of his current forgiving mood.

'Now see here,' Sullivan continued, his voice weak, his tone conspiratorial, 'I need you to do me a favor, Cap'n, need it more'n I ever needed anything. You can't tell Thompson or Montgomery or nobody about me being laid up here. You do, they'll put me on the beach, give my boat to someone else, an I can't have that. Couldn't live with it.'

You probably won't be living with anything for long, Bowater thought.

'You got to take over fer me, Cap'n, least until I'm on my feet,' Sullivan continued. He reached out a

431

hand – the move seemed almost delicate and fluttery – and clutched Bowater's arm. 'Send Tarbox over to the flag boat, have him tell Montgomery we gots to go to Memphis fer somethin. Need boiler parts or some such. Jest so's we're out of here whiles I convalesce.'

'Sullivan . . . you need a doctor. A real doctor. You should be in a hospital.'

'Ain't a thing . . .' Sullivan stopped, gritted his teeth, then sighed as the pain passed. 'Ain't a thing they can do in a hospital I can't have done here. But if we gets to Memphis, I'll get me a doctor to take a look. All right?'

Bowater frowned. A dying man's last request, or near enough. How could he refuse? 'Very well.'

Sullivan gave a smile of sorts, and seemed to shrink back into his pillow.

'Here, now, that's enough of the damned chitchat,' Doc interrupted, his reserve of pleasantness now expended. 'You get the hell out of here.' He half pushed Bowater across the cabin and toward the door. It wasn't until he had actually shoved Bowater out onto the side deck that he grudgingly added, 'Cap'n.'

Hieronymus Taylor sat amid the hissing, the clanging, the popping, the groaning, the *leit motif* of his life since he had spit on the refinement and wealth of his birthright and, at fifteen, picked up a shovel and begun heaving coal on a New Orleans side-wheel tug.

He sat on a stool, his wood slat-encased leg thrust out straight. It hurt, but not so bad. It was mending fast. He wondered if he would live long enough for it to actually heal.

His eyes moved naturally to the boilers, and in the dim illumination from the skylight on top of the fidley and from the few lanterns, he could see the pressure gauges and water gauges. All was where it should be, or near enough, but what was going on in the inside? In his mind he moved through the iron shells of the scotch boilers, probed the sides for weak spots, looked for stuck gauges, rusty corners, fire tubes ready to give out, pipes on the verge of blowing apart.

What was hiding in there, waiting to kill them all?

They had been under way, Bowater frantically ringing up three bells when he knew there was barely steam for one, some great emergency. And now they were anchored. Why that was, what was going on topside, Taylor did not know and did not ask. Not his concern. Just keep the steam up. Try not to kill us all. But could he do that?

On the ships where Hieronymus Taylor had served as chief engineer, and even as second and third, the machines became an extension of himself. He could feel a problem as surely as he could feel a pain in his own body or the onset of some illness. It was that realization, that he possessed such mechanical empathy, that drove him down into the engine rooms in the first place. His father had indulged him for years, seeing him tutored in the theoreticals of mechanical engineering, the emerging science of steam. He had hoped that his son would manifest his love of mechanics at a desk or drafting table, and not in an engine room. He had hoped young Hieronymus would not reject the station to which he was bred.

But in the end he had. Because he was an ornery

son of a bitch by nature, and because engineering did not happen in drawing rooms, but in engine rooms.

Eli Taylor, you old, pretentious, holier than thou bastard . . . He and his father had been at loggerheads since as early as Hieronymus could recall, and the prodigal son was pleased to reject everything the old man stood for – wealth, privilege, refinement. He resented the old man, and loathed him.

Or at least he had. But as the years mounted, the sharp edge of those passions dulled, and he began to see that maybe his father was not so wrong in everything. Eli, after all, had not inherited his wealth, but had fought tooth and nail for it, every penny, had pulled himself up from the docks around New Orleans, had made himself into a sophisticated man of the world. Only to see his son take exactly the opposite trajectory.

Hieronymus Taylor began to wonder how his father was doing, and his mother, began to toy with the idea of visiting them. Take a leave, Lord knew he had earned it.

He heard a pop and a hiss. *Aw, hell, Guthrie, what the hell have you done now?*

The second engineer, a hopped-up fireman named Burgoyne, ducked around the condenser. 'Got a steam gauge broke here,' he said.

'Can you fix her?'

'Reckon.'

'Go on, then.'

What in damnation else is waiting to let go? Taylor was sorry to see Mississippi Mike gored on that big bowie knife – and the emotion surprised him. He was more than happy to see Guthrie take a hard one to the head. He didn't mind an engineer who was a whining, sniveling malcontent, but he could not tolerate one who let his engines go to hell.

His mind raced over all the thousand things that could fail and make the boilers blow, like they had blown aboard the *Yazoo River*, and he felt the sweat standing out on his forehead, and he knew it was not the heat kind of sweat. At least no one else could know that, not when it was one hundred or more degrees down there. *Damn it, goddamn it . . .* It was bad enough without now having to be responsible for boilers that had been maintained by a lazy incompetent.

He heard steps on the ladder and was surprised to see Samuel Bowater climbing down the fidley.

'Chief,' Bowater said, stepping over to the work-bench where Taylor sat, casting his eye around the dimly lit boiler room and engine room.

'Cap'n. What brings you to the Stygian depths?'

'Thought it was easier for me to come down to the underworld than for Hades to come topside with a broken leg. Everything all right here?'

Taylor scratched a lucifer on the bench, lit a cigar. 'Good as can be expected.' His hand was trembling, but Bowater was looking the other way. 'Hard to know for sure, with a beat like Guthrie, what's ready to give out.'

Bowater nodded as he looked around. 'Sullivan's asked me to take command here, and not tell his commanding officer about his wound. He's afraid he'll be relieved of command.'

Taylor smiled at that, a genuine smile. 'Hell, he's gonna be dead in a day or so.'

'Most likely. Hard to say. He's a tough one, and Doc says he might make it.'

'Doc? You mean the cook?'

Bowater cleared his throat. 'Yes, well, in any event we can only wait and see. I agreed to Sullivan's request. It seemed the only decent thing to do.'

'Decent. Sure.'

Bowater turned and met his eyes and there was a vulnerability there that Taylor had seen only once before, when he had helped Bowater lift the body of Thadeous Harwell, his young first officer killed at the Battle of Elizabeth City, onto the boat that had come for them.

'I'll be honest, Chief,' Bowater said. 'I can't stand the thought of being on the shore and watching the fight. I can't stand looking at that damned *Tennessee* one more minute, wasting time trying to finish her when we never will.'

Aw, hell, don't go'n tell me none of this, I don't want to hear any goddamned confessions, Taylor thought. But he remained silent.

'I'm so eager to get into a fight I feel like I could explode,' Bowater continued, and Taylor wondered what had gotten into that patrician peckerwood. Where had his relationship with Bowater gone so terribly wrong that Bowater now thought he could confide his feelings? The only good thing about Bowater had always been that he kept to his damned self.

'After Elizabeth City and New Orleans . . . a sensible man would want to stay out of harm's way.' He paused. 'I don't know.'

'Damned if I know either, Cap'n. But I reckon you done the best thing.'

'Well, thank you. I . . . ah . . . I came down here to tell you, we'll be returning to Memphis if Tarbox can get Montgomery to agree to it. We'll get medical help for Sullivan and Guthrie.' Bowater seemed embarrassed now, as well he should. 'Are we set to make the trip downriver?'

Taylor looked around. He could think of a hundred reasons why they should not try, but how many of them were just excuses, how many were real? 'We ain't got enough coal in the bunkers right now. And I'd like to have a go at the air pump. I don't like the sound of it.'

'How long will the air pump take?'

'Half a day?'

'Very well. It will take that long to get coal, I should imagine.' Bowater paused, then continued. 'I had thought . . . my thought was, after we get to Memphis and get Sullivan and Guthrie squared away, I hope we can return upriver, rejoin the River Defense Fleet. The ship is in need of an engineer – I don't think Guthrie will be recovering soon. I would be most pleased if you would take that position. Assuming it is mine to offer.'

Oh, God . . . So here was damned Bowater the fire-eater, itching to get into a fight. Bowater the stick-up-the-ass, don't-get-coal-ash-on-my-white-gloves, night-at-the-opera patrician, dying to get into the monkey show with the Yankees, while he, Hieronymus Taylor, felt like jumping out of his skin from shear panic every time a pipe creaked.

'I'd be delighted to steam this here bucket into a fight, Cap'n,' he said.

He remembered once, in a frenzy of passion, telling a girl that he loved her. It was the last time he recalled his words sounding so completely insincere.

* * *

437

Bowater thumbed through the signal book, hoisted number fourteen, *Coal, I am in want of*. He dispatched Tarbox to the flag boat with requests and excuses.

It was not until late afternoon of the following day that they had coal aboard, the air pump rebuilt, and Commodore Montgomery's leave to go. Tarbox reported Sullivan down with a bad cold, unable to get out of bed, and Montgomery did not question him. By the time the anchor came up from the river bottom, Bowater was very eager to be out from under the flag boat's gaze. He did not like living with deception. He felt like a child waiting for his parents to discover the broken vase.

Tarbox might not have any inclination to take command, but he was pilot enough that, once under way, he could con the *General Page* though the river's tricky bars and shallows and snags. But Bowater could not ask the man to stand watch all night, so they tied up to the riverbank and posted a guard, and when the General Pages were done drinking, smoking, gambling, and brawling in the saloon, which was sometime after midnight, they slept.

Bowater, reluctantly, went to visit Sullivan, as he had done several times already. The river man looked even paler and more waxy than he had before, with beads of sweat standing out on his forehead. He drifted in and out of consciousness, and much of his talk seemed incoherent, though with Sullivan, Bowater found it hard to tell.

There were some people, Bowater knew, who had the words for just such a situation as that, the deathbed watch, but he did not. Should he tell Sullivan that everything would be all right? Should he

438

tell him he had better think about making his peace with God? The small talk he offered seemed facile and absurd, talking with a man who was facing eternity.

Finally, mercifully, Sullivan fell asleep and Bowater was able to sneak guiltily out of the cabin. He looked in on Guthrie, who did not look much better than Sullivan. His breathing was shallow and labored. He had not opened his eyes since Sullivan's hand guard had connected with his temple.

Bowater made his weary way back to his own cabin, aware that it really had become his own cabin, so much time had he spent with the River Defense Fleet.

In the early predawn hours, Guthrie died. He had opened his eyes once while Doc was there, opened them wide and in a strong voice said, 'Mind the damn feed water!' Then he closed them again and never said another word. Three hours later, he gave a gasp, a rattle, and he was gone.

Doc told Bowater all about it the following morning, up at the wheelhouse, with the first light breaking in the east. 'Fella's got to be real careful,' Doc said, staring at Bowater with an odd sort of intensity. 'Lotta ways a fella can git kilt. Look at ol' Guthrie there. Got liquored up, fell down the ladder into the engine room, smashed the whole side of his head right in.' He held Bowater's eyes, daring him to contradict that version of events. 'Got a dozen fellas saw it happen, be more'n happy to swear to it,' he added.

It would not have occurred to Bowater to bring Sullivan up on charges, but he did not care for the short cook's less than subtle coercion. 'Thank you . . . Doc . . . for your help with my memory. Please return

439

to your duties.' He turned his back on the man, the interview over.

They were under way with the rising sun, past a shoreline of hard-luck farms and wild places that looked like they must have looked before white men ever passed that way. Bowater knew the river fairly well by now, between Fort Pillow and Memphis, and he found he could pilot the boat himself in some places, having been up and down enough times to recall how certain stretches should be navigated. He and Tarbox took turns standing watch.

It was just getting on dark when they came alongside the levee in Memphis.

'Mr Tarbox, I must go to Shirley's yard and see what is happening there,' Bowater said. 'Please find a doctor to look in on Captain Sullivan, but he is not to be removed from the ship unless absolutely necessary. And please get Guthrie's body to the morgue. You may report his death in any manner you see fit.'

'Awright, Cap'n,' Tarbox said.

'Very well. Carry on.' Bowater was still astounded that these river rats would listen to him. But men like that, he knew, really craved leadership and discipline, deep down, and would latch onto it when it was offered.

Before stepping ashore, Bowater climbed down into the engine room, looking for Taylor. He found him at the feed water pump, a wrench in his hand, a coal passer standing by with half a dozen other tools. The fires were banked, the steam pressure down to three pounds, and Taylor looked much more relaxed.

'Chief?' Bowater had been dreading this moment. He was still burning with embarrassment over his humiliating confession to Hieronymus Taylor. Why

440

he had done that, why he had let the words come unchecked from his generally guarded mouth, he could not fathom. He wondered what breed of self-indulgent idiot Taylor now took him for.

'Chief, how'd the engine do?'

Taylor turned and looked at him, and his face revealed nothing. 'Not bad. Ran. Boilers didn't blow up. Don't reckon we could ask for much more.'

'Good. I am going over to the shipyard. Would you care to join me?'

'I best get this here feed water pump goin, or we ain't gonna be so lucky next time. I'll come by later.'

'Very well. Thank you, Chief, for taking over here.'

Taylor smiled, shrugged. 'You keep gettin my engine rooms blowed up or sunk, I got to find work where I can.'

Bowater left the *General Page* as the sun dipped away and the sky was lit blue and orange with the last rays of light coming over the horizon. He walked fast down the waterfront street to the open place that Shirley had turned into a shipyard. He felt guilty, as if he had abandoned his family.

He was brought up short by the crowd of men in the shipyard. At that hour he would not have expected more than half a dozen, finishing up for the day, with John Shirley rushing around as ever. But all the men were there now, his men, the yard workers. A small knot of soldiers in gray and butternut. An officer with a frock coat and gold swirls on the cuff.

Whatever was going on, Bowater suspected it was not good.

He hurried across the hard-packed ground to where the soldiers stood, about ten feet from the *Tennessee*'s port quarter, the focal point of the men

441

sitting and standing around. He could see now that the officer was talking with Shirley, the short man hidden behind the crowd around him.

'Mr Shirley, what is going on here?' Bowater said, pushing through, insinuating himself into the discussion.

The army officer turned to him slowly, with an imperious look. 'And you are?'

'Lieutenant Samuel Bowater, Confederate States Navy. I am the commanding officer of the ship building on the ways here.'

'Indeed?'

'It's bad news, Captain, damned bad news,' Shirley chimed in. 'Telegraph just brought word. Fort Pillow's abandoned. The *Golden Age* went up to get the last of the men out. Now there isn't a damn thing but sandbars and snags between the Yankees and Memphis.'

Bowater felt his stomach drop. 'Is there any word of the Yankees? Are they coming?'

The army officer, annoyed by Shirley's interruption, now commandeered the conversation. 'We believe they are on the move now. We don't know when they will be here, but we suspect soon. As Mr Shirley has said, there is little holding them back.'

'The River Defense Fleet's falling back to the city,' Shirley butted in again. 'The army officers are holding public meetings all over the city, see about organizing some defense, but it don't look good, not good at all.'

'Yes, anyway, that is not what we are concerned with,' the army officer said.

'And you are?' Bowater asked, not willing to be outdone in the imperious department.

'Captain van Reid, second assistant provost marshal. I am here by order of the provost. I . . .'

'He wants to burn the ship!' Shirley chimed in, like jumping on the punch line of a joke. 'He come here to order us to burn the damned *Tennessee*!'

'Is that true?'

'Lieutenant,' van Reid said with elaborate weariness, 'I have already argued the point with Mr Shirley, and I do not intend to argue it again. Unless you can launch this ship and tow it away before, say, sunrise tomorrow, it will have to be destroyed. It cannot be allowed to fall into Yankee hands.'

Bowater pressed his lips together, scowled, tried to think of something to say. Something insightful that would alter the situation. He could think of nothing, so he said, 'Can't the city be defended?'

'We have something in the neighborhood of two hundred troops to defend the city. You tell me, Lieutenant. Now if you will excuse me, I have a great deal to do. Launch your ship, and if you cannot, burn it. If it is not floating or burning by midnight, I will return and do it myself.'

He turned and marched off and the clutch of soldiers marched after him, leaving Bowater and Shirley and the rest to stare, open-mouthed.

Bowater looked at Shirley and Shirley looked at Bowater. There was not much to say. They might have launched the *Tennessee* in a few days, but not a few hours.

'There's some turpentine up in the paint shed,' Shirley said at last. 'That'll get things going along.'

Bowater knew the words he had to speak. Gather up flammable material, pack it around the ship, douse it with turpentine. But they would not come.

'Tanner, please see the ship ready for burning,' he ordered instead, and let Ruffin Tanner make the preparations.

The men did not move fast, not one of them was enthusiastic about the job at hand. But slowly, bales of cotton and straw and scrap timber were piled around the ship, the bare wood of her hull showing like white bone in the torchlight. *Like burning her at the stake*, Bowater thought. The ship was dying for his heresy.

Hieronymus Taylor appeared, walking on a crutch, and stood back in the shadows and watched.

It was full dark when the provost marshal arrived, expecting to find the men unwilling to burn the ship, or so Bowater suspected. But preparations were far enough along that the provost said nothing, beyond an introduction and 'Very good. Carry on.'

And then it was ready, there was nothing left to do, no excuse for delay. 'All right, you men.' Bowater turned to his crew behind him. 'Go ahead.'

The men with the torches stepped forward, solemn, as if they were part of a religious service. Up and down the ways they put flame to turpentine-soaked tinder and the fire roared to life, sprang up out of the cotton and hay and wood as if it had been there all along and was only waiting to be released.

Bowater stepped back from the heat, and the others did as well. Soon the shipyard was lit with the dancing light, yellow and deep shadow.

Oh, God, what a waste, what a waste ... Bowater did not know if he should feel guilty about his less than stellar effort at getting the ship ready, or angry that he had wasted precious time on such a lost cause.

They remained in the shipyard for a little more

than two hours, watching the great wooden edifice collapse into a pile of glowing coal, and then they left. Bowater took his men back to the *General Page*. Sullivan would get his wish in the end – Bowater's men would join his crew, Hieronymus Taylor would run the engine room. Bowater wondered if Sullivan would be alive in the morning so that he could enjoy his final victory.

But not a victory, not really. Sullivan might have got Bowater's men, but Bowater had Sullivan's ship. That thought stirred something else in Samuel Bowater, something deep. The Yankees would be there soon, perhaps in the morning. But he had a ship. He could fight them. He would not be watching from the shore, or holding his tongue as Mississippi Mike Sullivan gave orders.

And that, at least, was something.

CHAPTER 29

Without it was a strategic movement, it was useless to evacuate Fort Pillow. If we are allowed to place the mortars on rafts and permitted to use the transports and play strategy back on the enemy, I will contract to hold this river above Memphis for a month.

Brigadier General M. Jeff Thompson
to General Daniel Ruggles

Flag Officer Charles Davis, United States Navy, looked around his cabin and reflected on the lack of fiddles.

On the ships that he knew, the ones he had spent his career aboard, there were fiddles on everything, wooden lips around the edge of any flat surface to keep things from sliding off when the ship was rolling in a seaway. Fiddles on the bookshelves, around the tables, around the washbasin, little walls to keep non-secured items from hitting the deck.

There were no fiddles aboard the ironclad gunboat Benton. The *Benton* did not roll. She rocked a little, every once in a while, but the motion could not be

446

called 'rolling.' This was a different kind of ship, in a very different kind of war.

He sighed and looked down at his diary, open on the desk in front of him. The cabin was lit with several lanterns, enough light to read and write, but Davis missed the big stern windows of the captain's cabin of a proper man-of-war. This was more like a bunker than a cabin.

He picked up his pen and he wrote:

June 5. Colonel Fitch discovered several days ago a weak and assailable point by which he proposed to attack the enemy's works by land while I encountered the batteries in front. It was agreed between us that this should come off yesterday morning, but a foolish movement of Colonel Ellet prevented it in a way that could not have been foreseen. The movement was then to have been made this morning, as soon after daylight as possible. But the Rebels retreated yesterday and last night, after, as usual, destroying everything.

These works are very extensive and very strong.

I am now lying under the batteries of Fort Pillow, waiting for Colonel Fitch to return from some examinations he is making. As soon as he comes back we will make our preparations for going down the river. I do not believe that there is any force at Randolph. If not, there is probably no interruption between here and Memphis, except, perhaps, the enemy's gunboats, and they would detain us but a short time.

He heard footsteps in the alleyway, the inevitable knock on the door. 'Yes?'

A midshipman's voice. 'Sir? Colonel Ellet wishes to speak with you.'

Davis sighed. Ellet had been giving him a pain in the neck for the past ten days. He represented the worst of all possibilities: a civilian just recently turned army officer who was now playing at naval commander, with some bizarre notion he had dreamed up – flimsy little rams with which he hoped to run the enemy down.

Ellet had been badgering him since he arrived with various half-baked ideas for this foray or that attack. They had danced around the question of who had authority over whom, until they decided that neither had authority over the other, and then Ellet had started doing as he pleased.

Terrific bloody situation – two complete, separate waterborne commands on the same stretch of river . . .

Davis blew on the diary to be sure the ink was dry, and to make Ellet wait for a moment more, then closed it up. 'Come!' he shouted. The midshipman opened the door and Ellet stepped in.

'Colonel.' Davis nodded a greeting.

'Captain.' Ellet nodded back. 'Might I be so bold as to ask if you are ready to move on Memphis?'

'Have a seat.' Ellet's eagerness irritated the flag officer. The old man seemed to imply, with every word and action, that he, Davis, was not moving fast enough. Because Ellet the Upstart did not understand the need for planning and care. He did not appreciate the strategic importance of the gunboats, or how the advantage enjoyed by the Union would be wiped out if the ships were lost or, God forbid, captured, which they could be, if their commander did something rash and stupid.

When Ellet was seated, which Davis knew made him uncomfortable, which is why he had insisted, the captain began to speak. 'We will begin our move on Memphis this afternoon. We will not, however, rush headlong at the enemy. There is still a fortification at Randolph and we must make certain—'

'I have already been down to Randolph,' Ellet interrupted. 'I went down this morning with some of my rams to demand surrender. I sent a man ashore and he found the works deserted.'

Davis shifted in his seat. This was annoying in the extreme. 'On your own authority, you decided to demand the surrender of the Confederate works at Randolph?'

'Yes, on my own authority. Which comes from Secretary of War Stanton.'

'I see . . .' Davis stared at his desk for a moment, let the irritation pass. There would be time to deal with this later, but with Memphis hanging there like a ripe plum he did not have time now to waste on Ellet. 'Well, if that is the case, we shall get under way immediately. As I have related to you before, I see the rams in a role such as that of light skirmishers, whereas the gunboats would be more in the line of heavy artillery. For purposes of order of battle, I would like to see your rams on the wings of my squadron, and in the rear. Ready to dash forward, take the enemy in the flank if the opportunity presents itself, pick off stragglers, and the like. It would be folly to expose your . . . light craft to the brunt of the enemy's fire.'

'I see, Captain. Though I more imagine my rams in

the role of cavalry, charging forward, lightly armed but fast. However, in this I will yield to your authority.'

'Very good, Colonel.' Davis stood to make it clear he was done talking about this, and Ellet stood as well. 'The fleet will get under way in a few hours or so.'

'Very good, Captain. In the meanwhile the ram fleet will proceed downriver and meet up with you when you get down by Randolph.' Ellet held out his hand. The men shook, and Ellet was gone.

Davis sat again with a sigh. *In the meanwhile . . .* Bloody man.

He looked down at his diary. He had hopes of publishing it one day, when the war was over and he had achieved enough noteworthy accomplishments. He noticed a stack of paper on the edge of his desk. He squinted at it, trying to recall what it was. And then he remembered – the manuscript the Rebel spy had delivered to him.

He reached for it, smiled as he recalled that singular meeting. *Send the book to a New York publisher, honest to God!*

But in truth, he still did not know if the big secesh yahoo was serious or not. The Reb had given up a fair amount of intelligence regarding the situation in Memphis, revealed things that might or might not be helpful.

Not that Davis was starving for information about the enemy. Since the Rebels had instituted a conscription a few months back, deserters had been streaming north, and they all had a story. What the big Reb had said agreed with some accounts Davis had heard, contradicted others. It was hard to know.

He decided to let them go mostly out of appreciation for the outrageous nature of their story. It had given him hours of amusement, thinking on it and telling the other officers. Nor could the Rebels have gleaned any important information from their visit, even if they were spies. They didn't learn anything that a person sneaking through the woods on shore with a telescope couldn't have learned.

Taking them prisoner would have involved a big brouhaha over their flag of truce and their status at the time of their capture. Davis could envision the tedious correspondence that would result. In the end, it was less bother to just send them away.

He reached over and picked up the bundle of paper, smudged and dog-eared. He had tossed it on his desk and forgotten it, had not even looked at the title page.

Mississippi Mike, Melancholy Prince of the River. Davis frowned at the title. Was this a joke? Or were these idiots serious? He set the top page aside and began to read.

Chapter One – A Ghostly Tale. On the whole of the Mississippi, there is no man who would dare cross Mississippi Mike, best of the river-boat men. And of all of them, you'd reckon it was his kin would know best that the hardest drinkin, hardest fightin man on Western Waters was not a fellow to be done dirty.

By the end of the first page, Captain Davis was smiling. He read on. Ten minutes later he was laughing out loud.

During her wild run through Hampton Roads and

the Elizabeth River, Wendy Atkins had all but forgotten why she was doing what she was doing. Before, she would not have thought that possible. Risking everything to race across the country into the arms of one's lover – it was so romantic, she would never have dreamed anything could make her lose sight of that goal. But that was before she had been threatened with hanging or shooting or rape or burning to death.

Wendy Atkins discovered, during that short and brutal time, that, girlhood fantasies aside, even true love could not take precedence over everything.

Wendy nearly forgot her primary objective, but she did not forget it entirely. As she and Molly staggered up the dirt road, leaving the smoldering hulk of the *Virginia* behind, heading vaguely north toward Richmond, she remembered. Samuel Bowater.

When Molly finally collapsed at the side of the road, unable to go on after all the blood she had lost from the gunshot wound in her arm, Wendy remembered.

She dressed Molly's wounds, made her comfortable, sat with her in the shade by the side of the road. And as Molly slept, Wendy thought of Samuel Bowater, of the look he would have on his face when he saw her, after recovering from the shock of her being there. They would run to one another, wrap their arms around each other, kiss in a brazen and heedless way, careless of what the world thought, because they were in love.

Of course, Samuel was not generally the brazen and heedless kind, and Wendy was just starting to worry that perhaps he would be too reticent to kiss her in public that way, when she heard the sound of a

452

cart coming up the road. She left Molly where she was, walked back down the road, skirting the side, in case whoever it was coming up was not someone she wished to meet. Despite what she had seen with her own eyes, the specter of Roger Newcomb still floated in her peripheral vision.

It was not Roger Newcomb, or anyone who might be a threat, but an old cart loaded with a profusion of household goods, a farmer, his wife, their three children, a pig, and sundry chickens in wooden cages. Wendy waved them down.

'Gettin the hell out of here, afore the Yankees show and take every damned thing we got,' the farmer explained, when Wendy asked where they were bound.

'We have been trying to do the same. My aunt and me. Oh, we have had a terrible time. My aunt is hurt. Could we beg a ride of you?'

The farmer followed Wendy to where Molly lay. He had a notion that Molly's wound looked very much like a gunshot wound, but Wendy explained that it was from a broken sapling on which Molly had torn her flesh when she tripped and fell.

The farmer looked hard at Wendy. Finally he spat a stream of tobacco on the ground. 'All right, whatever you say,' he said. 'Let's git her on the wagon.'

It was not a comfortable ride, but it was better than walking, and the farmer took them to a place where they could catch a train to Richmond.

Molly slept a good deal of the time, but when she was awake she was lucid, and she told Wendy of a place in Richmond, the home of a friend, where they would be safe. It took them forty torturous hours of travel, rattling along on trains, waiting on benches at depots while the soldiers took precedence, jamming onto trolleys, before they finally arrived at Molly's friend's home, where they were welcomed in like family. Wendy felt as if she had been forty years in the desert, but now it was over.

She stayed for a week, sleeping when she could, between dreams that made her bolt upright, kicking at the bedclothes, cold with sweat. She tended to her aunt, whose recuperation was slow but steady. She helped in the kitchen when she had the strength. For a week she rested, recuperated, and then she knew it was time to go.

'Molly,' Wendy said, hesitant; she did not know how to broach it.

'You want to go to your sailor boy?'

'Yes.'

Molly smiled at her, brushed the hair from her face. 'You are a very different woman than you were the first time you set out on that mission.'

Wendy nodded. Molly sighed. 'I'm too battered to go on,' she said. 'A week or two, perhaps, but not now. Part of surviving is knowing when you must stop. But you are much younger than I am, and stronger. And now I know you'll be safe.'

Wendy was surprised, but she hid it. She had expected an argument from Molly, along the lines of 'Now you know what can happen . . .' but in fact her aunt's response was very much the opposite.

She left the next day. Some money in her carpet-bag, the bulk of it down the front of her dress, her pistol strapped to her thigh, she set out with none of the trepidation or uncertainty that she had felt in the carriage house in Portsmouth, packing her things.

She bid farewell to Molly. Their host took her in his carriage to the railroad depot.

She waited five hours there for a train, reading back issues of the Richmond *Whig* and the *Despatch*, reading the reporters' versions of the historic events she had just witnessed.

It was a long and exhausting eleven days of travel, west toward the Mississippi River. Terrible food, sleepless nights, excruciating delays. At several points she had to walk or beg a ride from one railhead to another because the lines did not connect. At other times she had to take a room in a hotel because the train was delayed for some reason – tracks washed out or torn up, engine broken down, cars diverted – and no one had any idea when it might arrive.

She wondered if the Yankee rail system was in such a shambles, and she had the sinking feeling that no, it was nothing like this. The shopkeepers in the North would keep their trains running on time.

Worst of all were the ribald suggestions of men who assumed a woman traveling unescorted as she was had to be earning her way across country in some manner, and they were willing to give her a job of work. There were times when she wanted to pull the pistol out of its secret holster and jam the barrel into some leering face, just for the satisfaction of seeing the lust dissolve into fear. But she resisted, and managed to satisfy herself with a few cutting words.

It was monotonous, irritating, unpleasant, uncomfortable, but it was a Sunday church picnic compared to the few days it had taken her to get free of Norfolk, and she never once even thought to complain.

Eleven long days, and then she was there.

It was midafternoon when the train arrived at the station and Wendy stood on protesting muscles, stretched as delicately as she was able, and retrieved her carpetbag. She stepped out into a beautiful day, bright and warm. She could smell the nearby river, the pungent smell of late spring flowers. She was there, after all she had endured she was there, and the elation was unlike any she had ever felt.

The fresh air was welcome after the train car, which reeked of tobacco smoke and too many people in too tight and warm a space. Wendy crossed the platform and pushed her way into the station. She did not imagine that anyone there would know Samuel Bowater by name, but she hoped perhaps someone might know where the navy men were employed. It seemed a wanton question, but Wendy had already left the bonds of propriety way behind, so she steeled herself and asked the ticket man.

'Oh, sure, ain't a soul here doesn't know that. They're pretty near heroes, 'round here. You just follow the River Road south an . . . well, hell . . . Tom! Come over here. This here lady needs a ride down to the shipyard.'

Tom, an old black man in an old black sack coat, nodded, smiled, took up Wendy's carpetbag. He led her out of the station to an old buckboard just outside the door, a tired horse standing in the traces. He set a crate on the ground for her to step on, then joined her on the seat, shook the reins, and the horse stepped off.

They rolled through the streets and then along the wide river, and Tom kept up a running narrative of everything they had done in town to prepare for defense, how the Yankee navy was closing in, but how they would be ready.

Wendy listened with half an ear while she took in the sight of the strange town. She had only been out of Virginia twice in her life, and once was just to Maryland and the other to Elizabeth City, North Carolina, to see Samuel Bowater. This was so different, so exciting – the travel, the new places, the reckless way she had run off to be with her love – it was absolutely intoxicating.

At last the shipyard came into view, a bustle of activity, men swarming around like ants on a hill of spilled sugar. Wendy felt her pulse race, felt a tingling in her hands and feet. After all this time and suffering, would she be reunited with Samuel Bowater, here, in the next five minutes? Would she have the courage to kiss him the way she had dreamed? She was not so certain now.

Tom pulled the buckboard to a stop, made to get out to help her down, but she leaped to the ground before he could even rise out of his seat.

'Thank you, Tom!' She handed him a coin.

'Thank you, ma'am! You enjoy you time wid you husband, now!' He tipped his hat and drove on.

Wendy took a few steps toward the yard and stopped. She looked over the men working there, but none of them was Samuel. Not that she would have expected him to be swinging a hammer or hauling on a saw.

A young officer standing in the yard glanced her way, glanced again, then approached. Wendy waited for him. 'Ma'am, may I help you?' He was wearing the uniform of a navy lieutenant.

'Perhaps. I am looking for Lieutenant Samuel Bowater, of the Confederate States Navy.'

'Lieutenant Samuel Bowater . . .' The lieutenant

looked away, screwed up his face. 'Name doesn't ring a bell, ma'am.'

'I was under the impression he was here,' Wendy insisted.

'Could be. It's not as if I know everyone. Let me take you to the captain.'

The lieutenant, whose name was George Gift, graciously took Wendy's bag and led her across the yard to a small wooden building, more of an over-large shed, which served as the yard's office. He led her inside, introduced her to a man seated behind one of two desks there, flowing with papers.

'Sir, perhaps you can help this lady,' he said.

The man stood, gave a shallow bow. 'Lieutenant Isaac Brown, ma'am. How may I be of assistance?'

'Lieutenant, I am Wendy Atkins. I am looking for a navy lieutenant named Samuel Bowater.'

Brown said, 'Hmmm,' and he squinted. 'Bowater . . .?' he said, unsure.

The man at the other desk in the room, who had not looked up from the journal in which he was writing, looked up now. 'Bowater? Sure, I know him,' he said. 'He was the one got command of the *Tennessee*.'

'*Tennessee?*' Wendy asked. She had heard nothing of that.

'Ah!' Brown said, as if all were explained. 'That's why you can't find him. The *Tennessee* is still up in Memphis. It was only this ship, the *Arkansas*, that was towed down here to Yazoo City.'

The Yankees were coming downriver. They were wasting no time.

The River Defense Fleet dropped down ahead of

them. By the light of the full moon and the huge bonfire that was once the gunboat *Tennessee*, the makeshift men-of-war tied up to the levee that lined the Memphis waterfront.

Confusion swept like a nasty rumor through the fleet; uncertainty was the only thing they knew for certain. The troops from Forts Pillow and Randolph had been sent away, there were no soldiers to defend the city. Was the fleet to make a stand? Try to hold the Yankees at bay? For how long? Were there reinforcements of any kind on the way? Or should the fleet preserve itself, make a stand farther downriver?

No one seemed to know. No one knew if anyone else knew, or if those decisions had even been made. The general feeling in the fleet was that they would not fight, that preserving the Confederacy's last waterborne fighting force on the Mississippi was more important than trying to hold on to Memphis, which would be lost eventually, no matter what they did.

'So, there will be no fight?' Bowater asked. Dragging himself back from Shirley's yard, exhausted, dispirited, he had met Tarbox up on the hurricane deck. The first mate was leaning on the rail, staring upriver.

'Reckon not. Feller on the *Colonel Lovell*, he told me we was gonna head downriver tonight. 'Course it don't look like that's gonna happen, so I don't know what the hell now. Ain't heard a thing from anyone who could actually make a damn decision, so I don't know what to tell you, Cap'n.'

'I see.' Bowater considered sending Tarbox over to the flag boat, but decided against it. It would remind those in command that Sullivan was still out of commission, and that might make someone overly curious. Besides, it was even money that they did not know on the flag boat what they were going to do, anymore than anyone else did.

Just wait and see. . . . Lord, after all his years in the service, it was one thing Bowater knew how to do.

'Word is, them Yankees is laid on Paddy's Hen and Chickens,' Tarbox added.

Bowater had no idea what he meant. He wondered if that was some kind of river man's insult. 'Paddy's Hen and Chickens?'

'Right up there.' Tarbox gestured upriver with his chin. 'Little cluster of islands, right at the bend of the river, 'bout a mile an a half above the city. Called "Paddy's Hen and Chickens." Picket boat brung word, them ironclads is tied up there. If it was daylight, we could see 'em from here.'

Bowater nodded. Two fleets within sight of one another, and no one knew what would happen next. Something, anyway. Make a stand or skedaddle, whichever it was, something would happen tomorrow. 'If we don't hear from the flag boat before, let's have all hands at quarters an hour before dawn, and a full head up steam,' Bowater said.

'Yessuh,' Tarbox said, and though he drawled the words, there was a note of approval there as well.

'And get some sleep, Mr Tarbox. I certainly intend to.'

The best laid plans . . . , Bowater thought as he lay in his bunk, sleepless, staring at the shadows made by the moonlight on the overhead. How many twists and turns had his life taken in the past year? After fourteen years of near stagnation in the United States

Navy, he had, in one year of warfare, more than made up for that monotony.

A little monotony would not be so bad, he thought. But he knew he would not get that anytime soon. Certainly not in the morning.

He thought of Wendy. Where was she? He had sent her several letters during the last week of April and the first week of May, telling her all about Memphis, the *Tennessee*, the River Defense Fleet, the Battle of Plum Point. The things he knew she would not really care about. And he also told her how much he loved her, missed her, wished he could hold her in his arms once again. The things she would want to hear.

He mailed them to her address in Portsmouth, the only one he had, and he never received a word in reply. He could only guess that she had returned to Culpepper and her mail was not being forwarded, or that his letters had not arrived at all. There were other possibilities, of course, but none that he cared to think about.

It was now June sixth, with midnight an hour past. Almost a month since the Yankees had taken Portsmouth and Norfolk and ended the hope of even a letter from Wendy. If she had not gotten out ahead of them, she was now behind enemy lines.

Where is she? What is she doing? he wondered. And as he did, he fell asleep.

After some time, someone shook him awake, and none too gently. His limbs were stiff and his eyes stung from too little sleep. His cabin was partially illuminated by a single lantern hung from a hook.

'Three in the morning. Hour to sunrise,' Tarbox's voice sounded in the dark.

'Thank you, Mr Tarbox.' Bowater swung his legs off the bunk, rubbed his eyes. He heard the click of the door as Tarbox left.

Samuel gave himself five minutes to collect his thoughts. He said a prayer, which he was not much in the habit of doing, and only by asking for help for everyone but himself was he able to avoid feeling like the world's biggest hypocrite. Then he stood, strapped on his belt and holster with his engraved .36 Colt, pulled on his frock coat, set his cap on his head and stepped out into the predawn dark.

Men moved like shadows around him, men stumbling to quarters, taking the places they would occupy if the *General Page* went into battle. The moon had set and it was quite dark, but still Bowater could see the shapes hunkered around the ten-pound Parrot rifle in the bow and loading small arms behind the wood and compressed cotton bulwarks.

He climbed up onto the hurricane deck. The morning was cool and damp and still. He could hear frogs and the call of wading birds, the buzz and chirp of insects around the levee. Lovely. He breathed deep, understood how a person could fall in love with that river.

Someone appeared at the head of the ladder, climbing up. He saluted. Bowater did not recognize him. 'Chief Taylor says steam's at service gauge, Cap'n,' he said. One of the coal passers. Bowater did not know his name.

'Very well. Tell Chief Taylor' – Bowater almost said, 'Tell Chief Taylor to listen for my bells' but he stopped himself. 'Tell Chief Taylor thank you. And Godspeed.'

'Godspeed,' the coal passer repeated, as if he would have trouble remembering. 'Yes, sir.'

They waited. Bowater, Tarbox, Amos Baxter, the helmsman. Doc arrived with coffee and hardtack smeared with something that might be construed as butter, and they ate and drank and waited some more.

The sky grew lighter, the dark pulled away to reveal the river, the town climbing up the hill, the levee, the ships of the River Defense Fleet, black smoke rolling from their chimneys.

'Look there,' Tarbox grunted, gesturing upriver. A great cloud of black smoke hung over the trees, a mile and a half away.

'Hope them damned Yankees done set their damn selves on fire,' Baxter offered, but Bowater knew it would not be that easy. The smoke was the collective output of the ironclad fleet's furnaces. They were getting up steam. Next stop: Memphis.

Bowater looked to the flag boat, the *Little Rebel*, wondered what decisions had been made. It was light enough now that he could see a figure at the base of the forwardmost flagpole. Bowater picked up the signal book just as the string of three flags ran up the pole. Numbers one, two, and four. Bowater ran his finger down the list. *Prepare for battle*.

'We stay,' he announced to the wheelhouse. 'We stay and fight.'

One by one the ships of the River Defense Fleet cast off and backed into the stream. The *General M. Jeff Thompson*, the *Sumter*, the *General Beauregard*, the *General Joseph Page*, the *Colonel Lovell*, and the *Little Rebel*. The *General Earl Van Dorn*, the *General Sterling Price* and the *General Bragg*, paddle wheels turning, kicking up the river white, their men hunkered down behind makeshift barricades of railroad iron and compressed cotton and pine planks, or clustered around the odd assortment of guns at bow and stern. The River Defense Fleet, the forlorn hope, steamed into the morning.

By the time Bowater could turn his concentration from conning the ship, getting her into the line of boats, like knights of old, ready to charge, the sky had gone from gray to the lightest blue. He could see people on the waterfront and gathering on the levee, the citizens of Memphis come out to watch the battle for their town, helpless spectators to their own fate.

Bowater gave the engine room a jingle. Dead slow ahead, enough to stem the current, keep them in place. He could see the Federal gunboats now, moving out into the river, forming a line from one shore to the other, much as the River Defense Fleet had done, a string of iron gunboats sweeping down on them. But it was still quiet, save for the working of the paddle wheels and the walking beam.

Bowater remembered Sullivan, down below.

'Mr Tarbox, I have to go below for a moment. Hold the boat here, watch the *Little Rebel* for orders, send for me if you need me.'

'Awright. Where ya gonna be?'

'I'm going to confer with Captain Sullivan.'

He rushed forward as fast as he could go and still maintain his dignity, down to the boiler deck and aft to Sullivan's cabin. He paused at the door and knocked, hoping there would be no answer, but instead he heard Sullivan's voice, 'Come!'

Bowater opened the door, stepped inside. Sullivan was sitting in his big chair, the one Bowater always pictured him in, the place he sat during their writing sessions. He was dressed in worn denim pants and a river-driver shirt and slouch hat. He had his gun belt with two pistols strapped around his waist. He was pale and sweating profusely, and his breath was labored, as if he had just run a mile or so, though he did not look as if he had the strength to stand.

'Sullivan, what in hell are you doing out of bed?' Bowater demanded.

'Doc told me . . .' Sullivan tried for a smile, but could not quite make it happen. 'Said we're gonna fight them Yankees. Can't sleep through that.'

Bowater was suddenly afraid that Sullivan meant to take back command of the ship. What could he say? It was Sullivan's ship to command. He tried to think of some argument that would not sound purely selfish.

'Don't you fret, Cap'n,' Sullivan continued, as if he had read Bowater's mind. 'You're still in command of this bucket. Hell, I don't know if I can walk, never mind take charge. But I got to be on deck. You can understand that, can't you?'

Bowater nodded.

'After all,' Sullivan said, 'I'm the hardest drivin, hardest drinkin . . .' He broke off in a fit of coughing.

'Yes, most dangerous son of a whore riverboat man on the Western Waters,' Bowater supplied.

From somewhere beyond the cabin, but not so far, a gun fired, a single cannon shot. Sullivan stopped coughing. The two men looked up, looked at nothing, focused their hearing. Another shot, and another. The River Defense Fleet, opening the ball.

'Come on, Captain Sullivan.' Bowater stepped over to the chair, offered Mississippi Mike a hand. Sullivan took it, and with a grunt, an involuntary sound ripped from his guts, he stood.

Sullivan draped his right arm over Bowater's shoulder and put his weight on it, and Bowater braced himself to hold the big man up. Together they stepped from the cabin, from their literary *salon*, right into the Battle of Memphis.

CHAPTER 30

The people in tens of thousands crowded the high bluffs overlooking the river, some of them apparently as gay and cheerful as a bright May morning, and others watching with silent awe the impending struggle.

Commander Henry Walke,
USS *Carondelet*

There was going to be a battle. A fight on the river. It was what everyone in Memphis was saying. It loomed like the Second Coming in people's minds, and it made Wendy Atkins so anxious she could scream.

Getting upriver from Yazoo City to Memphis had been no easy task. Even with money to pay her passage – and it was running low – it had been a job just finding a boat making the run. Wendy heard various takes on the same theme – *Boat to Memphis? Hell, there ain't no boats no more. Should a seen it before, hell, you could walk to Memphis on the damned boats. Now? With the damn Yankees, an Jeff Davis? You'd have better luck swimmin* – until she was ready to tear her hair out.

But she made it. Through perseverance, monetary disbursement, and shameless flirting she had managed to get upriver to Memphis, stepping ashore on the afternoon of June fifth with absolutely no notion of what she would do next, where she would go, how she would find Samuel.

She secured lodging first – it seemed practical – and then began to ask around. There were two things that she kept hearing. There was no naval presence in Memphis, no naval officers or men. And there was going to be a battle on the river.

Those two facts seemed to contradict one another. *How could there be a battle on the river with no navy?* she wondered. Finally she found a haughty assistant provost named van Reid, who explained to her that the Confederate squadron, a thing called the River Defense Fleet, was not under the command of the navy, but under army control, to the extent that it was under any control at all.

'I see . . .' Wendy said.

'And now, it is hardly safe for you to be abroad, ma'am. Might I escort you to your lodging?' the suddenly solicitous van Reid asked.

'I think I am safer escorting myself, thank you,' she said curtly and walked off. It was dark. She was very tired. She walked uphill to her hotel.

She was just stepping through the door of her room when another line of questioning came to her. The *Tennessee*, she thought. No one in Memphis knew where a naval officer might be found, but surely someone would know where this *Tennessee* was being built. With a refreshed sense of optimism, she went to bed and slept, deep and dreamlessly.

She was awake before dawn, dressed, and was out

the door. She woke the clerk at the desk, who was asleep on a tall stool and seemed in danger of toppling off.

'*Tennessee*? Certainly, ma'am. *Tennessee*'s building down to Shirley's yard. Along with the *Arkansas*, which they towed off. I can get you a carriage, if you want.' He glanced dubiously at the front windows, which looked like black marble with the night sky behind them. 'Don't know if anyone will be there. Besides, there's supposed to be a battle with the Yankees today.'

Wendy asked for the carriage. She could not wait another moment. She would rather pace back and forth in a dark, empty shipyard than sit in the hotel lobby, doing nothing.

The sky was lightening when they left the hotel, though the sun had not risen and the town was still lost in the gloom. Wendy sat in the carriage, swaying back and forth, stomach knotted. The old man driving the coach did not seem in much of a hurry, and Wendy wanted to lean out the window and tell him to get a damned move on, but she held her tongue.

Finally the carriage came to a stop, nearly tumbling Wendy headfirst. She felt it rock as the driver climbed down, opened the door. 'Shirley's yard, ma'am. Don't know as anyone's here.'

Wendy stepped out into the cool air under the now light blue sky. The air was thick with the odor of charred wood, an acrid smell that reminded her of the Gosport Naval Shipyard, which she had twice seen burned.

'This is fine, thank you.'

The carriage rattled away and Wendy stepped over

the bare ground into what she guessed was a ship-yard. There were makeshift buildings and piles of wood in sawn boards and uncut logs. And in the middle of the yard, a great pile of charred wood, a heap at least one hundred and fifty feet long and ten feet high of black charcoal and white ash. As she approached it, she could feel it was still warm, still smoldering. It could not have been burned very long ago. *What was it*? she wondered. *Could this have been the* Tennessee?

She heard footsteps and her hand reached down for the hem of her skirt, ready to pull it aside, yank the gun from the holster, a move she had practiced in the privacy of her room. She could see a man hurrying toward her, head down, moving fast. A small man, he did not seem to notice her.

'Excuse me,' she said when she saw he was going to walk right past her.

'Oh!' The man jumped in surprise. He stopped in his tracks, looked over at her. 'Yes? May I help you?'

'Hello, my name is Wendy Atkins.' She stepped toward the man.

'Pleased to meet you. I am John Shirley. I am the owner of the yard here.'

'Honored, sir. Perhaps you can help me. Do you, perchance, know a Lieutenant Samuel Bowater.'

'Bowater? Certainly I know Lieutenant Bowater. Right behind you, that pile of ash, that was his command. Burned it last night. Before the Yankees got it.' There was more than a little bitterness in his voice.

'Oh, dear. Will Lieutenant Bowater be here today?'

'Today? No, I shouldn't think so. No reason for him to come here now. Besides, there's going to be a battle, or so they say.'

470

So they say, Wendy thought. If there was going to be a battle on the river, she suspected that Samuel would be part of it, army command or no.

'Bowater was friendly with one of the captains of the River Defense Fleet,' Shirley continued. 'Don't recall his name. Big fella. Had the boat *General Joseph Page*. I imagine Bowater is probably with him today.'

'Yes . . .' Wendy said. Oh, God, this was terrible! She had finally found him, or near enough, and now he would be off to battle, perhaps without even knowing she was there.

'Do you know where this *General Joseph Page* is anchored? Or tied up?'

'The fleet was tied to the levee last night. Not very far from here. I could take you, if you like.'

'I would like that very much,' Wendy said.

From somewhere north of them, up the river, hidden by the cluster of waterfront buildings, a gun went off, the loud report of heavy ordnance. Shirley looked up quickly. 'Uh-oh,' he said. 'Reckon we better hurry.'

Samuel Bowater made his way down the side deck, bearing half of Mississippi Mike Sullivan's weight on his shoulders. By the time they reached the ladder to the hurricane deck, the firing had escalated from a single gun here and there to an all-out barrage, a solid noise of gunfire, a murderous cannonade.

Sullivan seemed to gain strength with each step, putting less and less weight on Bowater's shoulders, for which Bowater was grateful.

They came to the forward end of the boiler deck and stopped. The Federal ironclads were opening up all along their line. The ships themselves were beginning to look blurry and indistinct as they were lost from sight behind the wall of their own gun smoke. The gunfire was like the rumble of thunder, and cutting through that low sound came the terrifying whine of shells screaming past.

'Damn me! This is more like it!' Sullivan said, and though his voice lacked its characteristically excessive vigor, still there was life in it. As love's first kiss brought Snow White back to life, so the sound of flying metal seemed to revive Mississippi Mike.

'Can I help you to the hurricane deck?' Bowater asked.

'Thank you, Cap'n, I do believe I can get there under my own steam. You go on, now.'

Bowater nodded, bounded up the ladder and aft to the wheelhouse. Tarbox was working the cheroot in his mouth. 'Signal from the flag boat, Cap'n. Montgomery's sendin *Jeff Thompson*, *Sumter*, *Beauregard*, and *Lovell* forward, try and draw these bastards off'n the bar. Rest of us is back here. Reserve, like.'

Bowater nodded. He could see the four bigger steamers advancing on the line of gunboats, firing their bow guns, then steaming into their own clouds of gun smoke. The *General Page* was half a mile from the ironclads, the four Rebel boats in the advance were half that distance.

A shell flew by, close, with its terrible banshee scream, and Bowater and Tarbox both turned their heads and watched it hit the water astern. 'Reckon we'd be dead meat if them Yankees didn't have all that smoke in their eyes,' Tarbox observed.

'Let's head toward the Arkansas shore,' Bowater called through the open wheelhouse door to Baxter,

472

who was resting on the big wheel, 'see if we can get a clean shot at the gunboats.'

Baxter nodded, turned the wheel. Bowater stepped in and rang two bells. Mississippi Mike appeared over the edge of the hurricane deck. He was pulling himself up the ladder, it seemed hand over hand, red-faced and sweating, and Bowater wondered if this was such a good idea. But he knew Sullivan could not remain in bed, not with his ship going into battle. No captain could, who deserved that title.

'Cap'n Sullivan . . .?' Tarbox said. His tone was a mix of pleasure and uncertainty.

'Tarbox . . .' Sullivan nodded. 'I'm jest a sightseer,' he added. 'Cap'n Bowater's still runnin the monkey show.'

Tarbox looked from Sullivan to Bowater and back, then nodded.

The *General Page* was working her way across the river, and Bowater was looking for a place where they would have an unobstructed shot at the enemy. 'There!' he said to Baxter, stepping into the wheelhouse. 'Let's head up right there.'

Baxter grunted, gave the wheel a small turn. Bowater grabbed a tall stool that was pushed against the aft bulkhead and carried it out to the side deck.

'Captain Sullivan, a seat for you.'

Sullivan looked dubiously at the stool, as if it were too nancy for him to sit down, but as it was, he was leaning heavily on the rail for support, so he muttered a thanks and sat.

'Mr Tarbox, let's have the bow gun fire when ready. Tell them to keep it up, as long as they can find a target.'

Tarbox nodded and hurried forward.

'Aw, hell, Cap'n,' Sullivan said, settling on the stool, breathing hard. 'Here you're bringin all yer fancy navy ways to my boat. "Mister" Tarbox! Shit, now he's gonna expect *me* to call him that!'

'I'm not sure a little discipline—' Bowater's retort was cut off by the roar of the Parrott rifle, which sent a shudder through the deck and a blast of smoke out over the water. As if in response, a Yankee shell whistled past, taking out the boats on the starboard side in a great starburst of white-painted splinters. Shattered bits of boat flew high over the deck, like a flock of birds in disorderly takeoff, then came clattering down again, leaving only four bent davits standing and the torn ends of the boat falls swaying back and forth.

'Damn,' Sullivan said.

Bowater looked forward. The smoke was thicker around the ironclads, the gunfire more furious. *This is idiotic*, he thought. *We can't do this*. It was insane for the River Defense Fleet to remain where they were and swap gunfire with ironclads. They could never win on that ground. And the fleet had already proved that their rams could be effective against the Yankee gunboats. It was time for a cavalry charge.

He turned to Sullivan. 'We can't stay here. We'll be murdered.'

'You sure got that right.'

'We should ram them, go right at them.'

'Ram them? Hell, I was gonna say we should skedaddle to Vicksburg.' Sullivan gulped a few deep breaths, winced in pain. 'Naw, I'm jest joshin ya. You do whatever you want, Cap'n, an I'm with ya. Ain't like I got much choice.'

Bowater studied the Union ships. They were all but

lost in the smoke; it was hard to see which would make the best target. The *General Page*'s bow gun went off again, rattling the lightly built vessel as if it had struck a rock.

'How much water is up there, where the Yankees are?' Bowater asked.

Before Sullivan could answer, a ship burst from the bank of smoke, right between two of the Union ironclads, a side-wheeler charging downriver. It looked like a ghost come from the grave, as if it had appeared out of thin air.

'Damn!' Sullivan shouted.

'It's one of the rams!' Bowater shouted, forgetting to temper his excitement. Then, in a more controlled voice, added, 'One of the rams we saw upriver.'

'Well, now we got us a fight, ram to ram,' Sullivan said.

Colonel Lovell and *Sumter* were steaming up to the enemy, line abreast. They altered course with the appearance of this new threat, and made for the Yankee ram. The smoke rolled thick and black out of their chimneys, striking four dark lines against the sky, and Bowater wondered what the engineers were throwing on the fires. He frowned. He wanted to be at the enemy, or at least get a clear cannon shot, but the other ships were blocking his way.

He turned to Baxter. 'Follow *Sumter*!' he ordered. Perhaps there would be something left over for them.

And then a second ram burst from the fog, a roil of white water around her bow as she poured on the steam. Most of the River Defense Fleet was concentrating on the first ram; there was only the *General Bragg* between Bowater and the second Yankee.

You're my meat, Bowater thought.
'He's our meat!' Sullivan shouted.
God help me, Bowater thought.

CHAPTER 31

I saw a large portion of the engagement from the riverbanks, and am sorry to say that, in my opinion, many of our boats were handled badly or the plan of battle was very faulty. The enemy's rams did most of the execution and were handled more adroitly than ours . . .

Brigadier General M. Jeff Thompson
to General G. T. Beauregard

The Union ironclad fleet had let loose with a full barrage, the shots coming one upon another, by the time the Union ram *Queen of the West* cast off from the bank and backed into the stream. Colonel Ellet himself ran to the after end of the hurricane deck and hauled the ensign up the staff, the prescribed signal for the ram fleet to go into action. *Monarch* was moving off the bank, and upstream, *Lancaster* and *Switzerland* had not even put their lines ashore.

Ellet rushed back to the wheelhouse. The others would follow. They would understand, as he did, that this was their moment. It was time for the rams to go into battle and show the world that the weapon of the ancients was back, and ready to do great execution.

'Right between the ironclads, pilot, get us right downriver,' he ordered.

'Yes, sir.' The pilot paused. 'We'll be right under their guns, sir.'

'Who, the enemy?'

'No, sir, the ironclads.'

'Oh, they won't fire on us. Depend on it. Right between them, right for those Rebels.' He reached up himself and rang three bells. When they slammed the *Queen's* iron-shod bow into a secesh gunboat, they would need speed and momentum, all they could get.

Memphis was gone, lost from sight behind a great wall of gray gun smoke, the cumulative output of the Union gunboat's fire. Ellet could see the ironclads, low and dark, stretched across the river, and then in front of them a gray cloud that hung on the water and roiled up with every successive blast of the guns, and then nothing else. The smoke blotted out everything downriver, save for the blue sky, high overhead.

The *Queen of the West* was building her precious momentum fast, racing for the line of Federal gunboats. The flashes of the ironclads' guns lit up the smoke, orange and red, belched more smoke into the cloud.

The *Queen* charged on, right between *Carondelet* and *Benton*. Ellet could see startled faces looking out from gun ports as the ram swept past and plunged into the wall of smoke.

For a moment they were blind, like being in thick fog, a world of gray and dim, diffused light. Joseph Ford, first master of the *Queen of the West*, began coughing hard, doubled over, and Ellet coughed too.

He wondered how thick the wall of fog might be. He could not ram if he could not see.

And then they were through, bursting out of the far side like coming out of a tunnel, from gray smoke and blindness to brilliant morning – blue sky, brown water flashing in the rising sun, the steep hills on the Memphis shore, and the Rebel Defense Fleet, steaming for them.

'Here we go!' Ellet shouted. Upstream, the iron-clads kept up their fire, the shells screaming past, and Ellet wondered if the gunners could see at all through their own smoke. If not, there was as good a chance of them hitting the *Queen* as anything, but he was too gripped with the thrill of the thing to care.

'Sir!' Ford pointed downstream. Two of the Rebels were coming up fast, side by side, their bows aimed straight at the *Queen of the West*.

Ellet stepped back into the wheelhouse, stood between the pilots, Richard Smith and Joe Davis, their eyes locked on the action under the bows.

'Which one, sir?' Davis asked. The *Queen* and the two Rebels were closing fast, bow to bow. If they hit that way, it would shatter them all.

'I don't know . . .' Ellet said. They were charging right at one another. *We'll make a damn lot of widows this way . . .*

One of the Rebels began to turn, the one on the *Queen*'s starboard bow began to sheer off. Ellet stepped out of the wheelhouse. Behind them, the *Monarch* had broken through the smoke, was coming down on their starboard quarter. Ellet could hear the men on the ironclad gunboats cheering, cheering.

He pulled off his hat and waved it at *Monarch* and then at the Rebel who had sheered off. 'That one's for you!' he shouted, though he knew Alfred would not hear him. 'The other is my meat!'

The *Monarch* began to turn, to line herself up for a charging run at the second Rebel steamer. Satisfied, Ellet returned to the wheelhouse. Two hundred yards separated the *Queen* from the onrushing Confederate, two hundred and dropping fast, and still they came on, bow to bow.

Oh Lord, oh Lord . . . Ellet had played this scene out a hundred times in his head, a thousand, but here were difficulties he had not imagined, such as what he would do if the Rebel would not turn away from his bow-on attack.

And there was more to think of. If the *Queen of the West* hit the closest Rebel, then the Rebel right behind would have a clear shot at hitting the *Queen*, broadside. And there was a third secesh ram, just downriver. He could not hit one without being hit by the other. He could not hit bow to bow.

'Sir,' Davis began, tentative but urgent. The Rebel fired her bow gun and the water just forward of the *Queen* was torn up by grape and cannister.

In the instant the Rebel's bow gun went off, she began to turn, backing down and then sheering off, exposing a swath of larboard side, right under Ellet's bow and seventy yards off. The Confederates were unwilling to risk a head-on collision, but they had decided that too late. Incredible, it was a gift from heaven.

'There, there!' Ellet pointed toward the Rebel's side. The pilots were nearly dancing with excitement. Davis took the wheel from the helmsman, gave a quarter turn to larboard, following the turning Rebel boat around as the space between the ships dropped away.

The Rebel's stern wheel was really digging in. Ellet could picture the skipper laying on the bell, shouting for steam to get him the hell out from under the Yankee ram.

Too late, too late . . . Davis brought the bow around so the *Queen* was pointing first at her foredeck and then her deckhouse as the Rebel tried to steam away.

The *Queen of the West* struck just forward of the Rebel's wheelhouse. She did not even slow as she plowed on through. The side of the Confederate boat caved in like an eggshell. The chimneys leaned over, threatening to fall on the *Queen*'s foredeck. The whole vessel seemed to bend in the middle under the ram's crushing impact.

Then the *Queen* was brought up short, brought to a jarring halt by the mass of the ship impaled on her bow. Ellet was flung forward, hit the low wall and window of the wheelhouse hard, as tables, charts, instruments, crockery, and the pilots all flew across the space in a shower of debris.

The *Queen* twisted around, her paddle wheels still driving her into the rebel ship, which was filling fast and hanging on their bow. Ellet bounced off the wheelhouse's forward bulkhead and staggered back, but managed to keep his feet.

'Full astern!' Ellet roared, but he was the only one still standing. He crossed the wheelhouse, gave a jingle, three bells, *full astern*.

For a second the *Queen* was still, the terrible vibration in her deck gone, as the paddle wheels stopped. Then they began to turn again, churning in reverse. The ship shuddered as the paddle wheels struggled to pull the ram from the dying Confederate. Ellet could hear screeching and snapping sounds as the massive paddles drove the ship astern and drew the bow from the Rebel's side.

He turned to see what execution *Monarch* was doing, but he saw instead another Rebel rushing at them, black smoke churning from her chimneys, a mad bull charging a red cape. It was exactly as he had feared. Hung up on one ship, he was easy pickings for another.

He grabbed the bell and gave another jingle and three bells because he could think of nothing else to do. There *was* nothing else to do but brace for the impact.

The pilot, Davis, pulled himself to his feet, looked out the window at the Rebel ram, now looming over them. 'Oh, hell!' he shouted and then the Rebel struck them, right in the larboard paddle wheel. Painted boards and buckets and metal arms, bits of rail and parts of the *Queen*'s gig flew into the air and became so much debris as the Rebel drove the attack into the army ram's side.

The *Queen* heeled hard to starboard with the impact, and the paddle wheel made a terrible groaning noise as it was sheered clean off.

'Damn it! We're done for!' Ellet shouted. *So soon?* Was that all the battle for him? He did not think it was above ten minutes since he had cast off from the bank at the sound of the guns, and now the *Queen* was disabled and he would be lucky if she did not sink under him.

'Damn!' he shouted again and raced out of the wheelhouse to better see the damage. The sound of the battle was much louder on the hurricane deck, the low thunder of the ironclad gunboats as they poured their fire into the Rebels, the sharp crack of the Rebels' smaller guns, the shouting of men on the sinking Rebel ship and his own men on the main deck below.

It was bad. The larboard wheel was gone, there was nothing there. The water was littered with floating debris. It looked as if an entire ship had been blown to bits, right on that spot. Ellet turned to the deck-hand beside him. 'Billy, run below and see if we're taking on water!'

There was a thumping sound now that he could not identify. He looked around. Another Rebel was moving past, slowly, as if she were disabled. *Small arms!* They were firing on the *Queen* with small arms. Bullets were thudding into the deck.

Get the men behind cover, Ellet thought and then suddenly his leg was gone from under him, as if someone had hit him in the back of the knee with a club and sent him galley-west. He hit the warm deck planks with a grunt, hands down to break his fall, still not certain what had happened.

He rolled on his back and felt the pain shoot up his leg. He stifled a shout, gritted his teeth, looked down. Blood was spurting from his knee, and his leg from the knee down seemed to jut off at an unnatural angle.

'Sir! Sir!' Ford and the pilot Davis were kneeling beside him. 'Sir, you're hit!'

'It's all right, it's all right,' Ellet said, his teeth still clenched. He relaxed his jaw. Had to give orders.

'*Queen*'s out of the fight, larboard wheel's gone, I reckon we're going down,' Ellet managed, then a wave of pain hit him and he stopped for a moment, caught his breath, then went on. 'I think we can get to shore with the remaining wheel. Quick, quick, run her ashore while you can!'

'Yes, sir!' Ford said, leaped up, and rushed back to the wheelhouse. Ellet closed his eyes. Both he and the *Queen of the West,* disabled, knocked out. But not dead. It was as if their fates were intertwined, bound together, like vines twisting around one another. Hurt one you hurt them both. It was not the first time he had thought as much.

Bowater was seething and Mississippi Mike was cursing out loud. The river man cursed with a vehemence that did not seem possible for a man with a gut wound, as if the whole thing had been in his head, and now in the excitement of the moment was forgotten.

They had barely rung up two bells when the first Union ram hit the *Lovell* broadside with a crash that they could hear plain as could be, even over the gunfire, even a quarter mile away.

The *Lovell* seemed to fold right around the Yankee's bow, like a dishrag draped over a clothesline. She rolled hard and began to settle even as the Yankee was still driving into her.

'Oh, son of a bitch! They done for her! Son of a whore!' Sullivan ranted. He stood up from the stool, not quite straight, hand on the butt of one of his pistols.

Bowater ignored him. 'Baxter, come left. We'll make for the second ram. Tarbox, see that the gun crew in the bow fires into that ram, there, the one to the west. Keep them at it, fast as they can.'

It was like chess, a furious, waterborne game of chess, with the pieces all moving at once, the situation changing by the second.

'There goes *Sumter*! Damn me, there goes

484

Sumter!' Sullivan gasped, pointing. *Sumter* was racing for the first Yankee ram, which was still trying to dislodge itself from the *Colonel Lovell*. Bowater watched, transfixed. The actual impact was hidden from him by the wreck of the Lovell, but he could see the Yankee roll under its force, see the debris lifted in the air.

He imagined he would have heard the sound of the impact if the gunfire had not been so intense.

Then the *Colonel Lovell* sank, went right down as if it had never been meant to float. She settled on the bottom with only the upper deck still visible, an island in midriver on which the survivors of her crew huddled.

The smoke from the Union ironclads was spreading downriver, and the River Defense Fleet was adding its own, and visibility was getting worse, with patches of smoke like cotton batting hanging over the water. The second ram was lost from sight, but just for an instant, and then it burst out of the cloud that enveloped it, bearing down hard on the *General Bragg*.

Bowater could make out the big letter M hanging between the Yankee's chimneys. He searched his memory, pictured the rams anchored at Plum Point Bend. Monarch – *she was called* Monarch.

'Meet her, meet her,' Bowater called to Baxter at the wheel. They were four hundred yards downriver of the Yankee *Monarch* and the *Bragg*. If the Yankee ran the *Bragg* down, then the *General Page* would be there to do the same to the Yankee.

'Look here, Sammy, look here!' Sullivan said, with a renewed strength in his voice. 'There goes the *Beauregard* and the *Price*! Lord, they're gonna spit-roast that Yankee!'

The *Beauregard* and the *General Price* were racing for the *Monarch*, the *Beauregard* charging at her starboard side, the *Price* her larboard. They were like two hands clapping together to smash a mosquito between them, while the Yankee, seemingly oblivious, charged forward, bow still aiming for the *General Bragg*.

'Come on, come on,' Bowater caught himself muttering. The Yankee was going to be torn apart in this collision, smashed in on both sides. In a wild confusion of chimneys and black smoke, thrashing paddles and bow guns blazing away, the ships came together.

And suddenly there was empty space, just water and smoke, a gap between the Confederate rams as the *Monarch* slipped right between the two.

'No! No! No!' Sullivan screamed and the two River Defense ships hit, nearly head-on, bow to bow. The *Price*'s chimneys leaned forward, hesitated, then toppled over, as the two vessels, each still under a full head of steam, pounded against each other. The *Beauregard* smashed into the *Price*'s wheel box and ripped it away – box, wheel, shaft, everything – tore it clean off the side of the ship and dragged it along, hung up on the bow, a mass of iron and wood debris, nothing more.

'All right, here we go,' Bowater said. He was sickened by the scene. Nine Confederate rams against the two Yankees and the Yankees were decimating them. He rang four bells. Vengeance had no place in the heart of the professional naval officer, he knew, but this was different. 'Right for him,' he told Baxter. 'Just forward of the wheelhouse.'

The *General Page* surged ahead. Bowater could

hear the note of the paddle wheels go up as, some-where down below, Hieronymus Taylor cracked open the steam valve and let her go.

The *General Bragg* was just ahead of them, two hundred yards, twisting wildly to get out of the way of the *Monarch* racing down on her. Forward, the *Page*'s bow gun fired and a hole appeared in the Yankee's deckhouse, but the Yankee did not slow. Instead it turned with the *Bragg*, keeping its bow directed at the *Bragg* as the *Bragg* tried to circle away.

When they hit, it was a glancing blow, the *Monarch* striking the *Bragg* aft and sheering off, tearing up some wood, but little else. And now Bowater was looking right at the Yankee's broadside.

He rang four bells again, let Taylor know they needed it all. A hundred yards between them and the Yankee seemed to sense the danger. Bowater saw the paddle wheels stop, saw them reverse, the Federal ram trying to back out of the danger.

Oh, no, you won't, you bastard . . . Fifty yards. The fire from the Union ironclads was terrific, the shells shrieking past. Bowater felt a jar in the deck as a shell struck somewhere aft, a clanging sound as another struck something metal. He turned around. The larboard chimney had folded like a wilting flower, half the guy wires snapped.

Thirty yards. He could see men on the *Monarch*'s hurricane deck. Sharpshooters were peppering the *Page* with minié balls, he could hear the familiar thud as they struck wood. The far right window of the wheelhouse was shot out, the sound of breaking glass delicate against the backdrop of heavy guns.

Twenty yards and the Yankee put his helm hard over, paddle wheels full ahead, and the nimble ram spun around on her center, and the broadside disappeared as she came bow-on to the *Page*.

'You whoremonger bastard!' Sullivan roared at the Yankee ram. He had one of his pistols in his hand, a big army .44, and he was blasting away. Bowater thought he had better take it easy or he would kill himself before the Yankees did, but he had no time to dole out medical advice. He stepped into the wheelhouse and leaned over the speaking tube. 'Engine room, stand by!'

He grabbed a spoke of the wheel, twisted it around, with Baxter adding his weight. The *Page* heeled as she leaned into the turn, spinning toward the Yankee ram, bow to bow.

They hit with an impact that threw Bowater against the wheelhouse bulkhead. His arms came up to protect himself and he put his elbow right through the glass. He heard Baxter give a grunt as his chest hit the wheel, heard the horrible sound of the *General Page*'s bow crushing against the Yankee's.

The forward momentum stopped, the *Page* surged back, and Bowater was flung to the deck. He landed on his back in a pile of books and charts, and a half-eaten dinner that someone had left in the wheelhouse.

Baxter was clutching the wheel to keep to his feet. He twisted around, looked at Bowater, opened his mouth to speak, and a bullet blew the top of his head off. Bowater could only watch as the blood and bone flew out in a spray across the wheelhouse and the helmsman tumbled forward, a surprised look on his face, and collapsed right beside him.

Bowater climbed to his feet and looked out the glassless window. The two ships were grinding together, but the Yankee had called for *turns astern* and was extracting himself from the *Page*'s bow. Bowater grabbed the bell, gave a jingle, two bells. *All right, Taylor, get us out of here.*

Bowater stepped out of the wheelhouse. The minié balls were hitting like hailstones, but they made no impression on him. Mississippi Mike was lying in a heap, just forward of the wheelhouse, his arm moving feebly.

Bowater took a step toward him, heard a terrible screeching sound behind. He turned. The walking beam was making its rocking motion, up and down, pushing the paddle wheels astern, but it did not sound happy about it. *That can't be a good thing*, he thought, but there was nothing for it. He knelt by Sullivan, half rolled him over.

'Cap'n Bowater . . . give a fella a warning . . .'

'You shot, Sullivan?'

'Don't reckon . . .'

Bowater looked up. Ruffin Tanner was there, kneeling beside him. 'Bow took a good hit, sir. Sprung some planks betwixt wind and water. We're shipping it now, but I don't think it's coming in so fast the pumps can't keep up. The bow gun went right over the side.'

Bowater nodded. 'Can you take the helm?'

'Yes, sir.'

'Help me get Sullivan up first.' They each grabbed an arm and lifted, twisting Sullivan around until he was sitting up, and then leaned him back on a stanchion. The fall had opened his wound. There was a dark wet spot the size of a dinner plate on his shirt.

'Oh, hell, just when I was gettin better,' Sullivan gasped.

Tanner raced into the wheelhouse, pulled Baxter's body out of the way, grabbed the wheel. Bowater stepped in after him. The *Page* and the Yankee ram were still backing away from one another, the distance opening up between them. Ramming distance.

'We're going to circle around and give it to this son of a bitch broadside,' Bowater said. He grabbed the bell rope, rang up four bells. 'Put your helm hard to larboard.'

'Hard to larboard, aye!' Tanner said and spun the wheel. Bowater was happy to have a navy man, a deepwater sailor, on the wheel, and hear the familiar brisk response to a helm command.

The screech from the walking beam was even louder now as the paddle wheels stopped, then went ahead, changing the momentum of the ship from sternway to headway.

'Wheelhouse!' Hieronymus Taylor's voice came echoing out of the speaking tube.

'Wheelhouse here!' Bowater shouted back.

'Just thought you beats might like to know, things ain't lookin too almighty grand down here. You can ring that fuckin bell all you want, but I don't know how long it's gonna do you any good!'

Bowater paused. What did one say to that? 'Very well,' he shouted. *Very well.*

Hieronymus Taylor, as a rule not overly concerned with his own mortality, still had often wondered how a condemned man could march calmly to his death. It was, after all, the final moment, the dread end.

For in that sleep of death what dreams may come, when we have shuffled off this mortal coil, must give us pause, he thought, in Shakespeare's words.

There was a strange numbness that had accompanied him down into the engine room, that awkward climb down the short ladder from boiler deck to the lowest part of the ship, on which the engines and boilers were mounted. It was like a climb up onto a gallows.

He recalled the feeling, helping Guthrie replace that fire tube, the gut-wrenching, piss-your-pants fear in the face of that dubious boiler. It was a long time past. He was almost too tired to care anymore, so sick of being afraid that he barely had the energy for it.

That, he imagined, was how men went to their deaths. Since the Battle of New Orleans, since the horror of the boiler explosion that had wiped out his black gang, Taylor had pondered considerably on his reluctance to work around boilers. Now, in the middle of another fight, in a flimsy, unarmored ship, he was ready to admit the truth of the thing.

'I'm scared to death.' He said it out loud. He was marching up the gallows steps. He was a dead man. Why the hell not say it? 'I am plumb, outright, full-blown, goddamned scared out of my wits. I'm like to shit myself, right here.' It felt good.

'What was that, Chief?' Burgoyne was checking the water levels in the gauge glass on the boiler face.

'Nothin, nothin.' Over the hiss and thump of the engines, through the deck, they could hear the thunderous gunfire and feel the vibration through the water that enveloped the hull.

Bowater rang four bells and Taylor twisted the throttle open. None of it sounded good – the pistons, the cranks, the walking beam – but it was holding together.

If somethin would just let go, it'd give me some

damned thing to think about, he thought. As soon as that idea had formed in his head, he regretted thinking it – bad luck – but it was too late. The feed water pipe burst, spraying hot water all over the forward end of the engine room. A coal passer named Luke found himself right under the broken pipe. He screamed under the burning shower, dropped his shovel, and ran forward.

'Oh, come on, it ain't even steam!' Taylor yelled after him, but the sound of the man screaming unnerved him. He swallowed hard. 'Burgoyne, close that boiler up, get the steam down. Larboard boiler on line, come on now, stoke her up! We got enough water in there?'

Burgoyne slammed the damper shut and the third engineer opened the door on the second boiler, worked the valves to bring the steam on line. 'Enough water for now, Chief!'

Taylor hobbled back, fast as he could on his splint, shut off the feed water valve, and the spray of near boiling water dropped off to a trickle. 'Burgoyne, get a fish plate on that pipe, quick now!'

'Fish plate?'

'Yes, a damned fish plate. Please don't tell me you don't know what a fish plate is.'

'No, no. I knows what a fish plate is, hell yes. I just don't know as we gots one.'

'Well look for one, if it ain't too much trouble.'

Burgoyne hurried over to the workbench. The bell rang out, four bells again.

Taylor glared at it. *Ol' Bowater wants him some steam, huh? Got somethin in mind.*

He twisted the valve full open. *You can have all the steam I got, Cap'n, but it ain't gonna be what this bucket could do on her palmiest day*. The engine speed increased with the additional steam. The crank made a terrible sound. 'Someone get some oil on that!' he shouted, but the end of the sentence was lost when the gauge glass on the working boiler shattered with a tinkling sound like a little bell, which might even have been pretty if it hadn't been for the fireman's shriek as the boiling water sprayed his bare arm and chest.

'Shut that down!' Taylor shouted. 'An everyone stop screamin, goddamn it!' Burgoyne turned from the bench, took a step toward the boiler. 'Not you, Burgoyne, you find the damned fish plate! Luke, you done screamin? Shut off the valve to that gauge glass.'

Luke approached it with caution, the boiling water spewing out, reached under and twisted the valve fast. The water stopped spraying. But now they did not know how much water was in the boiler.

What the hell was I afraid of? Hell, I wish the boiler would blow right now and put us out of our damned misery.

A shell hit the deckhouse overhead and Taylor jumped and felt his heart pounding hard in his chest. *Well, maybe not*.

Another shot hit with a clanging noise that reverberated through the engine room. *Damn it, that's the chimney*, he thought. A shell had hit one of the chimneys.

Might not make any difference . . . Perhaps the fire-box flue would continue to draw, the chimneys would continue to suck the smoke and poisonous gas up out of the engine room. Then Taylor saw the first tendrils of smoke wafting around the tops of the boilers.

Ah, damn . . .

Burgoyne came ambling up. 'Got this here fish plate. It ain't quite the same size as the feed water pipe.'

'Wrap some gasket material around the pipe and clamp that son of a bitch on. We got to get water into that boiler.'

'Gasket material?'

'Find some, for the love of God!'

Burgoyne stood there for a moment, an unpromising look on his face. Bowater's voice shouted from the speaking tube. 'Engine room, stand by!'

'Stand by for what?' Taylor shouted back.

The *General Page* began to heel over in a turn, as much as the flat-bottomed boat would heel, enough to make Taylor grab onto the throttle to steady himself and Burgoyne stumble a step or two. 'Now what in hell is he doin?' Taylor wondered out loud. And then they struck.

CHAPTER 32

GENERAL: *I am under the painful necessity of reporting to you the almost entire destruction of the River Defense Fleet in the Mississippi River in front of Memphis.*

Brigadier General M. Jeff Thompson
to General G. T. Beauregard

The impact tore Taylor's fingers from the throttle valve and sent him careening forward. He slammed into Burgoyne, who was tumbling back, and the two men hit the deck, Taylor on top of the second engineer. He could smell the stale sweat and coal dust and residue of whiskey on the man. He could hear the wrenching sound of engine parts being torn from their mountings.

Taylor's arms and legs were flailing and Burgoyne's arms and legs were flailing and Taylor had a horrible image of the two of them, looking like they were copulating there on the deck plates. He pushed himself off and rolled away as Burgoyne scrambled to his feet.

Everything was moving. Lanterns swaying, men

rushing around, shouting, stumbling. One of the boilers was leaning at an odd angle. Taylor could see it move with the twisting and surging of the ship.

Oh, dear God, don't let that son of a bitch blow up . . .

He pushed himself up on his arms, but standing with his splinted leg was more of a trick. 'Secure that son of a bitch boiler! Git some shorin under it! Luke, Burgoyne, git some slice bars under that thing, hold her up! Eddy! Blouin! Git some shorin under that before it kills us all!'

The black gang recovered from their trance and scattered. Burgoyne and Luke grabbed up the long iron slice bars used for cleaning the boiler grates and levered them under the boiler, holding it in place. The others grabbed up wood planks and shoved them under the iron cylinder to stop it from breaking free.

Taylor crawled to the reversing lever and used it to haul himself to his feet. The engine room was filling with smoke. He could see the halo around the lanterns, hear the men begin to cough. The boiler that had been knocked out was the one they had shut down, so the steam pressure probably was not enough to blow the thing. That was probably why they were still alive and not scalded to death or shrieking their last few moments away. He twisted the throttle closed.

He was breathing hard, his mind racing, but he was thinking clearly, and the fear was gone. He did not realistically think he would live beyond the next hour, but he was not afraid, and that was something.

'Reckon that'll hold!' Burgoyne shouted aft, and on top of his report, a jingle and two bells. *Oh, hell* . . . Taylor jammed the shifting lever to astern, opened the throttle. Overhead the big walking beam paused and then began to rock the opposite way, with a screech and a clang and a banging sound. Taylor heard something pop.

Goddamn walking beam . . . Tolerant as walking beams were, they were not meant for that kind of abuse. He wondered if something had been knocked out of alignment. Knocked more out of alignment. The walking beam had been in no great shape even before they started bashing into other vessels.

'Hey, Burgoyne, get back to that feed water pipe!' Taylor shouted. Without water to the boilers they would be dead in the water in fifteen minutes.

The bell rang, four bells. *Four bells? What the hell they think's goin on down here?*

Taylor shifted the reversing lever, opened up the throttle, then hobbled to the speaking tube. 'Wheelhouse!'

'Wheelhouse, here!'

'Just thought you beats might like to know, things ain't lookin too almighty grand down here. You can ring that fucking bell all you want, but I don't know how long it's gonna do you any good!'

He heard a pause on the other end, then Bowater's voice. 'Very well!'

Very well?

Well, what else was the son of a bitch supposed to say? Taylor grinned. He looked down. There was half an inch of water over the deck plates. He started to cough. *Very well, indeed.*

The two rams were circling, the *General Page* and the *Monarch*, describing a quarter-mile circle on the Mississippi River as each looked for her chance to run at the other broadside. They would not try the headlong rush again.

The gun crew on board the fantail of the *General Page* had hauled their thirty-two-pound smoothbore around so it was trained over the larboard side, and they were taking shots at the Yankee when she would bear. But the Union ironclads upriver were also contributing their artillery, and the *Page* was getting much worse than she was doling out. There were gaping holes in the superstructure, and the one chimney still standing was riddled.

Bowater could not help but think of the boilers. In ships designed for this sort of thing, the boilers were well below the waterline. But not on board the *General Page*, which was built for nothing more dangerous than hauling cotton and passengers up and down the river.

One shot, one shot . . . The wheelhouse was nearly right over the boilers, with companionways that led right down to the engine room. It was not at all unheard-of for men in the wheelhouse to be scalded to death in a boiler explosion. Taylor would have it easy, never know what hit him. But the men in the wheelhouse? They would get the tail end of the blast. It might take them days to die.

Bowater kept moving. In the wheelhouse, onto the side deck, eyes on the enemy. Mississippi Mike Sullivan had pulled himself to his feet and was leaning heavily on the rail, and he didn't look well. They stood together, watched the Yankee circling around.

'That walking beam don't sound too good,' Sullivan said, his voice raspy. A shell from the gun-boats whistled by.

Bowater looked upriver. The ironclads were

broadside to, turning around. In just a few minutes they would be running downriver, bow-first, bringing their guns to point-blank range, firing from their impenetrable casemates.

He looked back at the ram. 'We don't have time for this horseshit.' He stepped back into the engine room, rang two jingles, all stop.

The paddle wheels slowed, the headway dropped off. Bowater leaned into the speaking tube. He could see threads of smoke wafting out of the brass mouth of the tube, could smell the acrid coalfire smell. 'Chief, get up all the pressure you can. When I ring four bells, let her go!'

'You'll get every damned ounce I have!' Taylor shouted back, then started coughing as his voice trailed off.

The *General Page* was stopped dead, and Bowater hoped the Yankee would think she was disabled. He had to make something happen. The Federal ram could steam around as long as she liked, waiting for the gunboats to come down, but if the *General Page* was going to do anything, it had to be now.

'Tanner, put your helm hard a'starboard. When this bastard gets close enough, we're going to pour on the steam, twist out of her way, and take her side wheel off. Just put our bow right into it.'

'Take her side wheel off, aye, sir,' Tanner repeated. He turned the wheel its full revolutions. They waited.

A quarter mile away the Union ram altered course, straightening out, turning her bow toward the *General Page. He must think we are disabled*, Bowater thought. How could he not? There was no other explanation for their stopping in midriver, exposing their vulnerable side to the ram.

The *Monarch* was pouring on the steam, putting everything into this charge. Bowater stepped out of the wheelhouse and stood beside Sullivan, who was standing straighter now. A few hundred yards separated the two vessels. They could see the water creaming white around the Yankee's bow.

'Cap'n,' Sullivan began, 'I ain't so sure . . .'

'I'm drawing him in. When he's close enough I'll go to four bells, turn hard, and take out his wheel box.'

Sullivan nodded. He looked as if he was going to say something, but he didn't. He nodded again.

Two hundred yards, and Bowater considered how fast the *General Page* could get enough headway on to answer the rudder. That was all he needed, enough headway to turn and aim for the wheel. The Yankee's momentum would do the rest.

He looked at the onrushing ram. You could not calculate mathematically such a thing as the exact moment to call for steam, the point when the Yankee was close enough that she could not escape, but far enough to allow the *Page* to turn. You had to feel it. And if you could not, you had no business commanding a ship.

Bowater drifted back into the wheelhouse. 'Get ready, Tanner.' Tanner nodded. Bowater walked over to the speaking tube. 'Get ready, Mr Taylor, about half a minute.'

'I'm ready!' Taylor shouted and muttered something else that Bowater could not hear.

Bowater's eyes were locked on the enemy ram. His hand reached up and grabbed the bell cord. He waited a second, another second, and then every nerve in his body screamed *now, now, NOW!*

He jerked the cord, four quick bells, and in an

instant the deck rumbled underfoot as down below Taylor let it all go, let all the steam he had rush into the cylinder, drive the piston with full force. The walking beam creaked as it began to move, the sound of gushing water came from the wheel boxes as the buckets dug in.

Bowater stepped out onto the side deck. The Yankee was one hundred yards away, but Bowater had timed it perfectly, he could see that. They would swing right out from under the ram's bows, circle up and hit her as she flew by.

Come on, come on . . . The *Page* was starting to move, starting to turn.

'Yeeeehaaaa! Here we come, you rutting bastards!' Mississippi Mike Sullivan shouted, then gasped for breath. He stood straighter, pulled his pistol, and fired, the shot loud in Bowater's ear. There was blood on the deck at his feet.

And then, even through the blast of Sullivan's .44, they heard the walking beam make an unearthly sound, a screech like something being horribly killed, but much, much louder than any living thing could produce. Their heads jerked around and looked up just as the shaft on which the walking beam pivoted snapped clean in two and the entire eight tons of wood and iron dropped and twisted and lodged itself in the A-frame, snapping bearings and connecting rods as it fell.

For a second the two men just stood there, dumbfounded, looking at the destruction. The *General Page* would not be twisting out of anyone's way.

Sullivan was the first to speak. 'Son of a bitch Guthrie, he's killed us all! Right from the damned grave he's killed us all!'

They turned back. The Yankee was twenty yards away. Sullivan began blasting away with his pistol. Bowater ran into the wheelhouse. He was three feet from the speaking tube, just beginning to shout a warning, when the Yankee struck.

The Federal ram hit them square in the wheel box. The entire half-round housing, thirty feet high, folded over the Yankee's bow, crushing under the impact, showering the Yankee with debris as the *General Page* was pushed sideways through the water. Sullivan was doubled over the rail, and only Bowater's staggering out of the wheelhouse, grabbing his collar, and pulling him back kept him from going over.

'Tanner! Abandon ship! We were towing the long boat! If it's still floating, get the men in it!' Bowater shouted. There was no need to assess the damage.

Tanner raced from the wheelhouse, forward and down, calling the order as he went.

'How are you, Sullivan?' Bowater asked.

'Been better. You go an get the boys in the boat, I'll see if they's any stragglers,' he said.

'You'd better come,' Bowater said. 'Come with me.' The vessel shifted under them. They looked up. The Yankee had reversed her paddle wheels and was backing out of the *General Page*, and Bowater imagined that her ram had been the only thing holding them up.

The Yankee's wheelhouse was only about fifty feet away. They could see the captain in his blue coat looking at them as they looked back.

'Go on now, Cap'n,' Sullivan said. His voice was not strong and Bowater knew he could not argue. Whatever Sullivan had in mind – attack the Yankees

502

single-handed, go down with the ship – he had to let him do it.

'Very well,' Bowater said. 'Don't miss the last boat.'

'I won't. An thanks, Cap'n, for puttin up with me all that time.'

Bowater paused. The *Page* heeled a bit. 'You're welcome.' He held out his hand. They shook. Then Bowater headed for the hurricane deck.

Taylor stood by the throttle, tapped his fingers on his leg. *When I ring four bells, let her go!* What did that peckerwood have in mind? It was the waiting Taylor could not tolerate.

He could feel a vibration in the deck plates, even through the water that was sloshing back and forth. There was another ship out there, coming close, and the vibration was made by her paddle wheels. *That would be the Yankee, comin to ram us,* Taylor thought. Put that together with Bowater's order and he could form a fairly good picture of what was about to happen.

'Hey, Burgoyne, what we got for steam, there?'

Burgoyne leaned toward the gauge. 'Twenty-three pounds.'

Taylor nodded. That was about as good as they would get. Not extraordinary, but it would do. *Damned good thing we got a walking beam engine,* he thought. A direct acting engine would have been knocked galley-west by now, but walking beams were more forgiving when the hull was wrenched around. *It's got limits, though,* Taylor thought. He had not been very happy with the shaft bearings from the start. He was less happy now.

He wiped his sweating hand on his pants leg,

double-checked the reversing lever, then wrapped his fingers around the throttle valve.

Son of a bitch is gettin close. Taylor could hear the other boat's paddle wheels, transmitted through the water and the fabric of the *General Page*.

Then the bell rang, four quick bells, so sharp and quick it made Taylor jump. He twisted the throttle open, spinning it around, letting the full brunt of the steam shoot down the pipes and into the cylinder. With a satisfying *huff* the steam drove the piston that pushed the crank that moved the walking beam connected to the crank on the paddle-wheel shaft. Taylor looked up, exalted, as the whole thing, towering over his head, began to move, to drive the *General Page* forward.

The crank went up and down and the water began to run over the deck plates as the ship gained headway, and Taylor smiled, because it was all holding together and turning the wheels.

And then from the top of the A-frame came a sound as terrible as any he had ever heard, a sound so wrenching it seemed it could only come from the mouth of some living thing – something that could feel pain, and express it.

Taylor looked up sharp, right through the hurricane deck overhead to the top of the A-frame. For an instant he thought some dumb-ass had got himself caught in the works, but he realized it was not that. It was the screech of metal fatigue.

'Uh-oh,' Taylor said out loud. Then he heard a snap, and the whole walking beam shifted and dropped. The crank bent in a big bow and then snapped. A section of the wooden arm was hurled forward as if shot from a cannon.

'Blow off that steam! Shut the boiler down! Let's get the hell out of here!' he shouted, limping forward. No sense in remaining in the engine room. All that machinery was so much ballast now. Burgoyne slammed the damper shut and twisted the blow-off valves and with a whoosh the steam exhausted up what was left of the chimney. Half the black gang was already up the ladder and out the fidley door.

Burgoyne turned and looked around. 'That all, Chief?'

'Yes, yes, git the hell out of here!' Taylor waved his arms toward the ladder and Burgoyne splashed across the deck plates, Taylor limping right behind.

Burgoyne took the ladder two rungs at a time. He flung open the door. The daylight flooded into the fidley, sunshine filling the place. In an instant the second engineer disappeared down the main deck. Taylor grabbed the ladder, swung his splinted leg around, and then the Yankee struck.

Taylor knew what it was – even as he was tumbling back, he knew it was the Yankee ram. He hit the deck with a splash and slid. The *General Page* heeled over under the impact, and in the bright light from the open door and the shadow of the engine room he could see the side of the *General Page* cave in as her own paddle wheel was literally pushed through the deckhouse.

The Yankee's iron-reinforced bow tore right into the engine room, right at the waterline. The deck plates parted as if a knife were cleaving them in two. The condenser toppled over and the main steam pipe shattered, and that alone would have been the death of him if they had not blown off the steam.

'Oh, hell!' Taylor shouted. He began to crawl up

the sloping deck toward the ladder, splashing like a seal through the rising water. He heard the high-pitched whine of metal under enormous stress, then a crack, then something fell across his legs, pinning him down.

'Oh, hell! Damn it!' he shouted again, with more enthusiasm. He clawed at the deck plates, tried to get hold of something to pull himself free, but there was only iron plate and water. He tried to move his good leg to kick off whatever was on top of him, but both legs were pinned tight.

Son of a bitch! He twisted around. The starboard crank had broken off the paddle wheel shaft and fallen across his legs. Had it not also fallen on top of other debris scattered on the deck, it would have crushed his legs under its weight.

Now, ain't that a stroke of luck . . . I mighta been hurt . . . 'Hey! Topside! Anyone up there? Halloa, you sons of bitches, come get this goddamned crank off my legs!'

No damned use . . . Those beats were too busy saving their own damned hides. Black smoke was filling the engine room and swirling up the fidley and Taylor started to cough.

He felt the *Page* shudder again, heard a grinding and snapping sound behind. The Yankee was backing away, opening up the hole that they had punched, and then stoppered, with their bow. He could see the water rising faster around him.

Well, this is fucking ironic. After being worried sick about a boiler blowing up, he was going to drown.

Guess I wasn't born to be hanged . . . the old man was wrong about somethin. Damn, Guthrie, you killed me after all. He pushed with his arms and tried to kick his feet but there was no chance of his moving the cast-iron crank.

The ship rolled and made a wave in the water filling the hold. It splashed into Taylor's mouth. He could taste mud and oil and coal dust. *Damn . . . reckon I don't care to drown, either.*

The light in the fidley dimmed, as if the sun had gone behind a cloud. Someone was standing in the doorway. Taylor heard them climb down the short ladder.

'Hieronymus Taylor, son of a whore, ain't this a fix!' Mike Sullivan loomed over him. He was breathing hard, hunched over. 'Didn't see ya topside, I was wonderin what become of ya.'

'Sullivan, ain't you dead yet?'

'No, lucky fer you.' The *Page* took a hard roll, ten degrees, and a ton and a half of coal shifted a foot to larboard. 'Not yet.'

He stepped past Taylor, a staggering, painful walk, bent over and grabbed the crank.

'Sullivan, go git someone! You can't lift that damned thing!'

'Come on, pard. River rats gots to look after their own.' He fixed his fingers around the crank. He was panting, his eyes wide, and Taylor saw the great patch of blood soaked into his shirt.

'All right, Taylor, all right . . .' Sullivan clenched his teeth, straightened his back, pulled.

'You dumb bastard, yer gut-wounded, you can't hardly lift your own fat ass!'

Sullivan's eyes went wider and Taylor saw his jaw tremble. A shout built in Sullivan's throat, a protracted sound that started like a moan and built to a crescendo scream as he lifted the dead weight of the crank. Taylor felt the weight coming off his legs. He kicked, almost free. 'Go on, Sullivan, go on!'

Then Sullivan fell, dropped straight down as if he had been hit on the head. The crank came down on Taylor's legs again and he shouted in agony, but Sullivan did not say anything. He did not move.

'Sullivan? Sullivan! Goddamn . . .' *The son of a bitch is dead!*

'Chief? Chief Taylor?' Now it was Bowater, standing in the door.

'Bowater, goddamn it, git down here!' The water was up to Taylor's chest and he was having a hard time keeping his head above it.

Bowater scrambled down the ladder. 'Sullivan? What the hell?'

'Fainted or dead, Cap'n, don't know, don't care!'

Bowater stepped across the deck, arms out to maintain his balance on the tilting deck plates. He rolled Sullivan out of the way, rolled him on his back. Eyes open, dead eyes staring out of his white face.

'You got to git someone to help lift that,' Taylor was shouting but Bowater had a slice bar in his hand. He shoved it under the crank and pulled up and Taylor felt the weight come off his legs once again.

Why didn't Sullivan think of that? Taylor kicked his way out from under the iron shaft. 'I'm out, Cap'n!' he shouted and with a crash Bowater let the crank go. The deck shuddered as the iron hit the deck plates and the *Page* took a hard roll to larboard.

Bowater offered Taylor a hand and Taylor took it and stood. Together they hobbled to the ladder.

'On the workbench!' Taylor shouted. 'The wooden box, grab her!'

Bowater opened his mouth as if to protest, but

instead scrambled the ten feet to the bench, grabbed the box, raced back. He grabbed Taylor by the shoulders, pushed him toward the ladder, hefted him halfway up.

'I can climb the damned ladder!' Taylor shouted, though a second before he had been wondering how he would do that very thing. He pulled himself up another rung with his arms and good leg, and from there was able to crawl out onto the boiler deck.

It was brilliant sunshine on the deck, and the planks were warm under his hands. He crawled along a few feet, dragging his splinted leg, which he was pretty certain was broken again. It hurt like hell. Every bit of him hurt like hell.

Bowater came up behind, helped Taylor to his feet. He draped Taylor's arm over his shoulder and Taylor wanted to object, but he knew he would not be able to walk otherwise, so he did not argue. Bowater tucked the box under his other arm.

'What the hell is this, Chief?' They stepped off, walking aft.

'Fiddle. I didn't reckon you could afford to buy me another, with what they pay you.'

CHAPTER 33

The battle continued down the river out of sight of Memphis, and it is reported that only two of our boats, the Bragg and Van Dorn, escaped. It is impossible now to report casualties, as we were hurried in our retirement from Memphis, and none but those from the Lovell escaped on the Tennessee side of the river. So soon as more information can be collected, I will report.

Brigadier General M. Jeff Thompson
to General G. T. Beauregard

Wendy Atkins was riding the same emotional seesaw as the thousands of others who crowded the levee and the heights of Memphis and watched the fate of their city being decided on the river in front of them.

It was pure elation to see the River Defense Fleet steam out to the fight, nimble warriors against the overbearing Yankees gunboats, which were hanging on their anchors with bows upstream to facilitate a quick retreat. She had heard enough stories about Plum Point Bend to understand that this was not entirely folly, the wooden boats going up against the ironclads.

510

The gunnery had started slowly, but soon it was murderous, and the town was in the line of fire. Shells screamed past overhead, and Wendy recalled with horror the time she had clandestinely sailed into battle with Samuel Bowater, and the Union shelling of Sewell's Point. It was frightening. The ironclads seemed omnipotent, and she felt her faith in the Confederate boats' ability to stand up to them wavering.

But still the Confederates advanced, boldly advanced right into the storm of shot.

'There, that one.' Shirley, standing beside her on the levee, pointed with a straight arm. 'That's the *General Joseph Page*. Good likelihood Bowater's on her.'

Wendy stared at the side-wheeler, hardly distinguishable from the other boats in the River Defense Fleet. She wondered about the captain, this fellow with whom Samuel had become such close friends. She was curious to meet him. She knew already that he must be a fellow of good taste, learned, well read, and erudite.

Four ships of the River Defense Fleet were pressing the attack, but the *General Page* was not one, for which Wendy was grateful. The ironclads fired and the Confederates fired back and no one moved. For some minutes, nothing seemed to happen. Stalemate. And then from out of the thunder and the smoke surrounding the ironclads came a single Yankee ship, unarmored, and everything began to happen at once.

Like metal filings to a lodestone, the Confederate boats were drawn to the Yankee ship. Then another Yankee came out of the smoke. The Yankees and the Rebels circled, slammed into one another, pandemonium on the water. Wendy saw one of the Confederate ships sink, slip away under the water as if the hand of God had pushed it under.

She felt the mood change on the levee, and a massive groan went up as the Confederate ship disappeared, a sense of despair that touched them all as if they were of one mind. She moved her attention to the *General Page*, still not in the fight. She began to pray.

Boats were crawling for the shore, including the first Yankee ram, but the second was unhurt, and making for the *General Page*. There was another boat between the Yankee and the *Page*, which Shirley said was the *General Bragg*, but the Yankee brushed her aside and struck Bowater's ship bow-on.

A great shout went up from the levee, and everyone held their breath because there was no telling who got the worst of it. And then both boats backed away, began circling.

'Look there!' Shirley pointed upriver.

'What?'

'The gunboats are getting underway! See, they're turning to come bow-down. Damn, that'll be an end to it.'

'An end?'

'The River Defense Fleet can't stand up to them. City can't stand up to them. It's over.'

'Over?' Wendy knew she sounded idiotic, but she did not know what else to say. She was stunned.

She looked back at the *General Page*, which was well south of them now, carried downstream on the current. To her amazement, the *Page* was stopped dead and the Yankee ram was rushing down on her, as if the Confederates were giving up, allowing themselves to be killed. The Yankee ram slammed into the *Page* with an audible crash, but the people on the levee had no reaction. It was over. They all knew it. They were too numb to react.

Except Wendy Atkins. 'Oh, those bastards!'

'She's done for,' Shirley said, mournfully. 'I'm sorry, Miss Atkins.'

They watched as the Yankee extracted itself from the *Page* and steamed away downstream, chasing after the remnants of the River Defense Fleet. They watched and waited and Wendy felt her terror mount. And then, from the far side of the sinking ship, a boat appeared, moving like a white water bug, pulling for the Tennessee shore.

'Look!' Wendy practically shouted, pointing at the boat, but Shirley's mood did not revive.

'It's too late. They'll just rot in some Yankee prison.'

'What? Why?'

'The Yankees will have Memphis in a hour or so. They'll round these fellas up. They got the city, they got the river. Nowhere to run.'

From despair to elation to anger. *Live through that, only to be made prisoner? I hardly think so.*

Wilbur Rankin, leading Memphis merchant, was not going to be a prisoner either. He was not going to be arrested, not going to be hung, not going to be killed by his fellow citizens in the panic. And most of all, he was not going to be poor.

Rankin had not spent the past twenty-three years cheating, embezzling, gouging, and extorting for nothing. He had not hoarded goods such as cloth, food, and shoes in his warehouse until prices became astronomical just to lose it all now, simply because the damned Yankees were here.

No, sir.

He loaded the wagon with whatever it would hold, whatever in his warehouse he could personally lift and toss in the back. Happily, the really valuable things tended to be the lightest – silk, for instance – and though the small hoard of gold coin was not light by any means, he had divided it into a few small boxes, which were manageable.

While the rest of the idiotic, sentimental citizens of Memphis watched their fate being decided from the levee and the hills, Wilbur Rankin was at his riverside warehouse preparing his exit. The war had been very good for him, so far. Blockades, shortages, wartime demand, he had made a fortune, but it was played out, at least as far as Memphis was concerned.

The Confederacy was done. Time to go north. He would return if Southern fortunes turned around again, but until then, he was a loyal Union man. Always had been.

He tossed the last box of tea in the back and climbed up onto the seat. It was a big wagon, made for hauling freight, and pulled by a team of four. He had managed to pile quite a lot back there.

He flicked the reins, got the horses moving. In the gaps between the waterfront buildings he could catch glimpses of the river, the thick blanket of smoke, the boats whirling about, limping for the shore in a sinking condition, paddle wheels shattered. He shook his head. *Stupid, stupid, stupid* . . . He did not understand why people even bothered.

He heard a voice calling, but he had expected that. Every fool who had not had the foresight to prepare an escape would be pleading with him. He would be Noah, and they would be the people with the water rising around them, and like Noah, he would tell them all to go to the devil.

'Sir! Sir!'

Rankin frowned and looked past the horses' heads. It was a woman, a young woman. Rankin slowed the team. A very attractive young woman, with long brown hair tumbling out from under a straw hat, and a shapely figure. She had a very worried look on her face. She had no baggage.

'Whoa!' Rankin pulled the horses to a stop. 'Miss, can I help you?'

The young woman ran over. *Very nice indeed. And desperate.*

'Please, sir, I must get out of town! Please, can I ride with you?'

Rankin decided to alter the plan. Desperation, gratitude, dependence, put them all together and they could render a young woman very liberal in the defense of her virtues. There was a hotel in Nashville he had hoped to reach that night.

'Certainly, miss. Hop on.' He did not offer to help her climb up onto the high seat. She had to understand right off the nature of their relationship.

'Giddyup!' Rankin snapped the reins. The horses moved out.

'Oh, thank you, sir,' the young woman gushed.

Rankin nodded his head. He did not speak to her. They rolled along, heading south to where Rankin would turn on the road to Nashville, now safely in Union hands.

They rode in silence for five minutes. Rankin was aware of a rustling of skirts and he glanced over and caught a glimpse of the young woman's ankle and calf, which he found enticing.

'Down there, sir, is that the city wharf?' she asked. Rankin did not have to look in the direction she was pointing, he knew the answer. 'Mm-hmm,' he said. 'Yes it is, darlin.'

'Very well,' she said, and her tone was quite different than it had been before. Lacking the desperation. 'You can stop.'

'Stop?' Rankin turned and smiled at her and found himself looking right into the barrel of a little pistol, aimed at his face.

'Yes, stop. And get off.'

Bowater and Taylor staggered aft, Bowater hoping to hell that the boat was still there. The one intact boat, the big one they had been towing astern. As Bowater had gone looking for Taylor, the men were massing on the fantail and crowding aboard the launch. Last Bowater had seen, there was not much freeboard left, and more men climbing in.

The *General Page* rolled again, another five degrees. Bowater grabbed the rail to keep his footing and keep Taylor from falling.

They made their way down the starboard side, the high side, Bowater looking for stragglers, but the men of the *General Page* were well motivated to abandon ship, and he found only a few dead men along the way, victims of small arms or shell fragments or splinters.

He heard footsteps on the deck. Tanner and Tarbox, Burgoyne and Baxter, they came racing aft. 'Let's git the hell along!' Tarbox shouted, like a parent who has lost his patience. They grabbed up

516

Taylor's arms, half dragged him aft, and Bowater followed behind.

They handed Taylor into the boat and climbed in after, and then it was only Bowater on board. He put a leg over the side, stepped awkwardly into the stern sheets, and jammed himself into the place by the tiller.

'Shove off! Ship oars! Pull together!'

Awkwardly, their work hampered by the men overflowing the thwarts, the oarsmen pulled and the boat gathered way. They pulled hard, getting distance between themselves and the sinking boat.

'Rest on your oars!' Bowater called and the men stopped rowing and leaned on the looms. Bowater turned the boat broadside to the sinking paddle wheeler and the men looked back at the place from which they had come.

The *General Joseph Page* was heeling over at a forty-five-degree angle, water lapping around her deckhouse, shot full of holes. With a groan the walking beam let go and tumbled off the A-frame, smashed into the deckhouse, and hit the water with a great splash that set the boat rocking in the circular waves.

The *Page* sat more upright with that weight gone, and then began to settle. The water came up around her main deck, then her boiler deck, and then up to the hurricane deck. Bowater watched the Confederate ensign, tattered but still flying, as it was swallowed up by the river. At last only the one remaining chimney was left, and half of that disappeared into the river before it stopped.

'Reckon she's on the bottom,' someone said, and that was met with a chorus of grunts.

Bowater looked upriver. The gunboats were coming down, and the rams had already chased downriver whatever ships of the River Defense Fleet were still floating. He wanted to make for the Arkansas side, try and get away overland, but one of the Yankee boats would catch them before they were halfway there. Besides, the overloaded launch would never make it.

'Oarsmen, pull together,' he said, and as the boat gathered way, he brought her head around to aim for the city wharf, the closest landing spot to them.

It was a ten-minute pull, long enough for Bowater to stare at the strange figure at the end of the wharf and deduce that it was a woman and she was waving to them. *Wife of one of these river rats, he imagined. Sweetheart . . . hooker that one of them owes money to . . .*

They got closer, and the only sound from the boat-load of hopeless and despairing men was the creak of the oars and the occasional groan of the wounded, and Bowater could not help but think that the woman looked a damned lot like Wendy Atkins.

Absurd . . . And the resemblance only made his loneliness and depression more acute.

They pulled alongside the wharf, which was a few feet above the gunnel of the boat, and Bowater had to admit that the woman looked very much like Wendy, but he had not seen Wendy in half a year, and so clearly his memory was fading.

And then the woman said, 'Samuel! Oh, Samuel!' and Bowater realized that it was Wendy Atkins, and then he did not know what to think. He stared at her. He said nothing. He feared for his sanity.

'Samuel, listen, I have a wagon, and I think it's big

enough to get all your men in, if we really crowd them in. I need help unloading it! Oh, Samuel, do hurry, we haven't much time at all!'

Her tone carried so much authority that it snapped Bowater from his stupor. 'Come on, you men. Up, up! Get that wagon emptied, we can still get out of here before the Yankees overrun us. Move! Do you want to rot in prison?' They could escape, they could do it with honor. They had not hauled down their flag.

The men moved. Exhausted, shocked, wounded, they pulled themselves from the boat, staggered over to the wagon, and began to unceremoniously dump Wilbur Rankin's goods on the ground, all save for the small, heavy iron boxes, which they guessed were worth hanging on to.

Bowater supervised the operation, seeing the wounded men loaded in first, made comfortable on beds of silk cloth, and then the others, crammed in like hands of tobacco prized into a cask.

When the last man was on board, Bowater looked around. He could not see Wendy and he was suddenly terrified that she had not been there at all. But there she was, on the driver's seat, reins in her hand. She smiled at him, that amazing smile.

He stepped quickly to the front of the wagon and climbed in beside her. She gave the reins a flick. 'Giddyup!' she shouted and the horses strained and the wagon gathered way.

Bowater looked at her and she glanced at him quickly, smiled, and looked back at the road.

How . . . how . . . He did not know where to begin, so he didn't. Too many questions. She handled the horses with a confidence he did not recall her possessing. Not the feigned confidence of her brash earlier self, but something real and solid.

Or perhaps he was just forgetting. It had been so long, and he was so tired. He closed his eyes.

CHAPTER 34

In reply I have only to say that the civil authorities have no resources of defense, and by the force of circumstances the city is in your power.
John Park, Mayor of Memphis,
to Flag Officer Charles H. Davis

Bowater slept fitfully and not long, lurching along on the heavy wagon. When he came awake with a gasp and looked around, they were rolling through open fields dotted with scrubby brush, little farms off in the distance. He could see birds and cows. It was as if the wagon had transported him to another country.

He swiveled around. The church spires of Memphis were still visible in the distance, peeking over the hills, the pall of battle smoke still hanging over the town.

For a long moment Bowater just stared. That cloud of smoke – the guns of the *General Page* had added to that cloud, he and his men had done their part in that orgy of riparian butchery. He pictured the wreckage of the *General Page* resting in the mud. He pictured the body of Mississippi Mike Sullivan

521

floating around the engine room. In his mind he saw the currents animating Mike's limbs so that even in death he was waving his arms in that frantic way of his.

'Hey, Captain . . .' The voice came from behind. Hieronymus Taylor. Bowater turned the other way.

'Chief. How are you doing?'

'Been better. Been a hell of a lot better. Fact, I can't recall when I felt worse.' Taylor paused, looked around the countryside. 'No, that ain't true. Day after our brawl in the theater I felt worse. So I reckon things are lookin up.'

'Have you taken to brawling now?' Wendy Atkins asked.

Taylor ignored the question, looked at Bowater. 'Now, Captain, if I ain't very much mistaken, this young lady drivin the wagon is none other than Miss Wendy Atkins of Portsmouth, Virginia. Is that a fact?'

Bowater looked at Wendy, suddenly unsure of himself. Wendy swiveled around. 'That is a fact, Chief Taylor,' she said.

Taylor nodded. 'My guess is that there is one hell of a story attached to your bein here.'

'You guessed right, Chief,' Wendy said.

'Awright. Let's hear her.'

'Where are we going, Captain Bowater?' Wendy asked.

Samuel had not really considered that, though it seemed an obvious question. He pictured the map in his mind, arrayed the Yankees where he knew them to be. 'I don't know,' he said at last.

'Well, it should take us some time to get there,' Wendy said. 'I guess there's time for my story. It started with the letter you sent, Captain, from Yazoo City . . .'

The tale spun out as the wagon rolled south, always south, deep into Confederate territory. There were more than a few times that Bowater and Taylor exchanged glances of strained credulity, more than a few times that Wendy said, 'You two must think I am a wicked liar, but in faith this is really what happened . . .'

Forty-five minutes later the story ended with a gun thrust in the face of the poor unfortunate who owned the wagon on which they were riding. They rattled on for a mile or so in silence. The men did not know what to say.

'I was going to tell you what we've been up to,' Samuel said at last. 'Two river battles, ship sunk under us, Sullivan killed. But frankly it seems pretty tame now.'

'So the mighty CSS *Virginia*'s gone, huh?' Taylor asked.

'Yup. Blown to the heavens. Molly and I were nearly killed when she fell back to earth.'

'She lived for four months and she changed the nature of sea-fighting forever,' Taylor said. 'We won't see the like of her again.' Bowater had never heard Taylor wax so sentimental, certainly not over any person.

They rolled on south, stopped in the town of White Haven because they were desperately hungry and thirsty. There was a store and an inn there, but between all the men crowded on the wagon they could come up with no more than a few Confederate dollars. That was when Ruffin Tanner suggested they open the little strongboxes, and they made the happy discovery of hoards of gleaming gold.

The innkeeper, who had regarded them with suspicion and fear, saw them in a quite different light when presented with actual specie, gold, the value of which only went up with the misfortunes of the Confederacy. The former General Pages ate well and were on the road again, because they all had the sense, unspoken, that they should get as much distance as they could between themselves and the Yankees.

They came at last to Commerce, Mississippi, though there seemed to be precious little commerce taking place. The sun was two hours set by the time they climbed wearily out of the wagon and stretched and groaned in front of the inn on the one main street. The inn was all but deserted, but still it was barely large enough to house all the men. They ate, another fine meal, and tumbled off to sleep, too exhausted to talk.

Samuel took a private room, as was fitting his status as captain, and saw of course that Wendy had a room to herself. In the dark he lay in his bed, staring up at the ceiling, a dull blue in the moonlight. Outside the windows the crickets and frogs were singing their opera, an ensemble cast of thousands.

The door creaked on its hinges and he did not startle, did not even ask who it was. He could see her in the muted light, her hair loose and hanging down her shoulders, a robe held tight around her. She paused and they looked at one another and neither spoke. Then Wendy slipped off the robe, slipped off her nightdress, and for a moment the light played over her naked body, her white skin. She stepped up to the bed, pulled back the cover, and slipped in next to Samuel.

Samuel put his arm out, wrapped it around her, pressed her tight. She lay her cheek on his chest and they seemed to melt together. They remained like that for some time, silent, serenaded by the crickets and frogs.

'God, I have missed you,' Wendy said at last.

'I have missed you too.' And he had, though he had not known until that moment just how much.

She propped herself up on her elbow, shuffled closer to him, kissed him on the lips. He ran his hands over her back, through that long thick hair he loved, cradled her face in his hands. They made love, as if they had been waiting their whole life for this and were not going to rush through it now.

Finally they lay side by side, their heads on the cool pillows, their bodies bright with sweat because it was June and it was hot and humid, even at two o'clock in the morning.

'What will we do?' Wendy asked finally.

'I don't know,' Samuel answered, the only true answer, but he knew Wendy needed more than that and it was not kind to leave her without it. 'We'll have to get to some city, someplace where we can contact the Navy Department. I reckon – I imagine we can find a steamer, something to get us down to Vicksburg. That's the last holdout on the river, and when that falls, the Confederacy is split in two.'

Wendy rolled over, flung an arm across his chest. 'Will that end the war?' she asked. There was a note of resignation, a touch of hope. Win or lose, she was ready for it to be over.

'No. Not immediately. There'll be plenty more war. The navy will have more work for me, of that I have no doubt.'

Wendy pressed tighter against him. 'I don't want you to go.'

And he did not want to go. For once in his life, it seemed, there was something better on shore than anything he could hope to find over the horizon. After years in the moribund United States Navy, where his coming or going was a matter of complete indifference to anyone, when he might have walked away at any point, he had at last found a reason to walk away, at the very moment he could no longer do so. Sometimes he thought God specialized in irony.

'The war will end someday,' he said, but the words did not sound as hopeful as he wanted them to. They had this day, and the next, and the next, and he would savor them and not think about the future. He knew how to cherish any given moment. It was one thing, at least, he had learned.

Epilogue

By June 30, 1863, the Battle of Memphis was a year gone. Time, that great if arbitrary healer, had come to the aid of Hieronymus Taylor. A broken leg had been the death of plenty of men, but not Taylor. It took him four months to recover from the third break to his leg, brought about by the falling shaft, and he was left with a permanent limp, but nothing worse.

Time was not so kind to Colonel Charles Ellet, Jr. The wound to the knee was not nearly so bad as the injuries suffered by others who survived, but he nonetheless suffered infection and died two weeks after his great victory.

And by June 30, 1863, all of it – Fort Pillow, Memphis, the River Defense Fleet – it was all history. Samuel Bowater's short tenure with the army was over, and he was a navy man once again, once again a

527

part of the Confederate States Navy that would fight on until the war was truly and finally over. Likewise Hieronymus Taylor. Ruffin Tanner. By the summer of 1863, those events at Plum Point Bend and Memphis were largely forgotten by everyone who had not been immediately touched by them.

In Pennsylvania they were worried about more than history. In particular, attention was focused on the gathering of armies in a place called Gettysburg for what had the makings of a major fight. The coming battle would throw the Southern invaders out of the North, or allow them to push on toward Washington, D.C.

And Lieutenant Tom Chamberlain of the 20th Maine, bone weary from the day's march, was hoping for a moment's reprieve. He longed for a moment during which he did not have to think about army things.

They had been marching hard, had covered eighteen miles the day before and twenty-three that day. They were marching north, pursuing Lee through Pennsylvania. The locals had been glad to see the Union Army, and had even obliged them by setting up roadside stands to sell food and drink at usurious prices. But Tom had noticed that the closer the civilians were to the Rebel army, the more obliging they became to the Army of the United States, and the more reasonable their prices.

He sat on his camp stool and leaned back against a small oak. He pulled his boots off and allowed himself the luxury of a groan. Around him, hundreds more men were doing the same, sitting around their little fires. It was hot, and no promise of rain, so the men eschewed their tents and slept on the ground.

They would not be there long. Ten hours if they were lucky.

Tom Chamberlain had driven a nail into the trunk of the oak and hung a lantern from it, which gave him light enough to read. He pulled the dog-eared book out of his haversack. It, like the 20th Maine, had seen hard use, being passed from man to man with a smile and a 'Hell, you got to read this.'

Chamberlain opened the book to where he had stuck a maple leaf as a bookmark the night before. *Chapter Fifteen – Mississippi Mike Turns the Tables on Rosencrantz and Guildenstern, His Hebrew Pards.*

He smiled in anticipation and began to read. Soon he was chuckling, he could not help it, and then laughing outright. It was perfect, magnificently crafted.

He read for the next hour, until he was done, then put the book down with a satisfied smile on his face. *Lord, that's funny. I cannot wait until Joshua has a go at it.*

Tom's brother, Joshua, colonel of the 20th Maine, would genuinely appreciate the genius of this subtle parody. Joshua was an educated man, a professor at Bowdoin College before joining the army. He knew his Shakespeare and would appreciate this skewed take on the bard.

He held the book up and read the title in the light of the lantern. *Mississippi Mike, Melancholy Prince of the River, or, The Rebels' Hamlet, written by a Union Officer Serving on Western Waters.*

Tom wondered who the officer was. There was good reason for him to avoid putting his name on it. The people back in Washington would not look kindly on an officer with so much time on his hands that he could write such a bit of doggerel.

And there was no doubt that Washington was aware of the book – it was immensely popular throughout the North, and particularly among army officers. Whoever that officer was, he had been in the South long enough to have a genuine feel for the colloquialisms of that illiterate, ignorant race of people.

He had to be a Yankee. Who but a New England man could be so thoroughly versed in Shakespeare, and able to craft so perfect a parody? No doubt he was making a small fortune off his royalties, with all the copies that had been sold. It was just too bad that the anonymous author would never get the credit he deserved.

THE END

HISTORICAL NOTE

THE RIVER DEFENSE FLEET

When New Orleans fell to David Farragut's fleet, it signaled the beginning of the end for Confederate control of the Mississippi, and a great blow to the Confederacy overall. Not because New Orleans was an active shipping port – the river had been sealed off from the sea by the Union blockade for some time – but because the city was still an important center for shipbuilding and the natural command center for operations on the Mississippi.

Despite its importance, and the obvious threat of Farragut's fleet in the Gulf, Secretary of the Navy Mallory believed that the greater threat to New Orleans was the squadron of City Class gunboats and the Union Army coming down from the north. Mallory insisted that Flag Officer George Hollins keep his small squadron in Tennessee to oppose the Union advance. It was only at the last moment, and largely on Hollins's initiative, that the naval forces of the river were moved south to oppose Farragut, a case of too little too late.

With Hollins's fleet nearly wiped out at New Orleans, the bulk of the Mississippi River defense rested with the River Defense Fleet.

This fleet was not a part of the navy, but rather of the War Department, and under the command of the general of the army in the Mississippi Department, Brigadier General M. Jeff Thompson. The fleet was first organized in January of 1862 and consisted of fourteen steamers fitted with rams in the bow and a single gun fore and aft. The ships were specifically not gunboats, as the army had no faith in the riverboat crews' ability with ordnance. They were designed to be fast rams, sinking their enemies in the manner of the ancient Greeks and Romans.

For command of the ships, the army looked specifically to experienced river men, captains and pilots. The men they found were fiercely independent, which is not usually a good quality for military men who must work in organized and concerted efforts. General Lovell, in command in New Orleans, recognized the potential for trouble when he wrote, 'Fourteen Mississippi captains and pilots would never agree about anything after they once get underway.'

THE BATTLE AT PLUM POINT

The Union Navy on the Mississippi had a bad record of letting Confederate forces take them by surprise. It happened at Head of the Passes, when Commodore Hollins caught Captain John Pope's Union fleet napping and sent them racing for the Gulf in a humiliating incident known as 'Pope's Run.' It happened later when *Arkansas* steamed out of the

Yazoo River and blasted her way through Farragut's fleet at Vicksburg. And it happened at Plum Point.

Plum Point was perhaps the least excusable, since the Federals were perfectly aware of the existence of the Confederate fleet just a few miles downriver at Memphis. And while the presence of seven 'cotton clad' rams might not have been reason to remain on high alert, still there was no excuse for being caught without enough steam up to turn the paddle wheels.

The much and deservedly maligned River Defense Fleet had its moment of glory on May 10, 1862, when they steamed around Plum Point Bend and found the *Cincinnati* and Mortar Boat Number Sixteen tied to the bank, the rest of the fleet upriver in various states of unreadiness.

Despite the Yankees' being able to get into battle quickly, the Rebels accomplished a great deal in their attack. The *Cincinnati* and *Mound City* were sunk by that most ancient of weapons, the ram. The ram had become unworkable when sail took the place of the galley slave, an early example of jobs lost to technology. It was steam that made it feasible again after several thousand years.

Union and Confederate reports of the fighting might lead one to believe they described two different battles. The Confederates elevated their accomplishments to the level of stunning victory, while the Federal officers brushed over the damage the River Defense Fleet did and laid erroneous claim to having damaged or destroyed a number of ships.

In his official report, Captain Davis, commanding the Federal forces, wrote, 'Commander Walke informs me that he fired a 50-pound rifle shot through the boilers of the third of the enemy's gunboats of the western line, and rendered her, for the time being, helpless. All of these vessels might easily have been captured if we had possessed the means of towing them out of action . . .' It is an absurd claim, but typical of the spin added to Union reports of the action.

There can be no question that the River Defense Fleet carried out a well-executed and successful surprise attack on the Union forces, a clear Southern victory. Unfortunately for the Confederates, the resources of the Union rendered the sinking of two ironclads little more than an inconvenience to the Union Navy.

The ships were raised and sent upriver to Cairo for repair, and soon were back in action. Even Captain Stembel of the *Cincinnati*, who was shot during the action, recovered, despite the fact that the bullet 'entered his shoulder just above the shoulder blade, on the right side, and passing through the neck, came out in the front of the throat, directly under the chin.' But the ability of the Union Navy to repair the damage does not change the fact that the Battle at Plum Point Bend, one of the war's few fleet actions, was a complete – and rare – victory for Confederate forces afloat.

THE IRONCLADS *ARKANSAS* AND *TENNESSEE*

Secretary of the Navy Stephen Mallory was a great believer in ironclads, feeling that their technological superiority would give the South an edge against the numerically superior Union Navy. He was not the only one in the Confederacy to feel this way. Soon after the start of the war, shipbuilders and aspirants to shipbuilding began to apply to the Navy Department for contracts to build ironclads.

One of those men was John T. Shirley of Memphis, a man who enjoyed the friendship of a number of influential people in the Confederate government and military. In August of 1861, Shirley contracted 'to construct and deliver to the secretary of the Navy, of the Confederate States, on or before the 24th of December, 1861, two vessels of the character and description provided. . . .' Four months was not an excessive amount of time to build two ships, but it was adequate. Adequate, that is, if the workmen and material had been readily available, which they were not.

By April of 1862 the ships were still under construction, with the *Arkansas* planked up and her armor being fitted, while the first planks were just being applied to the *Tennessee*. With General Grant and Admiral Foote, and later Davis, pressing down from the north, and Admiral Farragut gathering his forces in the Gulf of Mexico, there was a growing sense of urgency. Months before, Mallory had written, 'the completion of the ironclad gunboats at Memphis, by Mr Shirley, is regarded as highly important to the defenses of the Mississippi.' With the fall of Island #10 and New Orleans, urgency turned to desperation.

There is some question as to exactly when *Arkansas* was launched. It was some time around the fall of New Orleans, for immediately following that event, plans were made to tow the ship to the Yazoo River, where it was thought she would be safe long enough for her crew to complete her construction.

Arkansas, with the material needed to complete her loaded on a barge, was towed downriver, and then up the Yazoo. In Yazoo City, her new commander, the energetic and highly competent Isaac Brown, saw her finished. The following July, Brown drove the *Arkansas* straight through Farragut's fleet at Vicksburg, and assured her a place in the annals of naval history.

The *Tennessee* was not so lucky. By the time New Orleans fell, it was pretty clear that she would never be completed. So clear, in fact, that her engines – a rare and valuable commodity in the South – were sent away with *Arkansas* to preserve them from the Yankees. The night before the Battle of Memphis, the very last night that Memphis would remain in Confederate hands, the ship was put to the torch.

THE CAPTURE OF NORFOLK

The reader might well find the notion of Abraham Lincoln himself boarding a tug and scouting out a suitable place to land troops at Norfolk quite unbelievable, and understandably so. It is so unbelievable that it would not have been a part of this work of fiction if it had not actually happened in fact.

On a few occasions during the war, Lincoln took it upon himself to be a hands-on Commander-in-Chief, appearing personally at the front lines and even on occasion directing troop movements. To this end he had more motive and opportunity than any other President, save, perhaps, for James Madison. America's wars, as a rule, did not take place within a day's journey from the White House. Nor have many

Presidents been saddled with the kind of lethargic and incompetent military leadership that Lincoln suffered.

In early May of 1862, with McClellan stalled at Yorktown, unwilling to advance against a Rebel army half his strength and howling for more men, Lincoln took a steamer to Fortress Monroe to see for himself what was going on. With him went Secretary of War Edwin Stanton and Treasury Secretary Salmon Chase.

The men did not come as tourists. No sooner had they arrived than Lincoln began making decisions for Admiral Louis Goldsborough, who was not always quick to make decisions himself. Lincoln ordered *Galena* and *Monitor* to proceed up the James River and clear the way for Union traffic. On hearing that Norfolk was being abandoned, Lincoln ordered a bombardment of Sewell's Point to test the defenses there.

Lincoln and his party boarded a tug and watched the shelling from Rip Raps. Satisfied that Norfolk could be taken, Lincoln and Stanton scouted out a suitable landing place for Union troops. The ironclad *Monitor* participated in most of the action, and her presence was considered essential to prevent the *Virginia* from interfering with the forces on the ground. On several occasions the *Virginia* sallied forth and showed herself to *Monitor*, but they did not fight. Reading the official reports from both sides, it becomes clear that the commanders of both vessels each felt it was the other ship that declined combat.

On May 10, Union Major General John Wool with four regiments of infantry landed at the spot of Lincoln's choosing and marched unopposed into

Norfolk. The fleeing Rebels had set the navy yard on fire, just as the fleeing Federals had the year before.

As it happened, the Norwegian corvette *Norvier* did indeed show up in Hampton Roads at this time, bearing the Norwegian minister, though, for the sake of literary convenience, the author may have shuffled the date of her arrival by a few days, no more.

THE END OF CSS *VIRGINIA*

The final act in the life of that mighty ironclad was pretty much as portrayed in this book. With no port left to her in the Norfolk area, Tattnall ordered her lightened in the hope of getting her up to Richmond, where she could be safe, or at least could participate in the defense of the Confederate capital.

It was only when it was too late that the pilots, Parrish and Wright, explained that what they had repeatedly told the admiral – that a *Virginia* raised to eighteen feet of draft from twenty-two could make it to Richmond – did not apply with a steady westerly wind. The motives that Tattnall divined for this deception, as portrayed in the book, are taken directly from his subsequent report to Stephen Mallory regarding the loss of the ship.

It is certainly true that, let loose in Hampton Roads with nothing to lose, *Virginia* could have done extraordinary damage. Though Tattnall did not think Parrish and Wright to be traitors, they might well be considered heroes of the Union Navy.

THE BATTLE OF MEMPHIS

With Fort Pillow abandoned, there was nothing for the River Defense Fleet to do but drop down to Memphis and await the inevitable coming of the Yankee fleet (or fleets, actually, as the army rams and the navy gunboats were as separate as the River Defense Fleet was from the Confederate States Navy).

It was not a long wait. Fort Pillow was abandoned on the fourth of June, and the Yankees were ready to fight for Memphis on the morning of the sixth. The battle went as described in the book, the ironclads anchored in a line across the river, making a formidable defensive line, though it did not put them in a position to attack.

Luckily for the Yankees, Ellet was there and ready to bring the fight to the Confederates. Steaming through the Federal line, the *Queen of the West* and the *Monarch* boldly attacked the River Defense Fleet. The *Queen* struck the *Colonel Lovell* (sometimes called the *General Lovell*) amidships and sank her almost instantly. As the *Queen* was extracting herself, the *Sumter* struck her a blow that sheered off her paddle wheel and sent her out of the fight.

The ram *Lancaster* never got into the fight. The pilot, apparently for want of courage, backed and filled until he managed to disable her rudder. The *Switzerland* continued to obey her order to remain half a mile astern of *Lancaster*, and so she too did not get into the fight until most of the heavy work was done.

The chief of the battle was fought by the brothers Ellet in *Queen of the West* and *Monarch*. Between them, and with a little help from the gunboats' cannonade and the accidental collision of the *General Beauregard* and *General Price*, they managed to sink or destroy nearly the entire River Defense Fleet. Only *Van Dorn* was able to escape, running south to the last major Rebel stronghold on the river, Vicksburg.

Colonel Charles Ellet Jr., shot in the leg by small-arms fire, was described by Flag Officer Davis as 'seriously but not dangerously wounded.' Unfortunately, in the days before sterilization and antibiotics, even a minor wound could prove fatal. And so it was with Colonel Ellet. After fighting illness for a few weeks, he died on June twenty-first, in Cairo, Illinois, on his way home to recuperate. His wife, stricken with grief, died a few days later.

Command of the ram fleet devolved to his brother Alfred, and later his son. Ellet's army rams proved their worth again and again during the protracted battle for control of western rivers.

With the capture of Memphis, the Mississippi was entirely in Union hands, save for the heavily fortified town of Vicksburg. It would be more than a year before that town was taken, on the Fourth of July, 1863, the same day that Lee's battered army was retreating from Gettysburg. Only then would Lincoln be able to say that 'the Father of Waters again goes unvexed to the sea.'

GLORY IN THE NAME
By James Nelson

At the outbreak of the Civil War, the Confederate Navy must
defend nearly 3,000 miles of coastline with only a meagre
collection of ships and a handful of men. These include Sam
Bowater, a former lieutenant in the United States Navy, who
obtains his cherished first command in a tugboat turned
gunboat, the Cape Fear, with a ragtag crew. Struggling with
the pressures of his first command, in a naval service which is
still learning the ropes, Bowater finds himself and his men the
only defence between the Confederate shores and the massive
Union Navy.

From Hampton Roads to Roanoke Island, to an exciting,
bloody night time river fight for New Orleans, *Glory In The
Name* vividly brings to life the dramatic naval battles of the
Civil War.

'It is, by far, the best Civil War novel I've read; reeking of
battle, duty, heroism and tragedy . . . a triumph'
Bernard Cornwell

0 552 15097 5

CORGI BOOKS

THE *REVOLUTION AT SEA* SAGA
By James Nelson

Book One: BY FORCE OF ARMS

As the War of Independence begins in earnest, American merchant seamen prepare to strike the first blows. None strikes more deftly than Isaac Biddlecomb, captain of the *Judea*, whose smuggling activities are making a mockery of His Majesty's Royal Navy. Pursued by the HMS *Rose*, he sacrifices the ship he loved to the depths, together with the fortune he stood to gain, rather than surrender. On the run from the enraged forces of King George, Isaac disguises himself as a merchant seaman. He is reunited with Ezra Rumstick, a comrade and fierce rebel, as the revolution gathers momentum. On a brig bound for Jamaica, and now serving as a lowly mate, fate tests Isaac's mettle as he is captured by the enemy and faces a life of servitude under the deranged captain and sadistic crew of the HMS *Icarus* . . .

0 552 14960 8

Book Two: THE MADDEST IDEA

In the late summer of 1775, General George Washington discovers that his cache of gunpowder has dwindled to a mere nine shots per man. A desperate plan is hatched – to send a ship under the command of Captain Isaac Biddlecomb to Bermuda to capture the British powder known to be there. But the plan is a trap, set by a traitor among the patriots, and one from which even Biddlecomb cannot escape. Washington despatches his aide-de-camp, Major Edward Fitzgerald, to hunt the traitor down, while Biddlecomb must rely on cunning and seamanship to free his men and the ship, and to capture the gunpowder that is the lifeblood of the fight for liberty. Divided by an ocean but bound by the same cause, as well as by their own private fears, Biddlecomb and Fitzgerald must take on a common enemy – the greatest military power on earth . . .

0 552 14961 6

'NELSON WRITES WITH THE EAGERNESS OF A YOUNG MAN SAILING HIS FIRST COMMAND'
Patrick O'Brian

CORGI BOOKS

THE *REVOLUTION AT SEA* SAGA
By James Nelson

Book Three: THE CONTINENTAL RISQUE
In the winter of 1776 a decade of simmering tensions finally comes to the boil. The rebel government of Philadelphia, determined to cast off the chains of British tyranny, has authorised the creation of the United States Navy – a brazen act of American aggression against the greatest maritime power in the world. Still battered from her fight in Bermudan waters, the brig-of-war *Charlemagne* under the command of Captain Isaac Biddlecomb sets sail on a daring mission to raid the British store of arms on New Providence Island in the Bahamas.
0 552 14962 4

Book Four: LORDS OF THE OCEAN
General George Washington is preparing for the final destruction of the Continental army and orders Biddlecomb to transport to France the most dangerous secret weapon in the country's arsenal: scientist and philosopher Benjamin Franklin. Leading a new crew through the wintry North Atlantic, braving the cordon of the Royal Navy, Biddlecomb's seemingly simple mission to deliver Franklin to the court of Louis XVI is just the first volley in a grand scheme. While Biddlecomb is boldly raiding the English coast and Franklin is discussing strategy at Versailles, they both conspire to blow French neutrality out of the water – and turn the colonial uprising into a full-scale war.
0 552 14963 2

Book Five: ALL THE BRAVE FELLOWS
It is 1777, and Captain Isaac Biddlecomb, together with his wife and child, is bound for Philadelphia aboard the brig *Charlemagne*. His orders are to take command of the newly-built frigate *Falmouth* and take her out to sea before she is taken by Richard Howe's invading army. Unknown to Biddlecomb, the entire British fleet stands between him and the new nation's capital. Meanwhile, General Washington has yielded Philadelphia to Britain's might. As Biddlecomb and his crew battle to reach the prized *Falmouth*, only shipwright Malachi Foote and a ragtag band of deserters stand between the vessel and the seemingly unstoppable British army.
0 552 14964 0

'WILL APPEAL TO FANS OF C.S. FORESTER AND PATRICK O'BRIAN' *Mail on Sunday*

CORGI BOOKS

THE BRETHREN OF THE COAST TRILOGY
By James Nelson

Book One: THE GUARDSHIP
With the bounty from his years as a pirate Thomas Marlowe
purchases a Virginia plantation from a beautiful young widow,
Elizabeth Tinling. Soon afterwards, while defending her
honour, he kills the favourite son of one of the colony's most
powerful families in a duel. But in a clever piece of
manoeuvring he manages to win command of the *Plymouth
Prize*, the colony's decrepit guardship, and is charged with
leading the King's sailors in bloody pitched battle against the
cutthroats who infest the waters off Virginia's shores.
0 552 14838 5

Book Two: THE BLACKBIRDER
Thomas Marlowe, former pirate and captain of the
Guardship, lives prosperously on his tobacco plantation near
Williamsburg with his lovely wife Elizabeth. But when King
James, the huge ex-slave who is in command of Marlowe's
sloop, kills the crew of a slave ship – a blackbirder – and
makes himself the most wanted man in Virginia, Marlowe is
forced to go and hunt him down.
0 552 14842 3

Book Three: THE PIRATE ROUND
Thomas Marlowe is now a man of property, but the Anglo-
Spanish war has meant a decline in tobacco prices, and
Thomas decides to come to England to trade his wares, little
thinking that in the busy streets of London he will meet an
old enemy from his pirating days. Forced to abandon his
tobacco and flee, he has to take to sea and finds himself in
battle with the ships bound for the Moghul Empire, and in
Madagascar he at last comes face to face with his pirate foes.
0 552 14843 1

'A MASTER BOTH OF HIS PERIOD AND OF THE
ENGLISH LANGUAGE'   Patrick O'Brian

CORGI BOOKS